Moshe

Andrew Montante

Montante, Andrew
ISBN: 978-0-7443-2316-0
Moshe / Andrew Montante – 1st ed.

SynergEbooks
948 New Hwy 7
Columbia, TN 38401
www.synergebooks.com

Cover art by Andrew Montante

Printed in the USA

Moshe

*To my older brother Mark
and our mother Beatrice.
Thank you*

PROLOGUE

[23] And the LORD spake unto Moses, saying,

[24] Speak unto the congregation, saying, Get you up from about the tabernacle of Korah, Dathan, and Abiram.

[25] And Moses rose up and went unto Dathan and Abiram; and the elders of Israel followed him.

[26] And he spake unto the congregation, saying, Depart, I pray you, from the tents of these wicked men, and touch nothing of theirs, lest ye be consumed in all their sins.

[27] So they gat up from the tabernacle of Korah, Dathan, and Abiram, on every side: and Dathan and Abiram came out, and stood in the door of their tents, and their wives, and their sons, and their little children.

[28] And Moses said, Hereby ye shall know that the LORD hath sent me to do all these works; for *I have* not *done them* of mine own mind.

[29] If these men die the common death of all men, or if they be visited after the visitation of all men; *then* the LORD hath not sent me.

[30] But if the LORD make a new thing, and the earth open her mouth, and swallow them up, with all that *appertain* unto them, and they go down quick into the pit; then ye shall understand that these men have provoked the LORD.

[31] And it came to pass, as he had made an end of speaking all these words, that the ground clave asunder that *was* under them:

[32] And the earth opened her mouth, and swallowed them up, and their houses, and all the men that *appertained* unto Korah, and all *their* goods.

[33] They, and all that *appertained* to them, went down alive into the pit, and the earth closed upon them: and they perished from among the congregation.

KJV Numbers 16 23:33

CHAPTER 1
I See You

"Come out, stop hiding." She stood there waiting impatiently, tapping her toe, arms crossed. It was dark where she was, but her eyes were already able to see in near total blackness. She looked closer. Whoever was following her had a lantern. Obviously that person still needed a light source to travel into the darkest of tunnels.

The lantern's small light cast a shadow of someone that was creeping back and forth behind a tunnel corner she had just passed. She did not fear who had cast the shadow; since the altar incident, she feared very few. If anything, they feared her. She then used her mind-speaking powers to talk with her pursuer. *I see you. I know who you are, stop being silly.*

Bishtar, is that you? came the soft reply, also in her mind.

Bishtar, with a mock irritation, decided to speak aloud her next comments. "Of course it is. Now are you going to come closer? Are you lost? Or are you looking for lost sheep?"

The last question was something both youngsters could relate to and was directly relevant to their growing relationship. The lantern holder did not regret what he had done for her. The wounds he had received from protecting her lamb were all healed, even though the brutality of Gasheer's whip was indelibly etched into his mind. Nevertheless, he knew she did not intend harm in the 'sheep' question. He brought himself to stand before her, and shyly mind-spoke an answer. *Oh, okay, I'm glad it is y-you then. I-I wasn't sure.*

"Mosher," Bishtar chastised in a motherly way, "You are the only one I know that can still manage to stutter even when speaking in our minds."

"S-Sorry."

She rolled her eyes at his easy, gentle acquiescence. Then Bishtar got coy, something she was an expert at doing. "So tell me, why are you following me this time?"

"Oh n-nothing, it's just..."

"Out with it, Mosher. Out with it."

"Well, I, ah… I might have s-something for you."

At that comment, Bishtar's eyes lit up. And even though her eyes had grown to be large black orbs, her expression was clearly one of excitement.

"Ah, I don't know if y-you will like it. I ah..."

"Now, Mosher," she scolded while wagging a clawed finger at him. "Don't make me mad."

At first Mosher thought she was joking, but he also knew that making Bishtar mad was not to be taken lightly. Mosher, along with most everyone in their tribe, was witness to her growing powers. Her newfound abilities were, well, *scary* to say the least. So Bishtar's mild rebuke did, in fact, have a very serious side. "No, no, I s-sure wouldn't want to do that."

"Well then, let's see it," she prompted.

He looked at her, peering into those huge black orbs, thinking, feeling too. Although Bishtar was far from what he remembered her looking like in Egypt, he only saw what was in his heart. She was still Bishtar. Underworld on not, somewhere behind that unrecognizably pale, bulging black-eyed, hairless mask was the girl he loved... forever. She was still beautiful, no matter where they lived. And he intended on making her his.

"Very well then," he stated, his stutter momentarily forgotten. Mosher put down the lantern and reached into his pouch. He slowly brought out the prize that was hidden there. As the piece came out, the item gradually illuminated the stifling darkness that surrounded them. Bishtar's expression likewise became just as brilliant. He open-handedly held out the jewel before her. Its multi-faceted surfaces sparkled with glowing greens and vibrant purples.

"It's beautiful, Mosher. Where did you get it?"

"Stenrak."

"The Pon boy that helped rescue me from... from those creatures?"

"Yes." Mosher let her take the piece.

She scrutinized it better, twirling the jewel between her claws, smiling broadly while doing so.

Suddenly the stone changed shape, shrinking slightly and becoming more unified in its form. Its original green colors turned into bright ruby-reds. Mosher was slightly startled by it. But the magical transformation did not startle, or even frighten, Bishtar. In fact, she seemed intrigued by it, almost as if she had grown accustomed to seeing magic. The gem's light danced its colors across her face, and its ruby-red sparkles shimmered in her black eyes, making Bishtar look even more mysterious, and enthralling.

Then Mosher remembered what Stenrak had told him about the gem. Stenrak had said, *If the jewel changes shape and color, then the magical item has found its true master.* The thought of Bishtar wielding one of the twelve stones of power made him proud, and in other ways greatly frightened him.

"But," Bishtar voiced quizzically, "it has a beautiful necklace attached, made of gold. That wasn't Stenrak's doing, was it?"

"No."

"The necklace is so well crafted, and clasped to this glowing gem. It can only be the work of Darsheesh."

"Yes."

"But how? He is a master builder and always busy. How did you get him to craft such a thing?"

Mosher puffed up his chest a little, sucked in his slightly bulging gut, and bragged, "Well, y-you have to know people, don't you know?"

"So I see, so I see. You are indeed a young man that demands respect. It is clear that one day you will become a great man, and a great leader. Of that I am sure, Mosher."

If possible, Mosher's chest became even bigger, and his gut smaller.

Meanwhile, Bishtar held the gem delicately, admiring it and wondering about the boy she thought she knew. Mosher had changed recently. Yes, he still stuttered, and yes he was still very shy and humble, but there was something different about him. It was something she couldn't quite figure out – something she couldn't put her finger, or rather *claw,* on. Mosher's brutal scars had disappeared. That, in and of itself was surprising, but there was something much deeper to his change. Mosher was now more... confident... and forthright. He was taller in stature; from the inside mostly, not from the outside. The boy had somehow become a man, instantly. *How is it possible?* she wondered. *Will I ever know? But does it really matter after all?*

She looked deeply into Mosher's eyes, as if she was waiting for him to say something.

And for the first time in his life, Mosher didn't stutter and didn't hesitate. "Will you have it, Bishtar?"

She stared at him for a long second, then another second, and Mosher was not sure if he had made a mistake. Both of them knew what was at stake. They well understood what the acceptance of the gem really meant. Even though they now lived in the foreign and dark place of the underworld, they still believed in their culture, their heritage, and how such things spoke to the promise of having a future together.

When she still did not answer, Mosher started to feel deflated. *Why should she want s-someone like me? I have m-made a fool of myself. She doesn't w-want me and d-does not know how to tell me.* He thought about turning and running away. *I'll find a dark c-cave to hide in. They'll n-never find me. They'll forget I ever existed, the n-name of Moshe . . .*

Then suddenly Bishtar wrapped her arms around him, squeezing him tightly. Mosher was shocked at first and then reciprocated shyly. While they embraced, Bishtar generously mind-spoke, *Yes I will.*

Mosher smiled like he had never done before. He then whispered in her ear, "El be praised."

CHAPTER 2
The Chasm

2 Years Earlier

Calish ran to his tent as fast as he could, dodging past anyone or anything that stood in his way. He had to find his mother and sister. Something wasn't right. "Get out of my way! Look out!" he shouted while leaping over those who had fallen.

A streak of lightening suddenly burst through the sky, striking the individuals Calish had just passed. The unlucky souls were instantly caught up in smoke and flames, their bodies exploding into many fiery pieces. After seeing this, Calish realized that his present path was not a good option, so he decided to take a few shortcuts.

He crashed through his uncle's tent, knocking over all of their possessions. His relatives, mostly woman, children, and the old ones, cowered in fear as the tent shook from the mighty winds outside.

"Calish," one of them cried, "Help us!"

But Calish was already gone. Outside again, still madly running, Calish had to look up. The sky filled itself with the blackest of clouds. It got so dark that Calish could barely see, but by now he was so close to his own tent that having good sight was not needed.

"Mother!" he called as he sprang through the tent's entrance.

"We are here, my son. Hurry, please hurry!"

"Where is father?" he asked while scurrying to join his mother and sister beneath their dinner table.

"We do not know. He might be off to see one of the Elders."

"I must find him."

Calish started to get up, but his mother stopped him. "No, my son, it is too late."

Calish listened, for once, and quickly retreated to be by his mother's side. He was glad of it too, because the thundering sounds shook him to his core. Soon enough, the tabletop items tossed and tumbled from the vibrations outside. Plates, bowls, cups and candles flew off the table onto the trembling floor. Up and down went everything, here and there the pieces flew about. The family stared wide-eyed, hoping that the table could stand firm under the strain. They locked their arms tightly around one another, their hearts racing, pounding as much from fear as from the shaking ground.

"I'm scared, Mommy. Make it stop!" cried Bishtar, Calish's twin sister. But Hannah, their mother, did not respond. It was enough for her to merely keep from crumbling into as many pieces as that of her dancing dinner ware.

More thunder boomed loudly, and lightening glittered across the darkened sky. What should have been the tribe's bright sunny morning was nowhere to be seen.

Many of the congregate remained outside their tents; they huddled in small groups, or scampered beside their animals. And as the gathering wept, cried out, and got on their knees to pray, a sound unlike anyone had ever heard suddenly emerged from places no sound should emanate. It was the crunching sound of grinding, heaving rock. It was a noise as alien to a human's ears as the sound of a mighty sea that had been ripped open into two equal parts.

"What is that noise, Mother?" asked Bishtar as she covered her ears.

"It is the sound, my daughter, of the One who lives on top of the mountain."

"You mean Moses?"

"No, my dearest one. Not Moses; his God."

The ground then shook so hard that nearly all the humans and animals fell to the ground. After that, part of the ground opened wide enough so that some of the outlying tents and people fell into it.

The abyss, like a ravenously hungry maw, was growing, and becoming alive. Flames, smoke, and flashes of burning cinders licked their way up through the depths, touching many near the pit's edge, often stretching out to engulf those that were many feet from the opened ground.

Someone suddenly made a mad dash to run further away, and the fires transformed. No more were they just random flames; now they coalesced into a giant burning hand. The hand stretched

7

and towered over the pit. The fiery appendage reached to grab the crazed runner mid-stride. The runner, while being pulled back into the abyss, screamed in agony as his body turned to ashes.

"Tis the hand of Amheh!" a witness screeched, "delivering us to his lake of fire!"

After seeing this, many more tried to scamper in different directions, but those that did so only found another hole suddenly appear before them, ready to take them too. They were trapped, not only by the falling, but also from Amheh's flaming fingertips. Once captured, the fiery hand tore the runners into crisps as they were drawn downward. There was nothing for them but an even more cruel punishment for those who dared to defy their fate.

"Do not run!" they shouted to one another, "Stay where you are!"

But the orifice continued to follow a path that surely seemed predestined, gradually encircling the area where the three tribes of Korah, Dathan, and Abiram had centered their camps. Somehow the pit's fissures had only opened within those boundaries; not going outward, but slowly drawing themselves closer to where the Elders had pitched their tents. Nothing could stop the onslaught. Whole tents full of people slid below. Men, women and children shrieked in terror as the ground beneath them gave way to the rushing sensation of dropping into thin air.

The screams became so loud that they even drowned out the occasional thunder-clap. Many of the screeches were cut off only when one of the falling bodies suddenly crashed into a jagged rocky edge that outlined the abyss. Some fell instantly, while others who had not yet fallen scrambled to find something, anything, to grab hold of.

"Grab hold and tie yourself to the heaviest of beasts," one tribesman reasoned aloud. Others, thinking it an option, followed suit. But even the powerful oxen were propelled down, many of them clunking madly against the rock, their skulls and backbones making a gut-wrenching cracking sound as their flip-flopping bodies were shred to pieces. And of course the men who had tied themselves to the beasts were captive to a wild and bumpy ride into the void.

Upon seeing this, the survivors moved quickly to areas closer to the Elders' tents. And together they watched with terror as the fissures and fires progressed toward them, intent upon completing their mission.

"We're doomed!" they cried to one another. "What shall we do?"

As the chasm advanced upon the tents of Abiram, his tribe's bravest hunter, Asher, boldly approached the nearest hole. He carried the tribe's greatest weapon, a spear he had earned from Pharaoh. Asher stood tall and defiant upon the chasm's edge, defying the wind that pushed him about. Abiram and all his clan watched with great hope to see if Asher, with his mighty spear, could defeat the abyss.

"Watch out!" one clansman suddenly screamed to warn Asher.

Gradually a fiery hand grew out of the pit, expanding and stretching its flaming fingers toward him. But Asher did not cower or retreat. He looked at his spear with great pride. Then he pulled back the arm that held the weapon and with a mighty effort cast the lance into the heart of the red, flaming hand.

The spear ripped through the hand right before its fire reached to grab him. The red hot fingers retracted from the spear's hit. And while emitting a deafening howl, the hand turned into a ball of fiery smoke and fell below.

Everyone cheered with joy, for it appeared that Asher had defeated their enemy.

The spear thrower turned back to his Lord Abiram. Asher smiled broadly, as if to say he had done well. Abiram smiled too while saying, "Well done. Well done."

"Look out, Asher!" someone screamed again. But it was too late because another fiery hand even bigger than the first formed right above Asher's head. Before he could move, the fiery fingers swallowed Asher up and pulled him down into the abyss.

Abiram, with trembling breath, responded, "May the gods be with you, my son."

Soon after Asher disappeared, the ground shook some more and the opening that took the spear thrower spread to Abiram's tents. Within seconds, Abiram and all of his tribe were cast below.

Dathan was shocked to see these things, but not so much that he could not recover his footing. He grabbed hold of his tent's front support beams and stood tall. He wanted his clan to know that he would not give into the fear. He stared up at the nearby mountain with great anger. He raised his fist in hatred toward the lone figure that stood prominently upon a mountain's ledge.

Then Dathan spewed out his accusations. "You! You are the one that caused this. You would stand by, a witness that would do nothing to stop it."

The witness, the figure who stood on the mountain, looked down upon the scene, but did not, could not, stop the onslaught.

"Moses!" shouted Dathan, his voice seething with rage. "Moses, hear me!"

But there was no answer except that of the howling wind and crunching rock.

When it was clear that Moses would not listen, Dathan turned toward Korah's tent to see if his brethren would help. Above the crashing, thrashing sounds of the apocalypse, Dathan shouted, "Korah, do something!"

But Korah did not respond. He too looked up at Moses, but Korah's expression was one of great distress and sorrow. It was already decided; Korah now understood that. And even though the distance was great, Korah recognized that Moses was returning his gaze. Moses, whose face shown with the brilliance of the sun, stood out among everything else along the mountainside. This was a sign to Korah, pointing to the One Moses spoke of. In shame, Korah lowered his head while thinking, *If only we had heeded your warnings and remained obedient. If only we had believed in the truth behind our deliverance from Egypt.*

If only...

Once again, Korah lifted his eyes to meet the radiant face of Moses. And Moses was still there, a great man upon an even greater mountain, as it should be. Then Korah quietly, reverently pleaded, "Moses, my brother, do not forsake us. Ask Father to redeem us."

Moses's face glowed even brighter than before, and its light spread forth toward Korah. The Elder felt its warmth wash over and then flow through him. The gentle heat touched Korah's heart. The light's power went to the sacred object Korah had been given to protect, honor, and learn from.

"Korah, you fool!" screeched Dathan, "Why do you waste time? Call out to Moses. Demand he do something before we all perish."

Korah was distracted by Dathan's verbal assault. Korah took his eyes off Moses and turned to look at his fellow Elder. Dathan's face could melt iron. It was a heartbreaking sight. Korah could see in Dathan all that he himself had recently displayed: pride, avarice, and folly.

As a section of the pit, like a slithering snake, wove its way toward Dathan's tent, the angry man pointed at Moses and shouted, "Now, Korah, damn you. Now!"

"No, Dathan," Korah solemnly replied, "Damn to all of us... to all of us." And maybe, for a moment that was truly hard to accept, Korah understood why. While his wife and grandchildren wrapped their trembling arms around him, Korah clutched onto the sacred item he had hidden in his pouch. And the object, had it not been covered, would shine with a brilliance matched only by the luminescent face of Moses. But it was not yet time for that truth to be revealed.

"Kora-h-h-h-h!" echoed Dathan's screams as he and his tents full of his family fell into the abyss.

In the last seconds, as Korah could feel the ground beneath him start to give way, he looked up to the mountain one last time. To the shining figure Korah said, "Goodbye, my old friend."

Then the Earth all around them opened completely. Everything they knew, everything they had, everything they had ever created, fell into the pit. All that they once were was gone from the congregation.

CHAPTER 3
We Awake in Darkness

"Somehow we live," a voice whispered near him as if it did not believe it was possible.

The Elder looked all around, disoriented and dazed. It was dark, very dark. But even if one could not see, the numerous sounds of rustling bodies, moans of pain, and cries for help meant that many had survived. He got on his feet, unsteady at first, but otherwise whole. "Why can't I see?" he mumbled while touching his fingers to his eyes. He looked around again. Luckily there was a bit of light off to his left so he moved toward it.

As he did so, his foot bumped up against a lumpy form. The Elder reached down to see what it was. "God be with us," he exclaimed. Whatever it had been, or whoever, was now dead. The lifeless body felt stiff, cold and broken. Its arms, torso and head were riddled with smashed bits of flesh and exposed bone. The Elder touched a gaping hole in the corpse's head and sticky blood oozed onto his fingers. There was nothing he could do to help, so the Elder stood up while wiping the goo on his tunic. "God be with you."

As the Elder moved toward the light, he noticed other folks that were in varying degrees of motion as well. Some barely moved, while others had already regained their footing. The Elder kept moving. In the near distance he saw a fire pit, which was the light's source. The pit's arrangement was disheveled, but enough logs remained intact to keep the flames going. The folks who had regained their feet followed the Elder to the fire's light.

"Korah, is that you?" one of them said along the way.

The Elder Korah responded, "It is I. Who are you?" It was still too dark to be sure.

"It is I, Mishtas."

"Ah good, good." Seeing someone alive from his own camp was a hopeful sign. Korah and Mishtas soon held one another in solidarity and words of thankful greetings were exchanged.

"My Lord, what has happened?" asked Mishtas anxiously.

"I know not..." Korah decided to remain silent rather than explain to Mishtas what had taken place on the mountain. Nor did he wish to discuss the argument he had with Moses. He thought it best to keep those matters private; at least for now. "I'm not sure, Mishtas, I'm not sure."

"My head aches," complained Mishtas as he felt over his head and face. "I feel like I have slept a long time, too long maybe."

"Yes, I feel the same," agreed Korah, also still dizzy and unsettled.

"How long do you think we have been here, my Lord?"

"I know not, Mishtas. How say you?"

As Mishtas felt over his face, he suddenly noticed something, "My face has stubble on it. I remember now... my wife had helped me shave the morning the earth had opened up. And now I have this thick stubble."

"And... how long do you think?"

"I would say two days' worth."

Korah was startled by the news. How could they have been unconscious, or sleeping, or whatever they were for that long? What had happened to them while they *slept?* More importantly, where were his wife and kin?

He looked around again, but as nothing had really changed, he turned back to Mishtas, asking worriedly, "My wife? My son and daughter-in-law? My other sons? Have you seen them, any of them?"

"No, I am sorry."

"Oh," sighed Korah, visibly distressed to hear it.

"My Lord," prompted Mishtas, "if you want, I will go to find them."

Korah was at first happy to have the offer, but at the same time troubled to be left alone. Eventually though, the Elder took Mishtas up on his kind suggestion. "Yes, my son, please, if you will do your best to find them." Mishtas was not really a 'son' to Korah. He was actually a distant nephew, but since Mishtas was in Korah's tribe, it was not uncommon to refer to him as a son.

"I will, father, I will." As a sign of affection, as well as honor, Mishtas returned the familiar title. Mishtas grabbed Korah's forearms, smiled bravely, and moved into the darkness to find his kin.

Korah scanned the remaining folk that had gathered near him. Some he knew, but many were strangers.

"Korah, do something!" one of them exclaimed.

The assembled crowd seemed to like that demand. There were many voices but their murmurs indicated that the request was uppermost on their minds. The assembly pressed up against the Elder, surrounding him, peppering him with questions.

"Korah, Korah, where are we?" one of them asked.

"I know not," Korah answered, "But surely I say to you that we must be beneath what we once knew."

"Beneath?" another person asked quizzically. "What does that mean, *beneath*?"

"Beneath? How is that possible?" requested someone else.

"Korah, can you do something? Please do something to bring us home. Say something."

"Please, my friends, remain calm. I..:" stammered Korah, trying to find a free space, and a way to come up with the right words.

Luckily, before Korah could finish talking, Dathan roughly pushed his way to the front of the group. He was carrying a brightly lit torch. Dathan's best soldiers marched closely behind. Some of the people drew in closer, if not to hear better, then to be nearer to the light source. Abiram and two of his sons were soon to follow.

After the men jostled for position, the three Elders took the central spot and looked upon one another, waiting for someone to speak.

"We need to do something," Abiram blurted out.

"Yes we must, Abiram, but what shall we do?" asked Dathan irritably.

The Elders scanned one another's eyes with anxious expressions while they once again waited for one of them to take the lead.

Moans and cries for help then started to drift up from the dark space. Some were distant, some were close. It was hard to tell; the darkness was everywhere.

"Where are we?" one distant voice yelled.

"I know not. Do you know?" replied someone else.

"I am hurt, please, someone help me!" screeched another.

"Where are my children? Someone please find my children!" The voice of a very distressed woman wailed louder than most.

Others joined in, likewise calling out for lost loved ones. On and on the hurried and pleading voices from the dark filtered through the mysterious spaces. Confusion and sorrow gripped the people. What had started out as merely a few voices quickly turned into a mad chorus of despair.

Korah said nervously, "We must do something!"

Shouts and screams erupted, and the panic was spreading. Thrashing could be heard as some folks started fighting over lost items, lost people, animals, or anything else. Once again, the Elders scanned one another, waiting for some kind of decision to be made.

Abiram voiced unsurely, "We could collect ourselves first, I believe." Impulsively, he grabbed Dathan's tunic sleeve and fearfully stammered, "Before we end up killing each other!"

"Yes, I agree," said Dathan decisively. He removed Abiram's trembling grip from his sleeve and turned to Gasheer, his best soldier. "Take a group of men. Collect as many torches as you find. Quell any dissent, and tell the people to remain where they are until we can better manage the situation."

"Someone help me-e-e-e!" rang a loud shout from the dark.

"And please, if you will," furthered Dathan as he winced from hearing the peoples' wailing cries, "Do something to keep them quiet."

"Yes, my Lord," replied Gasheer. The man was a giant, nearly as wide as he was tall. His face was scarred, rugged, and homely. His arms and legs were all heavily muscled and puffy, like chunks of raw bull flesh. Over his torso he wore body armor that was made from the finest and most durable leathers. Those layers were overlain with thousands of overlapping brass scales. No other man could wear it, for the load of Gasheer's armor exceeded the weight of any of his soldiers. In his hand was a helmet made from shiny brass. Leather flaps fell from its sides and served to protect his broad neck. At the helmet's crest, above the summit, was the engraved image of his tribe's ensign, the Ox. Around his waist was a thick leather belt that sheathed his double-edged sword. And it also carried the cruelest of his weapons – a neatly bound bull whip. The man made an impressive and oppressive display.

Gasheer's personality well accompanied his titanic stature. He was coarse, harsh and ruthless. If anyone crossed him, Gasheer was not shy about introducing the offender to his unforgiving whip, what he called the Paingiver. Gasheer placed the helmet on his head, removed the bullwhip from his belt and turned to do as instructed. His foot soldiers, knowing their place, were close on his heel.

Korah watched Gasheer leave, thinking unkind things about him. The bully was well known to both the Hebrew nation and the Egyptians. And Gasheer's infamy was almost as impressive as that of his colossal stature.

Gasheer, a taskmaster for the Egyptian cause, had been given responsibilities that included running various building projects. Not many Hebrews rose to a ranked position among the Egyptians. Gasheer was an exceptional case because he had more than proven his worth to the Egyptian overseers by making sure their bricks were made, their enormous stones were moved, or their levers constructed. Most importantly, if schedules were not met, Gasheer was quite willing to demonstrate that there would be a heavy price to pay for Hebrew disobedience. Since leaving Egypt, while wandering in the desert, Gasheer had chosen men from various camps to create a militia. And under Gasheer's tutelage, they were well versed in war and aggressive tactics. So their immediate task of quelling the noisy tribesmen was something they were happy to do.

"Traitorous, foul-smelling brute," mumbled Korah under his breath.

The soldiers took up their clubs and in small bands ventured into the people's midst. Soon they could hear the soldiers shouting instructions. Those that were slow to comply were threatened, and more often than not, beaten into submission. Sharp cracking sounds soon shot forth from the darkness as the soldier's cudgels hit raw bones or body. Those sounds were

16

immediately followed by shouts of pain. The snap of Gasheer's whip also told its own unique story.

Snap!

"Awh!! Stop please stop. Gasheer, my Lord, I beg you..."

Snap! Snap!

After a few more snaps of the Paingiver, the noise level, beyond the echoing crack of Gasheer's whip, gradually began to dissipate. There were still moans, wailing cries, and sobs of pain, but Gasheer's men had done well to greatly minimize it.

The trio of Elders then conferred once again. They looked all about their position. Because the soldiers had commandeered many of the torches, then spread out to complete their task, the whole area had become more easily seen.

"We are in some kind of large cave," observed Korah as he looked up at the cavern's ceiling. In some spots the roof was lower to the ground than others, but overall it was a solid mass. There were no gaps or holes where one might see the sun, stars or anything they once knew. "We must be far beneath where our camps once stood at the mountain's base."

"We have fallen to our doom," sighed Abiram.

"We are still alive, Abiram," replied Dathan in a condescending way. "So obviously our *doom* has been postponed." Dathan turned to where he believed Gasheer was and shouted, "Gasheer! Come here!"

The soldier promptly did as he was told. "Yes, my Lord."

"Gasheer, take your men. And take Abiram's men too." Dathan stopped for a moment to see if Abiram would agree with his commands. Abiram quickly nodded his consent and gestured to his sons as if to say that they should obey Dathan. The men looked unsure at first. Then they acquiesced by bowing their heads toward Dathan.

"Yes, my Lord," one of Abiram's sons said to his new master.

Dathan was glad to hear and see this. With a confident smile, he continued to instruct all those under his charge. "Go about the area. Take stock of who has survived, who has died, who is hurt, and all supplies you find."

"The dead, what should we do with them?" asked Korah.

17

"Yes," agreed Abiram. "There are dead ones, I have seen it. It will cause panic again if the dead remain so close to the living."

"I agree, Abiram," said Korah. He too had already encountered the dead. It was unsettling, to say the least.

Dathan acknowledged the point with a thoughtful nod and turned to Gasheer. "Gather the dead. Find a secluded spot and deposit them there. That will have to do for now."

Mishtas appeared from the darkness and nodded to Korah. The Elder spoke to his companions. "Gentlemen, if you will excuse me, Mishtas and I have something to discuss." The two men went off to the side to discuss what Mishtas had found.

"My wife? My sons?" pressed Korah.

"Your wife was found. I... am sorry."

Korah looked very sad. He put his head down, and in between stifled sobs, he stuttered, "Please make sure you keep her separated from the other dead that Gasheer's men collect. I... we will find a resting place for her ourselves."

"I understand, father." To bolster Korah's heartrending mood, Mishtas offered, "Many of your grandchildren were found and are well. I have asked some women to see to them. Unfortunately your sons have not been seen, but one of Abiram's nephews tells me that they were in another distant valley when the earth opened, so they are most likely not among us."

"Yes, it is true, my sons where sent off on another mission far from our camps. I hope they are well, wherever they are."

"Yes, father, I hope so too."

"Hannah and her children?"

"Yes, father, they have been found near what remains of their tent. And they are well enough."

"Very good, my son. Thank you, thank you."

"But my Lord, there are still many unaccounted for... including my wife. I found our tent, but she was not there."

"I am sorry to hear this, my son." Korah held onto Mishtas's arm in a sympathetic way.

After a few moments, as the men consoled each other, Mishtas wiped away some tears, collected himself and continued to give Korah his findings. "There are many dark spaces that remain a mystery to us. I have asked others to help look for survivors in those places but they are too afraid to venture there. Some say they have heard loud screams."

"Yes, the lost are surely frightened and call for help."

"No, my Lord. They say there are screams of terror, as if something has attacked them."

"But what else could be here with us, Mishtas?"

"I know not, father, I know not."

* * * *

Somewhere in the dark recesses, far from where most of the tribe had awakened, survivors stumbled and reached out their hands, trying to find something familiar to grab hold of. Were they blind? How could everything be so dark? If it be night, where were the stars, the moon, or the fire pits? They were looking for anything to bring them back into the real world.

"Hashm, Meebel, Shemit? Where are you?"

One such woman, although bruised and battered, lurched forward, looking for her family, calling out their names in harsh whimpers.

She eventually came upon a soft form. She reached down and touched its surface, wondering what it was. Could it be her husband, or her two little children? She scanned over the whole figure. The size and shape seemed close enough to be that of her husband, but what was covering the form? It was like a very fine sticky thread.

"Husband, is that you?"

She clawed at the fibers, searching for a way through it. It was strong; she had to tear it apart. After that, she reached inside and felt cloth. Past it was flesh. It was an arm. She could feel a man's arm. She slid her fingers along the limb to its hand, her body trembling in anticipation and fear. She soon found the hand's fingers... a thumb, forefingers, and finally, as tears welled up in her eyes, a ring. It was the ring of promise and marriage. It was the band she had given her groom on their wedding day.

"Hashm. My husband." Sobs welled up to accompany her tears.

Then, a shuffling sound off to her left caught her attention. Could it be her little ones? She briefly looked but saw only darkness and more darkness still. A strange rapid-fire clicking noise then emerged.

Click, click, click, click, click, click, click, click. Hunched low to the ground and well within the darkness was a large shadowy form. Its spherical white eyes, rotating here and there, could not see. But this thing did not need to see. It twitched its jaggedly spiked mandibles, clicking them open and shut rapidly, as it felt the air for movement.

"Children, is that you?" she cried out.

The creature scrambled to the noise and pounced. It grabbed the woman with three of its forelegs, holding her in place. With a sudden lurch, the beast sent its thorn-like fang into her chest. The implement pierced her body; its pointy end soon thereafter emerged from her back. Shocked by the brute force, the woman was pushed hard to the ground. After catching her breath, she let out an ear-piercing scream. Then again, she shrieked even louder than before. "AAA-aa-HHHH!"

But the noise meant nothing to the monster, for it could easily shut itself off to unwanted sounds. The creature opened its toothy mouth. Then the glands that held its venomous mixture opened as well. The poison and acidic juices flowed down its fang and poured into the woman's body, liquefying her organs into a gooey sludge. The woman began choking as the bubbling blend of fluids filled her lungs and throat.

A bit of the slush touched the beast's undulating tongue. The creature could not resist the taste of it, so rather than spinning its prey into a food reserve for later consumption, the monster decided to first feed itself. Drawing closer to the source of food, the creature began sucking and slurping the thick substances into its cruel mouth. Some of the gooey mush spilled out, but by using one of its nimble forelegs, those bits were soon brought back into its waiting maw.

Nearby, two children now waking from their sleep, reached for each other and started to make noises. The movement so close by caught the monster's attention. Apparently it was not done hunting. Out of instinct, its blind eyes rotated in the direction of the sound.

* * * *

"Sheol," said the young warrior in consternation. He had heard the screams and ran as fast as he could to investigate. He arrived just in time to see the animal feeding on its prey. The monster was not to be trifled with, so he quickly took up a place behind a nearby alcove wall. From there he saw another prone form that was woven-up by the beast's thread. The second body was the monster's source of food for another time. He could also see two children moving about. Although he knew the creature was blind, he could tell that it was aware of the children's presence. The warrior, unlike the monster, could see very well in the dark. But that was but a small advantage against the hungry animal that hunted the surface dwellers. With his clawed hand he took up the stony hammer from his belt. He stood silently in the dark, waiting for his chance to do something to help save the little ones from the cruel beast.

"Striggitzz Sheol," he voiced quietly.

If only he had his brothers with him, the monster might be defeated. Alone, he stood little to no chance of success. The beast, a species of Mestalor, had victimized the warrior's people for eons of time. Their hard-shelled bodies were made up of two main parts. The front section had four multi-segmented legs on each side. Their heads were a tiny protrusion on its front part; sightless eyes sat on thin rods that shot out from its head. Its two pincers were clawed, hairy and covered the monster's fang-filled mouth. Inside its maw were the creature's most vicious weapons, a sharp puncturing spike, and acidic saliva that could melt its victim's insides into an edible slush. The Mestalor was a swift, nimble and powerful foe. Singular combat against a Mestalor adult was typically unsuccessful, and the specimen before the warrior was clearly a full-grown example.

"Mommy," one of the children cried.

The warrior cringed in frustration, knowing that the little one had made a fatal mistake. The creature, now very aware of its

21

prey's position, separated itself from its victim and jerked its segmented body toward the sound. The monster then started twitching its spiky pincers in anticipation. *Click, click, click, click.*

"Mommy!"

The monster's multiple legs jerked and skittered toward the ready food. Like a flash of light, the young warrior leapt into action, running with all his force at the creature. When he was near the back of the beast, he jumped up through the air, while swinging his stony hammer as hard as he could. Down went the club, directly striking one of the creature's hind legs. *Crack* went the hammer as it struck the beast's exoskeleton, splitting open a small part of it. The creature recoiled from the strike and swiftly poked out one of its other appendages at its attacker. The warrior was catapulted through the air, striking hard against a nearby cave wall.

"Oomph," he uttered as his body impacted the rocky surface. Stunned, but not so much he could not get up, he did so gingerly and slowly. He quickly accessed the situation. The beast faced him but otherwise made no moves to attack. He could retreat, but that would not save the small surface dwellers. The little ones sat helpless and within easy reach of the monster.

"Striggitzz," he said in anger. If only he had listened to his father and not run off alone to investigate the tremendous shaking of the underworld. But curiosity had gotten the best of him, as usual. And something inside of his recent Sklon-induced visions had told him to learn more about the strange beings that had been thrust into his world.

The creature remained facing the warrior, waiting for its attacker to give away his position. The warrior would not let the animal have that advantage, so he stayed as still as he could. It was a stalemate, but for how long? He could use his skills at mind-speak, but would that work against such a creature? There were stories, legends, of such things, but those were just tall tales, and he was still an apprentice in his quest to be a mind-speak master. He could use his hammer, but the monster would not be so stupid to turn its back again. *Besides,* he reasoned, *my hammer is not nearly powerful enough to kill the huge beast.* If only the horrific thing would just take its food and retreat, but the giant was too greedy and too stimulated.

The children called out again. "Mother, where are you?"

The creature twisted toward them.

"Striggitzz!" the warrior shouted. With all his might, he threw the hammer at the creature. The weapon bounced off the monster's head, shattering one of its protruding eyes. The creature shrieked in pain and turned away from the children and back toward the warrior. Abruptly, the creature flew at its attacker, its multiple legs jolting madly across the rocky floor.

In an act of desperation, the warrior extended his arm and instantly sent a mind-speak message into the monster's simple brain. *Home.*

The creature suddenly stopped at the very tip of his outstretched arm. The beast's rotating eyes were within easy reach of the warrior's trembling fingers. He could smell its rotten breath upon him as the beast's open mouth dripped sludgy drool upon the ground. The closeness of its bulging sightless eyes, one of them broken and bloody, and the twitching mandibles, was disgusting. The frightened warrior inwardly recoiled from it, but nonetheless he managed to remain motionless.

Sheol. The creature was, for the moment, frozen in place by his mind-speak's mental command. The message was designed to make the simple creature envision the place where it dwelt. The warrior had been to places where Mestalors built their homes. He had touched the filaments that covered their cold, damp spaces, and heard the strange twang-like sounds of the fiber's vibrations. His mind-speak message was visual, tactile, and audible. Although the beast was blind, it nonetheless could share in his understanding of the creature's habitat. It was the place where, in between feeding, Mestalors could sit motionless, quietly waiting for endless amounts of time.

Home. To secure the beast's stillness, the warrior once again sent the home-speak command. But this time, and for an unspeakably bizarre and disquieting moment, his connection with the beast was complete. He could sense what it was like to be in the creature's mind. It was a black, lonely, and unforgiving place, filled with strange sounds, disgusting tastes, and endlessly swirling emptiness. It was breathtakingly dreadful. Moreover, that bleak, lonely place wanted him to stay there. It began sucking him deeper into its desolate darkness, round and round, ultimately seeking to crush him permanently.

No, he determined willfully, *I must escape from here. I... Yes I am not this.* The warrior struggled mightily to return himself to his own awareness, reaching past the darkness, stretching his mind upward, beyond the blackness. He did see the light, at last.

"Sheol," he whispered in distress. After he had recovered his own normal consciousness, while still staring at the unmoving beast, the warrior brought his arm to his side. He cocked his head at the creature, as if to see it in a different way. The mind-speak experience had left him feeling a sad kind of empathy for the monster... almost that is, until he was drawn to the constant dripping sound of the beast's drool. He looked down at the small pool of slime as it burned into the ground. The awful smelling vapor filtered into his nostrils. The sight, sound and smell of it reminded the warrior that he and the beast were very different; and that he should not be taken in by his own mind-speak. His teachers had warned him of such things. He now knew that they had been very right. For the moment, at least, he felt secure in the mind-speak's effectiveness and the creature's immobility. He then slowly backed off, sliding along the cave wall. With a feather-like step, he began tip-toeing over the creature's numerous legs. Finally, when he had achieved enough distance, he scooted toward the creature's food reserves.

The warrior reached down. In an effort to attract the beast, he violently shook the dead form that was covered with the monster's thread. It was a warning aimed at threatening the beast's food reserves. Once again he cast out his mind-speak message: *Home.*

The beast suddenly jerked toward the warrior and shot through space. The warrior jumped out of the way just as the creature pounced upon the body. The animal quickly scanned the threaded form with its pincers. The monster then grabbed it up with one leg, throwing the lumpy figure along its back. From its hind parts the creature spun some more sticky fibers; two legs instantly grabbed the threads and wrapped the form securely to its back.

24

The monster turned and skittered across the ground toward a cavern corner. With no effort, the monster climbed straight up the cavern's steepest walls. Like a shadow, the monstrosity disappeared into a dark recess.

"Grizzlist," the warrior said in relief. He took in his first real deep breath since encountering the monster. He glanced at the tiny humans. For now at least, the little ones were safe. *But for how long,* he pondered? The Mestalor would be back. The surface dwellers were a food source that was too easy to capture.

The young warrior retrieved his weapon and returned to the area near the monster's prey. He knelt beside the corpse to better examine it. The dead body had been a female, and most likely the mother to the nearby children. With a quizzical expression, he whispered, "What are you? How can such a thing exist?" She was very strange looking to the warrior, notwithstanding the huge gaping hole in her chest. He studied her face. Her open, dead eyes displayed a shocked expression. "The eyes are so small, white, and have a small circle of color within them. And what is this on her head?" She not only had hair on her head, but it was long, and very thick. He ran his clawed fingers through it, wondering how the silky threads could have grown to such lengths. He picked up her hand. It was so light, delicate, and the fingers did not come to a sharp point like his. Her skin was a pale, pinkish color that was smooth and soft. He touched the female's clothing and was further amazed. Her garments were finely woven from a fiber that was very flexible, intricate... and so colorful too. *How could they have tailored such a thing?*

His mother, or even the greatest queen to have ever ruled, would have been envious of such attire. He leaned back, assessing what he was seeing. Suddenly he realized that he was a witness to something none of his people had ever encountered in real life.

"This female is what Ashkolon calls *human*." He voiced in wonder, "Surface dwellers. I am the first of my kind to see that his visions are real. Humans are not a myth, and they come from the surface world." The notion Ashkolon preached, and that some of his people held, was true. If that was correct, then the surface dwellers must be linked to his people's destiny. Age-old prophecy was shaping up to be a very real possibility.

25

"There will come a time when our peoples will be reunited," Ashkolon had advised. But after the world had mightily trembled, the warrior's tribe had been too frightened to act. Most of them could not accept, nor believe, Ashkolon's predictions. The young warrior, however, was different from the rest of his people. By acting on his own Sklon vision, the impulsive warrior had travelled to the place where the surface dwellers had fallen. He had arrived in time to fight the Mestalor, but beyond that he did not have much of a chance to truly study them. He now had that opportunity. "And I am the first," he voiced proudly.

He turned to watch the little ones as they continued to stumble about. They remained clueless as to how close death had been upon them. Moreover, they did not have the sense or ability to find a way back to their people.

Surface dwellers are so helpless, so fragile, he thought. After touching the dead woman's soft skin, and seeing how uncoordinated the children were, he couldn't help but believe that surface dwellers were innately inferior. Then he wondered if they could at least mind-speak. *Can they hear me?* he wondered. The warrior opened his mind to communicate with the children, as he would normally do with any of his own people. But he got nothing in return. *As my teachers described, humans do not mind-project thoughts.* He scanned the dead female's corpse again. *And their hides are so smooth, and easily damaged. How could they have ever survived? How long can they survive the underworld?*

A soft ticking noise caught the warrior's attention. He looked toward the sound. "Sheol," he hissed in irritation. Another threat, albeit an annoying one, was approaching the scene. The tiny creatures, attracted by the woman's blood, were finding their way along all surfaces and would soon be upon her corpse. Possibly they would be near enough, and frenzied enough, to attack the little ones as well.

"Striggitzz! Sheol." He had to do something quickly, otherwise the tiny insects would eventually find and attack the children. The warrior looked off into the distance. The surface dwellers had lit fires further into the caverns but the little ones could not see it. He would not reveal himself to the children by pointing out where to go. It was not the time to do so.

But he had an idea. Although he could not speak their language, the warrior believed that he might be able to project a special mind-speak image into their minds. So he reached into his pouch and withdrew a special mixture of Sklon. He quickly consumed it. The taste was truly disgusting, but his purpose far outweighed the momentary discomfort. Within a few moments he could feel the Sklon's energies filter up from his gut and then enter his mind. It was... exhilarating, powerful, and as always stimulating.

"Grizzlist." His body jerked, signaling that the Sklon had attained a kind of control over him. Transparent colors floated in front of his eyes. The hues transformed into nebulous blobs. The blobs morphed into strange beasts and even more bizarre looking humanoids. Places unknown to him also passed before him, gliding in and out of empty air. The collections of semi-transparent shapes even pressed themselves into nearby rocky surfaces. It was fascinating to witness, but nonetheless distracting. He had to allow the Sklon's power to help him before its energies waned. He readied his mental focus, bringing forth his self-identity, his will and his intentions. He stood up straight and stretched out his clawed hand toward the children.

"Sassitasss. Sassitass-s." Into their minds he sent images of light, fire, and walking. At first there was nothing, no response from them, and nothing to indicate they had perceived him. But then suddenly the warrior sensed that he was with them, in their thoughts. He immediately recognized that their minds were nimble, alert, and very receptive. For a moment he could sense what they wanted. They longed for the woman that lay dead and not far from their position. He could see through their eyes and they could also see what he saw. The warrior quickly turned his sights away from the woman so the children would not see her dead body. Rather, he directed his vision toward the fires in the distance. Then he sent a mind-speak command encouraging them to walk to the light.

Go there, he compelled. The two little ones suddenly looked at one another, confusion on their brows. Together they gazed into the expanse of the cavern. Although they could not yet see any light, they nonetheless started walking in the correct direction.

"Grizzlist." *'Success.'*

"This is strange," he thought to himself. A word unknown to him bubbled up in the warrior's mind. "Succ-s-ess-s." He spoke the word aloud, trying to repeat the sound he had heard in his mind. Could it be a word familiar to the surface dwellers? Was a Sklon induced mind-speak a sharing of knowledge that went beyond what he was told by his teachers?

While pondering the possibilities, the young warrior was forced to accept that there were many things he had yet to learn. "I will, however, keep that revelation to myself." If he were to reveal such an insight to Ashkolon, the prophet would probably get angry with him for taking so long to finally accept what the ancient teacher had lectured to him, over and over, and over, and yet over again. "Striggitzz Sheol, Ashkolon, I heard you the first 300 times."

Before too long, the warrior could feel the Sklon's effects fade. Thoughts of Ashkolon's sour face and of normal things helped to overcome the vision's influence. But the experience helped him realize that although it was a powerful tool in aiding visions, and now apparently communicating with other intelligent beings, Sklon was only a temporary ally. *No matter*, he reasoned. His Sklon had served its purpose.

As the dazed and confused children slowly walked to the lit areas of the cavern, behind them a flurry of activity soon swarmed over the woman's corpse. Small, creepy-crawly insects swamped the woman's lifeless form. They entered any opening they could find. If they couldn't find easy access, the little biters merely crunched their sharp pincers through her soft flesh. Digging their sturdy bodies into the skin, they soon thereafter disappeared, all the while eating anything and everything.

The young warrior once again looked upon the poor surface dweller. There was nothing he could do for her. He did, however, take solace in knowing that he had saved the woman's offspring. But the female was dead. While watching her being fed upon, he thought about his own hunger; he had not eaten in a while. Normally, if the woman had been of his species, many of his people would hold no reservations about eating her. But he put those thoughts from his mind. "Striggitzz."

28

Nonetheless, to relieve his hunger, he gathered a large handful of the tiny critters who were starting to eat the woman and stuffed them into his mouth. It was a temporary solution, not perfect, but then again not without its merits. One benefit was that it overcame the awful taste of the Sklon, for the tiniest of the insects had enough flavors to make the feeding enjoyable. There was another fortuitous side benefit. The bugs' flavors mingled nicely with the taste of the dead woman that was still within them. All in all, the combination was sufficiently rewarding. "Grizzlist."

While eagerly chewing on the bugs, he squatted down to ponder his next move. His closeness to the dead body encouraged some of the crawlers to scramble upon him as well as the woman. Soon enough they started to bite his skin too. But those opportunistic fiends were quickly impaled by his two-pronged black tongue. The animated little demons were drawn into his waiting mouth, kicking and squiggling all the way. *Delicious. Thank you, my little friends.*

The young warrior decided that he would stay a while longer, watching the surface dwellers. There was something so very curious about them, much beyond the obvious. There was also something that they had. It was an item Ashkolon had alluded to; it was a mystical object, and possibly transcendent. But the old prophet had also been very cryptic about it as well. *Nothing new there.* Nonetheless, the article had to be prophetically significant, otherwise humankind would have never appeared in the underworld. The warrior didn't know what that article was, but if he left, he would never find out.

But more importantly, his people were going to eventually discover the secret that the surface dwellers kept. The young warrior wasn't so sure that that was to be a good thing.

CHAPTER 4
The Valley

Very few knew of the place. Voice preferred it that way. If necessary, the spirit was most adept at finding the most unfriendly ways to discourage the curious. And Voice had help with this. The Valley's rather dangerous occupants did their part to keep the Valley hidden as well. Not that they did so at Voice's bidding, but rather because it was in their nature to do so. But not all the creatures that called the Valley home were brutish; some were actually serene, and in a few instances, quite charming. Nevertheless, a casual stroll along the Valley's tranquil shorelines could result in a much less than peaceful death.

Home sweet home.

The vast hole occupied by the Valley was deep within Father's blue sphere. Voice had discovered it soon after Father had banished His brightest angel to the depths of the underworld. At first the hole was just that – a huge, cavernous hole. But soon enough, life began to emerge. Pockets of plants sprang-up here or there: squiggly little things crawled through the muck and mud; slimy, boneless blobs swam through the waters; and then before too long, forests, rivers, waterfalls, mountains, valleys, and beasts of all kinds criss-crossed the expansive landscapes.

And light? Voice never really understood how it worked, but there was light. The radiant sphere was big by the Valley's standards: awesome, and yet somehow always muted in tone. It was reminiscent of the countless stars Father had spread throughout His cosmos. But the Valley's little sun shone much less brightly. It was like a mere tiny shadow of its celestial brethren. The yellow globe sat suspended in midair, well above the Valley's surface, not confined by limitations like gravity. Voice imagined that its essence was designed the same way.

Ultimately, however, the tiny sun and the lush Valley beneath it begged these eternal questions: *Father, do You mock me? Father, have You given me this Valley because You really love me? Yes, no, how say Ye?*

Father, for His part, was never very keen on answering. *Typical.*

Nonetheless, the Valley was a place Voice could call home. And it was place where Voice occasionally found very powerful allies to do rather ruthless things. *Ah, there you are, my beauties. I see you. Don't be shy.*

As Voice hovered above one particular meadow, three creatures of note popped their enormous heads above the tallest of trees. One of them roared, shaking the branches all around its area. The monstrous beast looked to its companions and they too roared in response.

Oh, how wonderful. My lovely titans. Aren't we talkative today?

Then one of the three titans lifted its flaring nostrils into the air. The monster took in a curious scent, then jostled its head to and fro, and like a thunderbolt shot back into the trees. The beast soon crashed through the branches and ran like mad into the open field, its companions close behind.

Smell something delicious, my dears?

Moving quickly to follow, Voice slid its translucent shape near the top of the biggest titan. 'Graxen', to be precise, was their formal name, according to the Pon. Voice had no quarrel with that name: Graxen was suitably scary and vicious enough. These particular Graxen models were nastier than most. They had brownish-grey skin that was scaly, rough and dense. Their forward-leaning bodies sat on two thickly muscled hind legs. At their body's end was a short, spiky tail. Two stumpy forearms protruded from their upper chest in an odd way. But the claws that sat on those arms were very strong and quite capable of holding prey still while the creature's fang-filled snout tore apart flesh, bone and just about anything else. All in all, Graxen had a wonderful design best suited to keeping the Valley's lesser beasts in check.

Ah, Graxen, my delightfully entertaining cohabiters, as it were.

Father had cast the giant species into the abyss eons ago. Most likely, Father, in one of His temperamental moods, had deemed them unfit to stay on the surface world. *So to the pit you go.*

Similarly, there were many other things – even higher beings – who had suffered the same fate.

But why me, Father?

The largest Graxen, the alpha, was moving fast, pounding his heavy feet on the meadow's tall grasses. Voice shadowed the titan, watching from above, compelled to see if anything deliciously destructive were to happen. *Perhaps I will join in on all the fun.* Voice could have easily outpaced the thunderous behemoth, but that didn't seem to be a sufficient way to enjoy the moment, so Voice morphed its transparent outline into a human-looking male.

Ah yes, Father's preferred design. Man. It suits me well. Voice couldn't help but review its new human body, admiring each and every glowing facet. *He* was immaculately robed in white, with flowing golden-blond hair, sparkling blue eyes, shiny golden skin, and handsomely chiseled features. Usually, when taking bodily form, the spirit's sing-song trick soon followed.

> *"Who is the fairest of them all?"*
> *Who in all the Valley can not see*
> *the reply is really very simple*
> *for the answer is quite clearly... Me!"*

Voice floated his golden body down near the running titans. He then drifted much closer to the alpha's head. He wrapped his newly formed legs over the alpha's broad neck, and in between the beast's numerous spiky thorns. Voice's hands grabbed hold of one of the alpha's spinal barbs. And then Voice hung on for dear life as the two of them bucked up and down with the beast's galloping rhythm.

> *"Yieollll!Yieollll*
> *I screech at thee*
> *excited I am*
> *tis Voice's decree!"*

The spirit didn't often make 'talking noises' like fleshy humanoids did by speaking out loud, but every once in a while, when the situation was right, Voice would make the effort. It was, however, a prickly proposition, because the spirit could not help but to occasionally have a strange sing-song word play when it made noise. For some unfathomable reason, sentient beings found the spirit's word play odd, so Voice almost never spoke aloud around Father's humanoid kind. They could be so insultingly rude. To not take superior beings such as Voice seriously was unacceptable.

Conversely, beasts like Graxen couldn't care less about Voice's noise, so... "Yieollll!"Yieollll!!" he shouted with wild abandon.

Voice's shrieks soon caught the attention of the alpha's two partners. The second largest Graxen male and a smaller female took note of the strange sight. As a matter of fact, they looked harder at the white robed figure than they did at the ground they were running past. And soon enough, the second male couldn't help but to investigate. The second shot like the wind at Voice, and as soon as it got close, it leapt up and snapped at Voice's body. But its fang-littered snout caught nothing but empty air, because Voice's golden figure could easily be nothing but an illusion of form.

"Ah, my friend
you want to play
so for this game
I'll surely stay."

Voice's human face took on a mock expression of total surprise as the second beast tried again to snatch its prize. The Graxen made some more unsuccessful lunges, but Voice eluded the biting creature by moving just out of reach. *Snap!* went the Graxen's snout.

"Almost, try again!"
Snap!
"Oh so close that time, do keep trying."
SNAP!
"One more and I think you'll get me."
SNAP! SNAP!

After that last attempt, the second growled in frustration and backed off a bit. Huffing and puffing, the snarling beast had to hasten its pace to keep up with the swiftly moving alpha.

In the meantime, Voice again began its noise making. After all, one never knew when proper noise making might be needed.

"Speak no more
the play on words
and act as if
they're vile turds."

Displeased by involuntarily speaking more word play, the spirit persistently added,

"Oops and
oops some more
shut your mouth
just like a do..."

No more, no more! Voice shouted in its mind, while cocking his human head at a strange angle. The spirit's handsome face became very calm and tranquil. "Steady, steady, stick to business, my fine fellow." Voice smiled broadly at its intellectual prowess and mastery of word-talking. For a superior being, such tasks were really very simple and easy. "You're doing very well."

"Well thank you for noticing."

"You're very welcome."

Naturally the second Graxen beast did not care what the odd creature was saying. But finding food so close at hand, and having no success at swallowing it was indeed causing the animal to grow in anger. The running Graxen could not help but to fiercely growl at the mocking, noisy figure.

Upon noticing the animal's frustration, Voice enticed the second beast by offering, "I'm really very tasty. Don't give up." Voice then hugged his body very close to the alpha's thick hide where its neck spikes were shallow and short, but also where the second beast could easily reach it.

The second Graxen eyed Voice carefully, but made no move to attack.

"Don't be shy
do not stew
here I'll stretch
and reach to you."

Voice began to extend his arm toward the second Graxen, wriggling his fingers in the process. Voice's face suddenly expressed surprise, and twisted in consternation at his failure to speak properly. *Stop doing that!*

"Very well, if you insist... There, are you happy?"

"Not yet, but soon..."

When the second beast did not attack, Voice elongated his arm further and further until his hand could weave itself in and out of the second's snout. The second Graxen crunched at the illusion, unsuccessfully. The crazed beast soon became more enraged. Voice then enticingly retracted his arm, gradually drawing in the monster. And with each crunch of its snout, the second beast was getting closer to the alpha.

"Almost... try again," Voice offered to the second beast. To himself he praised, "Ah, that's better, no word play."

"You really are an inspiration, aren't you?"

"Why thank you for noticing." Voice was happier about not sing-songing than he was about the Graxen game.

Finally, when the second beast was running side-by-side with the alpha, Voice waved his hand over the second's longest fangs, tempting the animal to make one mad lunge at Voice's whole body. To reinforce the deal, Voice made his body slightly larger. The whiteness of his flowing robe and the glowing color of his golden skin were in stark contrast to the alpha's dark hide. It should have been an easy piece of meat for the second Graxen to chew on.

"Here I am
can't you see

don't delay
come get me."

The hungry creature readily complied. *Crunch* went the second beast's huge maw at Voice. But the Graxen's fangs flew through Voice's illusive form and well into the alpha's neck.

The alpha recoiled from the attack, roaring and furious with its attacker.

The pair of Graxen males stopped running and came to a stop. The second quickly withdrew its teeth from the alpha's neck, with the alpha's blood and skin attached. Also stuck to the second's tongue were broken off spikes from the alpha's neck. The second screeched in pain as it tried to close its mouth without forcing the barbs further into its flesh.

The alpha, not caring about the second's dilemma, twisted its neck and rose up to make a lunging thrust. The alpha caught the second beast at the bottom of its neck, and the two monsters twisted and rolled over one another, chomping back and forth, each trying to get a dominant position.

Meanwhile, Voice gingerly danced and twirled in the air well above the alpha's crusty head, making merry at the violent display.

"La, la la, la
fiddle-lee dee
try as you might
you'll not eat me!"

The smaller female suddenly stopped running and roared, catching the attention of the two fighting giants. They popped up their heads to look at her. She lifted her snout high in the air, sniffing in the scent that had originally piqued their interest.

The alpha followed her as he too took in the distant smell. The alpha snorted and rose up, pushing past the second, stepping on his head in the process. The second followed, albeit while moaning in pain from the alpha's thorns that had punctured its bloodied tongue. Once again the giant titans took up the trail.

Shall we proceed?

The group, running together once more, pounded heavily past everything in their way. And Voice retook his mount upon the alpha's neck.

Soon enough, the biggest beast ran straight toward an enormously gnarled tree.

"Watchout!" screeched Voice as the titan rode perilously close to the tree's low-lying branch. Voice made a last-moment move to duck beneath the branch, even though Voice could just as well pass through it. But passing through the limb would not be nearly so much fun.

"Onward, my beauties, onward!" screeched Voice in exultation.

The trio of hunters strode over a ridge. Soon it became obvious as to what the hungry beasts were after. The titans suddenly stopped, causing dirt and stones to fly into the air. The beasts snorted and growled fiercely at the far-off target.

Oh my, oh my, what a fine morsel you will make... maybe.

Along a distant shoreline, a lone beast drank at the water's edge. The new animal was very different than the giants Voice rode with. The far-off creature was robustly round, soft, furry, and typically rather slow. It did, however, have one powerful weapon. Underneath its tail was an organ that could shoot out a very toxic, burning spray that could liquefy rock.

> *"Be careful my dears*
> *do not be remiss*
> *to forget the poison*
> *of a deadly Memtorsis."*

Most Valley beasts avoided the Memtorsis. Even the Graxen veered clear, if they had any sense. But the trio that now hunted were driven more by their hunger than common sense; not that Graxen were ever known to be the Valley's brightest to begin with.

Disregarding Voice's warning, the family of behemoths rushed to the Memtorsis' spot. The Memtorsis, seeing their approach, waddled further into the shallow waters. The Graxen followed.

The commotion shot up water, sand and debris everywhere as the furry creature turned to face its attackers.

The Graxen alpha took the lead, snapping at the Memtorsis' head, often getting very close to biting its furry ears and neck. The alpha towered over its prey. The titan's toothy snout was nearly the size of the Memtorsis' body. To distract it, the second male Graxen feigned to their prey's side. But the Memtorsis lifted its tail, positioning its weapon toward any beast that got too close. The smaller female snipped at the Memtorsis, but did not commit to any real aggression. When the Memtorsis pointed its tail at her, the female quickly ducked behind one of her larger companions.

Very Interesting, thought Voice as he watched the female execute its less-then-helpful strategy.

The second, still wounded from attacking the alpha, suddenly disregarded caution, opened its bloodied snout and in a fit of fury, flew at the Memtorsis. The furry beast quickly turned its tail, and in a burst of energy spewed a steady stream of its acidic poison right at the second's head. The second's open mouth was quickly met with the hot, sizzling liquid. The poison's searing pain should have stopped the aggressor, but the second's momentum could not be avoided; it slammed into the Memtorsis' body, sending both creatures down hard into the shallow waters. The two combatants tossed and turned, limbs flopping here or there, as spits and spurts of the Memtorsis' flaming hot liquid streamed over the second's body.

The second struggled to extract itself from the Memtorsis. It did so eventually; crawling, limping away as the poison scorched its way into the second's face and hide. For good measure, and as the second Graxen created some distance, the Memtorsis shot off one more gushing hot spray at the second's head.

The steaming hot liquid sizzled through the second's skull, melting flesh, bone and brains. The ruddy mixtures oozed down the Graxen's body, smoldering, and mingling into the shallow water below. The Graxen could not even cry-out, as its damaged throat made sound impossible. Now all that remained of its head was one eye, frozen in shock, as it peered into nothingness. The stunned beast haphazardly lurched forward and toppled onto the alpha's side. Some of the poisonous hot goo spilled onto the alpha's hind legs.

The smoking toxin sizzled and burned through the alpha's tough hide, and the huge monster roared in pain. The alpha bit onto the second's spine hard enough to lift the beast off its wounded legs. The alpha, in a tremendous display of strength, tossed the second's body far from the area. The second flew through the air and crashed into the shore head-first. Instantly, a loud cracking noise echoed through the air as the second's neck snapped in two.

"One dead
three to go
if this continues
there'll be no more show."

The alpha started to shake its snout and pick at its teeth with its front claws. Memtorsis poison from the second's body burned into the alpha's mouth, searing through its spiky fangs and melting its tongue into a black slag. The sludge then seeped between its broken teeth. Nonetheless, the alpha, in a final rage, clamped what was left of its wounded jaws hard onto the Memtorsis' torso, pressing the furry creature into a prone position. The alpha squeezed its jaws tighter than it had ever done. Blood, guts and gore exploded out from the Memtorsis' body.

The Memtorsis was now a heaping, smoldering mess. And the alpha wasn't much better off. The alpha fell to the shallow water on its side. It reared back and bellowed out a distressful call as the toxic acid continued to eat away at its flailing tongue and jowls.

The female Graxen, however, never came to the aid of either of her companions. This intrigued Voice even more than the violently entertaining devastation that had just taken place. He stared at her and asked, "What will you do now, my dear?"

The female spied out Voice suspiciously. She then cast her sights on the two creatures that lay close to her. She moved closer and sniffed deeply at the Memtorsis, but the furry thing's acidic blend of fluids was unappealing to her. She snorted the bad smell out from her nostrils. Then she turned toward the alpha and took in the huge titan's scents. The alpha's flesh, exposed here and there, was quite strong, pungent, and very much appetizing. She growled and snarled, lifting up her jowls, exposing her sharp fangs in the process.

"Oh my, oh my
a hunger to quench
beguiling the senses
from such a foul stench."

Then like lightning she tore into the alpha's exposed underbelly, savagely ripping open the softer tissue. The alpha twisted its head back to try and stop her but she easily scampered out of the way before being struck. The alpha lurched into the shallow water, trying to get away from her. The giant also folded its hind legs over its ripped-open belly, but she kept her snout near enough to attack at any time.

Meanwhile, the broken Memtorsis continued to unwillingly squirt dribs and drabs of its poison all over everything; except of course, the nimble and opportunistic Graxen female, who merely danced out of the way if some of the spray ventured her way. And if she did move out of place, as soon as the spray dissipated, she would ignore the Memtorsis and soon return to her spot near the alpha's bleeding belly.

Why bother with the poisonous Memtorsis when you have a ready meal for the waiting? This Graxen she-devil has a knack for devious, vicious cleverness.

Naturally, Voice thought to make the she-beast its new favorite. *I will remember you, my sweet... sweet?*

Hhmm. Voice suddenly had an inspiration. He levitated his golden body to be very near the female's head.

"I will, I will
call you my Sweety
as you crunch on his bowels
that are juicy and meaty."

40

Sweety stopped stalking the alpha for a moment and took a good hard look at Voice. But she did not make the mistake the second had made by attacking the prospective bit of food. She did, however, cock her head at Voice, in a way that said she was curious about the floating figure. She eventually decided to ignore the strange character, but not before snorting loudly at Voice in a less than respectful manner.

Now don't be rude, Sweety, my dear.

Sweety returned to stalking the prone and dying alpha. And when the alpha raised one of its hind legs a little too high, Sweety darted underneath it and started tearing at the open wound. The alpha cried out in agony, but before too long, Sweety's undulating head was well buried into the alpha's vulnerable belly. Sweety enjoyed her well earned meal, regardless of the alpha's moans and useless howls.

"Eat well, eat well
Sweety, my dear
for humans do come
but us they will fear

Just like the Pon
they will be mine
never redeemed
no prophesy aligned

I'll not be alone
enduring His hate
in Father's chasm
suffering this fate."

"Oh my, there I go sing-song wording again."

"And three verses, nonetheless! Why do you always ramble in threes? Are you stressed again? You are incorrigible."

"So says you, so says you."

Sweety soon thereafter had filled her belly and was ready to depart.

Voice flew in front of her and held out his hand as if to stop her. Sweety snarled in anger and was ready to run off, but then Voice sent a mesmerizing tone into her brain. It was the same noises Voice used to bend susceptible Pon minds to the spirit's will. *MMmmmmmm... MMmmmmmmm. . . MMmmmmmmm.*

Sweety tried to fight off the incessant sounds, shaking her snout back and forth, growling in frustration. But eventually she was overcome; the Valley's mighty king would not be denied. Sweety lowered her head in prostration before her master.

Voice smiled cruelly upon seeing this. He drifted above her and mounted his golden legs on top of her waiting neck.

> *"Very good, my love*
> *for together we go*
> *to crush the humans*
> *our greatest foe."*

In a regal and haughty manner, Voice then pointed his golden fingers toward a faraway place. Sweety took the hint, snorted, revealed her fangs, and made a rebelliously small attempt at chomping on Voice's outstretched arm.

Now, Sweety. Temper, temper.

Sweety soon thereafter sprang forward. And while galloping across the shallow waters, one could hear;

> *"Onward, my Sweety,*
> *forward, my dear*
> *don't bite your master*
> *and follow his steer."*

Voice screeched in jubilation as he bucked up and down on Sweety's neck. "Yieollll!" Yieollll!!"

As the odd pair left the scene, another beast approached carefully. It quietly stopped at the shoreline. The round furry creature had listened and watched the Graxen and its strange-looking rider as they strode off into the distance. When the dangerous beings were far enough away, the new visitor, a smaller version of the fallen Memtorsis, sniffed the air in the

42

direction of its kind. The acrid smell of the Memtorsis was not unfamiliar. But there were other scents; blood mixed with bile, mixed with scorched and torn-open flesh. It was most disconcerting. The beast cried out a moaning wail, and waited for a response. "B'lul, B'lul, B'lul-l-l-l."

When nothing came back, the furry beast waddled through the waters, going toward the motionless Memtorsis. The new visitor lowered its head, sniffing some more. Then the animal bumped the carcass with its snout, prodding the prone Memtorsis and looking for signs of life. The new visitor called out another wailing cry, then desperately, another. But the mangled and broken Memtorsis did not, could not, respond, because . . .

Her mate was dead.

She emitted a sound that was like a song; a long, deliberate howl of loss and longing. Her wails sailed over the shoreline, cascading over the waters, echoing back and forth, mingling with the sounds of the crashing waves. When the song was done, she looked up into the sky, then at the distant mountain range. She saw her path, well past a thick forest, up along the base of an enormous peak. Her destination was so very far; she had to leave soon.

So the female Memtorsis eventually moved off toward the beach. At the shoreline, she stopped again, and could not help to take one more look back. She blinked her sad round eyes open and closed, as if she could not believe what she was seeing. But all she could do now was to return to their lair and get ready for a task she should not have to complete on her own.

There was no other choice; her time had come.

CHAPTER 5
The Hunt

"Hurry up, Moshe, this way."

"It's too d-dark. I can hardly see."

"C'mon, don't be afraid. You're worse than my sister."

That comment was sure to get under Mosher's skin. Although Mosher knew Calish was using it as a ploy to get him to follow, it nonetheless worked. Actually, it *always* worked. "I'll show y-you who's afraid," Mosher countered as he bolted in front of Calish.

Soon enough, both boys were runnng like mad, busy doing what they had for the past few wake-cycles: exploring the tribe's new underground home. Their current adventure involved tracking down a loose animal that had not yet been corralled by Gasheer's soldiers. The fact that it was still free meant that Gasheer did not know of it, and therefore the beast was fair game.

"I think the animal is a goat. It is very tricky, the way it hides from us."

"Yeah Calish I've always wondered who was smarter, you or our g-goats."

"Ha, ha," replied Calish dryly. Not to be undone by Mosher's joke or his racing challenge, Calish sprinted past his friend in a sudden burst of speed and agility. "Hurry up, you're slower than Drinkel."

"Oh do shut up, Calish!" Mosher hated it when Calish compared his questionable running skills with that of his uncle's sleepy and listless donkey; the one the boy's had named 'Drinkel' because the beast did nothing but sleep, eat, and drink water all day.

"Drinkel, wake up. I think the animal went this way. Let's go! Wah-hooohhh!"

"It's not fair, Calish. You only run f-faster than me 'cause you're skinnier than a blade of straw."

"Whatever, Drinkel, my pal, whatever. This way, wahoo!"

The young warrior, startled by the sudden noise, woke up and moved to see what was happening. He saw two of the surface dwellers running across an open area near to where he had found a nice, safe niche to sleep in. He wiped the sleepiness from his eyes to get a better view. "Striggitzz… more of them," he complained.

The runners were young males, boys actually, and they were closing in on his position. Their appearance so near was unexpected; the warrior had to be very quick to hide from their sight, so he hunkered down into his burrow. He had picked the hiding spot because he didn't imagine that any of the surface dwellers were daring enough to explore so far from where they had collected themselves. The boys apparently had enough bravery, or stupidity, to traverse places that should have been off limits.

"Sheol," cursed the warrior. The boys ran right by the warrior's niche. Then they stopped suddenly and looked into the dark area where the warrior hid. The warrior ducked lower and peeked out, wondering what would happen. But soon enough the surface dwellers, seeing nothing but darkness, took off again. And of course the warrior watched them with great curiosity.

"Grizzlist." Intrigued by the boys' animated and spirited actions, the warrior decided to follow them. He slinked out from his niche and sprinted to stay near enough to the boys while at the same time always in the darkest of shadows. "What are they doing? Are they dim-witted?" The warrior couldn't imagine why the humans would go even further into the darkest of spaces. Dangerous creatures lurked there; his recent encounter with the Mestalor beast was proof of that fact. He had no intentions on saving their hides like he had with the little ones. *I'm done being a hero.*

"Striggitzz," the warrior suddenly gasped. Up ahead he saw a glimmer of whiteness pop out from a distant alcove. It wasn't as large as a Mestalor, but it was definitely there. The boys must have seen it too because they sprinted to chase after it. The white object stepped out again, noticed its pursuers, and immediately started moving very swiftly in and out of the nooks and crannies of the cavernous areas. The labyrinth of choices was endless. The humans were unaccustomed to it; they could not easily know which path to take, and soon they got misdirected. For the warrior, however, the mysterious places were all too normal.

Thinking fast, he took an adjacent tunnel to get a better view of where the adventurous humans were going and what they were after.

The warrior soon thereafter found an elevated ledge from where he could watch everything. Like a practiced hunter, in the darkest of shadows he waited, patiently.

Within moments, a small creature meandered into an open spot. The warrior was unfamiliar with the beast. *A surface world animal, h*e realized excitedly. *I am the first of my kind to see it.* The animal had a furry white body, a small tail that wiggled a lot, a long straight snout, and its head had two curved horns on top. The thing did not look dangerous; it had no fangs anyway. And it had only four legs, half as many as the Mestalor he had recently fought. But it was still an unknown, so the warrior decided to keep himself secret for the time being.

The two boys approached and stopped nearby. They could not yet see the beast, most likely because the funny looking thing hid in near total darkness. But the warrior could see it well. Unless the beast was really stupid, which was a real possibility, it could very easily stay hidden. The warrior then turned his attention on the boys. One of them was carrying a small vessel that had fire within it. It shed a small amount of light. Using it, the boys were doing their best to scurry around looking for the sly creature.

Not sure of where the beast was hiding, the searchers went off in a different direction. The warrior took one last hard look at the furry creature, thinking. His empty belly made him want to eat it. He could send a mind-speak to the beast, freezing it in place while he bashed it with his hammer. The thing's skull and horns would make for a fine fist-shield. But if he stopped to fill his aching belly, then he would miss out on what the boys were doing. Swallowing his hunger, the warrior decided to stick with the boys. "Striggitzz," he said in frustration. The warrior jumped down from his perch, running like mad, always finding a place from where he could watch them covertly.

The boys thereafter came upon a large pile of rocks. One of the boys, the slightly smaller of the two, started climbing the rocks with great nimbleness. His stout friend followed, albeit slower. The smaller boy held his small flame close to a particular spot. He then started moving some of the rocks aside, as if looking for something. The heavier boy joined his companion in the rock-moving efforts. After enough rocks had been moved, the smaller boy reached down and pulled out a long thin rod of some sort. Fascinated, the warrior quickly scooted closer to get a better look. The boy further examined his find. It had a very pointy top, made of a material that glistened brilliantly.

"Sheol." *It is metal weapon*, the warrior thought in amazement. His people had ways of forging things like metal. He had seen it before, but it was rare. Moreover, any metal his people had created was nothing in comparison with what the boy had found. The object's smooth, unblemished surface was quite remarkable. The warrior watched excitedly as the smaller boy held up the object like he had found something of great value.

"Yip, Yip. Wah-hooohhh!" Calish shouted. "Look what I've found." He held the thing up nearer the light of his lantern and declared, "It is a spear unlike I have ever seen."

Mosher asked deliberately, "Calish, do you not r-recognize it?"

"No, I'm not sure, but it is surely the finest. Is it not?"

Mosher moved closer and pointed at the object. "It is Asher's spear, Calish. There, see the red b-band at the bottom of the hilt. And look near the grip, there is the image of a snake. It is Asher's spear, for s-sure."

Calish prompted, "I have heard stories of it."

"True stories," cited Mosher with great pride. "They are true s-stories. The spear belonged to Pharoah. It is the finest lance, m-made from the rarest metal. The p-point is tipped by Electrum. The lightest yet s-strongest alloy in all the Kingdom."

Looking skeptical, Calish posed, "How did Asher, a Hebrew, get it then?"

Mosher, as always, was ready to review his knowledge of things. "Asher was Pharaoh's chariot r-runner. He could run alongside Pharoah's chariots and horses b-better than any other slave. One day Pharaoh w-was lion hunting. Pharaoh, while perched on his chariot, threw the spear at a lion, but m-missed, grazing the beast. The wounded animal turned on Pharaoh and was about to leap up and k-kill Pharaoh. At the last second, a spear pierced the lion in the heart, and the b-beast landed on top of the chariot's crossbar, d-dead. Everyone was shocked. They looked to see w-who had thrown the lance. It was Asher. After Pharaoh had thrown it and missed, Asher swiftly retrieved it. He then cast the s-spear at the lion."

"But would Pharaoh be so grateful as to give such a prize to a slave?"

"N-Not really. Asher was thereafter allowed to c-carry Pharaoh's spear on all lion hunts. It was a great honor."

"Then how. . .?"

Mosher answered knowingly, "Our people took m-much of the Kingdom's wealth during the Exodus. Asher... how shall we say, 'liberated' the spear from Pharaoh's lockers before our people left."

Calish was puzzled. "And what of Asher? I have not seen him."

"They say he was swallowed by the c-chasm after throwing the spear at AmHeh's hand of fire. Asher was a g-great warrior and the pride of my clan."

Then Mosher noticed something. It was nearby, so he climbed over some rocks to get a better look. Calish followed, bringing his lantern closer. A broken and bloody hand was sticking up through some stones and rubble. Mosher pushed some debris aside, exposing the hand's forearm. Upon the arm was a painted image. Mosher bent down to further investigate. The image was a snake wrapped around a spear. Mosher looked up at his friend with a sorrowful expression.

"What... who was this, Moshe?"

"Asher," Mosher said sadly. "This tattoo was a b-brand given to Asher, matching him to the spear. It was a gift from Pharaoh and a tribute to Asher's bravery."

"Asher was an uncle to you. Yes?"

"Yes."

Calish held the spear close to Mosher and offered, "Then maybe this is yours then."

"No, Calish. Y-You found it. Besides, I have this," answered Mosher while tapping the sling that was attached to his belt.

"Thanks, Moshe."

"You're welcome, m-my friend."

As the boys talked about their find, the warrior studied the long rod with a sharp gleaming tip. *With a weapon like that,* he reasoned, *I could do great things. I would demand respect and be feared. I could be first among father's sons. And if they try to seize, I will kill them.* The warrior had thoughts of taking the weapon. The boys were obviously agile, brave, and not much smaller than he was, but ultimately they would be no match for his fury, or his stony hammer.

"Grizzlist." The warrior's clawed hand went to grip his club's strong and rigid handle. He set his feet firmly on the cavern floor, ready to sprint and attack them in a flurry of deadly aggression. The human weapon would be his, no matter what.

As the young warrior was just about to take off, a sudden streak of motion caught his eye. He glanced toward it, but the thing was moving fast, even quicker than the white furry beast.

The warrior looked at the boys; they too had noticed the flashing figure. The boys jumped down from the pile of rocks and ran to give chase. The warrior sprinted as well, following from a distance, his mighty club ready for anything.

"Did you see that?" Calish asked in excitement.

"Yes, w-what was it?"

"Don't know, but let's find out."

"Where did it go?"

"That way, c'mon!" prompted Calish.

The pair scurried like crazy into the dark spaces.

After a while, the boys stopped. They had lost the running thing's trail. But Calish suddenly whispered, "Sshhh. I thought I heard something."

"What is it, C-Calish?"

"Not sure." After that, and when the boys were silent, a quiet growling and muffled chewing sound emerged.

"Did y-you hear that?" whispered Mosher.

Calish replied, "Yes. It came from that way. Let's go."

The boys soon came to an alcove corner; when they rounded it, the growling sounds got louder.

Calish carefully poked his head past another wall to see the noise's source. He whispered to Mosher, who was close behind him, "It is a wolf, feeding on a dead goat."

"Let's g-get out of here, Calish."

"No, Moshe, we can kill it."

"Are you m-mad?"

"You have your sling, I have Asher's spear, and we both have our knives."

"Calish," Mosher retorted evenly, "even if I manage to strike the wolf between the eyes, it will n-not be enough to kill it."

"Maybe not, but maybe we could scare it off."

"From its f-food? I don't think so."

"Wolves usually run from men, Moshe."

"Yes, *men,* Calish. Are w-we men?"

"Not yet, but doing this will make us so."

Mosher had his doubts but kept them to himself. Calish and he had hunted together many times, killing all kinds of small animals in the wilderness, but they had never gone after something as strong as a wolf. But deep inside, Mosher had to admit that there was something exciting about Calish's suggestion. "Maybe," answered Mosher finally. *Maybe.*

"Then it's settled," stated Calish. "Get the best rock you can find from your pouch and ready your sling."

Mosher poked through his collection and eventually found an excellent throwing stone. He held it up for Calish to see.

"Okay," began Calish, "I will come out from behind this wall and distract the beast. When you're ready, you come out too and take your best shot."

"Okay."

"Ready?"

"R-Ready."

"One... two... three."

On three, Calish stepped away from the wall while holding his spear across his body and pointing it at the wolf. He then gingerly bent down and placed the lantern as near to the wolf as possible. The added little light, along with the sheen from the cavern walls, illuminated the area enough to see everything, more or less. Calish then backed up a step and re-held Asher's spear with both hands.

The wolf stopped chewing on some of the goat's innards, and without lifting its head, suspiciously stared at the intrusion. Aggressively growling, the wolf spied the threat to its feeding.

"Moshe," Calish said quietly, "I'll move a little to the left. When the wolf's body is in full view, step out and take your best shot."

Mosher sneaked a peak from behind the wall. "What should I aim for?"

Thinking, Calish finally said, "The body... hit it hard. The strike might make it back off."

"O-Okay."

Calish moved to his left, drawing the beast to turn and face him. Mosher watched, and when he saw a full-body profile, he whipped the sling over and over as hard as he could. He stepped out from behind the wall and let loose his stone. Impact! Dead center along the wolf's ribs.

The beast jumped a bit and immediately glared at Mosher, snarling loudly. But the wolf did not move from the goat's side.

"Now w-what?" Mosher hushed-out worriedly. He put the sling around his belt and withdrew his small knife.

Calish took the spear and started making stabbing motions while shouting at the wolf, "Hey! Hey you, hey!!"

But the beast merely snarled again.

Then he had an idea. "At this distance, I am sure I can hit it." Calish poised himself to hurl the spear.

"You risk angering the wolf even m-more, if you miss," argued Mosher. "And you will n-no longer have the spear."

"I will not miss," countered Calish confidently. "Draw it toward you by pretending to attack, and when I see its full body, I will throw my spear."

"Okay." Mosher moved to his right a bit and pretended to jump forward as if he was going to rush the beast. The wolf turned toward Mosher, and Calish immediately tossed the spear as hard as he could. The spear's point penetrated the wolf's side. The wolf jerked around, trying to nip at the protrusion, but the spear's point had gone deep enough to get stuck. The wolf, with the spear still lodged it its ribs, jerked and jostled around, intermittently growling and snapping at both boys.

Calish blurted out, "I will try and grab the spear."

"No, wait."

"Why?"

"It is too d-dangerous."

But Calish disputed, "The wolf is hurt. See there, it is bleeding from the mouth. The spear must have punctured its lung."

Mosher countered with, "Don't you know that a wounded beast is the most d-dangerous."

"We must try anyway. Move over there, and when I say go, shout as loud as you can. Go!"

Mosher moved off a bit and started shouting. The wolf turned toward the noise and Calish swiftly lunged for the spear's long shaft. He grabbed hold of it, and then had to dance madly away from the wolf's snout as the chomping beast recoiled and twist-turned while snipping at Calish.

Mosher, seeing how close the wolf was to biting Calish, acted out another attack. The beast quickly turned to growl and snap at Mosher.

As Calish was holding onto the spear, the wolf suddenly made a jolting motion that loosened the spear from its body. The beast yelped from pain and then turned on Calish.

Calish immediately backed off a bit and directed the spear's point at the wolf's snapping jaws. The beast snarled aggressively, baring its teeth. Blood dripped from its mouth.

Then the enraged wolf snapped violently at the pointy thing in its face, while moving from side to side, trying to find a way past it. But Calish managed to redirect the spear accordingly, as he hopped and nimbly danced for position, staying just in front of the wolf's fierce snout.

Mosher, still off to the side, held onto his small blade, afraid, trembling a bit, and wondering what to do. "Shis-shtu, Calish."

Meanwhile, the warrior, watching carefully, moved in very close to the action and readied his hammer. He was still hidden within a dark crevice, but if needed he was within striking distance. A dark, hairy thing had killed the white animal and was presently aggressively defending it against the humans. The new beast had fangs, wonderfully chiseled and sharp fangs. It was a predator and therefore dangerously appealing. *Its toothy skull will*

52

prove I am a true warrior. Father will be proud when he sees it. But the question for the warrior was, who or what should he attack: the humans, the ferocious beast, or possibly both? A tough choice, but one he would ultimately put aside because curiosity once again primed his motivations. For now he would stay in the dark and observe how surface dwellers hunted. The warrior's people were very accustomed to surviving great adversity, and trained from the earliest time to defend themselves, and more importantly, to kill. He wondered if the humans had the same instincts. He reasoned that if the boys were smart – which was still in question – they could defeat the angry beast. So far the boys had made some interesting maneuvers, showing tremendous bravery, but the animal they fought was not yet defeated. In fact, the animal looked more dangerous than ever.

"Striggitzz!" Suddenly things took a turn for the worse. Out of instinct, the warrior readied his mental focus once again.

Calish, while poking with his spear and keeping the wolf at bay, didn't realize that the wolf would unexpectedly decide to attack the more vulnerable of its tormentors. The wolf stopped snapping at Calish's spear point and looked intently at Mosher. That threat was standing off a bit, alone, and rather timidly holding a small knife. The wolf suddenly burst into action, running hard at the boy.

"No!" yelled Calish, as he readied Asher's spear.

The warrior instantly sent a mind-speak command into the spear holder's brain. *Throw!* And the spear flew out of Calish's hand with a ferocity the young boy did not yet possess. And while the wolf was in mid-air, flying at Mosher's face, the spear's pristine tip ripped through the wolf's neck bone, practically severing the beast's head. Its limp body slammed into Mosher, knocking him down. The beast landed on top of him, its blood splattering all over.

"Grizzlist*!" Success. This word, 'succ-cess', realized the* warrior, *must be equivalent to being a good thing, or possibly meaning one had achieved a victory.* He had learned the human word when he had mind-spoke with the little ones. In both cases the word popped into his mind upon completion of a good thing.

"Moshe, you alright?" asked Calish anxiously as he ran to Mosher's side.

Moshe, still stunned, brought his hands and arms down from covering his face. With Calish's help, they pushed the wolf's lifeless form off from Mosher's chest. The animal's vacant eyes were still open; its bloody tongue then flopped out of its mouth to the ground.

After finally catching his breath, Mosher squeezed out, "Don't d-do that again, Calish!"

"Sorry, Moshe, sorry. Are you okay?"

"I guess so." Moshe looked at the blood splattered all over his arms and body. A very worried expression crossed his face.

Calish noticed the expression and started rubbing his hands over Mosher's torso. After examining his skin, Calish declared, "Don't worry, Moshe, the blood is not yours."

"G-Good," Mosher voiced with relief.

Calish then offered his hand, and guided Mosher to stand up.

"What happened?" asked Mosher in total disbelief.

Calish, with equal doubt, answered, "I'm not sure, really. I threw Asher's spear as the wolf leapt at you, but it happened so fast. Somehow I struck it so hard that the spear must have severed wolf's neck bone before it could hurt you."

The boys scrutinized the dead wolf. The spear's tip had gone clean through the creature's neck and was still protruding out from one side. And even though it was bloodied, the spears shiny metal glistened brightly past the stains.

"I didn't know y-you could throw a spear so well."

"Neither did I!" Calish retorted with surprise. He paused as if something was bothering him. "Moshe, all I know is that just as I was throwing, I had a funny feeling like..."

"Like what?"

"Like someone else was with me, helping me throw the spear."

Looking skeptical, Mosher asked, "W-Who?"

"Don't know." Calish was pensive for a moment. "Also, and I know this is going sound crazy, but I could see what was happening."

"Of course you could see what was h-happening!" snapped Mosher sarcastically. "So could I... unfortunately." He then took the spare cloth from Calish's belt and tried wiping away some of the wolf's blood from his tunic. When he was done, Mosher gave the bloodied rag back to Calish.

"No," argued Calish. "I mean it was like I was watching it from a distance. I could see you, the wolf jumping, and me throwing the spear. But it all happened so fast. I'm not sure if what I'm saying is real or not."

To consol his friend, Mosher advised, "This place, Calish, it is so s-strange for us."

"Yes, Moshe, but for some reason, I now get the sense that there is more to this dark place than we know, or can see. Much more."

The pair looked around their spot guardedly. As usual, there was only the darkness; and more black corners, niches and strange places. After a moment, when nothing happened, they moved to further examine the dead wolf.

As the boys stood over their kill, the warrior had the urge to get closer. He did so, finding another dark niche to hide in. He watched with envy as the spear-thrower jerked and pulled the lance from the beast's neck. The prized weapon was awesome in its effectiveness and he could not help but want the thing even more. It was a powerful tool that would serve him well. *When he tries to take it from me, I will stab Stilik in his throat, and watch him bleed out slowly. And father will make me his first son.* Once again, the warrior's thoughts ran to how he could easily take it from the surface dwellers. If he killed the boys, then so be it. For all he knew, his people would eventually kill all of the new arrivals anyway, so why waste a tremendous opportunity? One of his brothers – Stilik for certain – would surely claim the prized lance if this happened, and that would be unacceptable. He jostled his club, tightening his grip, and readied his stance to charge the boys once and for all. "Grizzlist. I will have it."

Calish, still concerned about his strange vision, pondered out loud, "Moshe, I still have this weird feeling that someone else is in my head."

As he was speaking, Calish suddenly could see himself and Mosher standing beside the dead wolf. "Whoa!" Calish exclaimed as he jumped from the shock of it. Just as unexpectedly, he was back in his own mind, seeing things normally. Calish held his spear tighter, defensively, as he suspiciously examined the vast darkness all around him.

"What is it?" asked Mosher.

"There's something out there watching us. I am sure of it, Moshe."

"W-Where?" Mosher took up his knife too, read to fight.

"Not sure, maybe straight that way." Calish pointed at a spot with Asher's spear. It was a black, cavernous corner. Calish stared intently into the darkness, sensing more than seeing, what or who was watching him. "There's something watching us right over there."

The warrior, startled by the sudden mind-speak connection, stepped further back into the darkness. His mind-link with the smaller of the boys had started on its own, without his active encouragement. *This is strange*, he thought and not something his teacher's had warned him about.

"Striggitzz," he whispered to himself. The surprised warrior looked hard into the spear-holder's eyes. The surface dweller was staring back as well. Somehow their minds were still connected and the warrior could still feel what the boy felt. And like when he had momentarily understood the Mestalor monster, the warrior could now gather what the surface dweller experienced. Unlike the dim-witted Mestalor, however, the surface dweller's thoughts were infinitely more complex.

The mind-link was gripping and unstoppable as images and emotions flowed like water into the warrior's awareness. The warrior was compelled to analyze the feelings and was most enlightened by what he was learning. For one, the human boy's sense of pride and will was strong. The human was sure of himself, no doubt. But what really struck the warrior was the boy's love for family... and most especially, for his companion. Within his mind the warrior could also see images of the other people the boy cared about. The warrior didn't know who they were but it was very clear that the human boy's love for those people was very intense. In fact, those emotions were just as strong, and deep, as the boy's sense of determination.

Not only do they look differently from us, they think, or rather feel, so differently as well. The warrior recognized some of the boy's emotions: pride and strength of will being only two of them. *I certainly have that,* summarized the warrior, comparing himself to the boy. But love for one's family or brothers? These were alien ideas to the young warrior's experiences. There was concern between the warrior's family members, and to a certain degree loyalty, but for only so long as survival dictated. Love was for the week-minded. Or for those who wanted to be victimized by stronger individuals who would exploit love-induced vulnerabilities. "Love?" voiced the warrior derisively. "Sheol to that." His world apparently was much more harsh and brutal as compared to that of the surface dwellers.

Or maybe humans are indeed as soft-minded as that of their soft skin. If so, they will never survive here. As I realized when I saved the little ones, they will be food for the taking before prophecy ever starts. "Striggitzz." *But does that make sense? There must be much more to this story. There must be more to them.* The warrior refocused his attention on the boy's spear. *At the very least, humans make weapons that my people could learn from.*

Again, as he watched the boy hold tightly to his weapon, the warrior could sense what the boy did. "Sheol, it is indeed spectacular." The warrior could feel his own clawed grip on the lance. The spear was truly matchless in its balance and weight. It made him want the thing even more. But the link he shared with the boy was too strong for him to disregard, forcing him to squash notions of taking it. While the two beings continued to gaze into each other's eyes, the warrior accepted, *There is something between us, human. It must have something to do with the secret your people carry.*

The warrior suddenly had an interesting thought. *Could the lance be that special object? It is so majestic. No,* he finally concluded, *the weapon is grand, but I sense nothing else from it. There is yet another object in their possession and I must wait to learn what those unknowns really mean.*

The warrior brought his mind back into itself, willfully shutting off the two-way link with the human boy. He withdrew deeper into the darkness. Eventually the mental connection disappeared and the surface boy stopped peering into a place that was for him nothing but a dark, mysterious void.

Nonetheless, the warrior kept watching his new companions, thinking deeply. *You are oddly compelling.* After seeing the combat skills of the boys, and sharing a mental link with one of them, the warrior had gained a respect for their bravery, and a begrudging kind of curiosity for their depth of emotion. Their attributes were a weird combination of great strength with dangerously soft feelings of love. Although the warrior didn't fully understand it, he sensed that their contrasting qualities were somehow a good thing, strangely enough.

The warrior returned the club to its place in his belt. He then felt for his pouch. He reached inside of it, making sure his special mixture of Sklon was still there. *They are definitely not stupid.* While being fixated on the smaller of the two boys, he resolved, *Nimble human you are... unique.* The warrior whispered to himself, "And I will find a way for us to meet, my new friend."

"What should we do with the w-wolf?" asked Mosher after accepting that there was nothing to see in Calish's mysterious cavern niche.

Calish eventually snapped out of his defensive posture. He glanced at the wolf and soundly proclaimed, "What else... we eat it."

"Shouldn't w-we tell the Elders of it?"

"And have Dathan and Gasheer take it away?" He used his spare cloth and started cleaning the blood from the spear's point. "No, Moshe, we killed this thing, it is ours. I say we split it, each taking half to our families. Is your family not hungry?"

"Yes, they grow hungry."

"Then it's settled; we split the carcass into two parts."

"Should we dress it h-here?" asked Mosher as he held his knife to the wolf's belly, ready to slice it open.

"No, let's find someplace closer to our tents, but still hidden. We will dress it and cut the beast into two parts. We'll take it home from there. Make sure you have your aunts prepare the fire before you arrive so they can cook the meat right away, before anyone tries to take it away."

"The s-smell will attract folks."

"Cook it in small pieces then, and have your family ready to eat it right away. I will do the same."

The boys grabbed up the wolf's hind legs and began walking off, dragging the animal behind them. The beast's nearly severed head was quite askew from the rest of its body, as blood continued to trickle onto the rocky ground.

While walking, Calish noticed that Mosher still clung to his small flint knife. "You used your knife well, Moshe. And isn't it amazing how bloodlessly clean it is after such a fierce battle."

"Ha ha, very f-funny."

"From now on we'll call it Moshe's mighty Wolf knife."

On cue, Mosher pretended he was fighting off an invisible enemy with it.

Calish then announced, "I don't know what I would have done without you and your Wolf knife, great warrior."

"If not for me, Calish, the wolf would be p-picking your skinny bones from its teeth."

"No doubt, my friend, no doubt."

Mosher used his Wolf knife to poke Calish's spear. "The way you threw the lance was really amazing. It would m-make Asher proud."

Calish smiled at the compliment. But inside he couldn't help but wonder as to how, or even *if,* he had actually done it. "Thanks, Moshe. And you were right. This spear's Lectum is truly unrivaled in quality. It severed the wolf's neck like a hot knife through mother's pot of oxen lard."

Mosher's face scrunched up. "Calish, it is called 'Electrum', not 'Lectum'. G-Gosh do you ever listen?"

"That's what I said, Drinkle… Lectum, okay?"

Mosher rolled his eyes.

After seeing the boys recover from the fight, talking amongst themselves, and then walking away with their kill, the warrior went to where the white animal lay. Without wasting any time, he grabbed up the dead creature and tore the head from its body. His hunger, now pressing him hard, got the better of him. He held the base of its skull to his mouth, picking and sucking out the creature's brains. He then turned the head over so he could dig out the eyes. He swallowed the round, stringy pieces whole, not really bothering to chew. He then threw his fingers into the empty skull, trying to determine the best spot for his grip, and for the purpose of turning the thing into a type of fist-shield.

Or this skull's horns might make for a good striking weapon. After finding a nice place for his fingers, through the eye sockets, and confirming that his grip was solid, he practiced swinging the weapon here and there. He hit his other arm to measure its force. *It hurts. Good. Or rather... 'succ-cess' as the humans might say.* He smacked a cave wall to measure the thing's durability. The weapon struck the rock solidly, without breaking. *The horns are strong. They could do real damage to one of my people. Stilik, to be precise. And the spiky ends could be further sharpened to penetrate an enemies' skin... or Stilik's throat.*

He picked up the creature's carcass and bit hard into the tail, ripping it free. He did not like the taste of it, so he spit it out. The aggressive beast that had killed it had torn open its belly, so the warrior grabbed what remained of the internal organs and quickly made food of it.

While greedily swallowing, the warrior looked to see what the two boys were doing. They had stopped. The smaller of the two boys was pointing in his direction. Obviously they were going to retrieve the other dead beast. *His* dead beast. The warrior threw what was left of the furry animal over his shoulder and calmly walked toward the far reaches of the caverns. The boys would find nothing for their efforts. It would raise questions in their minds, but there was nothing the warrior could do about that.

"Should we not also retrieve the g-goat?" queried Mosher.

"Yes, we'd better not leave anything behind." Calish pointed to the area where the goat should have been, and directed his lantern accordingly. The boys started walking, retracing their steps, following the bloody trail and dragging the wolf along. But when they got to the right spot, they found only a pool of blood and a severed piece of goat tail. Calish picked up the tail, examining it. "It looks like it was ripped apart."

"Yeah, see the torn edges. It's as if s-something bit it in two."

"Something with very sharp teeth, Moshe."

Calish quickly put his lantern down. They dropped the wolf and scanned their surroundings warily, suddenly very alert. Once again, Calish gripped Asher's spear, pointing it toward the dark unknowns. Mosher also held up his Wolf knife in a similar fashion. They circled their spot, back-to-back, ready for anything.

Calish warned ominously, "We're not alone, Moshe."

Before the warrior disappeared into a nearby tunnel exit, he took one more glance to see what the boys were doing. They obviously had discovered the mystery of the missing animal and were poised to take on whatever had stolen it. The warrior summarized to himself, "They are a brave lot. Small, but brave. And I am somehow pleased I did not kill them."

The warrior grinned at his bounty of beast flesh, shrugged, and rejoiced by saying, "Grizzlist, Succ-c-ess-s." Content that his belly was full, he had a brand new fist-shield, and that he had plenty more meat to keep him whole, the fearless warrior casually strolled into the darkness.

Mosher whispered in a hushed voice, "I d-don't like this, Calish."

Calish toed the lantern forward a bit in an attempt to see better. But the added light did little to illuminate the mysterious places all around them. Eventually, he whispered, "My brother, I agree."

Mosher said finally, "I think you're right, Calish, there is m-much more to this place than our eyes tell us."

CHAPTER 6
Asher's Spear

Calish tossed and turned. His dream would not let him wake up. There was something there with him, something he couldn't quite see, a shadow of sorts. And the phantom kept moving, sometimes closer, then withdrawing, every time Calish attempted to look directly upon it.

Wake up, wake up, he told himself. But he still could not. Calish was sure he was sleeping... even dreaming... but how could it be? The dream was so real; in fact, Calish knew where he was. So he further examined his location. The area was where his uncle's family had pieced together the leftovers of their tattered tent. His uncle's keep, the tent, was held up by the few pieces of timber that had not already been consumed in the fire pit. The pit, tent, and meager belongings lay in a distant alcove, far from the area where most of the survivors had settled.

Out of the corner of his eye, the shadowy companion moved in close, then veered to the left, toward the cavern's walls. The cloudy shape then ducked behind a large rocky outcropping. Calish's body followed, without his consent, gliding toward the area, then behind the large rock. But when he got there, the mysterious vapor had totally disappeared.

Calish looked down. A small boulder was wedged into a recess behind the outcropping. In a flash, Calish felt his body being whisked through the boulder and past it. Like being caught in a mighty river, his body was propelled through a long tunnel. Calish couldn't stop; his motion was swift, harrowing, and terrifying. Just as he was about to scream, he entered a large cavernous space. He abruptly stopped, and slowly started floating within the cave's vast spaces. The cavern was large, and there were glittering stones sprinkled all over the cave walls. Moreover, there were spots along the walls that were covered with some kind of plant life. The vegetation was green, red, and some places, black.

Then out of nowhere he glimpsed the ghostly shadow again. It was very near him, watching him. Calish dare not look directly at the thing. It was too frightening, too different, and it wanted something. Calish could feel that the phantom was after him for some unknown reason. The dark thing then suddenly lunged at him... "Aaaghhhh!"

"Calish wake up, wake up!" said Hannah as she shook her son. "You were mumbling in your sleep, moving about, and then you cried out. Are you well, my son?"

Calish stared at his mother, startled and confused. Her gentle presence helped him calm down a little. And even though it was dark, he could still see she was concerned, so he answered. "I am, okay, Mother." But was he, really? The dream was still with him, strong and clear. *Strange* he thought, usually dreams vanished from memory as soon as he woke up. This dream, however, was unique. If he didn't see the reality of his mother's worried face, he would think he was still in the dream.

"Calish," said Hannah with concern, "Are you well?"

"Yes, yes, Mother I am; it is just that..." Calish stopped talking. He thought twice about telling his mother of the dream. She probably wouldn't believe him. *But maybe* he reasoned, he should tell anyway.

"What is it, my son?"

Her concern was so genuine that he felt compelled to give in to her query. "I saw something, in my dream, Mother. It is... *was* so real. A figure, dark and fleeting, was calling me to go somewhere I do not know. It was like a ghost. It wanted something from me."

"Calish, my son, do not worry. It was only your imagination. This place," she said while indicating the darkness all around, "is so strange to us all. It is no wonder you are having bad dreams. Do not worry about such things. It is nothing; it will soon pass." She stroked his curly brown hair in a gentle way.

Calish was comforted by his mother's words. But something inside told him that there was more to the dream; it wasn't just his imagination.

As Calish pondered the dream's meaning he was suddenly interrupted by a terrible, relentless, and all too real enemy.

"Mosher is waiting for you," snarked Bishtar impatiently as she burst into view. Calish's twin sister stood before him, her arms crossed, her face fit to be tied.

"Moshe?" he asked excitedly.

"Who else would it be?" she retorted. The boys were inseparable, had been since the day they met twelve years before.

"Tell him I will be right out."

"You tell him; I'm not your servant!" Bishtar shrieked while storming away.

As Bishtar angrily pushed past the tent's fold, she passed by Mosher, who of course was patiently waiting there. She suddenly stopped to look at him, first with anger, then with a puzzled expression. "Mosher, why do you look at me that way?"

"Ah, what... wa-wa-way?" stuttered Mosher.

"Ah, ah, ah... this wa-wa-wa-way," replied Bishtar in a mock stutter. She mimicked a silly staring expression and threw it directly into Mosher's sunken eyes.

"Ah, I did n-not d-do that," he said defensively.

"Of course you did not," she refuted sarcastically as she flipped her hair. Having made her point, Bishtar walked off, knowing far too well that Mosher was stuck watching her every step of the way.

When Bishtar was out of sight, she turned back. Mosher was still standing there. His shoulders were slumped, as if he had been defeated beyond redemption. Upon seeing this, Bishtar's expression softened and she smiled warmly. *One day,* she mused, *one day.*

Calish leaped from the tent in his usual manner. Upon seeing his best friend looking depressed, he quickly gave him a gentle tap. "Snap out of it, Moshe."

"Okay, Calish, o-okay." Then Mosher inquired, "What shall we do today?" The idea of day and night had not yet disappeared from their customary speech, even though they now lived in constant darkness.

"Don't know. What do you wanna' do?"

"Don't know either."

They looked around and around. Suddenly Calish had an inspiration. "There is something..."

"Yes?"

"Well, it might be scary."

"S-So,"

"It might be tough."

"S-So,"

"I don't know, Moshe, maybe I shouldn't mention it. It will be too much for you, my friend." To egg Mosher on, Calish acted uninterested. "Forget it."

"C'mon, Calish, w-what is it?"

"You sure?"

"Yep,"

"Sure?"

Mosher rolled his eyes. He knew Calish was teasing him, but curiosity got the best of him. "Go a-ahead, out with it."

"Okay, you asked for it." Now that he was with his best friend, Calish had the nerve to explore the dream's implications. By himself, Calish probably wouldn't have ventured anywhere near the area of his uncle's keep, but with Mosher by his side, nothing seemed impossible. Besides, it was something to do. "C'mon then, Moshe, I have something to show you."

"What is it?"

"You'll see."

Thinking of the possibilities, Mosher's expression soon shifted to one of excitement. They smiled together, for the day's adventures were about to begin.

Calish picked up one of his mother's lanterns that contained burning oils and a small lit flame. Now that they were ready, the boys took off like a shot into the cavernous spaces.

Soon thereafter, they came upon Calish's uncle's keep. Calish led them to the place where the cave wall appeared to stop. No, in fact it *did* stop. It was a dead end of a rocky cave wall.

"There is n-nothing here but a whole lot of nothing," said Mosher jokingly. "Is this what you wanted to show me? Wow, more rock. I'm really impressed, Calish. What else do you have in store, a tour of your m-mother's tent?"

"Just wait, my friend, and we shall see." Calish held the lantern closer to a large boulder-like outcropping. Luckily, the stony surface had some of the reflective sheen; it enhanced the lantern's tiny flame enough to make the area easier to see. Calish moved to the boulder's side and then around it to the back. Behind it was another large stone at the base of the boulder. Calish held the lantern close to the stone in question. There was a small hole behind the top of it. Calish peered into the hole. "There is a larger space behind this rock. If we move this thing, we can squeeze through the space back there."

"Okay, to what, or rather w-where?"

"We shall see, brother, we shall see."

"Oh, g-great."

Calish put his lantern off to the side, and encouraged Mosher to grab hold of the stone like he was doing. "Alright, push, Moshe, push!"

The boys put their muscle into it. But the stone didn't budge.

"Why aren't you pulling, Moshe?" asked Calish out of breath.

"Pulling? What are you saying Calish? You said p-push, not p-pull."

"Can you not hear as well as pull, Moshe?"

"Listen, Calish, I clearly heard you say p..." Mosher cut himself off and rolled his eyes. There was no point in arguing with Calish. It was always a losing proposition. "Alright, Calish. What is it then, *p-pull?*"

"Yes, Moshe, and give it all you've got." The boys set their hands on the obstacle and readied their stance. "Okay, Moshe, on three. One... Two... Three!"

The boys pulled mightily, but nothing happened. The stone remained unmoved.

They sat down breathing hard. "It's no use; the thing is wedged in there too tight." Calish got up, sat his butt upon the disagreeable rock, and tried to come up with a good answer.

But Mosher surely had a solution. "We need a lever of s-some sort."

Calish, ignoring his friend, suddenly said, "You know, Moshe, I think if we had a timber of some kind, we might be able to budge this thing loose."

You mean like maybe a... *lever?* quizzed Mosher mockingly.

"Yes, Moshe, very good, that is exactly what I was thinking. We need a *lever.*"

Mosher just rolled his eyes again. Calish was impossible. "Where can we g-get one? Gasheer's men have confiscated all the remaining timber. They'll never let us use one for this. Unless w-we tell them, then maybe..."

"No, Moshe, no one must know of this. We will take what we need. It is between us only, okay?" Calish studied his friend with an expression that said he expected agreement; and a certain kind of agreement as well.

"Okay, Calish, this will remain b-between us."

Calish nodded. He then spit in his hand and offered it to Mosher. Mosher followed suit. They looked at each other and readied their tradition.

"Cal-Moshe," they said in unison while shaking hands. As was their custom, the boys kept secret agreements by doing the spitting ceremony while reciting their secret code word: 'Cal-Moshe,' which was short for Calish and Mosher combined.

"Okay then, what's the p-plan?" asked Mosher.

"We go find Gasheer's camp and see what we can see."

They soon reached the center area of the settlement. Gasheer's men, as instructed by the Elders, had confiscated all the most important commodities: spare timber, cattle, cattle feed, weapons, extra food, anything that was needed for the survival of the tribe. Those items were quickly becoming scarce, so the Elders had decided to collect them all. The items were gathered by kind; timber in one place, cattle in another, and so on. Beside each pile lay a well-tended fire pit. The fire's light helped Gasheer's soldiers keep a watchful eye on the tribe's bounty.

The boys wandered past the various collections, in between the soldiers, looking and assessing the situation. "I see a nice p-piece of lumber there," said Mosher.

But Calish had his eyes on something entirely different. Mosher followed his friend's gaze and suddenly saw what Calish was spying. "You cannot b-be serious," Mosher said in disbelief.

But Calish would not be deterred; he had that *look* on his face. Mosher knew it all too well. "Calish," exclaimed Mosher. "G-Gasheer will never let us have it. He will c-crush us for sure."

"It is not his."

"It sure looks that way to m-me."

"He took it from me," argued Calish. "You were there. You saw him take it. Why should he have it?" Calish did not lie. Calish and Mosher had found the item buried under some rubble. Calish had brought the item to show his grandfather, but Gasheer, who just so happened to be nearby, had torn the prize from Calish's grip.

"Why shouldn't he h-have it?" replied Mosher, repeating Calish's question, "Ah, maybe because he's ten times bigger than us!"

"So? That doesn't give him the right. Besides, who is he anyway? A bully? Grandfather says he is more ox than a man. He is a Philistine and not really a Hebrew. So it should belong to the finder. Not to a beast."

"You m-might be right, Calish, but I don't know..."

"I want it, Moshe. It is mine, and I will have it."

The two boys studied the item. Calish tried to come up with devious ways to get it, while Mosher wondered how he would be punished once they were caught. Gasheer, the brute, would never let it be taken from him. Mosher could already feel the snap of Gasheer's whip striking his bare skin.

Nonetheless, Mosher joined Calish in scoping out the prize. Mosher finally uttered what he was dourly thinking, "Calish, you are insane."

The item in question, Asher's spear, glistened brightly in the firelight. And regardless of the oppressive cavern darkness, the unique tool outshined every other metallic weapon nearby.

"Shishtu," muttered Calish angrily.

The lance stood propped up on a lumber stand, alongside other spears that Gasheer's men had placed side-by-side. When the soldiers were sleeping, they would set up their weapons in one place where they could be well guarded. And by seeing the heavily armed soldiers surrounding the weapons, 'heavily guarded' would have been an understatement. But Asher's spear stood out from the other lances. It was the tallest, the shaft made from the best of lumber. Its metal top was forged from the strongest steel. Over that, the spear's pristine layer of Electrum made it perfect.

"Shish-shtu," repeated Mosher in his own way, "How can we p-possibly get it? We cannot do it."

"No, my friend, we *can* do it. All we need is a proper diversion."

For a moment Mosher wondered if he was to be that 'diversion'… and a sacrificial goat at the same time. Meaning that while Mosher, the goat, gets Gasheer's men to chase him, and of course eventually catch him, Calish sneaks away with the prize scot-free. Mosher could once again feel Gasheer's whip.

"I have a plan," announced Calish boldly.

"Oh g-great," sighed Mosher. He couldn't wait to hear it.

"Retrieve your sling, Mosher."

"Why?" Not that he was opposed to it, for Mosher was very fond of the device, and he typically carried it anyway, but he couldn't quite fathom where Calish was going with his supposed plan.

"We will need your skill with it."

"Nice," voiced Mosher in wary anticipation.

CHAPTER 7
The Diversion

"Wait, not yet," Calish said in hushed tones. The boys hid behind some spare tent-parts and other debris, waiting and watching. It was an alcove devoid of the slick surface that enhanced any light source. So the area was dark and barely discernable. In front of them was an animal pen full of what remained of the tribe's herd. Beyond that was a fire pit that the guards had erected, both for light and for cooking food. Five guards were stationed between the pit and the main entrance to the animal pen.

Mosher stood ready, his sling loaded, its long tethers wound between his fingers. At Calish's signal, Mosher started his whirling motion. Around and around Mosher twirled his sling with well practiced precision.

"Steady, steady. Now!" stated Calish.

Mosher whipped the sling a few more times, and let loose the rock. It sailed with a perfect arc at one of the guards that stood around the animal pen. The projectile struck the guard in the back of his helmet.

"Who has done this!?" the guard shouted as he jerked from the hit and looked all around him. The beasts in the pen were startled by his sudden outburst, but other than that, nothing happened.

"What are you complaining about now, Cabesh?" asked the lead guard.

"Did you not see? I was struck by something?"

"All I see is you whining about something, as usual. Are you upset because your wife refused your advances again?" At that comment, the other guards started to laugh. "Maybe if you bathed more often..."

"Again, Moshe, now." And Mosher let loose another perfectly placed stone. It struck the lead guard in his exposed leg.

"Who has done this?" bellowed the angry guard.

Calish turned to his co-instigator. "Now comes the tough one, Moshe. You ready?"

Mosher nodded his answer. He reached into his pouch and readied his sling with another stone. It was the best one of his choices, and the one he had been saving. Mosher stood up fully and began to whip the sling around and around, faster and faster. It would be a difficult shot, but Mosher was confident he could hit his target. In the wilderness he had made much more difficult shots than the one he had his sights on.

Calish watched the guards as they moved about, looking for answers to their quandary. When the guards were sufficiently distracted, Calish signaled the go ahead and Mosher released the last stone.

In a flash, the projectile streaked over the animal pen, past the guards, to strike the cooking pot that sat perched from a tripod above the guard's fire pit. The pot shattered apart, sending bits of meaty stew all over.

"Quickly, you fools!" yelled the lead guard, "Gather up the meat before we lose it." Some of the guards scrambled to the pit. They then unwisely reached into the fire to recover the food. Yelps of pain commenced as they often reached too far.

The lead guard sent two other guards into an adjacent direction. "Find who has done this and bring them to me!"

The guards flew off as instructed.

As the meat-grabbing guards clumsily gathered up the burnt bits of food, the lead guard soon got impatient with their unsuccessful efforts. He turned to Cabesh and ordered, "Stay here. It appears that I must do this myself." The lead guard then went to the pit to oversee the food recovery. He looked about the flames and was quick to find a choice meaty piece that had not yet been recovered. So he greedily reached into the flames. But he did not have much success either as he also stretched too far; he subsequently shrieked in pain while clutching the morsel. "This piece is mine!" he cried while holding up the prize. He then plunged his hot fingers in his mouth to cool them off.

Cabesh, closely watching the scene, mocked, "Who is the fool now?" He turned to see where his other companions had strayed.

Calish peered at Mosher. "Now's our chance. I will see you soon."

Mosher nodded understanding. He picked up his lit lantern and readied his stance.

"Go!" prompted Calish.

Mosher ran as fast as he could. The animal pen was fenced in by a collection of stones that acted as posts. Ropes were used to tie the posts into a round-about pen. Mosher ran toward the closest post, easily ducking under the rope. The animals jostled at the sudden intrusion, but soon settled down. With his wolf knife, Mosher cut the rope and tossed the end on the ground, revealing a gaping hole between two of the stone posts. He then stealthily crawled between the animals to somewhere in the center of the small herd. He readied his lantern and watched to see when Cabesh would turn the other way.

Very soon Cabesh did.

"YEEiOUUU!" Mosher shouted. He stood up and threw the lantern on the ground with all his might. The clay pot, with the burning oil within it, exploded into a fiery ball of flames. The animals jumped from surprise and rushed like mad through the fence's new opening. Mosher quickly grabbed hold of two of the nearest beasts – one sheep, and the other a goat – and ran like the wind through the opening. He squeezed hard on the animal's furry manes in an effort to match their excited pace. And with that, the collection of beasts, plus one wild-eyed boy, ran into the darkness of the caverns.

"Come back!" Cabesh called out to his companions. "Our beasts escape!"

But by the time Cabesh's comrades had reached the animal pen, Mosher was already hiding in the darkest tunnel he could find. He watched with joy as the guards scrambled to figure out where the animals had gone. For now he was safe; it looked like he had been successful. He only hoped that Calish had been so lucky.

Calish, by this time, had snuck up on Gasheer's tent, most specifically, within striking distance of Asher's spear. He ducked behind Gasheer's tent, watching and waiting for his moment. A soldier suddenly appeared from the darkness. He ran to Gasheer and immediately explained what had happened at the animal pen. After hearing the story, Gasheer told the men on duty to quickly go help round up the stray beasts. The men took up their spears and made haste toward the site.

Gasheer turned to the running soldier and commanded, "Go to the other camps and wake the soldiers there. I will sound the alarm." The soldier nodded his understanding and flew out toward the other camps. Gasheer then entered his tent to retrieve the shofar ram horn.

Calish seized upon the opportunity. Sprinting like lightening, he ran at the lance post, and without slowing, grabbed Asher's spear and flew away into the darkness.

Gasheer returned from his tent, put the shofar to his lips, and blew away. As he did so, Gasheer looked all around him. In mid-blow, he suddenly stopped. There was something wrong, something was amiss. Were his eyes playing tricks on him? His spear was not in its place. He again studied the area around his position. Maybe it had fallen. *No*, it had not. Had one of his soldiers taken it by accident? *No,* they dare not touch it.

"Where is my spear?" Gasheer muttered. Eventually, as the chain of events played out in his mind, understanding bubbled to the surface. And then it dawned on him. He had been duped, and his brow furrowed into a monstrous display. "Arrrghhh! I will get you!" he shouted to the open air.

Gasheer then put the shofar to his lips, and this time he blew the alarm louder than it had ever been blown before. "Birrrrrr, Birrrrr, Birrrrrrrrrrrr-r!"

Calish and Mosher soon thereafter met at the rendezvous place, behind Calish's uncle's keep. Calish was first to arrive, and as he watched Mosher approach, he put his lantern down near the obstructing rock. Mosher got there, stopped and faced his friend. Calish had a huge grin on his face. He also had one hand that was hidden behind his back.

"Well?" asked Mosher, trying to see what his friend was hiding.

When it was clear that Mosher was paying close attention, like magic, Calish made his prize appear in front of him. He lifted the grand and glistening spear up high like a mighty... warrior. "Eureka!" Calish shouted with joy.

Mosher smiled broadly. Thinking not to be outdone, Mosher took a handful of goat and sheep fur, and he too held his hands up high like a mighty... sheepherder. "Eureka t-too!"

And they laughed with glee like only two mischievous boys could.

CHAPTER 8
The Crystallight and Maana Caves

"C'mon, hurry up, Moshe."

"Okay, okay, Calish, but how do you know where we are g-going?"

Calish was moving through the tunnels too swiftly, as if he already knew the route; which should have been impossible. "Never mind that now, Moshe. Just try to keep up."

Mosher hurriedly scrambled over the tunnel's jagged obstacles to close in on Calish's position. In one hand Calish held the lantern, their only light source. In his other hand was Asher's spear. The boys had done well to use the spear's strong shaft to wedge the obstructing rock out of place. They then pushed the stone aside and entered the tunnel behind it. After that, the boys had ventured through the tunnels at a very rapid pace, going deeper and further than Mosher would have liked.

"Yike-shtu," Mosher said with apprehension. Since the Tribes had been cast down, he and Calish had explored many dark places, but the one they were now in was by far the most distant from the settlement. Mosher glanced up at his friend, wondering if he should ask to go back.

"Shi-shtu," muttered Mosher, as he watched his friend brave the unknown spaces like it was a normal thing to do. Calish's face was steady, determined, and fearless. Going back, it appeared, was not an option.

Where are we going? whispered Mosher to himself. *Why are we doing this?*

Calish's shadows cast themselves across the tunnel walls. The shapes danced eerily; so dark, and so foreign to anything Mosher had ever imagined. The boys had ventured into caves during their journey across the Arabian deserts, but those mysterious places were nothing compared to the one they were presently in. Mosher briefly looked behind himself and saw only the blackest of spaces from where the pair had just passed. Unfortunately, the tunnel walls did not have that shiny substance that made the settlement area brighter. The tunnels were ominous indeed, and if it hadn't been for Calish's insistence, Mosher might not have been brave enough to journey further. Mosher swallowed hard and jumped forward to reach his friend.

After some time, and many twists and turns, Mosher accidentally went off in a side tunnel. Upon realizing his mistake, he tried backtracking to where he was before, but the darkness made the true way unclear.

"Calish?" he called. But there was no response. Louder he voiced, "Calish!" And again he cried, "C-Calish!"

Mosher stumbled and fell. It was too dark and he couldn't see where Calish had gone. Crawling, he probed this way or that way, but there was nothing but rock, solid walls, and more rock. *Where is Calish?* he fretted. Had his friend abandoned him in the tunnels? It couldn't be. He looked everywhere but the blackness surrounded him. There was nothing, and nowhere, to go.

He soon found it hard to breath; it was as if the darkness was crushing him. Mosher started to panic. Tears started welling up.

Just as he was about to scream for help, he heard the most wonderful sound in the world.

"Moshe."

Mosher turned toward the sound, but still saw nothing but... nothing.

"Moshe."

"Here! I... I am-m h-here!" His voice must have given away how scared he was, but Mosher didn't care.

The slightest sliver of light appeared from somewhere ahead of Mosher's position. Then slightly more light appeared. Behind it was Calish, holding his little lantern. Calish stopped when he saw Mosher. He held his lantern higher to show his friend where he was. "Moshe, what are you doing, taking a break? C'mon, this way."

Mosher swallowed the fear that gripped him and quickly wiped away his tears.

"What are you waiting for? C'mon, let's go."

Mosher got up and moved forward, but stopped short of getting so close that Calish could see that he had been crying.

Calish, for his part, ignored it and said enthusiastically, "It is not far, my friend. Follow me."

"Okay, I'm w-with you." Mosher reached out and grabbed Calish's tunic, gently at first and then harder. Calish didn't seem to notice as he led Mosher forward.

Soon thereafter, the tunnel took a sharp turn. As they rounded the corner, they noticed a dim ray of light casting itself along the tunnel wall not far from their position. Calish looked back at his friend and smiled brightly.

Mosher asked, "Calish, have we g-gone in circles? Are we back at our settlement?" The amount of light being shed could only have been from the fires that sprinkled the tribe's encampment.

"No, Moshe, no. You shall soon see where we are."

Within seconds, Moshe could tell that they were coming upon a large opening. Strangely, beyond it was a lot of light; too much in Mosher's mind.

Calish's excitement suddenly got the better of him as he bound forward, leaving Mosher behind. But that was okay, because Mosher had no other intention than to follow his friend into the light.

"Shi-shtu," gasped Mosher, clearly stunned, as he crossed the tunnel's threshold and entered the large, open space. With mouth agape, he stammered, "Calish, what, h-how... w-what is this p-place?"

Calish stood before Mosher, and joined in with his friend's amazement. Together the astonished adventurers scanned their breathtaking surroundings and smiled with effervescent joy.

* * * *

"How could this b-be?"

Calish shrugged his shoulders, grinned some more, and waved his friend deeper into the cavern's vast spaces. Calish then put his little lantern down. Its feeble light was no longer needed; in fact, it was soon forgotten.

Mosher was caught up in the moment. With a wide-eyed stare, he circled his spot. The whole area was as bright as the hours just before dusk. Glittering gemstones littered the cavern's walls. In some spots it was packed with tightly knit collections and in other areas the gems were sporadic and random. Some jewels were small, while others protruded well out from their anchor point. The ornaments projected a sparkling light, and colors that defied Mosher's vocabulary. Some were blue, or green. There was yellow, turquoise, red, even violet. And some were colors Mosher didn't even know existed.

"Watch this," said Calish as he readied his spear. Calish walked over to the nearest wall and poked at the gemstones. A slight clinking sound emerged, but nothing else changed. Calish then took a good swing and struck a jewel with great force. This time an eerie ringing sound came forth and lighted sparks flew out in all directions.

With great curiosity, Mosher approached the place where Calish had struck the gemstones. He touched the spot. It was slightly warm, but otherwise unchanged. "It does not m-move," Mosher observed, as he tried to pry free the sparkling stones.

"No, the gems like to stay where they are. But let me try again." Calish took his spear, and with all his might struck at a gem that was sticking out from the cave wall. A loud clink rang out and then a glittering shard flew off and down to the ground.

"You b-broke Asher's spear, Calish!" Mosher said worriedly.

Calish brought up the tip of the spear. Both boys examined it carefully. Its fine point was as smooth and perfect as when they had first seen it.

Mosher smiled knowingly. As if he had invented the substance, he proudly proclaimed, "Electrum. The finest metal forged by the best craftsmen in all the kingdom."

Mosher bent down, picked up the shard and brought it in close for study. "They are like crystals. I r-remember seeing such as this once in Egypt. It was owned by a shopkeeper, who had g-gotten it from a free trader. But those gems did not s-shine nearly as bright as these crystals." Mosher gestured at himself with the jewel and asked, "Do you m-mind?"

"No, go ahead, it's yours."

With Calish's approval, Mosher placed the fine jewel in his pouch.

Calish looked around, thinking about Mosher's description. "Crystals, yes. I like that word, Moshe. We will call them Crystals. And we will call this place the cave of the Crystal-light."

"The Crystallight C-Cave, it is then, Calish."

"Now come, Moshe. I have more to show you."

"More? You mean there is m-more than this?"

"Oh yes, my friend, much more."

Running more than walking, they soon came upon an area where the Crystallight jewels had dissipated. There were still gems here or there, but for most part they were not nearly so densely packed. Calish used his spear to point out something else that covered the cave walls. A form of mossy plant-life had grown up where the spear pointed. For the most part, the plants were shortly cropped and close to the surface, but in certain spots the stems rose as tall as grass. Some of it was green, some red, some purplish, and others blackish in color. Where the gems were the brightest, a strange multi-colored flowering occurred. Where there were almost no gems, the blackish colored vegetation looked even darker and thicker.

"Watch this," prompted Calish in a daring way. He put down his spear, walked up to the tallest of the plants that had flowered, and plucked some of the stuff from its footing. He then promptly stuffed it in his mouth and began to happily chew away.

Very surprised, Mosher stuttered, "Calish, are you m-mad?"

"Why is that?"Calish asked with a muffled voice.

"Do you not know that some p-plants can be poisonous?"

In mid-chew, Calish stopped. His face suddenly lost its cheerfulness and he proceeded to spit the stuff out of his mouth. Some of it, however, was stuck to his tongue, and Calish had to claw at it to fully remove it. And Mosher couldn't help but laugh.

"What are you laughing at, Moshe? Do you want me to die?"

Still laughing, Mosher replied, "Is this the first time you've eaten the p-plants?"

"No," Calish replied sheepishly, "I tried it once while you were still in the tunnels."

"Well then, have y-you died yet?"

Calish looked at himself up and down, arms and legs, wiggling his toes and fingers, and reported, "No I seem to be okay, I guess."

"You see then, n-nothing to fear. What does it taste like?"

"Well, I cannot say it is as sweet as my mother's honey bread, nor as filling as goat meat, but in a pinch it will do."

"Well, then m-my brother, since you discovered it, what shall we call this plant?"

Calish mulled over the request for a moment and finally announced, "Maana. We shall call it Maana."

"Do you mean *Manna?*" asked Mosher, doing his best to correct Calish's mispronunciation.

"Yes, that's what I said, *Maana*. Are you deaf, Moshe?"

Mosher rolled his eyes and gave up. "Alright, *Ma-ana* it is then." If Calish wanted to call it Maana instead of Manna, who was he to argue?

While trying to swallow what was left in his mouth, Calish sputtered, "Eating this plant has made me thirsty, Moshe."

"Well, ah, sorry b-but we didn't bring water, so..."

Calish scanned the area. Very soon he found something else interesting. He pointed up at the cavern ceiling. "Look, I see droplets of water flowing down the side of the Maana wall.

Mosher concurred. "It m-must be what feeds the plants. Look closely, there are cracks up there. The w-water is coming through."

They walked to a place where they could touch a wall that was clearly damp from the trickling water. They tried catching some of it in their hands, and licked what they could, without much success.

Less than happy with the results, Calish muttered, "There's not really enough here to drink from."

Mosher, pondering the possibilities, put forth, "No, but maybe our b-builders can find a way to better draw it directly from its source."

"Somewhere within the ceiling's rocks, then?"

"Or b-beneath the cavern floor. In any event, Calish, our people w-will surely find a way." Mosher looked thoughtful again. "What now? We must be m-missed. Should we return to the s-settlement and tell them of our... *your* Crystallight discovery?"

"Not yet, Moshe. I would like to explore a little more before we go back. We still might find other things to help our people. You never know."

"Okay," Mosher replied. Truth be told, Mosher was in no hurry to return to the dark tunnels anytime soon.

"Good then." Calish pointed in one direction. "Moshe, you go that way, and I'll go this way. We'll meet up back here in a little while. Okay?"

"Are you s-sure we should split up?"

"Why, are you scared, Moshe?" While pretending to clutch onto his own shirt like his life depended on it, Calish asked sarcastically, "Shall I extend my tunic so you can latch onto it again?"

"Why ah, no... n-no way. I didn't d-do that, by the way."

"Sure you didn't, Mr. Tunnel Rat, sure you didn't." Calish picked up his spear and stated, "Well then, let's meet back here in a little while."

Sounding as confident as possible, Mosher answered, "Okay, see you s-soon."

After that, Calish followed a path that led to a series of more tunneled-out spaces. Enough gems covered the walls so that the area was relatively well lit. He soon found another large cavern. No matter where he looked, the whole area was a labyrinth of small alcoves, adjacent tunnels, and numerous archways that, if the pattern held, could have led to other unknown spaces. It was very intriguing, and Calish imagined that it would take years to fully explore and map them all. *Moshe and I are gonna' have fun going through each and every one of them.*

"Moshe, is that you?" A sudden shuffling noise off to his side left Calish surprised. But how could Moshe have followed without him knowing it? Mosher had clearly gone in a different direction, and his stout and less-than-graceful friend was not the stealthiest of creatures.

Once more the shuffling sound happened, but this time it was closer, and Calish started to get nervous. "Moshe, stop playing games. Come out." The sound emerged again and Calish tensed, gripping his spear tighter. The noise was coming from an alcove not far from his position.

Suddenly a strange shape popped out from behind the alcove wall. Calish was stunned, and he instinctively took a few steps backward. It was a hand. A hand with clawed fingers had reached over from behind the wall. Following that was a big round head. The head had two eyes that stared at Calish. The eyes were huge black orbs and the head had skin that was as pale as a lamb's white fur.

"Shishtu!" he gasped. Calish moved his spear to a defensive position, and quickly searched for a place to run.

Just as he was about to bolt, a sound entered his mind. Calish looked around but could not find the source of the sound. Were there others watching him? Was he surrounded? He readied his footing once more. And then the sound entered his mind again. It was music-like and this time the sound carried a feeling attached to it. The feeling was not at all aggressive; in fact, it was soothing, and it matched the melodious sound.

Calish reviewed the strange creature, knowing that somehow the big-headed thing had created the sound.

"What do you want?" he asked the strange being, "Who are you?"

The creature cocked its swollen head at a strange angle, as if it was trying to quiz-out Calish's words. The creature blinked its enormous black eyes. A strange expression crossed the being's brow, and once again the pleasant sound entered Calish's mind. The music was most pleasant and peaceful.

"Okay, friend, okay." Calish relaxed his stance and lowered his spear. The creature took note of the move. As if the gesture was a good thing, it stepped out from behind the wall.

"Yikeshtu." The thing, the creature, was hideous. *How can such a thing be?* Calish quizzed to himself. The monstrous thing's whole body was the same pale color as its bulbous head. The creature's thin arms and legs were like sinewy leather with tightly packed muscles. The thing's feet were bare and claw-like, just like its hands. The individual was clothed, in a fashion. Covering its groin and hip was a type of material that matched its leathery pale skin. There was a strap crossing its bare chest. Attached to the being's hip cloth was a belt, where on one side there was a small pouch. On the other side, there was a corded strap that held a thickly boned handle. At the end of the bone was a sharp stone. *Whoa,* realized Calish guardedly. It was a club-like weapon. But the creature made no move toward the weapon; in fact, the being's posture was not aggressive at all.

Calish whispered, "Are you a Nephilim, as in the stories my grandfather has told me?"

Calish then took note of the creature's size; it wasn't much taller than he was. If it had been any bigger, Calish might have not been so eager to be so close to the thing, soothing music or not. He then remembered that Korah had told him the Nephilim were giants! The being before him, although strange, was definitely no colossus. It was, however, male in appearance, its covered groin and bare chest made that fact very clear. But the creature; *the boy,* Calish recognized, was not yet a full grown man. If Calish had to guess, he would say the strange boy was not much older than he was.

Very slowly, the white-skinned boy reached into his pouch and brought out a substance that looked like the plants Mosher and he had recently discovered. The material was very dark and course. The boy put the stuff into his mouth and swallowed it without chewing.

Food, is it food for you? thought Calish. "What do you want?"

The boy once again made the funny expression, and the melodious sound followed. Then, in his mind, Calish saw images that were reminiscent of his recent dream; the one that had encouraged him to explore the Crystallight caverns. He saw the tribe's settlement, the rock that would not move, the tunnels, and then an overview of the Crystallight caves. "How do you do this? How do you put images in my mind? You are the one that brought me here, aren't you?"

The strange boy's expression twisted again and Calish saw something different. In his mind he was whisked away through very dark tunnels, twisting and turning, until he ended up in another cavern. The place contained crystals, enough at least to readily see the area, and it had many objects strewn about the cavern floor. There were hides of strange animals, bones, hut-like structures, and pits that once housed fires. There were also broken weapons that were similar to the one carried by the creature.

Calish's mind-tour suddenly shifted and he once again found himself gliding through the same tunnels. The trip ended at one particular tunnel's entrance. The entrance to the tunnel that led to the cavern was high on a ledge. For a moment he was standing on the ledge, looking down. Then suddenly he was flown down to the base of the ledge. He turned his eyes up. From below one could not at all see that there was a tunnel opening beyond the ledge. The wall before him was steep and high, but if one looked close enough, they might say that the climb to the ledge would be difficult, but not impossible.

Through his mind's vision, Calish focused his sights on the strange boy and asked, "You want me to go there? To the place you are showing me in my mind?" Calish pointed to his eyes, then his head.

The strange boy tilted his head and the music became a little louder in Calish's mind.

"I guess that's your way of saying *yes*."

The creature turned to go back behind the cave wall from where he had been hiding. Calish tensed, because he could not see what was there. But the strange boy soon reappeared, carrying a package wrapped in a leathery cloth. He held it out at Calish as if he wanted him to take it. But when Calish would not move, the boy knelt down and placed it at Calish's feet. The strange boy gestured at the package, but Calish still wouldn't budge, so the strange boy reached down and removed the leathery material around the package. Suddenly everything became as clear as day.

"Yikeshtu. What is that?" There was light, an unbelievable amount of light, emanating from the object within the cloth. It was so bright that at first Calish couldn't see what the light's source was, but as soon as his eyes adjusted he could tell that there was a fist-sized gemstone that was at the light's center. Calish couldn't help but be drawn to it; he moved closer. The jewel glistened with many colors, mostly green, that were more intense near the gem's insides.

Calish looked back up at the boy, who was using his arm to cover his face and eyes. The light's brightness obviously made him uncomfortable, but the strange boy remained nearby. Then he made a gesture that told Calish to take-up the lighted gem.

Calish put down Asher's spear and picked up the jewel. It was warm, but not overly so. It was beautiful, and Calish was drawn to the mysterious facets of color that swirled deep within the jewel's surface. Calish smiled and glanced at the strange boy. He was still hiding his face, but he made a weird grin, like a smile, only different. He opened his mouth a bit, exposing his teeth.

"Shishtu!" The boy's teeth were hideous: sharp, like fangs, but tiny ones, and too many for one mouth. The color was a dark grey, almost black. Even the gem's intensity could do little to brighten their darkness. The grey teeth were in stark contrast to the creature's pale skin. The strange boy then pushed out its tongue. It was long, black, and... *El help us*, it had two points! The boy wiggled his tongue, and again Calish decried out loud, "El help us!" The twitching tongue reminded Calish of a snake. There seemed to be no end to the strange boy's surprises.

Thankfully, the boy retracted his slithering tongue. His toothy grin, however, stayed in place, as if to say that he wanted Calish to really see it, and to really know him for what he was.

"Okay, friend, I guess you are happy. Ah, I'm not sure why you're showing me this, but here you go." Calish held out the sparkling gem, as if to give it back. Then the musical sound was heard again and Calish, in his mind once more, saw himself carrying the stone to the dark place his people had settled. The creature gestured openly to the cavern where they now stood.

"You want me to bring my people here, with this alighted gem to guide us. Yes, I understand."

Calish bowed his head slightly. "Thank you."

The strange boy copied suit and while still covering his eyes, bowed also. The gesture made him appear much less strange to Calish. *Gestures*, Calish supposed, sometimes transcended cultural differences... *Well, in this case,* mused Calish, *species differences,* because the strange boy was like no human he had ever seen. But no matter what the boy was, he had made it possible for Calish's people to have a chance at surviving in their new underground world.

Suddenly, in his mind's eye, Calish saw the cave that sat beyond the ledge.

"Yes, I understand. I will go there, soon. And meet you there."

Just then a loud voice interrupted Calish's interaction with the strange boy.

"Calish! Calish, where are y-you?" It was Mosher, trying to find where his friend had gone.

Calish peered at the boy, wondering if he wanted to stay to meet Mosher. But something in his posture said that he was not ready to meet more of Calish's people. The boy was starting to look tired and he made moves as if he was going to retreat into the tunnels. Calish partially wrapped the sparkling gem, picked up his spear and turned to face his new companion.

"Here, Moshe, I am here!" shouted Calish. He and the boy exchanged glances.

As they could hear Mosher approach, the boy showed his toothy grin once more and gave a slight bow. Calish returned the gesture. He watched as the mysterious boy disappeared into a nearby tunnel.

"What happened?" asked Mosher as he ran to where Calish was standing. "I w-waited for you. What w-were you..." Just then Mosher stopped talking, because he noticed the foreign object in Calish's hand.

"What is that?"

Calish smiled at his friend. While still marveling at the jewel's brilliance, he answered, "It is a beacon of hope, Moshe. A great Crystallight gem to guide us to our new home."

CHAPTER 9
Is There Hope

Korah looked up, and all around. The cavern's ceilings and walls were growing much dimmer – not because of the walls themselves, but because of something the people could do nothing about. When the tribe had first landed in their underground world, the fire pits were numerous and strong. But with the resources being quickly used up, the level of lighting, as with the amount of wood to feed the fires, was fading fast. It wouldn't be long before the people would be in total darkness.

"Our world darkens, Father," warned Mishtas.

"Yes, my son, I see it."

"How can we survive without light?"

"We might never know, for surely we will starve to death first," Korah said sadly.

"I also see it," sighed Abiram, as he too scrutinized the cavern walls while approaching Korah and Mishtas. Mishtas bowed his head in deference to the Elder.

Korah responded, "Our sky, such as it is, grows darker and darker."

The sky, the cavern's ceilings, had a sporadic covering of a substance, slick and shiny, that took firelight and enhanced it. The effect was to make the general area much easier to see in. After the tribe had located where the greatest concentration of the slick substances was, they moved the fire pits and their other belongings nearest to those areas. The glossy areas were also found on some cave walls and even the strange cone shapes that hung from the ceilings. The discovery had offered some hope, such as it was; a sky of dim light that gave them something to look up to.

"How goes our food supplies?" asked Abiram, quick to change the subject.

Korah studied his old friend and thought back to better times. It had been so long since they had other concerns, and joys. Now all that seemed left to discuss where the grim realities of their common dilemma. "Dathan tells me the herd numbers are falling quickly. The bread, grain and flour is nearly depleted. There are no more fruits. There is water from cracks in the cave walls, but that too is not enough for all of us."

Abiram took in the reports. Then he added his own bit of doom and gloom. "I hear some people telling stories of finding small bugs. Some are trying to eat them. But the taste is very bad and they say the insects are dangerous and will bite your skin off. If not squashed very hard, they will attack. In any event, the people will soon starve. What then?"

"Panic will spread," stated Korah factually, "and our food centers will most certainly be overrun. Gasheer's men might not be able to stop them."

"Many will die."

"Dathan, I believe, is counting on just that," relayed Korah.

"It cannot be. He would never say such a thing."

Korah stared into Abiram's eyes. "Does he have to say it for it to be so? Think about this. Is it not Gasheer and his men that guard our centers of food? Are they not in possession of all weaponry? Have they not made it their business to decide who gets what resources and when?"

Abiram could not find fault with Korah's point. In a hushed, mistrustful way, Abiram said, "My family and their other kin have complained about not receiving a proper allotment of food. They are hungry and need more. But I had hoped that all had been fair in such matters."

Korah interjected, "When has it ever been fair, my brother? Have we not seen this in Egypt? Have we no experience with the strong over the weak?"

Both men, if they were to so choose, could disrobe and provide stark evidence pointing to the truth of those sentiments. The scars from the task master's whip would never heal.

Abiram whispered, "Gasheer and his men do not grow thinner."

Korah nodded knowingly to that observation.

Abiram then prompted, "It was Dathan that first offered the suggestion to confiscate all important resources and collect them into distribution centers."

"And we all agreed to the proposal; it seemed the prudent thing to do." Korah had told his people to cooperate with the collection efforts. When the tribe had been first cast down, the people had caused a great deal of uproar as they fought over anything important. In an effort to secure food and other consumables for future use, the Elders deemed it necessary to gather the goods in one place. It was a hard thing to do; most people will not hand over their last bits of food willingly, so a forced confiscation was the only real solution.

"Gasheer's men took too much, however," Abiram said like a conspirator. Before he spoke again, he looked around warily. Apparently he trusted Mishtas to hear his complaints, but Abiram still feared that someone too close to Dathan would catch wind of his griping. "Many have complained that their private belongings were rifled through, and things were taken of personal importance. Not all that was taken was of communal value."

Korah sympathized, but choose to not reveal that his people had complained of the same thing. He calmly slid his hand down to his pouch to where he had hidden away his secret possession. Luckily, the sacred object was still there.

"And why can't the collection centers be closer to our tents?" asked Abiram, as if he found fault with the arrangement.

Once again, Korah could do nothing but remind his fellow Elder of what was already known. "The distribution centers are situated separately from our main settlement. Dathan choose those spots. Normally I might tend to agree with that policy, but Abiram, my friend, maybe all is not as it might appear to be. I have noticed, as I am sure you are also aware, that when our people walk too near to a pile of debris that is designated for a fire pit, Gasheer's men display a threatening stance. It scares many. There needs to be further attention brought to this matter."

Korah did not like the direction that the conversation was taking, but Abiram needed to show solidarity with him if they were to effect any real changes, especially with Dathan. So far Abiram appeared to be with him; if not in action, then in spirit at least.

"Maybe we should have this discussion with Dathan present," Abiram said softly.

"I agree," snapped Dathan, as he appeared suddenly from a nearby dark space. And further in the darkness, behind Dathan, was Gasheer. Unfortunately, it wasn't too dark to see the frown on Gasheer's face. If it was possible, the brute's scowl was more pronounced than usual.

Dathan bowed his head to each Elder, and then eyed Mishtas, who was standing there quietly. Dathan glared at Mishtas as if his presence was unwanted. Mishtas recognized Dathan's intentions, so he looked to Korah for instructions. Korah gently guided Mishtas to stand back a few feet.

After seeing Mishtas give way, Dathan squared himself up straighter. He smoothed out his fine robes and pronounced, "Shall we open a formal meeting, my brothers? I will, of course, take up your suggestions with the utmost importance."

Korah recognized the condescending tone in Dathan's voice. And it was only getting worse. At first Dathan's haughtiness was bothersome, but it was quickly becoming standard fare. Korah pondered to himself, *How long will it be until Dathan decrees himself to be our sovereign ruler? A king... and tyrant to boot. The Pharaoh of the underworld. El help us.*

"We need another solution," stammered Abiram, trying to sound brave in Dathan's presence. "Our people will soon starve." After saying this, he glanced at Korah, in hopes of getting his support.

Korah took in the look and turned to Dathan with confidence. "How say you, Dathan?"

"Well, first of all," began Dathan imperially, "based upon the premise of the statement, and the fact that for some unknown reason I was not privy to your earlier discussion, I can only surmise that you are referring to our arrangement for the distribution of consumables. Moreover, from what I recall, what needs to be pointed out is that we all agreed to our present arrangement. Did we not?"

"Not all that has transpired has been agreed upon, Dathan," argued Korah.

At first Abiram nodded in agreement, but when he saw the seriousness in Dathan's face, he quickly retracted his nods.

"Should we not discuss the details of how our 'common' goods are being shared?" asked Korah.

Dathan asked, "And what is it that is troubling you, brothers?"

As if on cue, Gasheer stepped forward to stand directly behind his Lord.

Abiram, upon seeing the giant so close, took a small step back. Abiram's apprehension did not go unnoticed by Dathan. If anything, it appeared to make him happy. Gasheer, for his part, took no note of it. Inspiring fear in others was a normal occurrence for him.

Korah scrutinized Gasheer's enormous torso; it was near impossible to miss. The behemoth showed no signs of shrinking due to hunger. *No wonders there.* The undiminished strength in Gasheer's stature made Korah think twice about persisting with his inquiries, but the subject needed a thorough vetting, so he bravely proceeded nonetheless. Korah put forth his question in an accusatorial manner. "The distribution of food... is it equal?"

"Of course, why do you ask?"

"There are complaints."

"There always are." Dathan turned his stern and domineering eyes on Abiram and stated, "Abiram, how say you?"

Abiram started to speak... then he saw the grimace on Gasheer's face. The brute grinned, opening his mouth slightly; most of his front teeth were missing and the few that remained were broken, and crooked. Moreover, bits of stringy meat were still hanging from the cracks. Abiram swallowed hard and finally spluttered, "Well, Dathan, I ah, ah, ah, everything seems to be in order, I suppose. W-We are doing what we must."

Korah couldn't believe what he was hearing. Abiram was softer than his wife's pot of mashed gruel.

Dathan smirked at Abiram. "We are indeed, Abiram. We are indeed. And to that end, what else concerns you, brothers? As I already said, I am open to suggestions, of course."

Korah was not happy with Dathan's controlling manner, and dismissal of questions about food, but he decided to ignore that for the moment and pursue another important topic that needed exploring. "Perhaps we should offer prayers for our return to the surface. We said we would do so, and as of yet have not done it."

"Yes, yes," shot Abiram, glad to be done with the food subject, and even happier to be free from Dathan's wrath. "Please let us do that. Ah, ah… how should we begin?"

"We begin," stated Korah plainly, "by appealing to the Gods, or rather *God*. The true one named by Moses, who led us out of Egypt and bondage."

"Yes, yes" agreed Abiram hopefully, "and surely by now our brethren above will ask Moses to pray for us as well."

Dathan, trying to remain calm contested, "Moses? Moses? He will hear their prayers? He will hear us? Is it not Moses who caused us to be here?"

"But Moses talks to God," cited Abiram. "Surely he is the one to help us now."

Dathan refuted, "To bless us, or curse us, I wonder?"

"To bless, to bless," furthered Abiram. "In the blessing prayer, for example, Moses called on El to seek blessings and offer thanks. Perhaps it would be foolish to do otherwise."

"Foolish?" interjected Dathan angrily. The Elder gestured to their dark environment. "You would give thanks and call on a power that has done this so called 'blessing' to us? And for what? Not obeying Moses, who thought himself better than us." Dathan, ignoring Abiram, glared at Korah. "That is what is foolish, and only a fool would follow such a path."

"I am a fool? I think not," said Korah. "And there are other prayers to consider. For example, I was standing three feet from Moses when he taught the prayer of redemption. Is this not the prayer we now need? And did I not hear him say God's name, El, as Abiram rightfully remembers, and that we all must repent before Him?"

Dathan was ready for this argument. "We do not know of this redemption you speak about, and can only take you at your word. Do you have another witness to this so-called prayer of redemption?"

Korah thought for a moment. He finally realized that he had broached a subject that he did not have good answers to, so he finally stated, "No."

Dathan, being persistent, said, "Tell me, Korah, if this is what you learned while you were alone with Moses, while Abiram and

I were not present, then what else did Moses share with you? Is there something you hide from us, your tribal brethren?"

Abiram, following along with Dathan's accusations, quickly decided to turn on Korah. "We all agreed to stand together against Moses. Yet if I recall, it was Dathan and I who stood at the base of the mountain while you alone, Korah, ascended the peak to parley with Moses. Do you think we can forget this? Are we fools for you?"

Returning the favor, Korah turned on Abiram and spat, "Yes, you are a fool. And because of your spite for Moses, we will all die!"

"Spite?" argued Abiram, suddenly finding his voice. "Are you not the one who originally instigated our rebellion against Moses?"

"I was," admitted Korah, saddened to be reminded of it.

"Furthermore," chimed in Dathan, glad to capitalize on the moment, "on the day when the Earth opened up, was it not you that stood by and did nothing as Moses watched us fall to this place?"

Upon hearing this, Abiram stared with astonishment at Korah, wondering if Dathan's statement had merit. "Is this true, Korah?"

Korah did not answer Abiram, but looked at Dathan with a rising anger. Dathan's face was hard, steady and accusatory. Korah disregarded Dathan's glare. "You don't know what you're talking about."

Dathan mocked, "I do not know what I'm talking about? Did I not demand of you to appeal to Moses moments before we fell below? Was I blind? Could I not see that both you and Moses shared a connection... was it a light that passed between you both? Tell us truthfully, Korah, what secrets are you keeping from your fellow Elders?"

Korah hesitated, his lip trembled a bit, but he did not give in to Dathan's challenging allegations.

"Korah," probed Abiram, "what is Dathan talking about? Could you have prevented this? Could you have appealed to Moses? What is this 'light' you shared with Moses?"

"Yes, Korah, do tell us," pressed Dathan.

"There was nothing I could do to stop this," Korah said while gesturing to the dark cavern. "And I *did* appeal to Moses. Speaking to myself in prayer, but by then it was too late."

Not to be dissuaded, Dathan prompted, "And the light between you?"

As if in ignorance, Korah asked, "Light? What light?"

"Am I blind? Did I not see a bright light pass from Moses and go to you?"

Korah had seen the brightness of Moses's face, and he had felt the light's warmth. But Korah was unaware that Moses's glow had somehow been transferred to him in a way that it could be seen by others. Thinking quickly, Korah asked, "Is it not true that when Moses ascended the mountain to speak with El, that he would return to us with his face glowing? Is this not what we first feared in him, and later came to covet for ourselves?"

"And?" Dathan prodded cynically.

"What you saw… what you *think* you saw… was merely a reflection of the power given to Moses. I could not have created such a thing."

Abiram asked, "But did you share in it? Did Moses communicate something with you?"

Korah avowed, "There were no words passed between us."

"Was there another type of communication?" asked Dathan as if he already knew the answer.

Korah paused to calculate a response. He didn't want to keep things from the other Elders, but if he gave in to their insistent questions and told them of the light from Moses, then he would also have to explain how he had the sacred item. The light's warmth had washed over him and channeled itself onto the object in his pouch; the bond between the light and the object was undeniable. This proved that the oracle of El had unknown and mysterious properties. If revealed, those would-be powers would surely cause a great rift between the Elders. Moreover, unbeknownst to the other Elders, Moses had given the item to him alone. Moses had not told him to speak of the object with others. In fact, Moses had said, 'Korah, this sacred oracle is for you. There will come a time when you will need and value it greatly. Take heed that you protect and treasure it always.' At the time,

Korah didn't understand what Moses meant, and he still didn't fully know what the object was for, but there was one thing Korah knew for sure: Dathan must never know of it.

Thinking quickly, Korah said, "How do you imagine I could have communicated without words? Am I not a man just like you?"

"So how do you explain what I saw?"

"I cannot. But maybe, in the heat of the moment, you... imagined it."

Dathan's face turned very dark.

"Or maybe," chimed in Abiram to ease the tension, "there was a sudden streak of sunlight near to Korah. It was, if I recall, a most sunny day before the dark clouds formed and the Earth opened up."

Korah nodded at that suggestion, glad to hear another explanation, even if it was from a less than reliable source that had somehow stumbled upon a feeble, yet feasible, excuse.

Dathan harrumphed.

Abiram and Dathan looked at one another, assessing what Korah had said. Of the two, Dathan was by far the most distrustful; his face was tight, his eyes squinted and one of his eyebrows was raised to the hilt. He did not believe a word Korah had said. Abiram's face was merely a puzzle, as usual.

"Perhaps," proposed Abiram, "we could offer a prayer to the God of Moses and at the same time to the ones familiar to us from Egypt."

Korah responded, "As far as praying to the gods and the God of Moses, I would agree..."

"There then, you agree with Abiram," responded Dathan, cutting Korah off. Dathan was happy with his progress in fomenting dissent between his brethren, but that only worked if he ended up as the ultimate arbiter. To that end, Dathan quickly changed the subject. "We must do something to offer hope for our people."

"How?" queried Abiram, in his doom and gloom mode once again. "Our food is nearly gone. We will all surely die. What shall we do?"

"We have not yet 'died', Abiram," lectured Dathan. "As I said before, we still live. There must be a reason. And I put forth to you that our survival has nothing to do with Moses; as confirmed by our very forthright brother Korah. But as to what we should do..."

"Ask for forgiveness is what we should do," interrupted Korah.

Dathan exploded, "No! We will do no such thing. Gods will be worshipped, yes. But it will be the ones, as brother Abiram says, we're most familiar with." Dathan stood tall and arrogantly declared, "And in this matter, you will do as I say."

Gasheer then stepped forward to back-up his Lord's statement.

Abiram, frightened again by Gasheer's sudden closeness, moved involuntarily to grab hold of Dathan's tunic sleeves. Gasheer, seeing the act as hostile, unsheathed his sword and pressed it hard against Abiram's throat.

"Dathan!" shouted Korah, "you have no right to threaten an Elder. Tell your man to stand down." When Gasheer or Dathan did not respond, Korah glared at Gasheer and barked, "Now!"

When Gasheer still did not move, Korah leapt up and grabbed Dathan by the collar. Dathan responded by pushing Korah, but there was not enough force in it to separate the two. Then a few clumsy punches and elbows were thrown. But since the men were old, the force of the blows was relatively mild. More shoving commenced and both men stumbled to the ground. They ended up in a slow-moving wrestling match, grunting and groaning, making much more exaggerated noises than necessary.

"Fool! Stop twisting my arm," one of them complained.

"Aough! You old goat, let go of my leg!" the other griped.

The commotion was quickly attracting a crowd of tribesmen. Many were shocked. But others were fascinated to see their leaders tussling like children. They should have intervened; after all, this did concern their high and mighty leaders. But they did not. No, the remnant survivors were not inclined to stop the wrestling match simply because many of them blamed the Elders for their predicament.

"Maybe we should stop them," said one bystander.

Another person responded, "Why should we? Let them have a taste of what we face."

"You could be right."

"Of course I am."

"I got five shekels on Dathan."

"I'll take that and raise you one goat horn mug."

"Deal."

The surrounding guards seemed in no hurry to end the show either.

Eventually, however, after Gasheer's signal, two of the soldiers separated the combatants. Both Elders got up wheezing and coughing, neither one of them very eager to resume the fight. One of Dathan's men held onto Dathan, and Mishtas supported Korah.

"Where's my five shekels?" asked the bystander.

"It was a draw, fool; you get nothing."

"Figures."

Dathan recovered his breath. As for his dignity, he straightened out his robes and huffed, "Very well, no need to get so excited, my brother." He then turned to Gasheer and said calmly, "Gasheer, my good fellow, please remove your sword from Abiram's throat."

Gasheer sneered into the sunken eyes of Abiram, as if to say he was not so sure about carrying out the orders. Abiram recoiled at the sight, and pinched up his nose from the monster's foul breath. Gasheer sheathed his sword.

"Very good, very good," deemed Dathan. "You see, my brothers, we can all agree once again that everything is fine. All is well."

But Korah, although still tired from the tussle, would not relent. He had had more than enough of Dathan's patronizing tone. Summoning up all his courage, and his shallow breath, he stormed into Dathan's space, saying, "All is not well, you fool. We will all die soon. Can you not see, Dathan?" Korah paused, then charged, "Or is this what you always wanted?" Gasheer be damned if he was going to accept the injustice, or Dathan's blatant grabs for power any longer.

"Are you accusing me, Korah, of somehow masterminding this entire debacle?"

"Did we not, in Egypt, have a saying: If the sandal fits..."

Dathan glowered at Korah, his expression filled with hatred. With the slightest movement of his fingers, Dathan gestured at Gasheer. Of course the bully knew exactly what was expected from him. Gasheer stepped up toward Korah, sword at the ready. Mishtas, following suit, also stepped forward to stand in front of Korah.

Abiram at first acted as if he would mediate, but he quickly changed his mind. He looked wildly about for a place to hide. Gasheer and Mishtas puffed up their stance.

Just as another fight was about to erupt, a man pushed his way to the front of the crowd and shouted to Abiram, "My Lord, my Lord!"

Abiram, with a quivering voice, prompted, "Yes, my son, how say you?"

The man exclaimed, "Animals have been stolen. Eaten. And Gasheer's men have killed folks they claim have done the stealing. There is much blood."

Abiram turned to Dathan and asked, "Is this true?"

Dathan, without missing a beat, replied, "This is the first I'm hearing of this, like you."

But that retort was not good enough for the crowd. Murmurs of discontent spread throughout the flock. Soon enough, voices shouting for justice rang forth. The crowd started jostling for position, and soon threatened to overtake Dathan's soldiers.

"That's not good enough," argued Korah. "Your men go too far. Our people are hungry. You have no right ordering your men to kill our people." Angered by this troubling news, and bolstered by the heated voices in the crowd, he once again approached Dathan. Mishtas followed, close by Korah's side.

Seeing this, Gasheer stepped up too. The unruly crowd was a problem that his men could deal with, but Gasheer felt it more important to personally take care of the most pressing of the issues. He stared down at Korah with a menacing glare.

Just as Gasheer was ready to once again unsheathe his sword, someone in the crowd shouted, "Look! Look there!"

The whole clan turned to see where the shouter was pointing. In the distance they saw a beam of light streaking across the cavern's vast expanse. The light was very vivid. It had a greenish tint and it was brighter than anything that could be cast by a lantern or torch. It was a sparkling dance of radiance that bounced along the cave floor and simultaneously glittered along the cavern's shiny ceiling. The crowd, with wide eyes, was taken in by the strange sight.

"What is that?" one person asked in wonder.

"I know not," another answered.

"Is it Moses?"

"I pray you are right."

"I pray I am wrong." ·

"Why?"

"Cause that means he's stuck here with us."

As the strange light grew stronger, someone in the outer part of the assembly shouted, "It is Calish and Mosher. They come this way!"

The bright light soon reached the outer perimeter of the crowd. The people, from back to front, readily parted to let the light bearers pass by.

Finally, the folks nearest the gathering's center stepped aside. Calish, along with Mosher, walked through the gap to where the Elders stood. As soon as he got close enough, Calish stretched out his arm. Then he fully opened the hand that held a luminous stone. Instantly, the stone's green light burst open with a great force, shedding enough radiance to brighten the whole area. The multi-colored sprinkles of light flashed and sparkled around everyone, as if suspended in midair.

Upon seeing the magical display, the Elders, soldiers, and the rest of the crowd marveled at the sight of it. Even Dathan, behind his typical smirk, could not help but be impressed by the spectacle.

Calish, seeing the peoples' surprised expression, gave Gasheer his most intimidating sneer. Then, facing his grandfather, Calish produced his most winning, victorious smile.

Korah returned the smile and nodded with affection. While gesturing to the congregation, Korah encouraged, "Go forth, my son."

Calish rotated toward the flock and raised the shimmering stone as high as he possibly could. The stone's radiance seemed to stretch forever, overcoming their dark home with its dazzling and brilliant light.

The people shouted with joy. For the first time since being cast down, the remnant survivors raised their voices in a most wonderful cry of hope.

CHAPTER 10
Sneaky-Sneak

"Bishtar, is that you?"

The girl smiled but did not answer. She moved forward toward the tunnel exit looking around suspiciously, then scooted back into the corner where the old man had first seen her.

The old man tried again. "What are you doing there in the dark? Do you not want to go to our new home? Come follow us, it is not far. I can already see the light. The Crystallight cavern is close. Look there, our new home awaits. You are welcome to make your home near ours. They say we can choose where to set up our tent. Our clan must have already chosen a spot by now. I hope it is a good one." The old man, a member of Bishtar's tribe, pointed to the nearby exit, to where a fair amount of light was being cast into the tunnel. He was walking slowly, his skinny body carrying packages full of his belongings.

"No, thank you," answered Bishtar shyly. "My family and I have already set up our tents, and ah... I am waiting for someone."

"Very well then." The old man turned to his wife and said cheerfully, "Come, my dear, let us be on our way. The line is long. There are many waiting to pass security."

The old man's wife sighed, rolled her eyes and picked up the bulkiest of their belongings. Being the stronger of the two, and easily the broadest, she was tasked with hauling sacks nearly as big as she was.

After the old couple left, Bishtar reached down to the parcel she had hidden away. She had to jostle the clumsy bundle, wrapping it better so that the contents beneath its covering remained hidden, and hopefully quiet. "Hush now," she whispered to the bundle. She picked it up gently and moved to an out-of-sight place where she could watch the old man and his wife as they entered the Crystallight cavern.

As the old couple got to the front of the inspection line, when enough folks were assembled in front of her, Bishtar scooted closer, hiding behind them all, and at the same time very close to the old woman. Bishtar carefully put down her bundle, making sure the wrappings covered everything. She then ducked low, watching and waiting for her chance.

"Stop there!" commanded a soldier to the old couple.

"What is it?" the old man responded. "What do you want? As you can see, we have nothing but our meager belongings."

"Stand aside for inspection." The guard pointed nearby. "You, old man, stand there. Put down your stuff. Your wife, go over there." The old woman quickly stepped to an area in front of a group of people who were also waiting their turn.

"Very well, no need to shout," griped the old man.

Since finding the Crystallight caves, the tribe had managed to ferry all of their belongings through the tunnel Calish had discovered. Carrying their personal effects was often managed by wrapping them in blankets, and if they were too heavy, they tied them with rope and pulled them through. Luckily for the old couple, the old man's wife was strong enough to heft the heavy stuff upon her broad, rather manly, shoulders.

"Are you carrying any animals?" queried the soldier as he suspiciously watched them.

The animals were a slightly different story. Pulling the beasts by a rope tied around their neck was usually sufficient. Pushing them through also helped. The rams had been the most difficult; their horns were constantly bumping into the tunnel walls, and when the ornery beasts would get particularly frustrated, the ram-pusher got a swift kick, and plenty of bruises along with it. Ram-pushers soon became scarce, so lots had to be drawn to choose between the less-than-eager candidates.

When the old man did not respond quickly enough, the soldier repeated, "Are you deaf, old one? Do you carry any beasts?"

The sheep and goats were generally easier, although noisier and a lot messier. Many of the folks following the flock could attest to bruised hips and twisted ankles after slipping on the creature's generously dispersed waste products. The oxen, unfortunately, being much too large to fit through the tunnel's narrow corridors, had to be slaughtered. Their meat, bones, and horns did, however, make it through without a scratch. Living animals, upon entering the Crystallight cavern, were instantly segregated and collected by Gasheer's soldiers.

"No," answered the old man, "as you can see, these are just our personal items and supplies."

"We shall see, old one," grunted the guard. He bent down and started rifling through the old man's items.

In any event, the tribe, either separately or in small groups, had left the dark place where they had first awakened and without too much trouble made their way to the lighted cavern. Well, maybe there was some small degree of trouble.

"Where did you get this?" demanded the soldier as he unwrapped a particularly interesting article.

"This pot is mine!" yelled the old man.

The lead soldier replied curtly, "The Elders have deemed it communal." The soldier looked into the jar, stuck his finger in, and tasted its contents. "You have salt in here."

"So."

"So, we need salt to preserve our meat; you should have already given it to us. Why do you need salt? Are you hiding meat from us as well?"

"We have no meat. You soldiers have already taken our beasts for yourselves."

"Never mind that, old man," the soldier said crossly. "You should have given me the salt without wasting my time."

The old man countered, "The Elders have nothing to say of such a small thing, so why are you taking issue with it?" He turned to his wife. "Have we not carried this from Egypt? Is this not our pot since the day we married?" His wife nodded in agreement but was too scared of the soldiers to actually speak. The old man reached to take back his property, but the guard held tight.

"The Elders are not here, citizen. But I am. Now let it go before we get angry."

"No, the Elders must say so."

"They just did." With that statement, the pot was forcibly taken by the lead soldier. He pushed the old man aside as a second guard made use of his club on the man's back.

In between yelps, the old man cried, "I will tell my lords of your treatment."

"Go ahead," replied the soldier as he clubbed the complainer once more for good measure. Meanwhile, the lead guard put the pot in a pile of communal objects that had already been confiscated.

Once everything had made it through the tunnel, the settlement had dispersed throughout the Crystallight's spaces, more or less at their own discretion. They grouped themselves according to family, and clan, some taking alcoves that had enough room to accommodate all the family members, some pitching their tents out in the open. However, choice locations, such as near the best Maana fields, were reserved for Gasheer's soldiers. But no matter where they ended up, most agreed that the Crystallight caverns were much better than where they had first arrived in the underground world.

A world of light... *Crystallight* was now theirs.

The lead soldier then eyed the old man's very quiet wife. Noticing the soldier's hostile demeanor, the woman became very frightened, and she dropped her heavy packages. They fell like a sack of potatoes, clunking loudly as they hit the ground.

The soldier was about to examine her belongings but because the sacks looked rather disheveled, unappealing and somewhat smelly, he retracted a bit. He finally said to his helpers, "Let the old woman pass. She is too scared to defy us by hiding anything."

As soon as Bishtar heard this, she took her bundle and neatly aligned it to be hidden directly behind the woman's bulky sacks. The little girl then backed away while looking casually around and acting as if she was not even there. *Oh, please let this work,* she wished, *and please be silent,* she projected to her bundle.

Luckily the guards did not take note of her, or maybe they ignored her because she was covered by the bulky torso and thick robes of the old woman. One of the guards barked, "Hurry up, be on your way, woman."

The old woman nodded apologetically. Then, forgetting herself, she smiled, thus revealing her mostly toothless mouth. The unsightly vision was made even more bizarre because there were two broken and stained teeth that emerged at impossible angles. She soon realized her mistake and quickly closed the gaping, dark crevice.

But the horrid mysteries had already been exposed, and the guards recoiled from the sight. "Yikeshtu," they mumbled to one another. "I just lost my appetite," griped the lead guard.

The woman grunted as she hefted her load up to her shoulders. She turned and waited for her husband to follow. Just as Bishtar was sure she would be noticed, the old man interjected . . .

"I will tell Korah of this!" he screeched, still very upset about his pot.

The guards happily turned away from the old woman's scary face to look at the loud complainer. They waved at him angrily as if to say *Go, before we hit you some more*. The old man grumbled under his breath, picked up what remained of his stuff and took some slow, unsteady steps into the cavern, hobbling because of the beating he took. He accidentally dropped a small item, but his wife, seeing him stumble, picked it up, thus making her burden greater as she too moved forward.

"Go on then, do as you please," replied the lead soldier dismissively.

As the lead guard's focus was stuck on yelling at and watching the old man, Bishtar, making herself as small and sweet-looking as possible, picked up her bundle, and like a shadow, took up her place directly behind the heavily-laden and auspiciously large old woman. Together the old man, his wife, and the quiet little shadow meandered into their new home.

CHAPTER 11
Transformation

"I wish to sleep more, Mother," complained Bishtar.

"No, my daughter, it is time to wake. There is work to do. It is our turn to receive our Maana allotment. If we are late, we might not receive our share. There is nothing to eat. We finished all our Maana before we slept. Calish has already left to find places where the plant grows unbeknownst to Gasheer's guards."

"Who cares what he does," she grumbled while turning to sleep some more. "I ate too much. Now leave me be."

"No, now get up!" Hannah grabbed Bishtar's arm and turned her around. Bishtar suddenly opened her eyes, angered by her mother's insistence.

"Agghh?!!" shrieked Hannah in horror at what she saw. Looking back at her was a ghastly sight. Gone were her daughter's beautiful blue eyes; now they were black orbs as dark as the night sky. Hannah recoiled from the sight.

"What is it, Mother?" queried Calish as he burst into the tent.

Without taking her frightened eyes off of Bishtar, Hannah directed Calish to see his sister. Calish did so and was likewise startled.

"What is it, Calish?" asked Bishtar anxiously. "What do you see?"

"Ah, ah, nothing, I'm not sure. Your eyes are different."

"How so?"

"They are black, all black. There is no whiteness at all."

"Is this a trick? Stop playing games, Calish!" Bishtar glared at her mother, but Hannah was still shocked into silence.

Calish grabbed the shiniest metal plate his family owned. He brought it over to Bishtar and held it to her face. Bishtar gasped at the strange reflection. Then she gingerly touched her eyes, to see if it was real. "How can this be? Mother, what is happening?"

Hannah just shook her head in worry. Finally, she asked, "Are you ill, Bishtar?"

"No, Mother, I feel fine."

At least that was something. But Hannah was still worried, so she answered as best she could. "I don't know, my daughter, I do not know."

Calish knelt down in front of Bishtar to better see. As he did so, Hannah was suddenly drawn to the back of Calish's head. His hair was thinning. Bald spots appeared, and the revealed skin underneath was a very pale, ashen color. Hannah studied Calish's fingers as they held the plate. His hands were growing distorted, knobby, and his fingertips were becoming claw-shaped and almost bird-like.

Calish felt his mother's stare, so he turned to her and asked, "What is it, Mother?"

But Hannah could not speak. All she could do is cup her face in her hands to hide her tears.

Calish looked at his sister with puzzlement. Bishtar studied him too, carefully and deeply. Then she slowly brought her pointy fingers to touch his face, and his eyes. She pushed the plate away from her and toward her brother's face. Calish brought the plate in front of him, and saw what they both did. His eyes had also become nearly as black as his twin sister's.

"Shishtu," he muttered. As Calish stared at his strange new appearance, Bishtar reached up to hold his hand: claw-to-claw, in solidarity. Together the stunned and newly transformed siblings listened to their mother's weeping cries.

CHAPTER 12
Joseph's Cup

"What is it, Mother?" asked Bishtar.

Hannah was sitting on a stool, her head and shoulders slumped forward. Bishtar sat down at her mother's feet, respectfully. The black-eyed little girl gazed up at her mother's sad face, wondering why the woman appeared to carry the weight of the world.

At first Hannah failed to meet her daughter's wanting eyes, but then she dared to look back. Upon doing so, Hannah's heart was broken all over again. Her spirit reeled from seeing her beautiful little girl looking more and more unrecognizable. *Nae,* monstrous might even be said, for Bishtar's golden hair was all but gone. Her head had swollen so much that it seemed too big to sit on such tiny shoulders.

"El, give me strength," Hannah whispered to herself. Somehow Hannah held back her tears, but it wasn't easy. Then she glanced down at the small package in her trembling hands, drawing a little hope from what the item represented. Oh, how she dreamed that the action she was about to perform would somehow reverse Bishtar's awful transformation. Would giving the magical gift to Bishtar make her human? Could it make her the real Bishtar once again? Deep inside, Hannah knew better; it was merely wishful thinking of a desperately scared woman. But what else could she do? The transfer of ownership had to do something good. On some level, it had to work. At the very least the bequest would give Bishtar a connection to her ancestral past, and to her culture. Maybe it would help to remind the extraordinary little girl of her true self.

Summoning up more courage than the woman really had, Hannah nervously exposed the item from beneath a white cloth. She then held out the gleaming metallic silver object so that Bishtar could get a better view.

"It is Joseph's Cup!" Bishtar voiced in surprise.

"Yes, my daughter."

After a pause, where both of them stared in wonder at the old and ornately designed object, Hannah began her practiced explanation. "Joseph was the twelfth son of Jacob. Jacob, along with his father Isaac, and Isaac's father Abraham, were all blessed by El. Joseph, Jacob's most beloved son, was the first of his clan to come to Egypt. He became a great prince of Egypt. His eleven brothers, our ancestors, followed Joseph to Egypt. Four hundred years later, we had become a collection of twelve tribes known as the Hebrew nation." Hannah then offered the cup to Bishtar.

Bishtar had listened intently to her mother's inspiring story. She took the cup to herself and rotated the item carefully, as it was of great importance. "But how did you get it, Mother?"

"Daughter, as you know, I served in Ra's temple. You were to serve as well, when you were a little older. You were allowed to witness me perform duties in the high priest's rituals, with the cup, because you had to learn what to do."

Curious, as always, the little girl turned the cup on end. Under the handle's base were strange letters that had been neatly engraved into the metal. "What are these letters, Mother?"

"They say the words, El Nachash or El's Divination."

"Oh," sighed Bishtar, but not really understanding.

"You were meant to follow me in servitude to Ra's temple."

"Did Ra give you the cup then?"

Hannah smiled at Bishtar's innocent question. "Daughter, when we escaped our fate as slaves, we freed ourselves and also much of our oppressor's belongings. We took the objects as recompense for our four hundred years of loyal servitude to the Egyptians. I knew the priests hid the cup at the base of their statue of Ra. And while the Egyptians were busy hiding from El's wrath, I took the cup. It was never theirs to begin with, after all; it belonged to Joseph, our forefather."

"But how did you ever get such a thing past Gasheer's soldiers guarding the Crystallight cavern?" Bishtar's question was important to her because she had a difficult time smuggling her own secret package into the cavern. *Maybe,* she reasoned, there had been a better way, if she had only known about it.

"Daughter, do you remember when we first arrived here?"

"Yes. We travelled with father Korah. And they searched our belongings."

"But did they search Korah's personal things?"

"I'm not sure; I did not see with all the fuss. I guess not."

"You are correct, they did not. Korah is an Elder. Gasheer dare not touch father Korah's personal items. So before we left, I hid Joseph's cup in one of father's sacks."

Bishtar thought about that. She wondered if that trick might have worked with her lamb. Then she would not have to have gone to all the trouble of going back to retrieve the beast on her own. But on second thought, she realized, hiding a small cup on Korah's person and having him unknowingly transport it was a lot different from trying to stash a squiggling, bahing lamb. Father Korah, although very old, would have surely noticed a living creature amongst his belongings.

But that story was not the issue at the moment. So Bishtar focused again on the cup asking, "Why show me, Mother?"

"Because I took it, we must keep it. And Joseph's Cup now belongs to you. As my daughter, it is yours."

Bishtar, still very curious, asked, "El's Divination? What does it mean?"

"It means that the God of Moses sometimes shares visions with mortal man."

"What kind of visions?"

"Legends say Joseph used it to help his eleven brothers to live, prosper, and find their destiny; a destiny of El's vision for our people. But that was long ago. In our time, the priests of Ra kept the cup secret from our people. Only they and the specially chosen servants were allowed to know of it. If one were to speak of anything they saw in Ra's temple, they were to be instantly killed. The priests sacrificed beasts, and sadly, horribly, sometimes people. They used the blood to fill the cup. And then the priests gazed into the cup to see from afar, or to see what the enemies of Egypt were doing. Ra's priests did magic; it was evil what they did and not of Joseph's El. I do not know myself if what they saw is totally true; I, being a slave, was never allowed to see into the cup. In any event, it is best to never speak of the cup's existence, for there is surely dark magic within its grasp."

"But what shall I do with it?"

Hannah leaned forward and once more dared to look into Bishtar's deeply black-filled eyes. With intensity, Hannah answered, "Keep it, and its secrets, just as I have done, just as my mother did, and as hers before that. Let Joseph's Cup remind you that no matter where you go, or what you might look like, that you are, and will always be, a descendant of Joseph's forefathers and a Hebrew daughter of the proud tribe of Benjamin."

Bishtar met her mother's gaze and solemnly swore, "I will, Mother, I will."

CHAPTER 13
The Diseased

After the congregation had settled in the Crystallight cavern, and everything seemed to be fine, Korah, Dathan and Abiram met to discuss a new problem. Something very strange was happening... beyond, of course, what had already occurred. A few of the people, all the younger ones, were changing. The reports had come in from various camps. Not all the families that had little ones had experienced the changes, but so far three families had seen it.

"Why is this happening?" asked Abiram worriedly.

Korah answered bleakly, "It is part and parcel of our being cast down."

"No, ah yes, oh... I am not sure," rambled Abiram, increasingly unsure of just about everything. "What do you think, Dathan?"

Dathan paused. "I believe..."

"Well, I believe it is this," stated Korah, interrupting Dathan. Korah held up some of the Maana plant.

The Elders had established protocols for the collection and distribution of the Maana plants. Some was for eating raw, some sat well in a soup dishes, some could be ground into a powder for baking, and some of the courser material was reserved as animal feed. It was soon discovered that some of the plant that had rotted to a thick mushy paste was flammable, so lanterns could be replenished.

"Why do you think this, Korah? Have we not done well to tend to it?" asked Abiram.

There were places where the Maana was particularly fruitful, but those spots were well protected by Gasheer's men. Teams of plant collectors were given the task of gathering the plants by their respective size and color. The pickers were closely monitored, and the plants were brought, under guard, to a distribution center for dispersal. Over the course of many sleep cycles, the tribe had managed to establish a working system that fed the whole settlement. Eventually the people learned to eat their new food, accepting the allotment process without too much complaint.

"Yes, we have tended to it well. But what else could it be? When we lived in the dark place, where we first woke up, we did not see the aberration. Besides the Crystallght cavern itself, the Maana is the only variable that is unique and different."

"You could be right," agreed Abiram finally. "Ever since we have been eating the plants, things have changed. Do you think the vegetation is poisonous?"

"No," Korah answered. "As far as we know, although some children have a changed appearance, no one has gotten ill."

They all nodded in agreement. The reports had also confirmed that fact. It was a bit of good news amongst a plethora of concerns and issues the Elders were ultimately responsible for.

"But why haven't any of *us* changed?" quizzed Abiram. "The older generations, I mean."

"Maybe we will," declared Korah. "Maybe with us it will take more time. In any event, there appears to be nothing we can do about it. The Maana is nearly all there is to eat. The animals are nearly all gone. The grain is, in fact, gone. We will soon have to depend on the Maana alone. And as I said, maybe it is just a matter of time."

"Or maybe there is a curse," warned Dathan, "that if necessary, we can stop before it spreads, like a disease."

"What are proposing?" asked Korah, very suspicious of Dathan's motives.

"If we cull the infected, the cursed, out from the rest of us..."

"Are you mad?" claimed Korah in disbelief. He looked at Abiram wantonly, but the Elder merely shied away from actually having to take a stand against Dathan's proposition.

Dathan appeared pensive and directed his comments accordingly. "Have we no experience with the coughing disease in Egypt? Do you not remember how it spread from hut to hut? Did we not have to isolate the sick into one place before it stopped? Did the infirmed not all die, eventually? And then the remnant survived."

Korah refuted, "That was different."

"How so? Have we not been told that the recently infected show strange, unnatural signs: blackened eyes, hair loss, limbs that are stronger than normal, bigger too, and fingers that are claw-like? Is this not a sickness? So how is this different?"

"I don't know. It just is."

"There you go. You have no proof."

"And neither do you."

"Maybe not, but I am merely taking precautions." Dathan faced Abiram and gave him a stern glare. Expecting a certain response, Dathan asked, "Abiram, how say you?"

Startled by Dathan's intimidating stare, Abiram stumbled, "Well, ah, ah, I guess you could be right."

"Abiram!" decried Korah, incredulous at Abiram's weak-kneed surrender.

"I... ah, guess you too could be right." But after relooking at the grim face of Dathan, Abiram stammered, "However, should it not be best left for Dathan to decide? After all, he has kept us safe to this point. His men have shown strength... Have they not?"

"*His* men? *His* men?" responded Korah distrustfully. "Abiram, as you well know, many of my sons were not among the cast down, and many of your best soldiers were lost in the chasm. So if Dathan has *shown strength*, is it not because many of his soldiers were lucky enough to have survived our ordeal?"

Abiram was about to respond when Dathan raised his hands to calm the heated exchange. "Gentlemen, please, let us not quarrel over such matters. The fact that many of my tribe's soldiers survived was no doing of mine. Regardless, we must recognize that the soldiers are carrying out our agreed-upon decrees." Dathan pointed to the workers gathering and carrying Maana, and the guards closely watching them. "Are they not protecting us from chaos? Are they not, after all, doing a good job?"

"Maybe too good," stipulated Korah.

"And what is the alternative, Korah? Do you not remember how close we were to killing one another over scraps of bread and grain when we first arrived here? Many were driven to eating straw!"

"Yes," furthered Abiram, too quick to agree, "And remember some even tried eating those nasty bugs. They got cuts all over their face and mouths for trying."

"And Abiram, is it not true that Gasheer has integrated what remained of your guard into our tribe's army?"

"Yes, I suppose so, Dathan. Yes, yes you are correct. I ah, do thank you for that."

Dathan, like a high and mighty nobleman, nodded graciously to accept the thanks.

But Korah couldn't look upon Abiram at that moment; the man was turning into a sniveling coward. Moreover, Korah could not be so easily intimidated. So he directed his indignation at Dathan. "And to whom do Abiram's soldiers now hold their final allegiance, Dathan?"

Dathan put a coy expression on his face and said smoothly, "Gentlemen, we are all Elders of our tribe. Each one of us shares in that tremendous responsibility. But perhaps, if I might suggest, we could vote on an ultimate authority figure, a leader among the leaders, as it were..."

Abiram eagerly jumped in first. "Dathan, in Egypt you were chosen to lead us in worshipping our god Osiris. Maybe you should lead us now."

Dathan answered knowingly, "Yes, how apropos, Abiram. Osiris, the god of the underworld. And lest you remember that I also helped our Egyptian overseers tend to the temple of Isis as well."

"Yes, yes, brother Dathan," agreed Abiram, "I remember it well. You do speak the truth. Isis, the goddess of helping people in need. And are we not in dire need?"

"Well, yes," continued Dathan, "thank you brother Abiram. And seeing how some of our children are changing, the need is even greater for us to do something."

"Yes, yes," groveled Abiram, "I have to agree." Abiram peered at Korah as if to say everything was fine with Dathan being in charge.

Korah knew he was being out-maneuvered, but for the moment he could do nothing. He reached down and without calling attention to himself, felt for the hidden object in his pouch.

115

Somehow the devise had to save him; save them all. He had to believe it. "Very well, Dathan, and Abiram, I will leave it for you to decide... for now."

Dathan was pleased with Korah's acquiescence. "Although this sounds harsh, we must be prepared for solving an imminent danger within our ranks. If the diseased are allowed to spread their sickness, then we are all at risk."

"Meaning?" asked Korah warily.

"Meaning that, if upon our worship to the gods, an animal sacrifice is deemed insufficient, then we will give to the gods that which they require. The diseased among us prove that the time for worship is even more pressing. The answers are in humble obedience to our gods. Perhaps sacrificing just one of the diseased will be sufficient."

Korah stood straight, and in defiance declared, "An animal sacrifice might be acceptable, Dathan. But we can go no further. We are not pagans. El will not have it."

Dathan was very displeased to hear references made to the God of Moses. He faced Abiram and asked, "Abiram, how say you?"

"Well, I ah, ah, very well then."

"Very well to what exactly?" bullied Dathan.

"Just ah... very well," responded Abiram as he sheepishly studied each Elder.

Dathan rolled his eyes and pivoted back toward Korah. "For now I can agree to your terms, brother. But know this, if the gods give us a sign, then we must act as they see fit, no matter what the cost."

Korah pondered that for a moment, reached to his pouch, and concluded, "There are many signs, brother. Let us make sure we only follow the true one."

* * * *

Gasheer came to stand by his master, attentive as always. Both men watched as Korah and Abiram left for their own camps. Dathan kept a sly smile on his face until it was clear that the other Elders were out of sight. After that his face twisted into its usual

116

stern, foreboding and arrogant appearance. He turned to Gasheer. "Tell me more details of the children showing the most change."

"There are three so far. One in the Ruben camp, one in the Levi tent, and..."

"Yes, go on."

"The grandchild of Korah... her name is Bishtar."

"Yes, this one I know; I have seen her before. Why do you hesitate to speak of it?"

"No, my Lord, I do not hesitate. It is just that she is related to an Elder and..."

"It matters not, my fine fellow. In fact, it is actually very interesting. Tell me more of her."

"She has changed the most of all the children. Her eyes are as black as coal, most of her hair is gone, her skin is an ashen pale color, and her head appears to have grown too large. Many are scared when they look upon her."

"Fascinating," responded Dathan. In a cold way he furthered, "And maybe, my good friend, we could, as they say, kill two birds with one stone."

Gasheer was confused so Dathan elaborated. "We could diminish Korah's authority by openly sacrificing one of his own, while simultaneously showing the remnant who is really in charge. And possibly, although unlikely, we could also be helping to remove the diseased among us, thereby playing on the peoples' fears and cementing my control over them. The flock must have their shepherd, after all, my good fellow. And there is only one shepherd per flock. There, you see," Dathan said proudly, "Two birds, one stone... Well, upon further thought, that is more like killing three or four birds with one stone. But the idiom stands nonetheless."

Gasheer still appeared stymied, but he managed to say, "Yes, my Lord, what will you have me do?"

"Watch her, ask your men to do the same. Look for anything abnormal, beyond what is already happening, and if an excuse, *any* excuse arises, we shall have to capitalize upon it... to our advantage, of course."

"You mean to kill Bishtar, my Lord?"

Dathan was truly puzzled by Gasheer's lack of comprehension. "Of course. Do you have a problem with that?"

Gasheer grinned meanly. "No, my Lord."

CHAPTER 14
The Lamb

"Mosher, what are you doing here? Are you following me?"

"Ah... ah... no."

"Of course not," Bishtar said dryly. She had seen him out of the corner of her eye, and only stopped to confront her pursuer after she couldn't shake him. She then quickly used her shawl to cover over some material she had stuffed into her pocket.

As he walked closer, Mosher noticed her odd move, wondering why. Since some of the stuff was still sticking out and quite easy to recognize, he asked, "What are you d-doing with that hay, Bishtar?"

"None of your business," she snapped. Then, thinking better of it, she glanced at him curiously and offered, "Do you want to see something?"

Mosher looked around suspiciously because she had asked the question in a strange way. "Okay, I g-guess."

Bishtar smiled. "Follow me then." They ran together to a secluded spot in a distant alcove. Behind a pile of rocks and debris was a tiny lamb. The creature was tied by rope to a heavy stone. The lamb gently went to them as they approached it, and proceeded to *bah* upon seeing the bits of hay in Bishtar's hand. "Baah, Baaaah."

"How did you g-get this?" Mosher asked in disbelief.

"I found it."

"Where, when, ah, ah, h... how?" As usual, when he was with Bishtar, Mosher couldn't help but stutter much more than usual. He chided himself for being so foolish sounding, but what could he do? Bishtar was, well... Bishtar.

"When we were first sent below, before Dathan confiscated all the animals, I found it astray. So I took care of it."

Most likely, thought Mosher, *it was one of the beasts that Calish and I had freed when we had released the animals as a diversion to take back Asher's spear.* He was glad to know that their adventure had done something nice for Bishtar. But telling her the Asher story wasn't necessary; it was enough to know that the lamb made Bishtar happy. "Yes, in our dark home you c-could hide the lamb, but h-here in all this light," he said, while indicating the Crystallight cavern, "it is much m-more difficult. And how did you get the animal past G-Gasheer's soldiers guarding the M-Maana cave's entrance? They inspected everything as it entered this p-place."

She cocked her head as if to say that the answer was easy. "Have you not seen how they behave, Mosher? How many times have they beaten one of our people to take our possessions away from us? I merely waited until the guards were busy doing what they do best, and when they weren't looking, I snuck by." She put on her most child-like face and tilted her body as if she was nothing more than a sweet little girl. "I can be very innocent looking, if don't you know..."

Mosher could only marvel at her acting skill, and once again be reminded at how much he was taken in by her charm. "G-Gasheer will be angry if he finds out."

"Will he, Mosher? Will he find out?" She scrutinized him closely, expecting a certain answer. He returned her gaze. Even though her eyes were as black as coal, underneath it all Bishtar was still in there, somewhere. Mosher noticed only what his heart was telling him to see.

"I will keep your s-secret, Bishtar."

"Good." Then Bishtar suddenly grabbed Mosher's hand and kissed him on the cheek. Mosher was taken aback, but at the same time he could feel a spark of energy flow through his body at her touch. He immediately blushed and looked at anything else so she wouldn't see his clumsy reaction.

"Baah, Baaaah," went the lamb.

Abruptly, Bishtar stopped staring at him and focused on her furry little friend.

Yes, perfect timing, thought Mosher.

Bishtar reached down to stroke the beast, giving it what little food she had. "He is hungry, Mosher, but I don't have enough hay."

Mosher also bent down to touch the creature, and while doing so he noticed a discoloring along its belly. He went closer; it was the branding mark of his tribe, Abiram's tribe. The animal belonged to his great uncle. Mosher quickly decided to say nothing of it. Bishtar claimed the beast; that was good enough for him.

Then he had an idea. "I will find h-hay for your lamb, Bishtar."

Bishtar smiled. "How? Gasheer's soldier's guard all animal feed."

"I will find a way," he said trying his best to sound confident and brave.

"Thank you, Mosher. I also might have a way and will look for something as well."

"B-Be careful."

"You too."

* * * *

After Mosher left, Bishtar went to a nearby alcove. She stopped and looked all around to make sure no one was there. Satisfied that she was alone, she went to where there was a shallow hole set within the cavern floor. She bent down and reached inside the cavity to retrieve the item she had hidden there. She uncovered the item from its white cloth, and just like the first time she had seen it, the object's silver metal glistened brightly. After reviewing Joseph's Cup, she looked back at her little lamb, while thinking about the stories her mother had told her.

With less-than-overwhelming confidence, she uttered, "Perhaps I could find feed for you using this."

"Bah Baaaah," came the lamb's reply.

"Okay, if you agree, let's try, shall we."

She took out a small flint knife from her tunic apron and approached the beast. She placed the cup below the lamb's belly. The gentle lamb jostled a little bit, but otherwise let her do what she will. She grabbed its leg to hold it still and with the knife carefully nicked the creature's soft belly skin. She cringed, the lamb jumped, but nonetheless the operation was a success. Within moments, a few drops of blood started falling into the challis. She looked inside. Sadly, there was not much blood, not nearly enough to fill the cup. Not wanting to cause more damage to her lamb, she decided to add water to the blood so that it might be better filled up. She walked to a nearby cave wall, where drops of water were pouring in from ceiling cracks. She positioned the cup to collect some of the flowing water. Soon enough, there was enough water to fill the cup half-way. The water mixed with the blood, making it a transparent reddish color.

She stared into the cup, not knowing what to do. Finally, she determined, "Perhaps if I speak my wish, it will come true. But I must say it like the Ra priests did. They were always so serious when they said stuff."

Bishtar put on a serious expression and gazed into the liquid. She waved her free hand over the cup's lid. Then, with a grave voice, as if summoning a magical incantation, she chanted, "I seek hay, please help me find hay. I wish for hay, where can I find hay? Oh, great Cup of Joseph, where can I find hay for my little lamb?"

"Baah, Ba-aaa-aah," went the little lamb, as if on cue. But beside that comment, nothing happened.

Not ready to give up, she swished the blood around with her index claw, while thinking that if she wanted results, she needed to say something much more meaningful. So she tried again, this time with a bit more robust, yet dramatic sincerity. "Oh great El, I am Bishtar, the daughter of Benjamin. El Nachash, please help me find hay for my lamb. He is hu-ungry."

As she swirled and spun some more, she suddenly found that using her finger was no longer necessary; the liquid was spinning around and around on its own. Startled, she nearly dropped the cup. But somehow she held onto it, and stared with amazement at the magical swirling liquid in front of her.

"Shishtu!" she decried in shock. The reddish blood changed, becoming as clear as water. The spinning stopped and the water became very still. Within the liquid Bishtar could see two figures come into view. She soon recognized them: one was that giant Gasheer, and beside him was that mean old Elder, the one called Dathan. They were talking. She could barely make out the noise of their voices, because it was too low. So she moved her ear closer. She could then understand what they were saying!

"Yes, my Lord, what will you have me do?"

"Watch her, ask your men to do the same. Look for anything abnormal, beyond what is already happening, and if an excuse... any excuse... arises, we shall have to capitalize upon it... to our advantage, of course."

"You mean to kill Bishtar, my Lord?"

"Of course. Do you have a problem with that?"

"No, my Lord."

Bishtar was shocked. She quickly dropped the cup, and its bloody contents went splashing about. She trembled greatly as an anxious fear gripped her to the core. "No!" she exclaimed.

She stared at the lamb. "What will I do? Tell mother? Will she believe me? Tell grandfather? Will he be angry that I used a tool of Ra's priests and did their evil magic? Grandfather Korah tells us of Moses's El and how we are commanded to have nothing to do with the ways of the Egyptians. If that be so, then is what I saw even true? How can it be?"

"I must be wrong; this thing tells lies. Grandfather would never let them kill me. The cup was a tool of Ra and they corrupted it to their evil ways. It is all a lie!" She looked toward the lamb for support.

The lamb, for its part, did not respond one way or the other. *Figures.*

She desperately wanted to abandon the cup and thought mightily about walking away from it. But then she remembered what her mother had told her, and she paused. She nervously picked the cup up and quickly covered it over with the white cloth, saying... no, vowing to herself... "I must never use this evil again. Never!"

Bishtar buried Joseph's Cup back in the crevice from where it was found. She covered over the hole with rocks so that no one would think anything of it if they were to see the spot.

She picked up her lamb, stroking it lightly, saddened that she had not found her beast what it needed, still frightened by the whole experience. But after a few moments, she braved a glace back at the covered up crevice. She continued to look, finding small hints of curiosity with each passing moment. Somehow a part of her was intrigued by what lay beneath the stones. But those things were still deeply buried within her. It was not the time for those concerns. Bishtar was not yet ready to brave the mysteries of the unknown, at least for now.

She resolved herself by holding the lamb tighter, gazing into its gentle eyes and saying, "Perhaps Mosher will have better luck. Yes, I know he will find you hay. Mosher is a special person. If anyone can do it, he can."

"Baah, Ba-aaa-aah," responded her lamb in agreement.

* * * *

From behind, Mosher approached the soldier that stood guard over the tribe's animal feed. The soldier turned to see what the intrusion was. *El be praised,* thought Mosher. It was Cabesh, the soldier he had struck with a stone when he and Calish had recaptured Asher's spear.

"What do you want, boy?" barked Cabesh.

"I was wondering if you could spare s-some hay?"

"No. Now be gone."

Mosher looked around to make sure no one else was present. "Perhaps we could m-make a trade."

"Stop bothering me," Cabesh responded angrily, "Get lost before I get mad." The soldier waved his hand dismissively.

"Oh, okay kind sir, but you m-might be missing out on something very valuable..." With that little inducement, Mosher turned and started walking away.

After a few moments, and when Mosher started to think his gambit had failed, he heard, "Stop, boy!"

Mosher stopped and casually turned back. "Yes sir, how can I help y-you?"

"Come back here."

Mosher did as he was told. The soldier scrutinized his surroundings, and when it was clear no one could overhear, he said, "What do you offer... and it better be good."

Mosher reached into his pouch and retrieved the small Crystallight gem Calish had dislodged from the walls when the boys had first found the caverns. Mosher held it up; the tiny jewel sparkled and glowed with brilliant purple-red colors.

Upon seeing it, Cabesh's face lit up. But soon thereafter, he retracted that expression. He was not going to show his interest in the glistening prize. Cabesh tried to act as if he didn't care when he said, "What could that tiny rock do for me, boy?"

Mosher, remembering how Cabesh's colleagues had mocked him at the animal pen, decided to play on that incident. Mosher twirled the gem around, enticingly. Then he made the mistake of moving closer to Cabesh. "El, give me strength," Mosher whispered as he scrunched up his nose. Being too close to Cabesh meant being victimized by the soldier's foul smell.

"Perhaps," Mosher tendered, in between gasping for fresh air, "If you are m-married, and I do not know if you are, then maybe your wife might like this. Perhaps she m-might like it so much that she will favor you with kindness... or s-something else along those lines."

Cabesh was intrigued by the possibilities, but became suddenly skeptical. He wasn't going to let a mere boy fool him. "Tell me, boy, what do you want with a bit of hay?"

"Well, kind s-sir, if only you knew how fond my grandmother is of a proper sleep. I simply want to take the hay's bits to create a fluffy pillow. Would you be so kind as to take this meager g-gem in exchange?"

Suspiciously, Cabesh asked, "How much hay do you want?"

"Whatever you c-can spare."

"Well," replied Cabesh insincerely, "I don't really want the stone, but seeing that you want the hay for a good reason... very well, I will give you a small portion."

The soldier took another good look around, to check for witnesses, or lack thereof. Then he grabbed up a nice sampling of hay and gave it to Mosher. In exchange, Mosher handed him the gem. The soldier quickly pocketed the jewel in his pouch, and Mosher stuffed the hay in his tunic.

The extra padding made Mosher's round torso slightly rounder, but for Mosher, or rather for Bishtar, looking a little fatter was well worth it. "Thank y-you, kind sir," said Mosher as he walked away.

"Hmpphh," grunted Cabesh.

As the boy left, the smelly soldier grinned broadly, thinking he had struck the better deal. Cabesh brought the jewel to his mouth and bit into it, checking to see if it was real, saying happily, "My wife will surely grant me favors now."

* * * *

Dathan appeared from his tent. A frown crossed his brow as he surveyed the scene before him. A group of his men were gathered at the tent's entrance. The lead soldier was beside another person; a girl, who was most disconcerting to look at. If Dathan had his way, she might have already been dealt with. Once he recognized her, Dathan quickly realized that this could very well be his perfect "two birds with one stone" moment. But he would have to navigate those waters carefully, so he straightened his robes, looking authoritative, and asked the soldier, "What is it now?"

The soldier held onto Bishtar's arm with one hand, and with the other he held a rope that was attached to a baby lamb. The lamb was compliant and peaceful; the struggling and twisting girl was far from it.

"Let me go, before I scream!" she screeched.

"It sounds like you have already accomplished that," said Dathan. He looked at the soldier and ordered, "Report."

"We followed the girl after she was seen picking up scraps of animal dung. She was picking through it, weeding out any undigested straw. We thought it odd, so we decided to find out what she was doing. She led us to a distant alcove where we found the animal tied up behind some rocks. We then brought the two of them to you."

"Very good," Dathan told the soldier. He pointed to the lamb and asked the girl, "Can you explain this?"

At first she just stared back with a mean scowl on her face.

Dathan returned her glare, thinking that Gasheer was right; her big black eyes were strange indeed. But Dathan, refusing to be frightened by the sight, stood straighter and closed in on the girl. "Well?" he asked, much louder. "Speak up."

"The lamb is mine. Now let me go!"

126

"The lamb, my dear, is not yours. And we most certainly will not let you go."

The commotion was quickly drawing a crowd. Some of them, having recognized Bishtar, ran off to tell Abiram and Korah.

Upon noticing that the crowd was growing, Dathan whispered in one of his soldier's ears. The people were much too eager to hear what was being said, so he asked the soldier to get back-up... meaning Gasheer.

Within a few moments, Korah and Abiram showed up. They were followed by members of their families. Korah and Abiram went forward through the crowd to stand before Dathan.

"Dathan, what is the meaning of this?" barked Korah.

"The girl was caught keeping a lamb that does not belong to her."

"She is my granddaughter, Dathan, and whatever you think she has done, it doesn't matter."

"It *does* matter, my brother."

"No it doesn't!" screamed Hannah as she came to Bishtar's side. She and Mishtas had pushed their way to the front of the gathering. She tried to remove the soldier's grip from Bishtar's arm, but could not do so.

"Release her, I demand it!" she screamed at Dathan.

"Woman, you are in no position to demand anything."

One of Dathan's soldiers stepped in between Hannah and Dathan. The soldier made a menacing expression at Mishtas. But Mishtas did not back down as he stood by Hannah.

"Wha- what are proposing to do, Dathan?" stuttered Abiram, visibly distressed.

"What else can I do? The girl must be punished. Look at her. It is obvious that she is diseased. See her eyes."

Everyone turned to set their sights upon her. Some of them reluctantly recoiled from the girl's strange appearance.

Dathan acknowledged the people's fear by advancing on her. "Something must be done to cleanse the tribe from what infects us."

"No!" shrieked Hannah. "You will not touch her." She turned to Korah and pleaded, "Father, do something."

The crowd was getting tense; there were heated exchanges on how to deal with the situation. There were some murmurs flying about that corresponded with the fact that they did not like what was happening. And yet many agreed with Dathan. To them the changed children were a danger to them all. But the people were split; and there was no real consensus on what to do.

Mishtas, knowing that Hannah's husband had died in the chasm event, had decided to watch over Hannah and her children. He could not let Dathan do anything to harm them. So he puffed up his chest and pushed his way past the soldier who stood between Dathan and himself. "Dathan," Mishtas voiced confidently, "I cannot allow you to do this. It is one thing to have Gasheer man-handle adults, but this... this I will not stand." Mishtas took an aggressive stance in front of Dathan.

Mishtas' argument had swayed many into action. The folks that agreed with Mishtas... those who had had enough of Dathan's oppressive dictates and confiscations... started pushing their way forward, angrily raising their fists and shouting at the soldiers that guarded Dathan. Soon enough, the anger spread to include some who had originally been on Dathan's side. The crowd moved closer and closer, forcing Dathan and his guards to back up.

Dathan's men were clearly outnumbered. He knew that a fight was sure to take place. The soldiers worriedly glanced at him for orders.

Just then Gasheer showed up, followed by some of his closest men. Gasheer easily pushed himself through anyone in his way, knocking them aside as if they were made of straw. The tall giant went right at Mishtas. Gasheer shoved his massive chest right up against Mishtas' face, forcing Mishtas to give way, even if a little.

"Now leave here. All of you!" Gasheer commanded, first at Mishtas, then to the rest of the gathering.

But Mishtas stood his ground, holding his chin a little higher to match Gasheer's height, even though the chin-lifting did little to improve the discrepancy.

His family and some of Abiram's family, seeing Mishtas's bravery, would not leave; they gestured to each other as if to say they were united behind their kinsman.

"Do not make me angry," growled Gasheer menacingly.

Very good, very good, thought Dathan, relieved to see the latest development. Having Gasheer nearby meant that the tide had dramatically turned in Dathan's favor. The angry crowd, albeit reluctantly, stopped shouting and looked up at Gasheer. The mountainous man scowled at them again, bringing fear to their hearts. They soon backed away enough to allow Dathan's guards to retake their protective positions around their master.

Dathan stepped forward and poked his head past Gasheer. After noticing that the people were now much more compliant, he produced a disingenuous expression, as if to say there was no other alternative to the actions he had already called for. "I am sorry, but there is nothing I can do. Gasheer, take the girl away."

"Stop!" shouted Mosher as he pushed his way through the crowd.

"What do you want, boy?" asked Abiram. Seeing his grandnephew, Abiram went to stand near Mosher, if not slightly behind him, after seeing Dathan's angry glare.

"Speak!" Dathan was quickly losing his patience with the whole incident.

"The lamb, the l-lamb..." stuttered Mosher, "does not belong to Bishtar. It is m-mine."

The crowd inhaled at the statement.

Dathan grimaced at the boy and demanded, "Prove it."

Mosher took out some hay that he had secreted within his tunic.

Dathan argued, "That does not prove anything except that you knew of the beast and were possibly helping feed it."

"No, it is the o-opposite," Mosher retorted loudly.

"Meaning what?"

"I am the o-one who asked Bishtar's help in feeding the l-lamb. She knew n-nothing of it until recently."

Dathan scrutinized the two children, trying to assess the truth. Bishtar's abnormal black eyes, the lack of hair, the whole strange package, did very little to dissuade him from finding fault with her. But the boy had, for some unknown reason, already confessed. For Dathan, however, the confession wasn't good enough. "You are lying, boy."

129

Knowing that he had to say something more substantial, Mosher revealed what he knew of the beast's ownership. "Look at the lamb's b-brand. It is from my g-great uncle's herd."

Abiram was startled and equally dismayed to be included in the middle of the controversy. He darted his eyes back and forth as if searching for the quickest escape route. But eventually he found the courage to bend down and see the brand.

Dathan glowered at him, waiting for a response.

"It is true," Abiram stammered meekly, "The beast was once mine. But seeing that we now have rules governing such matters, I am not sure as to what to make of all this."

"Well, I am," cited Dathan. "It is obvious that the two children were complicit in this endeavor. Therefore..."

"You are an old fool," someone muttered under their breath.

Shocked by the statement, everyone looked to see who dared to say such a thing. Dathan, who was the most surprised, knew who had said it. He stood up straighter and went to stand incredulously before the insult-thrower. But the culprit had to do something to take Bishtar out of the realm of blame; the rebuke, if nothing else, would foster that result. By the sour expression on Dathan's face, one could easily see that the ploy had worked.

Dathan hovered over Mosher and spat with fury. "You would dare speak to me this way, boy!" When Mosher remained silent, he said, "First you steal, then you lie, and now you have the unmitigated audacity to insult me!"

He turned on Abiram and demanded, "Brother, your charge has shown nothing but contempt for our traditions. If you have anything to say in defense of your descendant, do so now."

Abiram studied Mosher with a pained expression, then a submissive one as he turned back to address Dathan. "Since his parent's death in Egypt, I have done my best to see to his welfare. But obviously that was not enough. Maybe this will help teach the boy our ways. Dathan, do as you will."

The people nearby inhaled upon hearing Abiram's easy compliance.

"Abiram!" scolded Korah. "You cannot possibly find fault in the boy; your own grandnephew?"

Abiram at first looked like he agreed with Korah, but then he shied away after seeing Dathan's stare and Gasheer's evil grin.

Seizing on the opportunity of Abiram's acquiescence, Dathan ordered, "Seize the boy! Hold him."

A nearby soldier grabbed Mosher from behind, clasping him by his two arms. Mosher struggled at first, and when he could not get free, relaxed and remained still, but only after he had moved his shawl to a better position covering his tunic.

Gasheer, ever watchful, took note of the boy's odd movement. He unsheathed his sword and approached the boy. Everyone, including Dathan, was wide-eyed, wondering what the brute of a man was to do next. As gasps could be heard from the crowd, Gasheer took the point of his sword and jabbed it at Mosher's side. But he did not use it to stab Mosher; rather, he used the sword's tip to pull back the shawl and reveal the tunic beneath it. Gasheer gestured knowingly to his Lord. Dathan stared hard at Mosher's tunic.

"Blood," declared Dathan. "That looks like blood stains." To Mosher, he asked, "Boy, how did these stains get there?" When he received no answer, he signaled to Gasheer, and the soldier tore the covering shawl completely off Mosher's torso.

"Your tunic, boy, is covered with blood stains." Dathan touched the cloth. It was dry. "It appears that you tried to wash the stains away, but you were unsuccessful. Now speak!"

But Mosher would not answer. The dried up wolf's blood was none of the Elder's business. Besides, telling the story would only cause more trouble for him and Calish. So Mosher stood there staring up at the Elder with a scared yet defiant expression.

Calish, who was watching the whole thing while standing next to Korah, made a move to go to Mosher. But Korah held him back. Mosher looked to his friend for guidance. Calish stared back and gave a slight shake of his head, as if to say nothing. Dathan took note of the exchange between the boys. Then he spied out Korah. The Elder held onto Calish protectively.

Very telling, thought Dathan. The two boys were both involved in the whole mess; of that fact Dathan had no doubt. But Dathan was no fool, and would not complicate the matter by implicating Korah's beloved grandson. Opening a war with what remained of

Korah's tribe was not prudent; at least for now. The boy Mosher, however, was a different matter entirely.

Dathan smiled unkindly at the boys and then addressed the crowd. "My fellow tribesmen, it is clear that we not only have a thief among us, but also one of the culprits that has been eating our communal property. The blood stains prove this beyond question. We know some of our heard has been stolen and eaten. Well, we now have solid proof of the dastardly deed. This is a crime against all of us. This cannot go unanswered."

Once again the crowd was split between those who agreed with Dathan and those who wanted leniency for the boy. Their shouts were loud and heated.

Dathan raised his hand to quiet them. "My friends, we do this for all of us, please know this." He turned to Gasheer and commanded, "Take the boy and tie him to the nearest post."

Upon hearing this, many in the crowd exploded with anger. But Gasheer's men took out their clubs and threatened anyone who spoke too vehemently.

"Dathan, do not do this," pleaded Korah. He scanned Abiram's face for a sign of support, or any indication that the Elder would do something to protect his own grandnephew. But the old man looked defeated, dejected, and humbled into submission by Dathan's cruel nature.

"I will not let you!" shouted Mishtas as he moved in on Dathan's space.

Dathan nodded at two of his soldiers and pointed at Mishtas. The men quickly surrounded Mishtas, grabbing him firmly enough to keep him from causing any more trouble.

Korah, emboldened by Mishtas's loyalty, and by the number of clansmen who clearly wanted leniency for the boy, muscled his way to stand face-to-face with Dathan. Korah drew in close to Dathan's ear and whispered, "Tell your man Gasheer to restrain his hand against the boy, and to meet out only what is minimally necessary. For if the boy dies from his wounds, there will be a rift between us that will not mend. And there will be retribution... my *brother*."

Dathan took in Korah's steadiness and gradually pulled away, smiling that twisted, duplicitous smirk of his. Dathan then called

Gasheer over to him. Gasheer bowed his head so that Dathan could whisper in his ear, which he did. Gasheer then nodded as if in understanding.

Dathan leaned into Korah and Abiram so that only they could hear. "Gasheer will do what he must." To the people, he said loudly, "We do this for all of us. We have survived up to this point because of our willingness to maintain order and discipline. I... I mean *we*," while indicating the Elders, "have taken it upon ourselves to make rules that have kept us alive in this terrible place. We can only survive *if* we agree to those rules."

Hannah and Mishtas held tightly on to Bishtar. So Dathan turned on them and said forcefully, "Do not think we are done here. The girl, or whatever she is, must be dealt with."

"You must kill me first!" shouted Hannah.

"Woman, mind your tongue."

"And me," added Mishtas.

Dathan *harrumphed* at Mishtas's rebuke. He gazed into the crowd to further make his case. "Are we going to live? Or are we not obliged to root out the evil among us?" He said this while indicating Mosher and Bishtar. The crowd understood the reference, and by playing on their fears and confusion, Dathan was masterfully fermenting dissent. Shouts of agreement with Dathan sprang forth while others shouted for an end to the scapegoating of children. Once again, the people were split, and very boisterous in voicing their opinions.

Dathan raised his hands to calm the noise and lectured once again. "My fellow citizens, sooner or later the time will come for us to decide on how best to manage the larger issues raised here. But for now, let us deal with an obvious breach of protocol. The boy has stolen communal property and therefore should be punished."

After that rational-sounding statement the voices of agreement slightly outweighed those of dissent. Dathan took the crowd's jaded approval as a good sign and summarized, "Very well then. Gasheer, tie the boy to the post and proceed to carry out said punishment."

Calish was unable to contain himself. "No!"

But he was easily manhandled into silence by one of Gasheer's men.

Korah tore the soldier's hands off of Calish and pulled the boy close enough to whisper in his ear. "Do not fret, my son. Please trust me for now."

Calish glowered into his grandfather's eyes, but saw only compassion in return.

When Korah looked deeply into Calish's eyes, he soon became frightened from something he did not expect to see. As with Bishtar, his grandson's eyes were showing signs of turning all black; the normal whiteness was nearly gone.

To save the boy from Dathan's wrath, now more pressing than ever, he forcefully pushed the boy to stand behind him. Luckily, Calish did not resist too much. Korah then turned to the Elder. "Dathan, do what you must, and make haste with it."

"As you see fit, brother." Then to Gasheer, Dathan ordered, "Do this."

Gasheer grabbed Mosher by his tunic collar and dragged him to the nearby tent post. Gasheer tied Mosher up facing the post and pulled his tunic down from around his back. The crowd took up places all around the site, waiting for the punishment to begin. Many held onto one another in fear, comforting themselves with mournful expressions. But they would not – could not – interfere.

"I cannot believe this is happening," one of the onlookers sadly said.

"I cannot believe it has taken this long *to* happen." responded the other. "So believe it, my friend, believe it."

Korah, with Bishtar and Calish by his side, took up their place very near to where Mosher was tied up. They held each other, unified in their disdain for what was happening. Calish watched Gasheer move in on Mosher; a seething hatred crossed his young brow as the giant stalked his victim. Bishtar watched Mosher's face carefully, staring at him as if she could somehow give to him what little strength she had.

Mosher returned her gaze. He knew what was coming but decided that it didn't matter. All that really mattered was her, like always.

Gasheer took some calculated steps back and readied his bullwhip. He took a few practice shots into the open air. *Snap! Snap!* The loud cracking sound caused gasps of shock from the crowd. Their shock was equally partnered with empathy, for many of them had felt the whip as well. Gasheer then turned to stand behind Mosher. The monster of a man aimed, and like he had done countless times before, let loose his Paingiver.

Snap! Snap! And again... *Snap!*

Bishtar watched in horror as Mosher jerked violently after receiving each blow. *Snap!* Suddenly Mosher nearly lost his balance, his legs buckled and he almost fell. *Snap!* But rather than giving in, somehow the little boy righted himself, even though his tied-up hands mightily trembled as they grasped at the pole for support.

Snap!

If only I could help him. Bishtar thought to herself. *If only that were possible. If only...*

Suddenly something inside of her emerged into existence. She didn't understand it, but there was a tickling feeling deep in her stomach. It went along with something she could see as well. There were strange colors that gradually appeared over Mosher's back. Some were peaceful-looking colors, soft blues and greens, that moved here and there right over Mosher's bloody and broken skin. When Gasheer's whip struck, the colors turned reddish, and became agitated, and after that they retreated into the air. Then they circled around to resume their place, floating just above his skin, once again turning blue and green. Strangely, Bishtar felt connected to the colors, and as if she could move them too. She wanted to move them, not knowing why, but with her mind she did, especially after Gasheer's whip had struck. She made the blue-green colors return to Mosher's torn skin, more quickly and more evenly. Mosher's skin responded to the gentle colors by relaxing ever so slightly, as if the soothing hues wanted to heal his wounds. So after each of Gasheer's damaging blows, Bishtar shifted the restoring colors over Mosher's damaged skin as quickly as possible.

Snap!

135

With each of Gasheer's whipping blasts, Bishtar directed her thoughts and her control of the soothing colors accordingly. It appeared to help Mosher, but the effort was making her tired physically, mentally and emotionally. Her face began to twist in turmoil, and her feelings were tearing at her heart. She wanted to scream. Instead, she started to sob and shake. She held onto Calish desperately, clutching at his slim but strong shoulders.

"I am here for you, sister," Calish whispered as he took note of her struggle.

As Gasheer's whip ripped open his bare skin, Mosher fought back the tears. With every ounce of strength in his body, he remained standing, refusing to fall; trembling, jerking nervously from each blow, but still dry-eyed. Even though he thought himself to be a weak little boy, he nonetheless could not allow the one he loved to know of it. Bishtar, however, could not be so strong, because she could not stop her tears from falling. They fell like a river, streaming down her face. But Mosher would not, could not, let her see him do the same.

Snap! Snap! Snap!

Mosher took it, and took it again, because he would never let Bishtar see him cry. Never.

CHAPTER 15
The Hidden Place

Calish picked up a wound-up rope. He flung it over his head and around his shoulder. Mosher didn't bother to ask about the rope's purpose; as usual, Calish must have had his reasons. Calish then handed Mosher the lit lantern and they walked toward the place Calish wanted to go.

"This way," directed Calish with Asher's spear.

The boys entered a tunnel, a dark one, where the lantern's light was needed. Soon thereafter they emerged into an alcove that had enough Crystallights along the cavern walls that the lantern's light was not needed. Mosher put it down. He looked around but could not discern any other exit from the place. It appeared to be a closed space.

"There is n-nothing here, Calish."

"Oh yes there is," Calish responded while pointing up and over to a far corner.

Mosher squinted to better scrutinize for details. "Okay, I see a ledge up there, b-but nothing else."

"Just wait and see."

The adventurers approached the spot beneath the ledge and gazed straight up. The shelf was well above them. There was no obvious way to climb the steep wall to reach it, if indeed that was why they were there.

"We need to get up to that ridge," determined Calish.

Yup, thought Mosher, *Calish wants that ledge... Figures.* "Okay, sure thing. Ah, do you have any more s-surprises that might help us fly?"

"In a way, yes, Moshe." Calish pointed to a spiky protrusion that was just below the ledge's lip.

Mosher glanced at the thorn-like stone, then looked back at Calish with a 'so-what' shrug of his shoulders.

Calish smiled and removed the rope from around his shoulder. He clumsily knotted one end of it. Then he took up some rope strands and whipped them around in some less-than-graceful circles. He threw most of the package at the spike. It missed, badly. He tried again, and missed even worse than before.

"Nice s-shot, Calish."

"Okay then, you try it."

"If you insist, I will." Mosher took up the rope. He unwound Calish's primitive knot and created a new, *proper* one. Mosher held fast to one strand and rotated the rest of the rope into a flamboyant circular motion. When ready, he tossed the appropriate part at the spike. The knotted end barely grabbed the spike's point. Mosher gently jiggled the rope until the knotted end slid nicely over the spike's shaft. He tugged on the rope to secure the knot and turned to Calish with a proud smile.

Calish quipped, "Okay, rope-boy, you win."

Mosher motioned at the sling attached to his belt. "I did try to teach you. M-Many times, if I recall."

"Whatever, Moshe, whatever."

The daring duo looked up again hesitantly. Even with the rope in place, the climb was still very steep and daunting.

"What n-now?"

"One of us has to climb the rope, and once we get there we must hold onto the spike while reaching for the ledge."

Of course, Calish, sure thing.

It was hard to tell from below, but the ledge's lip appeared to be close enough to the spike that Calish's idea might be possible. Mosher took his eyes off the ledge to see his friend. But Calish was peering back and pointing his chin enticingly at the rope.

"One of us?" Mosher asked incredulously. "Oh n-no, I'm just rope-boy, remember? This is your idea."

"Very well, Moshe. Let me show you how it is done."

Mosher gestured generously to the dangling cable as if to say, *Go ahead, show me.*

Calish handed Asher's spear to Mosher. Then he took a few deep breaths, and dramatically flexed his arms and shoulders. He grabbed the rope firmly, pulling on it twice to check for its purchase, and started climbing. Strangely, Calish's nimble arms and legs seemed well suited for the task; he flew up the rope as if he was weightless.

"Yike-shtu," muttered Mosher in amazement.

When Calish reached the spike, he grabbed onto it and pulled himself up a bit. He then stretched his right hand up to meet the ledge. "Got it!" Calish declared. With a combination of pulling and pushing, Calish shimmied his way onto the shelf. His head popped-out from over the edge. "Toss up the spear."

Mosher flung the object very high, in a perfect arc. Calish deftly caught it. Looking triumphant, he called out, "Well, Drinkle, what are you waiting for?"

Mosher shrugged and began climbing the rope, very slowly. After many fits and starts, combined with a whole lot of huffing and puffing, he eventually reached the spike. He grabbed it with one hand and stopped to catch his breath. He was already exhausted and barely able to hold his grip steady. His feet were scratching here and there, trying to find a secure spot. One foot suddenly slipped, forcing him to furiously grab the spike with both hands. Mosher, starting to get scared, braved a glance at the ledge above him. From the cavern floor, the ledge looked close to the spike, but Mosher could now see that the distance was too far for him to reach. Furthermore, he could not see a way to release one of his hands without falling. "Shi-shi-shtu," he mumbled. Mosher looked down while thinking about how he would find his way back to the cave floor.

"I'm gonna' fall. I can't d-do it," he grunted.

"Yes you can." came his reply.

"I'm g-going back down."

"No, look up. Moshe, trust me... Look up!"

Mosher did so reluctantly, uncertainly. Calish extended his hand down to meet his friend. With great confidence, Calish affirmed, "Grab it."

Mosher tensed. He took a deep breath, released his right hand, and lunged up to meet Calish. Mosher couldn't tell how it happened, but by some means their hands suddenly connected. All at once Mosher could feel the strength in his friend's grip. Calish's grasp felt like a vise, as if it could crush Mosher's fingers. Calish immediately started pulling. Mosher could sense the power in Calish's arms as well. Calish pulled some more while saying, "Push, Moshe, push." Mosher did his best to help, but could do very little; in fact, he felt as heavy and cumbersome as a sack of sand. Regardless, Mosher was gradually making progress.

Just as Mosher was close to overcoming the ridge's lip, Calish gave another unusually strong pull. Like magic, Mosher was catapulted well onto the shelf. Mosher rolled over onto his back and gazed at his friend, wondering how such a thing was possible. Calish was too strong. Mosher studied Calish up and down, thinking that his best friend was becoming something unfamiliar to him.

Slightly winded, Calish asked, "You good?"

"I'm g-good," Mosher answered while sucking enormous gobs of air.

"You're heavier than you look." Calish pointed at Moshe's round belly, which just so happened to be exposed because of all the ledge-scrambling.

"And you're s-strong for a skinny little muskrat."

Calish laughed.

As both boys got up, Calish patted Mosher on the back, and Mosher winced in pain. "Sorry," said Calish quickly, remembering the scars on Mosher's back from Gasheer's whip.

"It's okay. Now w-what?"

"We go through there." Calish pointed to a small tunnel not far from their position. From below, the small opening was truly hidden; it could only be seen if one was on the ledge.

"What of the lantern?"

"We won't need it. The distance is short."

"The r-rope?"

"Yes, we need to pull up the loose end and leave it on the ledge. We will need it to get back down."

Calish then got on his belly. With Mosher holding onto his feet, Calish was able to stretch Asher's spear far enough over the ledge to scoop up the rope and pull the loose end up to where they were.

"Now no one can follow us," Calish stated. "You ready?"

Mosher nodded.

Calish scooted into the tunnel and disappeared. Soon thereafter, he called out, "Moshe. Come quickly, you must see this!"

140

"Wait, Calish," pleaded Mosher, "I cannot see as well as you. Wait for me." He too scrambled into the narrow space, right behind his friend, marveling once again at Calish's fearlessness and aptitude with strange places.

What's going on? How is he doing all this? pondered Mosher, clearly perplexed by Calish's transformation. Since Calish had shown the people the Crystallight and Maana caves, he had changed much more than the other children. Calish's eyes had gotten much darker and bigger. With the changes came the corresponding knack to better see in near total darkness. Moreover, the top of Calish's head was greatly swollen and his once long brown hair was thinning; mere strings of it hung loosely from spotty patches. His mouth and nose had shrunk to near slits. His skin was a pale white color. Calish's limbs had grown thinner, more muscular, and obviously stronger. His hands looked more like claws.

You are so different now, my friend.

Mosher accepted Calish's bizarre appearance; they were best friends and that was all that mattered. But could other people do the same? Could they really see Calish inside of that distorted and alien shell? That was a question that had yet to be fully answered.

"You never could keep up with me, my friend."

"You always cheated in our races," refuted Mosher as he scrambled faster to catch-up.

Calish called back, "It is here, the place I was telling you about. We are here."

Mosher crawled through a narrow tunnel that opened up into a moderately-sized space. Crystallight gems were sporadically placed along the cave walls, allowing the boys, or rather Mosher, to better see. It was still a dark place, but not overly so. Nonetheless, Mosher's eyes needed more time to adjust than Calish's.

Eventually Mosher could see his surroundings. "Shi-shi-shtu!" he exclaimed in surprise. The boys had a habit of exploring the tunnels together, but the place they were in was surely unique. *Maybe,* mused Mosher, *this is even surpassing the strangeness of the Crystallight caverns.* There was only one entrance/exit from what Mosher could see. But what made the place really unusual

141

was all the stuff strewn about. Scattered over the cave floor was a collection of torn raw-hides, dilapidated and simple hut-like structures, dead fire pits, broken tools, and dried bones.

"Who left these things h-here?" asked Mosher in amazement. "Have our people been here? I do not remember them s-speaking of this place."

"No, these things are not from us."

"Then w-who?"

Calish paused for a moment, choosing his words carefully. "Moshe, there are others who live here, with us, in this underground world."

"Others?" quizzed Mosher in disbelief. "Are you m-mad? How can that be? The Elders said the God of Moses cursed our three tribes because of our disobedience. Only *our* tribes were cast b-below. They said we were lucky the gods did not kill us outright, as they had done to so m-many others. They said we are alone down here to suffer our fate."

"Moshe, the Elders are fools... well, some of them anyway. They are wrong about our new home. This is proof." Calish confirmed his statement while pointing at the man-made objects.

"Well then, w-where are the ones who lived here?"

"They are nearby. They watch us. They will soon reveal themselves to us."

Mosher pondered that statement's implications. "What do they w-wait for?"

Calish held up his claw-like hand to Mosher. "Maybe they wait for this to finish changing."

"I don't understand. Are they waiting for your hand to become even m-more gruesome?"

"No, I think they are waiting for *all* of our hands to become as gruesome as mine."

Mosher studied his own hands, taking note that the digits were slowly becoming very unfamiliar to him. He could tell that before too long his fingers would be the same as Calish's. "Why would they w-wait for this?" asked Mosher, while holding up his knobby hand.

"Because, my friend, that is what some of us are becoming. And this..." Calish used his clawed fingers to envelop his own dreadful face, "is what they look like."

Mosher wasn't sure if he was okay with that declaration; it was a lot to take in. Bishtar had changed drastically in her appearance. Now Calish was looking more and more like her. The thought of it scared him.

And this place scares me. Mosher glanced over all the debris; it was so old-looking, abandoned even. Whoever had left it behind was long gone. That was comforting in a way, and yet still provocative and most likely dangerous. If he was alone, Mosher would have been trembling with fear, but because Calish stood with him Mosher felt confident and secure, more or less. Regardless, and fear or not, Mosher couldn't help but be curious so he asked, "Calish, how did you know about this p-place? And all the other stuff we've been doing lately?"

"A vision."

"A vision? What does that m-mean?"

Calish paused again before answering. He wasn't yet ready to tell Mosher of the strange boy. He couldn't quite identify why he wasn't ready, except to say that it just didn't feel like the right time. In the Crystallight cave the boy didn't seem ready to reveal himself to Mosher either. Luckily, his friend Mosher had always been a kind soul, and had never tried to pressure him into defining his reasons for things, or for his leadership in whatever they did together. Moreover, how could he explain what he himself could barely understand? So Calish decided to leave the 'vision' question up in the air for the time being. "I'm not really sure."

Mosher, looking skeptical, eventually acquiesced. He trusted his friend implicitly: always had, and always would. But inside Mosher could not help but be reminded that his best friend was growing to be as extraordinary, unique, and as mysterious as their new underground home.

Calish pronounced, "This place, Moshe, will be our secret, hidden place." He held up Asher's spear. Thinking well about the threat of Gasheer taking it again, he said, "When we don't need it, this will be where we can keep Asher's spear. We can hide other things here as well. And Mosher, no one can follow us here, ever. Deal?"

Mosher would not, could not, go against Calish's request. It was how they had operated since day one. So, in typical fashion, they spit into their hands. Their claw-like digits enveloped each other firmly. Mosher instantly felt his friend's powerful grip. For the first time ever, Mosher did his best to reciprocate. Calish grinned in acknowledgement. In unison, they spoke aloud their solemn oath. "Cal-Moshe!"

CHAPTER 16
Sky Rock

The two boys ran like the wind. Well, one of them did anyway. The other did his best to keep up, but as usual could not compete with his lean, agile, very swift and sometimes annoying friend.

"C'mon, Drinkle, the mysteries await!" called out Calish excitedly.

Correction: *Make that 'always' annoying friend.* "You're such a cheater, Calish." Mosher yelled in response.

At that comment, Calish suddenly stopped. He leaned on Asher's spear, while taking deep breaths, thinking about what he had heard. He couldn't let the claim stand; he just had to argue with Mosher's accusation, "What are you talking about, Moshe? I didn't cheat. You're as crazy as you are slow, Drinky-drink."

Mosher caught up to Calish, stumbling a bit, catching his breath, and started the drama by saying, "Yeah, but you know I'm still sore from Gasheer's whip; it hurts, and well..."

Calish took note of Mosher's statement, and feeling sorry for his companion, allowed Mosher to get very close to him. Mosher's face, a mixture of exhaustion and sorrow, suddenly changed to surprised joy. He hit Calish on the shoulder, shouting, "You're it!" and ran off into the area they were originally exploring, laughing like a hyena.

Calish, realizing he had been thoroughly duped, set off to reach his fiendishly clever foe. He sprinted like mad to not only catch Mosher, but to surpass him in an unparalleled display of speed. *I'll show you...* And of course that is exactly what Calish did. As he easily passed Mosher, Calish turned around, and while running backwards he taunted, "You're slower than my sister, Moshe. No, I take it back, my *grandma* could beat you, ha ha."

"You son of a Caanon dog!" groused Mosher while huffing and puffing in hot pursuit. Calish laughed at the insult, and chuckled even more at Mosher's sad attempt to catch him.

Then Mosher suddenly stopped and said, "Hey, look there, Calish." Mosher was pointing at something as if it was really strange.

Calish slowed down a bit, shook his finger, and warned, "Oh no, ol' buddy, you're not gonna' fool me twice."

Mosher countered, "No really, look there, I think we found something."

Calish, after realizing that Mosher was not going to follow him, also stopped. He ambled back to Mosher's spot, suspicious, ready to bolt before Mosher could tag him again. "What is it this time, Moshe?" Calish cheekily threw out, "Find more hay for Bishtar's lamb?"

Mosher disregarded the reference, knowing that Calish intended no harm in the remark. In fact, it was Calish and his whole family that had been instrumental in Mosher's recovery from Gasheer's Paingiver. Mosher had stayed in one of Korah's tents while his wounds healed. Calish, his mother, and sister had done everything possible to see to his needs. While he lay on his stomach, unable to really do much on his own, Mosher soon realized that if there was a silver lining in being punished for defending Bishtar, it was having much more time alone with the one he loved. He naturally would never tell her such a thing, but deep down Mosher believed that Bishtar knew what he felt for her. So maybe in a strange way Gasheer's whipping blows were a *good* thing. Odd but true. Yes, the scars were still deeply ingrained into his body and mind, but without Calish's family, and most especially Bishtar's tender care, Mosher might have never survived at all.

Within a score of sleep cycles, Mosher was well enough to once again resume having adventures with Calish, exploring the Crystallight cavern's mysterious realms.

"Do you s-see what I see?" Mosher peered into an area that was darker than most of the alcoves they had been running through. But there were enough Crystallight gems to see a little bit. If one looked hard enough, they could see strange vegetation that was sporadically popping up along a dim cavern wall.

Calish took a quick peek. "Just more Maana, Moshe."

"No, there's other stuff b-beside it." Mosher walked around, finding more of the dissimilar plants. Then Calish started to take notice, as it became clear that Mosher had indeed found something new.

"Hey, those plants look familiar," voiced Calish.

They moved closer and Mosher bent over to pick up one very identifiable sample. He then announced, "Mushrooms!" Later he pointed out another nearby growth. "And that looks like f-fungi; we've seen similar things b-before."

"This is great news, Moshe. Our people will have more than one thing to eat."

"If it isn't p-poisonous, that is." Mosher chose another prime example, plucked the monster from its roots and held out the big fat mushroom right in Calish's scrunched-up face. In a tempting way, Mosher prompted, "Give it a t-try."

"Oh no. You just said it's poisonous, no way."

"Scared? It's just a m-mushroom, Calish. We used to eat them all the time in E-Egypt. S-Scared, huh, scared?"

Calish frowned a bit. Then, taking the dare, he grabbed the mushroom, took a bite of its beefy sides, and cautiously chewed away. He swallowed grudgingly, his face crumpled up more from the effort.

"How does it taste? Oh, don't tell me. Not as fine as your m-mother's sweet bread, not as filling as g-goat meat..."

Without missing a beat, Calish finished with, "But in a pinch, it will do."

They both started laughing.

Calish made another sour face. "I'm thirsty, Moshe. All this running and eating dry mushrooms, ya know." Then he proposed, "Maybe if we look around we'll find a stream or pond." Calish used Asher's spear and pointed to a certain place. "Let's go over there to try and find one. As far as I know, none of our people have been in those areas. Maybe we'll have luck there."

"Okay, b-brave mushroom eater, lead the way."

Thinking quickly, Calish disputed, "Listen, Moshe, don't even think you fooled me into eating it. Remember, I'm always one step ahead of you, Drinkle, ol' pal." With that, Calish sprang a few steps forward, just to show Mosher who was the fastest.

"I might be Drinkle, but you're the one w-who's thirsty from eating it." Mosher smiled widely on what he believed to be the winning retort.

"Whatever," snarked Calish, making sure that he got in the last word.

After a few moments of wandering toward the uncharted locations, Mosher stopped walking. Calish also stopped. "What now? What's wrong?"

Mosher, looking very pensive and somewhat confused, pointed off in another direction. "We must g-go there."

"Why?"

"I d-don't know, I ah, just have a feeling."

Calish's expression was quite skeptical as he studied his strange-acting friend. But he finally relented. "Okay, Moshe, you're the boss. Lead the way."

Following Mosher's recommendation, the explorers walked through a new alcove. Then they entered another cavern that had a very high ceiling. After walking a short distance, they could see a massive boulder. The monument was impossible to miss; it dominated a very large cavern niche. The colossal stone was flat and smooth along its forward-facing side. The whole thing sat on a mild angle that was pitched up from the cave floor. At the boulder's base, the ground was cracked; whereas rubble and small stones littered the behemoth's thick sides.

"Wow, that thing is huge," declared Calish.

"It looks like something p-pushed it into the Earth with g-great force.

"Yeah, like it came from some other place."

Mosher added, as if inspired, "Or from the s-sky. A big giant r-rock from the sky."

"Yeah, I like that, Moshe, I like it. We'll call it Sky Rock. Good idea, rock-namer."

"Sky Rock? Hmm, I like it t-too, Calish, thanks." After that, Mosher stared at the monument's peak and reverently whispered, "Sky Rock."

Mosher then got real quiet. He approached Sky Rock's front side, scrutinizing its details. He looked up, down, and all around. The boulder's smooth surface was set at a steep, yet climbable incline. On impulse, Mosher chose a relatively accessible spot and started scrambling up onto Sky Rock's face. When Mosher got near the middle point, he stopped. He glanced down beneath his feet as if he was searching for something really important. Mosher then turned back at Calish.

What's going on? Calish pondered. Mosher was acting quite odd, like he was beside himself.

Then, as if in a trance, Mosher ceremoniously pointed to Asher's spear. He gestured as if he wanted Calish to throw it up. Calish shrugged and gently tossed the lance to Mosher, who deftly caught it. Mosher then climbed a little higher along the monument's wide, smooth plane.

Calish called out, "What will you do, oh great and powerful Moshe... smite the rock?" He laughed at his own joke.

Mosher, ignoring Calish's remark, glared at the Asher's spear as if it was a magical device. Using the spear, he singled out a particular spot on the boulder's surface. Suddenly, Mosher swung the lance very high and swiftly brought it down, striking the rock face very hard.

Ping! A loud ringing echoed throughout the cavern. To follow was a rumbling noise that soon got louder, which was then mixed with a grinding sound. After that, Sky Rock started shaking. Mosher, startled awake from his stupor, quickly jumped down and off of Sky Rock. He then took up his place standing beside Calish. Together they watched in awe as Sky Rock's face developed a crack in its otherwise pristine facade.

"Shishtu. What have you done, Moshe?"

"N-Nothing, I swear."

The fracture widened a bit. There was another rumbling sound and suddenly a fountain of water gushed up through the crack, gurgling and bubbling high into the air. The sprout of water then flowed from the middle of the rock and down into a shallow indentation along the cavern floor. A large puddle was formed as more water poured into the inset. The puddle soon turned into a stream. The stream grew more, eventually following a path that stretched as far as the eye could see, until it disappeared into the cavern's darker spaces.

Mosher handed Asher's spear back to Calish. They checked it, and its shiny tip remained unharmed by Mosher's Sky Rock strike. Mosher smiled knowingly again, but this time Calish beat his friend to the punch.

149

"I know. I know, don't say it... Electrum."

Of course, Mosher followed-up with, "The finest m-metal forged by the finest craftsmen in all the kingdom."

Calish rolled his eyes. As the boys marveled at the sparkling waters, Calish asked, "What made you think to do it? I was only joking about the smiting thing."

Mosher, deeply absorbed by the miraculous display, finally uttered, "I don't know. I ah..."

"Had a feeling?"

Mosher shrugged and stammered, "I g-guess so. I think I heard the w-water, or felt it or, gee, I'm not sure."

"El be praised. It's magic." Calish patted Mosher on the back; his friend winced from pain.

"Oh, sorry, Moshe, sorry."

Mosher's wounds had not yet fully healed, but he didn't want Calish to feel bad about the mistake so he smiled and said, "It's okay, Calish."

Calish smiled upon seeing his friend's generosity. Then he gestured to the bubbling liquid. "Give it a go, Drinkel, my pal."

"Ha-ha, Mr. Skin and B-Bones." Mosher bent down to scoop up a sample. He brought the water to his lips, sipping it, carefully at first. Soon enough, Mosher took another sample, and another, as it was obvious that the water was cool, clean, and most refreshing. "It's delicious, Calish. I have n-never tasted anything like it."

Calish grinned, and he too grabbed up some refreshment. "You're right, Moshe." Calish continued to drink, washing the dry taste of the mushroom from his mouth and quenching his thirst at the same time.

"And w-what shall we call this?" asked Mosher while gesturing to the whole watery area.

In a mock stutter, Calish mumbled, "You mean, besides w-water?"

Mosher shook his head in frustration. "C'mon, Calish."

"Okay, okay, brave rock smiter. I have an idea... how about *you* name it."

Mosher was intrigued by the offer, so he thought for a moment, and declared, "How about the Fountain of Moshe?"

"Oh brother," sighed Calish. "Very well then, Moshe's Fountain it is."

Suddenly the gurgling sprout of water erupted, and a much stronger geyser shot straight up into the air, nearly hitting the distant cavern ceiling. A very loud, thunderous, vibrating sound emerged. Mixed with the sounds came grumbled words. "That is not the water's name!"

Shocked and surprised, the boys grabbed onto one another while staring wide-eyed at Sky Rock.

"Did you hear that?"

"Yeah, d-did you?"

"Yes, where'd it come from?"

"Don't know, d-do you?"

"No."

Just then, from the midst of Sky Rock, the bubbling water once more exploded upward. Again its noise was like thunder. But mixed within the sound the boys heard a very angry voice shout, "Who are you?... Well? Lest I not ask again. Speak, young ones, speak."

Mosher shakily whispered, "It's Sky R-Rock... talking!"

"I know, Moshe, I know," Calish murmured back as if it was obvious.

Then the angrier-sounding Sky Rock demanded, "Speak, I tell you!"

Calish swallowed hard. He stepped forward and with a trembling voice croaked, "C-Calish, I am Calish and this is Moshe, ah... I mean Mosher." Calish looked behind him to see Mosher hunkered down directly behind him, hiding like a leech that clung madly to his tunic. Calish tried to shake him off but the leech hung on tight.

There was then silence, except for the bubbling waters. They waited, and the boys started to think the episode, whatever it was, had ended.

But then, after a few more harrowing moments, came the booming voice again. "Mosher! Step forward and be recognized."

Mosher jumped nearly as high as the gusher of water. He stared at Calish, wanting comfort, but finding very little. Calish pried Mosher's hand from his tunic and pointed his chin toward

151

Sky Rock. Mosher reluctantly took one wobbly step around Calish, and another tiny step forward. He glanced back at his friend. Calish shrugged, giving him a very shaky thumbs-up. "Gee, thanks," whispered Mosher. He turned uneasily toward the gusher of water and waited.

"Mosher!" Sky Rock's omnipresent voice said. "What you call me is nothing. I am that I am. But this is how you shall call Father's divine liquid: The Water of Life. Do not forget this, young ones. Never forget this."

Calish and Mosher simultaneously nodded their heads in agreement.

"I cannot hear you!" boomed Sky Rock.

So Calish stammered out, "Yes yes, we understand it. The Water of Life. Yes, we will remember. Right, Moshe?" Calish anxiously gestured to his friend as if to say something... anything.

When Mosher hesitated, Calish said, "Hurry up, say something before he gets mad."

"Ah, you m-mean he's not already m-mad?"

"Just hurry."

A trembling Mosher haltingly complied. "Y-Yes, the W-Water of L-Life. G-Got it, sir, Sky R-Rock, sir. Sure, w-whatever you s-say. We got it. S-Sure thing. We totally u-under . . .

"That's enough, Moshe, I think he heard you."

"G-Good, El be praised."

"You have been chosen!" continued Sky Rock.

Mosher scooted behind Calish again. After a short interval, he poked his head out from the side and whispered in Calish's ear, "Say s-something b-before you piss him off m-more."

"Me?" answered Calish incredulously, "You're the one he called out, so you pissed him off."

"No I didn't, y-you did."

"No, you did."

"No, you d..."

"Silence!!!"

After they stopped quivering from fright, Calish eventually moved up a little. Mosher clung to his back collar, the little leach following every step of the way. Calish called out, "What are we chosen to do? I mean, okay, Mr. Sky Rock, sir; could you please tell us what we're chosen for?"

Sky Rock, appearing to have calmed down, explained, "I am here for you. Over untold eons of time I have waited to give you this gift: Father's Water of Life. I do His will. The Water of Life will give you strength to carry on and fulfill prophecy."

Very abruptly, Sky Rock's rumbling noises quieted, the fountain water receded, and the vibration lessoned. Speaking pleasantly, almost tiredly, Sky Rock seemed to sigh. "I will return to my sleep now."

After that, there was silence. The fountain of water continued to diminish until it was a mere trickle. Just as the boys started to relax, the water suddenly gushed higher one last time and once again Sky Rock's voice exploded, shaking the entire cavern. "Moshe!"

Mosher jumped even higher than before. He popped his head from behind Calish's shoulder and stammered, "Oh Shis-shtu. Y-Yes, I am here, sir Sky R-Rock."

Sky Rock declared, "Thus Saith El, our Lord. The time will soon come, Moshe. You will know what you must do."

Calish and Mosher exchanged quizzical stares. Calish elbowed him in the ribs to get Mosher to answer, while mouthing *Say something.*

Mosher haltingly stuttered, "Okay, I w-will know what to do kind Sky R-Rock, s-sir. Yes sir, I will d-definitely know what to do. Got it, sure thing, absolutely, will do, n-no problem, I totally unders..."

"Silence!"

Calish poked him in the arm and Mosher swiftly closed his mouth. Both boys gazed at Sky Rock, hoping that the scary dialogue had finally ceased.

Serenely, Sky Rock said, "Goodbye for now, young ones."

The awestruck boys innocently responded in unison, "G-Goodbye."

The gusher soon withdrew back into Sky Rock, bubbling less and less until nothing else came out. The shallow pool, however, remained. The boys approached it with curiosity and wonder.

"Should we d-drink more?"

"Sky Rock didn't say we couldn't. Plus, we already did. The water is still there, so..."

The boys drank. After drinking their fill, they lay down beside the pool. Within a few moments their eyes closed and the two explorers, the impulsive rock smiter and his brave trail-blazing, somewhat annoying friend, ventured into the mysterious realm of dreamers.

* * * *

Mosher stood up, stretching and broadly yawning. It was contagious, so Calish did the same. They both wiped the crust from their eyes… at least most of it, anyway.

While rubbing away, Mosher looked around a bit, eventually noticing the obvious. "Hey. The W-Water of Life is gone. What does that m-mean, Calish?"

Calish, with eyes still half-closed, took a glace. He yawned again, disinterested. After realizing that they had fallen asleep, he reasoned, "Maybe there was no water to begin with. Maybe it was just a dream, Moshe."

"Maybe what was a d-dream?"

"You know the whole..." Then Calish stared at Mosher as if to say *Are you thinking what I'm thinking?*

Mosher duly completed Calish's sentence. ". . . the whole Sky R-Rock thing?"

"Yeah. Hey, wait a minute. Are we talking about the same thing?"

"You mean Sky Rock, the smiting, the g-gusher of water, the s-shaking ground..."

"The Water of Life..."

"The mean old b-boulder that talks in a scary v-voice..."

"And you holding onto me like a frightened little girl."

"Oh brother," sighed Mosher as he rolled his eyes.

Calish laughed, "Well then, I guess it wasn't a dream if we both saw it."

Mosher shrugged. "Guess not. But if it was n-not a dream, then where is the pool of w-water we drank from?"

Calish thought for a moment, and then offered his opinion. "Maybe it was only for us, Moshe... the Water was for us. And it means grandfather is right, we are not alone. El is with us. Sky Rock's Father, our Father, is here with us."

Mosher nodded in agreement.

"In any event, this must be our secret forever." Calish spit into his hand and extended it forward. Mosher, as always, followed suit.

"Cal-Moshe," they said in unison while shaking their saliva-slathered grips.

After the vow, Calish couldn't help but pat his best friend on the back. "Oh sorry," Calish said in a hurry, "I didn't mean to..."

But strangely Mosher didn't flinch, as he should have done. Mosher reached behind himself curiously. He touched on top of his shoulder and then below it along his back, rubbing harder, as if looking, or rather feeling, for something.

"What is it, Moshe?"

"I d-don't know."

Calish reached over and pulled back part of Mosher's tunic. Calish lifted one eyebrow when he didn't see what he should have seen on Mosher's back. "Moshe, lift up your shirt."

Mosher did so. Very curious and anxious, he asked, "What d-do you see, Calish?"

"Nothing..." Again, Calish said, "nothing." While gently touching Mosher's smooth skin, he proclaimed, "Moshe, your scars are gone!"

"B-But how?"

"El be praised, my friend. It could only be Sky Rock's Water of Life."

"It's true then, it's all true. It *did* h-happen." Mosher's face took on a very thoughtful expression. "And you know s-something? I do feel different."

"How so?"

"I don't know. I feel b-better than I have ever felt. I feel changed inside, somehow. Do you feel the same?"

Calish became introspective too. "Yeah, Moshe, I do, but I can't explain it."

"Sky Rock. Remember? He said s-something about the Water giving us the strength to carry out p-prophecy?"

"Prophecy?" queried Calish as if he was unfamiliar with the word. "What does it mean, Moshe?"

"It means we are m-meant to do something, in the future, s-something that is really important."

"Us?" Calish was very surprised.

Moshe stretched to look at his back and got Calish to do the same. "If Sky Rock could do this, then he m-must know what he's talking about, so I g-guess so."

"Shishtu."

"I'll second that, Calish. I'll s-second that."

CHAPTER 17
The Altar of Light

"We should build an altar now. We have been here long enough. That is to say, if you agree?"

"Yes, yes, Abiram, you are right. We must build an altar to give thanks for this place ... and for the *Maana*." Dathan was careful to pronounce their food the way Calish had when the adventurous boy first described it. He didn't want the people to think the food was a gift from El, so a slight change in name was fine with him. Besides, the food's mispronunciation was quickly catching on.

Happy that Dathan had agreed with him, Abiram then pivoted to the surrounding crowd and called out, "Fellow citizens, start gathering the materials needed to build our altar!"

There were murmurs of consent as the people went to their given task. They started by gathering stones that looked like they might be appropriate. The assembly went from here to there, bumping into one another, picking up all kinds of debris, only to discard it as soon as it was lifted. Often the gatherers selected a stone that someone else had recently thrown away. This led to clipped comments that served to illustrate how stupid some people were. Arguments and shoving matches soon erupted over what to do.

"Stop!" commanded Dathan as he held up his hand. When they had stopped, Dathan eyed Darsheesh, who was nearby. "Darsheesh, see to it that our people build a proper altar."

Darsheesh, the best builder in Dathan's tribe, well known among the people for his skill, nodded his consent. "Where shall I build it, my Lord?"

Dathan scrutinized the Crystallight cave. It was immense; some parts were so vast that the ceiling could not readily be seen. Picking a good place was at first a challenge, but Dathan finally chose a spot that had a series of elevated steps. The steps led to a raised platform. Immediately behind the platform was a narrow tunnel, that as far as Dathan knew had not yet been explored. But more importantly, the raised platform made it a perfect site for an altar.

Dathan pointed up to the platform. Saying to Darsheesh loud enough for all to hear, he ordered, "There, build our altar there." He paused for a moment. When he saw that the people were attentive, he added, "You all know Darsheesh. His building skills are unmatched. You will now take instructions from Darsheesh in this matter."

The people nodded in agreement and then looked to him for direction. Darsheesh, now in control, went about his business of organizing the people for the task.

Dathan faced Abiram and Korah. The trio stood together watching while the people gathered things under Darsheesh's authority. There was, for the moment, peaceful unity. *Well,* thought Dathan as he studied his fellow elders, *Peaceful, yes. But unity? Maybe not.* "Korah," prompted Dathan, "you look troubled."

Korah rubbed his rough gray beard in thought. "Brother, do you not remember the last time we did this?"

Abiram gestured in solidarity. He then waited for a response from Dathan.

"Korah, my brother," Dathan answered, "that altar was Nathan's doing, and Aaron's. This is a different situation. This time we will honor our true gods. This time we will build an altar to Osiris and Isis."

Korah was incredulous. "Are you insane? It will end up being the same thing. Do you not know what folly Nathan's shrine was?"

"If memory serves me, did I not see you, Korah, dancing and making merry at the sight of the golden calf?"

A spark of outrage crossed Korah's brow. He tightened his stance and readied himself to launch a punishing blow.

Dathan prepared to defend himself.

Just as the two were about to fight, Abiram stepped in to quiet the dissent. "Korah, Dathan," he pleaded, "we should not reopen old wounds. Let us come together to find solutions."

Korah opened his fists; Dathan did the same. The old men, at some point, had to accept their finite limitations. Brawling was best left to the young bucks. More importantly, the aches and pains from their first fight had not yet dissipated, so each man was actually quite glad to give in.

Still breathing heavy, Korah asked scathingly, "What do you propose, Dathan, *my brother?*"

"As we have already discussed, this time I will lead the prayer and I will make sure our gods hear us." Dathan indicated that the trio should look upon the beginnings of Darsheesh's craftsmanship. The man was busy carefully fitting the stones into place. His skill was indeed masterful. The gatherers seemed inspired to help even harder after seeing the work take such a good shape. "Besides, we need to give them purpose. Can you not see that this is a *good* thing? Our people are united."

Korah, for his part, couldn't quite bring himself to argue the point. The people were indeed unified for once. And who was he to quarrel with the situation, such as it was. There was already too much darkness, death and despair; maybe this altar of Dathan's was somehow a good idea.

But what if we're wrong... again? thought Korah. He reached for his pouch and was reminded of what it truly represented. In the back of his mind Korah couldn't shake the feeling that there was something terribly amiss. His people were being led astray, like before. The altar would not, could not, be an ultimate solution. Nothing good would come of such a thing. As with the golden calf, disobedience could never save them. "We shall see," Korah sighed solemnly, "we shall see."

* * * *

"It is done, my Lord." Darsheesh announced to Dathan.

Abiram, Korah and Dathan went to the base of the elevated steps to inspect Darsheesh's work. They all gazed up toward it, nodding in approval. The altar was well designed, having many stones that were interwoven enough to give the appearance of a very solid looking single unit. The base was rounded, leading to a column-like vertical shaft. In total, it stood over four feet tall. At its peak was a raised platform made of a large stone tablet. The tablet's edges were flat. Its central area was inset, forming a bowl shape. The bowl leaned forward a bit so that one could see its hollowed-out structure, even while standing at the bottom of the steps.

"Darsheesh," marveled Dathan, "you must have worked very hard to chisel out the altar top's tablet so quickly."

"I did as I was told," answered Darsheesh humbly.

Dathan beamed with pride and glanced behind him. The tribe was starting to gather, as instructed once the altar was finished. When everyone had taken up their places, the Elders climbed the steps. Dathan, Abiram and Korah took their spots near Darsheesh's altar.

Dathan nodded magnanimously to his companions and took a few steps forward to address the people. He grinned brightly, smoothly, and began to pontificate. "Our work is nearly done here. Thanks to you, and especially to the skill of Darsheesh, we will see our prayers answered in our new center of worship. This will be a holy place for our people. We will bow to this altar, and the gods will hear us!"

The crowd reacted well to hearing those words. They smiled, clapped, and gave shouts of approval. Dathan basked in the moment as if the tributes were to him, rather than to the gods.

He then held up his hand to enlist the people's attention. "When we first found ourselves here, we awoke into darkness. The world we once knew was gone to us. The people we once knew were gone to us."

The crowd took in Dathan's tone and were saddened to be reminded of their recent past.

Dathan was playing to their emotions like a master performer. "The man who led us out of Egypt abandoned us, left us to die here in this underworld pit."

At that comment, the crowd started shouting angrily in agreement, just like the speaker wanted.

Dathan was far from done. "In fact, this so-called leader is the reason we suffer here. He orchestrated this entire disaster. It was he, along with his so-called god, that caused the earth to open and swallow us. Like we were nothing!"

More shouts erupted. Then the rabble quieted down just as quickly in order to listen to Dathan's hostile and inflammatory words.

"But I say, we are not nothing. We are *great!* The God of Moses will hear us. He will hear our outrage, our indignation, and our triumph over his so-called power!"

Thunderous applause and greater shouts followed.

Korah and Abiram looked upon the raging crowd, then at one another, somewhat baffled. Above the din, Abiram asked, "Did we agree with this?"

Korah shot back, "No. Never."

After raising his hands to quiet the tumult, Dathan continued, "Proof of what I say, you ask? Look around you. Are we not in a much better place now? Of course we are. And I will tell you why. Our true gods heard our prayers and have answered them. They inspired one of our Elder's sons to find this Crystallight cavern, full of light, water, and food: the *Maana.* So we should give thanks to brother Korah here, and his grandson Calish, for listening to our true gods."

The crowd started to call out thanks to Korah. Those that were near Calish patted him on the back generously. Calish looked up to Mishtas, who was by his side, and said above the clamor, "That is not what happened, Uncle."

Mishtas answered, "I know, Calish, I know."

Dathan started up again. "Our true gods, Osiris and Isis, will be thanked. And after that they will bless us with even greater gifts. And we will not only survive, but triumph over the evil that has cast us into this dire fate. I tell you here and now, we will be great once again!"

The crowd went berserk, shouting out in unison, "Osiris, hear us... Isis, hear us!" Dathan commandeered the chorus of praise by waving his arms to go along with their chants.

After the ruckus had settled, Dathan cast his gaze upon Calish. "And please, if you will, grandson of Korah, let us once again see the gem of light our gods have given us."

Calish hesitated, but was so pressured by the surrounding people that he retrieved the jewel from his pouch. Its green glow sparkled to life, as it had when Calish had first presented it to the tribe.

Dathan gestured to Gasheer and the huge man stepped forward. The giant grabbed up the Crystallight stone from Calish's hand. Calish went to get it back but Gasheer merely pushed him aside.

"Give that back!" shrieked Calish. He was more than ready to go at Gasheer, but Mishtas held onto him. "Uncle, please, let me go, it is not his."

"Be patient, Calish. Now is not the time."

The two of them then glared up at Gasheer. Mishtas' expression was one of steady defiance; Calish showed great anger, as thoughts of revenge crossed his mind. *One day, bully, you shall meet Asher's spear. One day . . .*

Gasheer returned their stares, grinning at their impotence. Then he went up the altar steps and handed the gem to Dathan.

Dathan nodded, studied the stone in his hand, and put forth, "We thank Korah and his grandson for taking care of this for us. The gift from our gods has found its way to us, from youthful exuberance to the wisdom of the Elders. It is time for our leaders to use the gemstone to benefit all our tribe through a proper ceremony." Dathan's tone became more casually persuasive as he put forth, "Before we commence with the worship, however, let us take some time to prepare. We will need a suitable sacrificial offering, among other things. Plus, we are tired from building this fine temple of worship. So I propose that we first eat, and rest. While doing this, let us also take time to contemplate how to ask the gods to bestow their favor upon us."

That was a reasonable suggestion; many were hungry or tired from the work, so they all agreed to leave.

Smiling charitably, Dathan interrupted their exit with, "And my fellow clansmen, it has been decided that because you have successfully completed our magnificent altar, each family will receive an extra allotment of Maana."

The people were joyous to hear it. They hooped and hollered and called out words of profuse appreciation: "Thank you, Lord Dathan. May Isis bless you, Elder Dathan. Great Osiris' light is upon you, brother Dathan."

Dathan, of course, absorbed their gratitude as if it was he who was personally handing out everyone's Maana portion.

Korah and Abiram could not help but share expressions of disbelief. "Did we agree to *this?*" queried Abiram again.

But this time Korah merely shrugged as if to say: *So what else is new?*

After celebrating the refreshing news of having more food for once, the tribe cheerfully collected themselves and started to return to their tents.

As they were leaving, Korah held back Dathan. "How can you have made those promises to our people? How do you know this altar will work?"

"I do not," admitted Dathan in hushed tones, so that no one might overhear. "But look around you. And think of the great miracles we have already seen. We were hungry; we found the Maana. We were thirsty; we found water. We were in darkness; we found this wonderful Crystallight cave."

Korah responded, "Did the altar do those things? I think not."

Dathan became thoughtful. "Is it not fitting that we thank the gods for our recent good fortune? Is it not the gods that led us here? Is it not *they* that wait for our thankful prayers and worship?"

Once again, Korah was left unable to argue the point. "I hope you are right, Dathan."

Dathan said in a light-hearted way, "Do not worry so much, my brother. It makes you look much older than you already are." His tone then became serious. "Just think, Korah, maybe the gods Isis and Osiris are waiting for our worship." Dathan held up the Crystallight stone, pondering its magical brilliance. "Maybe once we do so, they will reward us with even greater gifts."

Or maybe, mused Korah worryingly, *our 'gifts' will not be as rewarding as you think.*

CHAPTER 18
The Sound of Voice

The people ate well, and when they had their fill of the Maana, they retreated to their tents to sleep. As they slept, some of them dreamt of things no one should imagine.

Hear me. Hear me. Hear me. Hear me. Into their minds, Voice sent a sound meant to mesmerize the humans' awareness into compliance and reverence.

Very few could actually perceive the sounds; human-kind had always been segregated from Voice's influence. But those that could hear it jostled restlessly in their sleep. The agitated dreamers shared one obvious quality; all of them were children that had shown signs of the transformation.

I am with you. And you are with me. We are near one another. We will be one.

Over and over, throughout the sleep period, Voice repeated the same message. Some of the transformed that responded to the sounds were ripe candidates because they and Voice shared something in common. It was a trait Voice had in spades; and it was a peculiarity that had dogged humans since their inception. For sure, there were many of the transformed who could resist Voice's temptations; in fact, Voice's call barely registered with them. Unfortunately, mankind had fallen away because there were always those individuals whose ears could be pried open a little too much. Whether they be Pon, man, or a little of both, Voice wanted those sentient beings that, like the spirit, shunned the light and embraced the dark.

I am with you. And you are with me.

Most notably, there were two humans that could heed the sounds very well: one little boy, and one girl. The boy listened carefully to Voice's call. In fact, he actually quite liked it. Unfortunately for Voice, he was still much too small to be of interest... yet. The girl, however, she was older, and she was... well, she was special.

Maybe too special.

CHAPTER 19
The Worship

Mishtas entered the tent and said to Korah, "Dathan and Abiram await for your arrival at the altar. Dathan says that it is time to worship, and thank the gods."

"Very well," replied Korah as he gathered up his pouch.

"Do you think the gods will hear Dathan's prayers?"

"Mishtas," replied Korah grimly, "I most certainly hope not."

* * * *

Voice's spirit hovered above the Holy Place, watching the humans do their busywork, angry at its inability to control them directly. *Father, why do you taunt me with their presence? Father!? You do not let me talk to them upon the surface world. Why are they here, in my world? Father, answer me... please.*

When no word was given, Voice determined. *Very well then, I will show them what a god can do.*

* * * *

The tribe took up places surrounding the altar; some sat, while others stood. Korah and Abiram, along with their immediate families, were closest to the raised steps.

Dathan, in ceremonial garb, exited from his nearby tent, and in a grand display of pomp and circumstance, ascended the steps. He walked behind Darsheesh's altar and scanned the people before him in a serious manner. When the people were eventually hushed into silence, Dathan began to speak, most reverently. "Osiris, Isis, we thank you for protecting us in your underworld, and for bringing us to this oasis among a darkness that threatened to smother us, your chosen people. Oh great Osiris, hear our prayers. Thank you for saving us. And thank you for the bounty we have received in your great and wonderful world. Isis, grant our request for your intervention. Your power is truly great, and we wish to show our thanks and praise by offering up this blood sacrifice." Dathan raised his arms and slowly bowed his head in reverence.

The remnant also bowed in compliant unison. Tied up on top of the altar's tablet, Bishtar's lamb, however, objected by calling out, "Bah. Baaah." After hearing the animal call out, the congregation returned their focus upon Dathan, ignoring the lamb in the process.

Once again, before he spoke, the gathering lowered their heads at Dathan's command. "As a sign of your love for us, you have given this great gem of illumination." Dathan lifted up Calish's Crystallight stone. Its normally greenish hues started glowing with purple-black colors. The change alerted the crowd, and they were quick to take in the strange sight. Dathan was surprised too, but soon enough the stone's sudden changes merely served to inspire him. As the people made sounds of awe and worship, he quickly made the most of it. "This illumination is another sign that you hear us, oh great Osiris. We know you demand a sacrifice. And you shall have it!" Dathan spied out Bishtar, wanting to make her the sacrifice, thinking to himself, *Soon little diseased one, soon.*

But Bishtar met his gaze, with equal if not greater hatred.

With his free hand Dathan pulled out a dagger he had hidden under his cloak. He raised it to be near the lamb's throat. As he started to cut through the lamb's neck, the beast cried out, "Bah! Bah-h-h!"

Infuriated, Bishtar's mind exploded with energy. The little girl balled up her right fingers, turning them into a claw shape. She raised her arm and extended her index finger at the lamb. She then directed her thoughts like she had never done before, making her desires real. The elements of air became surrounded by swirling colors. Her lamb was engulfed by it. Her mind could see and move the colors, as she had done to help Mosher. She quickly directed her little fore-claw and guided her will accordingly. Suddenly the lamb lifted up above the altar, floating in midair, and away from Dathan's knife.

Voice quickly took note of this. *That small human girl... she has mind-motion power! And I will make her mine!*

Some people around Bishtar also noticed her unusual behavior. They were stunned by the floating beast, but not so much that they could not prompt others to look at the strange, dark-eyed little girl who appeared to be in control of said flying lamb.

"How is she doing that?" one onlooker asked in amazement.

"The little one is possessed!" they fearfully declared to one another.

Dathan was at first shocked by the hovering beast, but he hurriedly recovered and loudly pronounced, "This is yet another sign by Osiris that we must make a sacrifice to him in worship!"

Osiris, Osiris! shouted Voice. *Foolish humans, giving worship to spirits I vanquished long ago. They think their so-called gods control a power stone. I will show them a god they should worship.* Voice sent a message to its nearby brood. *Cultists, get ready to kill them all!*

After that, Voice channeled its power into a mass of energy. The force sparkled into flashes of light and color that cascaded out of the Crystallight gems housed within the cavern walls. The sparkling colors coalesced and compressed into a bolt of lightning that struck the top of the altar, obliterating Darsheesh's tablet into a thousand flaring pieces.

The lamb was flung through the air. It sailed across and over many people, and was eventually caught by a very unassuming bystander. He stared at his little white package with shock, then with hunger, for he had not tasted meat since the day he had been cast into the underworld. He looked around guardedly. Luckily for him, everyone was still distracted by the exploding altar, so he swiftly ran to the furthest, darkest corner he could find. "Eureka!" he cried out to the lamb.

"Bah! Bah-h-h!" came his reply.

Voice's lightning shot out again, hitting the Crystallight stone in Dathan's hand, causing sparks of light that criss-crossed everywhere. The stone was also immediately turned too hot; it burned into his skin so Dathan quickly threw it away.

Calish, wide-eyed like everyone else, was not too surprised to take note of where the stone fell. While the crowd watched Dathan jostling to and fro, he gingerly made his way over to the precious jewel.

167

The people, startled and shaken, held their breath while they waited anxiously to see what would happen next. But what *did* happen was surely something no one could have possibly imagined, or prepared for.

Suddenly emerging from the hidden passage behind the altar, they heard, "Mmm... Mmm... Mmm." The loud moaning sounds echoed into the whole cavern.

"What are they!?" someone screamed.

"What is that!" shrieked another.

"Tis monsters from the pits of Sheol!"

Creatures too strange to describe shuffled their way into the area. Panic ensued as the tribe scrambled to get away from the monstrous intruders.

Take them, Voice commanded to the Cultists.

The dead-eyed creatures meandered into the people's midst. Their naked and disheveled bodies lurched forward, claws raised as they moaned loudly, salivating upon seeing all the flesh before their hungry eyes.

Voice focused its commands on the Cult's leader and best fighter, the spirit's First – Telek. *Telek, take the girl and kill as many as you wish. Make haste, I am sure Storn has his spies watching this. We must hurry before he sends his soldiers.*

Yes, Master, replied Telek.

Gasheer, ready to battle as always, stomped his way in front of Dathan, protecting his Lord. A few Cultists lurched at him and Gasheer immediately started bashing at the creatures with his arms and fists. The Cultists screeched in pain as they were being tossed back and down to the cave floor.

"Gather the men, prepare for battle!" shouted Gasheer to his First soldier. Instantly Gasheer's First, his second-in-command, ran off to round up their army. Gasheer thought about retrieving his armor, but the situation was too threatening; there was no time.

Within a few moments the shofar's trumpeting blasts echoed throughout the cavern's spaces. *Brr, Brr, Brr, Brr, Brr, Brr, Brr!*

The few men assigned to the altar duty took up their swords, jumping over the tribe that stood between them and the strange attacking creatures, shouting, "Get back!"

Most did try. But some stumbled, and those that fell were taken up by the cruel creatures, who clawed at them viciously. Like wild animals, the Cult beasts sank their sharp fangs into the people's bodies, ripping through their soft flesh, crunching bones in two, drinking in the flowing blood, and eating them alive. The monsters moaned louder and louder the more they fed.

Amidst all the chaos, Telek shuffled to the girl, taking her up like she weighed nothing.

Bishtar tried to stop him by using her powers, the way she had with moving the lamb, but could not. It was as if her mind was tired, exhausted from holding the lamb in the air, even though her body had plenty of energy. So instead she scratched at the giant, ripping at him, clawing and screaming, "Let me go, aghhhh!"

Telek stretched his one good eye to look at the squirming thing in his arm. But because he barely felt her swipes, Telek merely groaned in annoyance and turned to go. He stepped toward the tunnel exit to leave and was suddenly stopped dead in his tracks.

Gasheer stood in his path. The giant was all too eager to tear apart the strange interloper.

Voice saw it and commanded, *Give the girl to another Telek while you kill the huge human.*

Yes, Master. Telek quickly handed Bishtar to another nearby Cultist, who at first was happily salivating to have a ready bit of food. But after Telek slapped him in the head, the Cultist shuffled toward the tunnel exit, with Bishtar screaming at the top of her lungs all the way.

Telek rotated toward the obstacle in front of him. Voice's First readied his posture to take on the enormous human.

Gasheer circled his opponent, readying himself too. But before doing battle, Gasheer examined the odd being before him: the beastly thing was definitely a man-like specimen, much larger than the other strange creatures, and nearly as big as he was. The intruder's skin was a leathery gray color. But unlike the other naked monsters, this one was clothed in a torn loin covering. The beast's head was hairless and bulbous; his one good eye was black, enormous, and he had a huge purple scar crossing his gruesomely repulsive face. The man-beast had a necklace made of

169

fang-like bones, and around his waist was a belt that held a stony club... a weapon that the hostile creature soon took up.

Good for you, thought Gasheer, happy for the challenge. Following suit, Gasheer retrieved his short sword from its sheath. Gasheer grinned, thinking more of his mean, simple thoughts. Man-beast, monsters from the pits of Sheol, it mattered not to the champion of the Egyptian princes. They all fell to his power, and the snake demon would be no exception. Gasheer could already taste his delicious victory; the man mountain would show his foe what a warrior descendant of the Philistine titans could do!

"Grooah!" bellowed Gasheer, enticing the beast into action.

They flew at each other like rabid dogs, punching, grabbing, pounding away, blocking hits as they swung their weapons, looking for an opening, striking glancing blows in the process.

What are you waiting for, Telek? Stop dilly-dallying. Kill him.

Yes, Master.

Hissing loudly, Telek reared up and flung his body at Gasheer, knocking both of them to the cave floor. In the process, both fighters lost grip of their weapons. Gasheer, a practiced wrestler, grabbed Telek by the head and neck, squeezing hard. Gasheer then muscled Telek over, onto his face. After that, Gasheer pulled his thick frame on top of Telek's jerking body.

Voice, getting more impatient with its First's lackadaisical performance, decried, *Telek! Get up now before I feed you to our Mestalor.*

Telek complied. While being punched mercilessly by Gasheer's meaty fists, Telek rose, taking the blows, slowly bringing up Gasheer with him. Once on his feet, Telek turned to face Gasheer. He grabbed onto Gasheer's sides, sinking his claws into Gasheer's thick skin. In an unparalleled display of strength, Telek lifted the big man high in the air.

Gasheer's shock at being levitated was short-lived, for Telek, in an even greater demonstration of shear power, tossed Gasheer through the air. Impossibly, the man was suddenly like a bird in flight... graceful, weightless and free.

The witnesses to this phenomenon were quite possibly more surprised to see the flying titan than they were by the bizarre attacking monsters. "What is that?" queried one surprised bystander.

"'Tis the rising phoenix, Gasheer," replied another.

In any event, Gasheer's buoyant freedom was fleeting, for the giant soon came crashing down to Earth, very hard. Luckily for Gasheer, the brunt of his heavy fall was cushioned by landing on some of Voice's Cultists. Unluckily for them, the cushions were summarily crushed, squished into a flattened and bloodied pulp. Soon thereafter other nearby Cultists were quick to notice the prone and deliciously enormous piece of meat right in front of them. They swarmed over Gasheer, sinking their teeth and claws into his profusely abundant flesh.

But Gasheer was not nearly done. Their meager scratches served only to fuel his rage, and his desire for revenge. He kicked, punched and slapped his attackers away like they were mere toys.

Meanwhile, the tribe's army had assembled. They took up strategic positions around their opponents and were making a successful counter-attack. The soldiers used their weapons to kill Cultists left and right. Arrows, swords, spears, and shields were striking the Cultists from all sides, knocking them to the cavern floor. Once down, the nearest soldier used his short sword to hack the wounded Cultist to pieces.

Seeing the humans' successful assault, Voice shouted to its brood, *Retreat, you fools! Retreat!*

The still mobile Cultists took up some of their closest victims and slunk their way back into the same tunnel they had arrived in. Telek retrieved his club, and was quick to follow after them. He then masterfully used it to beat back any soldier that dared to impede the Cultists' retreat. The soldiers soon became wary of Telek's obvious prowess and gave him a wide berth.

After forcing the soldiers away, Telek ascended the elevated steps and stood alone at the tunnel entrance. Then he started to enter it.

Before disappearing, Telek suddenly turned around, and with his one black eye he spied out Gasheer. Telek stuck out his snake-like tongue and hissed loudly at the giant human, as if to say, *Anytime, anywhere.* Telek then retreated into the darkness of the tunnel. Left behind were only the shrill sounds of Bishtar's screams, echoing further and further away.

"Groahhh!" roared Gasheer in impotence as he watched his opponent vanish.

A few brave soldiers doggedly went after Telek, but because of the darkness and close quarters of the tunnels, they soon returned.

Gasheer's First then ran up to the giant and asked, "Sir. Should we follow?"

"No, not yet," Gasheer answered grudgingly, obviously unhappy. "Let us regroup. Post guards at every nearby cavern entrance."

"Very well, Sir."

Soon thereafter the survivors took up the wounded and dead. The hurt shrieked in pain; family members cried out for their dead or missing, and the rest did everything they could to alleviate the worst of it.

As that process continued, the Elders ascended the steps of the altar. Abiram nervously scanned the tunnel where the monsters had fled. "We must do something!" he bawled, obviously scared and unsure.

Korah ignored Abiram and focused on Dathan. Determined to make sure that soldiers be sent to retrieve his granddaughter, he pointed into the tunnel and demanded, "They have taken Bishtar. We must get her back!"

"And we will," declared Dathan hurriedly. He called over to Gasheer. "Gasheer, ready your men and gather the needed supplies. In the meantime, send your best scouts ahead, to follow the beasts."

"Yes, my Lord."

Mishtas came forward and climbed the altar steps. He went to Korah worriedly asking, "Father?"

Korah answered while clutching his pouch, "Yes, my son, I know. We will get her back. One way or another."

CHAPTER 20
Rescue

"Wait, my sons, wait."

"Grandfather, I will not. Moshe and I are ready. Please trust me."

But Korah put his arm gently on Calish and Mosher's shoulders. He then guided the boys to sit beside him on their bench. Korah said kindly, "You know things that you have kept hidden from the tribe... and from me."

Calish and Mosher exchanged glances, and Calish put forth, "Grandfather, I..."

"It is okay, my son. For there are always secrets; it is a sad truth of human nature. Be that as it may, there are things I have kept hidden as well, things that you must hear of, my son... my sons."

Mosher smiled broadly upon hearing that he was included into Korah's family. Since the lamb incident and his punishment from Gasheer, Korah had informally adopted Mosher, allowing him to reside in one of his tents even after Korah's healer had finished tending to his wounds.

"Yes, Grandfather, what do you wish to tell us?" asked Calish.

Korah directed his eyes most specifically at Calish and began his explanation. "Do you remember Moses?"

"Yes, I saw him talk with you many times."

"As an Elder, he and I shared communion with the one true God... El."

"On the mountain?"

"Yes, yes... good, you remember."

"You argued about things up there."

"Yes, and I truly regret those things now," Korah said sadly.

"But what has that to do with us... with Bishtar?"

"Calish, our God is not the gods that Dathan had us pray to at the altar. Dathan's gods are false. They are what kept our people in bondage in Egypt. El delivered us from the Egyptians. There is much of this to tell you, my son, but for now you must know this. El has given to our people gifts, wonderful gifts. To help us."

Korah produced the Minthuru stone that was hidden within his pouch. It was mostly black with reddish highlights near the edges. It shone brightly as Korah brought it forth and nearer to Calish.

"What is it, Grandfather?"

"It is called the Minthuru. It has great power. If needed, it will guide the stone's true bearer. It has told me of your... special knowledge of our new home." Korah wanted Calish to know that his secrets were not necessarily a bad thing. "It has shown me that you, for your present quest, will need this." He offered the stone to Calish. "This is for you, Calish. Guard and protect it with your life, for our very existence will depend on it."

As Calish took up the object, he said, "Grandfather, I do not know how..." Suddenly, the stone glistened, and Calish was struck by a vision. He was shown a place where he could find his sister; and he was shown a path that would lead him to her.

"I know where she is," Calish said, wide-eyed.

Korah nodded his understanding. "Before you go, take this as well." Korah produced a lantern that he had kept hidden.

"Where did you get this?" Calish had never seen such a nice lantern. Anything that fine would have been confiscated by Gasheer's soldiers.

"Sometimes, my son, secrets can be a *good* thing."

As Calish and Mosher got up to leave, Korah said, "My sons?"

They turned to look at the old man. "Mishtas will be joining you."

The boys glanced at one another again; Calish skeptical, Mosher looking somewhat relieved. "He is an expert bowman and hunter. You will need his skills, I am sure."

Calish, would not, could not, argue. Korah was still his grandfather and their tribe's Elder.

"He will be most welcome," responded Calish. "Thank you, Grandfather."

"Good hunting, my sons. Bring me back my granddaughter."

"We will, we will."

* * * *

Mosher met with his friend outside of Calish's tent. Mosher had his sheathed wolf knife, a jug of water, and his sling. Calish had his flint knife, and of course Asher's spear. He also revealed that, in another pouch which was different from the one holding the Minthuru stone, he had the Crystallight gem.

"How did you get it Calish?"

"During the fight with those creatures, I took it from near the altar. We will need it. Remember what grandfather said, 'sometimes secrets can be a good thing'."

"Far be it from m-me to argue with that," replied Mosher.

"Are you ready?" asked Calish.

Even though Mosher was very keen to find Bishtar, he was still uncertain as to how they could accomplish such a difficult task. "How can we defeat such m-monsters, Calish? Even Gasheer and his men could not overcome them."

"I have a plan my friend."

Oh no, not another plan, thought Mosher. "G-Great," he said while trying not to roll his eyes.

Calish peered intently at his friend and proclaimed, "And I will rescue Bishtar."

Mosher could see that 'look' in Calish's eyes. Knowing that Calish held his strong belief gave Mosher hope. If anyone could do something improbable, it was his friend Calish.

"Let us go this way." Calish picked up his spear and pointed in an unusual direction.

Mosher was confused. While pointing to the place where Gasheer had gone, he countered, "Gasheer and his men went that way, toward the altar, following the b-beasts that took Bishtar. Why do you want to go this other way?"

"First we must find someone."

"Who?"

"You will see." Calish brought out the lantern from behind a pile of debris. The flame had already been lit. Calish picked up his rope and gazed at his friend.

Now Mosher knew exactly where they were going, but he was still confused. "But w-what of Mishtas? Where is he?"

"Don't worry," answered Calish, "he will join us upon our return."

Soon thereafter, the boys used the rope to climb the ledge that led to the hidden place. They scrambled through the small tunnel. As soon as possible, Calish went to stand near one of the dilapidated huts.

Mosher followed him. "Now w-what?"

"We wait."

"For . . ."

"You'll see, very soon."

Within a few moments, Mosher could hear the sound of footsteps. He tensed up and reached for his wolf knife. Calish put his hand on Mosher's arm as a way to get him to relax. Mosher did so. Then, from a very dark place behind the old hut emerged a dark figure. It moved toward them. The lantern's small light gradually brought the strange character into better view.

"Shish-shtu!" declared Mosher in shock. He instantly took a step back, thinking he should run, but Calish held him back. It was one of those creatures that had attacked the tribe at the altar. This one was smaller, but nonetheless, it looked the same as those monsters that had carried off Bishtar. As the creature moved even closer, Mosher turned to Calish and asked nervously, "Do we know w-what we're doing, Calish?"

"Yes, we do."

"Oh g-good. Glad to hear it."

"Moshe," stated Calish, as the young warrior stopped in front of them, "this is the 'person' that showed me how to find this place."

After what he had witnessed at the altar, Mosher wasn't sure if Calish's new friend was nothing but more trouble. "That's nice, b-but..."

"He also gave me this." Calish held up the Crystallight stone. It glistened, and upon seeing its sudden brightness, the young warrior had to cover his eyes.

"Oh, I see." But Mosher was still doubtful. He whispered, "Can we trust... him?" Mosher scrutinized their new companion's physique and was sure that the 'him' designation was correct. His thin, yet muscular torso and the leathery groin covering all pointed to it being male. But his facial features were still very odd. "He looks so, ah… weird."

Calish smiled. "Don't worry, Moshe, he doesn't understand our language. But to answer your question, he's also the one that told me how to find the Crystallight caves, and the Maana. So..."

"So we might all be dead if it wasn't for h-him."

"Yup."

"Wait a minute. If he doesn't understand us, and I'm guessing that means y-you don't understand him, then how did he tell you how to find the M-Maana caves?"

"In a vision." Mosher still appeared skeptical, so Calish tried to explain. "I really don't understand it too well, but I had a dream that showed me how to find the tunnel behind the rock we moved with Asher's spear. And the rest you basically know, except that when we eventually reached the Maana cave, we separated. Remember?" Mosher gestured that he did. "Well, that was when I met our friend here for the first time, and he gave me this gem." Calish said this while indicating the Crystallight stone. "Then there was another vision as to how to find our hidden place here. Do you remember that I tried to explain how I knew about our secret place?" Mosher nodded again. "Well, I guess I kind of understand it better now, because he is the one who gave me the visions all along."

Mosher stared at the strange creature. He had to ask, "So why would he be so willing to help us? Is it n-not the case that when people give something, they usually want s-something in return?"

Calish looked hard at Mosher, mulling over what he had said. Then he turned back to see the young warrior, who was still an unknown factor, regardless of the vision's promises. Comparing the two them, the warrior was a person he had just met – an unknown factor – but Mosher was someone he had known all his life. He trusted Mosher completely. "As usual, you have given me something to think about, Moshe."

"Glad I could help."

"You always do, my friend, you always do."

"So w-what do we do now?"

"Not sure, but..."

The young warrior stretched out his hand. Calish, seeing what he wanted, gave the Crystallight stone to him. As soon as it was in the warrior's palm, the gem started glowing, much more than usual. A moment later, Calish could sense that the Minthuru gem, within his other pouch, was vibrating. So he retrieved it.

"Are you s-sure we should show father Korah's stone to him?"

"No, but what choice do we have, Moshe?"

The Minthuru stone was vibrating enough to tell Calish that something had activated it. By chance he moved the stone closer to the young warrior and the Crystallight gem. The Minthuru stone started to vibrate more, and simultaneously it made a humming noise. Calish looked at Mosher, wondering what was happening.

"I think the two s-stones are linked, Calish. Maybe they are supposed to be closer. Try it." So Calish did, and the humming increased. "Is that a g-good thing?"

"I hope so."

"Me too."

The young warrior cocked his head at the humming sounds. "Glagisst."

"What does that m-mean?"

"It means 'gligatzz'. Don't you know?" mocked Calish, mispronouncing the warrior's word.

"Oh, okay, thanks for that."

The warrior then made a gesture as if to say *Come closer*. Calish looked at Mosher; Mosher looked at Calish. They both stared at the warrior and the warrior stared back. Calish and Mosher shrugged and took a small step forward. The warrior smiled; his teeth were a dark grayish black, and sharp like fangs. He was most fierce looking. He glanced briefly at Calish. Then the warrior focused his bulging black eyes on Mosher. Suddenly his slithering forked tongue came sticking out. Then of course, it jiggled.

"Sheol!" exclaimed Mosher, clearly dumbfounded by the weird sight.

Taking note of Mosher's choice of words, the warrior reacted by raising one of his eyebrows. But he did not speak to hearing the word 'Sheol', just yet. He also did not retract his tongue; seeing Mosher's shocked reaction somehow made him happy, so he added a few extra tongue wiggles for emphasis.

Mosher eventually tore his eyes from the sight to glance at Calish with astonishment. But his friend was ready. "I've already seen the wiggling tongue show. Now it's your turn. Surprise!"

"Thanks a b-bunch for warning me."

"That's what friends are for, pal." Calish reviewed Stenrak again. Noticing that the strange boy seemed keen on focusing his attention on Mosher, Calish said dryly, "I think he likes you."

"As what, d-dinner?"

"Be serious, Moshe."

"Okay, sorry." Mosher bowed his head at the young warrior. The creature graciously retracted his tongue and bowed back. Calish and Mosher smiled at that.

Because the group was now closer together, the humming stones got louder.

As they listened, Mosher asked, "Okay, now what?"

"I think we should move even closer." Calish stepped forward, holding the Minthuru stone in his right hand. The warrior held the Crystallight stone in a similar way.

"Here we go," said Calish.

Eventually the two stones met. There was a flash of intense light, and near to them a shimmering doorway of colors appeared. The three adventurers were amazed at the sight. The stone holders, most especially, were drawn to the doorway's mesmerizing appearance. They walked toward it slowly as if in a trance.

Before Mosher could object, they stepped through its threshold, side-by-side. All at once, everything was gone.

CHAPTER 21
The Meeting

"Where am I?" said one boy.

"I'm not sure," said the other boy. The two figures studied at one another, surprise etched on both of their faces.

"I know you," said the first boy.

The second boy answered, "I know you too." Then he became very pensive. "How... ah... how am I talking to you? Do you understand me?"

"Yes?'

"Where are we?"

The pair took in their surroundings. They were standing along a cliff's edge, high above a vast open landscape full of plains, valleys, mountains, bodies of water, and a big, expansive sky. The sun was up and everything appeared magical, brilliant and splendid.

"Do you know this place?" asked the second boy.

"No, do you?"

"I have never seen such a place, never in my wildest dreams, or visions."

The first boy reviewed the sights again. After scrutinizing some of the landscape's details, he reported, "This place is like Egypt in some ways, but there are strange differences."

"Like?"

"Well, first of all, the sun is wrong."

"The sun?" asked the second boy, clearly perplexed by the word.

"Yes." He pointed to the bright orb in the sky. "It is too small and not nearly as bright as it should be. And around it I see a funny mist that extends... well, it looks like it goes everywhere."

The second boy glanced straight into the sun; its brightness caused him to cover up his eyes and turn away. The first boy was about to question the other boy's strange response, but then a loud roaring could be heard. Both boys searched out the sound's source; at the same time they saw an enormous beast that roamed the valley beneath their spot. Its neck and tail were as long as a cedar tree and its round body was bigger than a small hill.

"And what is that?" asked the first boy, obviously surprised.

"That I know. We call it a Graxen beast."

"A what?"

"A Graxen," the second boy repeated. "I have only seen one alive before. I have seen their bones more often. But I have never seen one in a place like this."

"A place like what?"

"A place so open and bright. And a place with one of those." He pointed at the sun. "What did you call it? A sun?"

"Yes. And how come you don't know about that?"

"Because, well..."

Suddenly it dawned on both boys that they had skipped a few steps in their dialogue.

The first boy, with a sudden understanding, started piecing things together. "I... we were standing in the hidden place. I remember now. You and I held stones that touched. Do you remember?"

"Yes, I do now."

The first boy said, "There was a doorway we stepped through, there was a flash of light, and now we are here."

The second boy nodded in agreement. "You are the boy I gave our gemstone to. You brought with you another stone that I had never before seen."

"Yes, and you are the person who showed me how to get to the Crystallight caverns. You met me there in person, scared the Shishtu out of me, and then gave me a vision of where to meet you again."

The warrior bowed his head in acknowledgement. "I am Stenrak."

"I'm Calish. I don't know how, but somehow we are speaking the same tongue."

"It must be this place; this valley."

"Yes, Valley, that is a good name. I like it, Stenrak. How did we get here?"

They turned around toward where they heard a slight buzzing noise. A short distance away was the doorway of colors they had recently breached.

"Through that, I suppose," guessed Stenrak.

"What is it?"

"A product of the stones, I gather."

They both looked down and noticed that the stones were still in their hands.

Calish walked to the doorway and peered into its various surfaces. But he could not see much beyond broken slivers of swirling colors and shapes. He thought he could see, in one of the bizarre facets, his friend Mosher, but the image was distorted so much that he wasn't sure. "My friend Moshe must still be back there." He tried reaching into the wall, but something like a gentle force kept him from entering any further. He turned back toward Stenrak, wondering what to make of the situation.

Stenrak walked closer to Calish and extended his hand that held the gemstone. Once again, the humming noise increased. "I reason," said Stenrak, "that the only way back is to do what we did to get here."

"Well, before we try, I need to talk with you, Stenrak."

"Very well, proceed."

"My sister Bishtar has been taken by your people."

"Not by *my* people, Calish."

"I saw them. They, ah were just like you." Calish said this while indicating Stenrak's body. "Your eyes, everything about you. I am not sure, but to me you all look alike."

"I see you as being strange too, and similar to one another, but there are differences between your people. It is the same for us. The attackers might have looked like me, but that is where the similarity ends, I can assure you."

"Meaning what?"

"I imagine that in the world where you are from, what my people call the surface world, there are many tribes and many differences between those tribes, as well."

"Yes, there are many, and differences between them are just as many."

"It is the same for us, Calish. My people call themselves the Pon. My particular tribe calls itself the Helon. We have lived in the underworld since the time of the First Ones."

"The First Ones?"

"Yes, the first to enter the underworld; humans like you, who became Pon, like me."

"What? I do not understand?"

"It is a long story, my friend. Suffice it to say it was long ago. Many of my people do not believe it. We only know Pon. We only know the harsh reality of our dark world."

"How do you know of the surface world then?"

"Legends, stories, and on rare occasions, visions."

"Okay, but those things that attacked us, what..."

"They are called the Cult. They are led by an evil spirit we call Voice. My people have done war against Voice's Cult since time began. They are powerful, deadly, without mercy, and hard to kill."

"Why would they take my sister?"

"They only take those chosen by Voice, or those that they will feed upon."

Calish was suddenly very nervous upon hearing that bit of news. "Feed upon?" he asked excitedly, "What do you mean? Are they going to feed on Bishtar!?"

Stenrak was somewhat surprised by Calish's emotional reaction. For him the Cult's practices were well known and accepted as fact. Worrying about it was a waste of time. "I am sorry if you do not understand us, or them. Our worlds must be very different, because to us the Cult's ways are not surprising. When they go too far, we merely kill them, as much as possible."

"But Bishtar is my sister. I, *we* must..."

"I will say something to you now," interrupted Stenrak, "but know this... it might or might not elevate your anxiety concerning your kin."

"Bishtar is not just kin, she is my *twin* sister," interjected Calish.

"Very well. In any event, in my estimation Voice had the Cult take her for reasons other than a source of food. There were many adults present at the battle that would have provided much more meat than your sister. The Cult did take adults, so taking your sister was unnecessary. Voice wanted her for some other reason. Therefore, she must still be very much alive."

Calish thought about that. He was glad to hear the good news, but he still had questions. "Hey, wait a minute, how do you know about the adults being there?"

Stenrak paused. "Because, Calish, I was nearby as the battle raged."

"You were there?"

"I was."

"Well then, you saw them take her?"

"I did."

"Then you can help me find her."

Stenrak walked to the edge of the cliff, carefully calculating his response. He finally turned and offered, "If I help you, I must ask for something in return."

It suddenly occurred to Calish that Mosher had been right. People didn't just do good deeds without expecting something in return. Calish would have to remember to listen to Mosher more attentively. "Okay, name it."

"I want your... 'spear'. You call it a spear, yes?" asked Stenrak, surprised that he somehow knew the word.

Oh, is that all? Calish thought suspiciously. He didn't want to give up Asher's spear, but what choice did he have? Bishtar was his sister and saving her was all that really mattered. Without Stenrak's help, the task would not be possible. But giving up the greatest spear of all time was still tough. Beyond that, as Mosher had warned, the spear might be the first of many concessions. Calish hesitated, deep in thought.

When Calish did not answer, Stenrak added, "And there is more."

Oh great, there's more. I really need to listen to Moshe better. "Okay, what else?" voiced Calish somewhat skeptically.

"Your people are powerful fighters with weapons my people do not have. At first, when I encountered your people, I thought you to be frail and weak; your mind-speak abilities were obviously very limited. Our legends say your world is lush and soft. I thought you to be equally soft, your flesh smooth and your willingness to kill just as yielding. But after seeing your warriors battle the Cult, I realize I was wrong. You are brave, swift, very clever, and well organized."

"Ah, thank you, Stenrak, I guess."

"And I see in you, Calish, a future leader. So I ask for your promise."

"Go ahead."

"There will come a time when I will need allies, powerful ones. I ask you to be those allies."

Luckily Calish had an easy answer for that promise. "You have done much for us, Stenrak, there is no doubt. I am not my people's leader, but if one day I do become one, then I will grant your request."

"And the spear?"

Calish knew he had to answer. Fortunately, deal-making was a skill-set well known to his people. Thinking quickly, he came up with a fair compromise. "You get the spear only after I have done something very important with it."

"That, my friend, Calish is a very open-ended proposition. It might take a lifetime to fulfill."

It looks like deal-making is well within your skill-set too, realized Calish. "No, what I have in mind is very specific, and I will not wait a lifetime to see it."

"Ah, I see," responded Stenrak knowingly. "It is a mighty weapon that has only one purpose. Therefore I can perceive that you intend to use it to kill someone. An enemy, and a powerful one at that. A mighty weapon to take down an equally powerful prey."

"You could say that, Stenrak, you could say that. The spear is yours as soon as my use for it is done."

Stenrak nodded graciously. "Then we are in agreement?"

"We are."

"And your companion, how can I assess his cooperation with our deal?"

"Do not worry, Stenrak. His name is Mosher. I call him Moshe for short, and he can be trusted completely."

Stenrak nodded his understanding. Then he thought about something. "Moshe stared at me strangely and then spoke to you."

185

"Well, to us, you look... odd."

Startled a bit, Stenrak retorted, "It is good to know we have so much in common."

"How so?"

"To me, you are just as... odd." Stenrak curled up his lips, bore his sharp teeth, and stuck out his pointy black-forked tongue. Then he started hissing. "Hiss-ss, hiss-ss, hiss-ss."

Even though Stenrak's behavior was alien, Calish had to take the hissing sounds as something akin to humor. *Pon humor,* he reasoned. So Calish quizzically smiled, while leveling a raised eyebrow, especially after seeing Stenrak continue to stick out his jiggling, wiggling snake-like tongue.

"But I don't look at you like Moshe. No, I don't think you're odd looking, Stenrak. No way."

Following suit, Stenrak replied, "And I think you look as normal as I do, my friend."

At that comment, both boys started laughing in their own unique way.

After a few moments, Calish asked, "Shall we then proceed to rescue my sister?"

"I am ready, my surface-dwelling friend."

Just before they clasped together their stones and entered the shimmering doorway, Stenrak stated, "Calish, I don't know the exact place she is being held."

Calish took on a serious expression, brought his stone to touch Stenrak's gem, and declared, "Don't worry, I do."

* * * *

The rescue party traveled through dark, often tight tunnels, following Stenrak's lead. Although there were many passageways, Stenrak eventually chose one that brought them closer to their target. He often made his decision after conferring with Calish as to the general direction. Calish didn't know the specifics of which tunnel was best. All he knew was what his gut was telling him: pointing left, right, up or down. Stenrak took it from there.

Mishtas, speaking of the strange being they followed, whispered, "How does he know which path to take? They all look the same to me."

As they closed in on yet another three-pronged fork in tunnel directions, Mosher answered, "He sees in the darkness, m-much better than us, Uncle. This is his w-world. And we have been a witness to his other powers."

The group then stopped and started peering into the three dark and mysterious tunnel choices set before them.

Stenrak hesitated, as if he was unsure as to the best option. Once again it was Calish that was sure of the correct path. "She is this way," he said, while pointing out a particular tunnel. "I can hear her." He pushed forward his lantern, but the small light did little to illuminate the area.

Stenrak similarly positioned his Crystallight stone toward the tunnel Calish had pointed to. His gem provided more greenish light, but it still did not help very much. Stenrak, not really needing the added light, did it more for his human companions. Nonetheless, it was clear that the path was leading downward.

From first glance it looked like there was enough room for all four travelers to navigate side-by-side, if they squeezed up close together.

"I do not hear anything," responded Mishtas, cocking his ear as if he should hear something.

"I hear Bishtar in here, Uncle," answered Calish while pointing to his head.

"Is she far?"

"She is near, very near. We must be quiet." Calish glanced up at the man respectfully. "Uncle."

"Yes, Calish."

"I want to thank you for coming with us, and for accepting Stenrak, our new friend." He gestured to Stenrak and smiled.

Stenrak, knowing he was being discussed, peered at Mishtas, cocking his head in the process. The Crystallight's green glow made Stenrak's pale face and bulging black eyes even more bizarre and unsightly. Mishtas took it in, swallowed hard, and tore his eyes away from Stenrak to look at Calish and Mosher.

187

"You, Mosher and Bishtar are my kin," Mishtas declared. "Korah charged me with your care. Besides, Hannah knew you boys were up to something. She came to me and I could not refuse her. I could not stop those beasts from taking Bishtar at the altar, but I'll be damned if I will let them hurt her."

"And as far as your 'friend' is concerned, I trust your instincts, Calish. And Korah told me that you boys know things. Things that have kept our people alive, so I am fine with Stenrak here." Mishtas braved another glance at Stenrak and shyly smiled.

Stenrak acknowledged the smile by producing his own fang-filled grin. Through his sharp black teeth one could see his pointy forked tongue wiggling here and there. Luckily for Mishtas, Stenrak kept the snake-like probe in his mouth.

"Yikeshtu," Mishtas voiced in surprise. His smile quickly turned into a wide-eyed, one brow raised expression of disbelief. Somehow he managed to not express how odd Stenrak was. He did, however, quizzically glance at the boys, and they surely knew what was on his mind.

"We know, Uncle, we know," responded Calish dryly. "We've both seen the tongue show."

Mosher, returning to the original subject, voiced thankfully, "It is g-good to know we have an adult with us. I trust Calish and Stenrak, but I too am glad you are h-here, Uncle."

Upon hearing the words, Mishtas took his eyes off of Stenrak while patting Mosher warmly on the shoulder. He then gripped his bow tighter, retrieved an arrow from his quiver, and loaded the weapon. "I am not a soldier, but I am an accomplished hunter. I was unprepared at the altar for the attack. I will not let that happen again."

Mishtas noticed the object Stenrak had tied to his belt. The horned thing was hard to miss. It made Mishtas curious as to how it came to be. Beyond being a hunter, Mishtas was an expert herdsman, so the item was very familiar to him, regardless of the Crystallight's greenish light that made it look almost as strange as the person wearing it. "And where did he get that? I'm sure Gasheer never gave it to him."

The boys and Stenrak followed suit to review the object in question. Stenrak covered it with his free claw as if to say it was his and no one should have any thoughts of taking it. His grin disappeared and his facial expression took on a protective stare.

Calish nodded knowingly to Stenrak. The Pon warrior relaxed, and Calish began his explanation. "Uncle. Moshe and I kind of met Stenrak soon after we fell to this underworld."

"Kind of, meaning?"

"Moshe and I were chasing a lost goat. We encountered a wolf that had caught it. We fought the wolf and killed it. Somehow Stenrak was there in the shadows watching us, and helping us." Calish and Moshe exchanged meaningful glances. Calish continued. "Later, Moshe and I realized that Stenrak had used his mind-powers to help us defeat the wolf."

"So did you meet him then or not?"

"No, not really. We, or I, sensed that he was there, in the darkness, but we never saw him until later on."

"Then how did he get the goat's head? Did you give it to him?"

"Stenrak here is most resourceful, Uncle. While our backs were turned, he took it. He ate the goat and as you see, he kept the skull for some reason."

"And look," furthered Moshe, "he has r-removed the lower jaw, and hollowed out the skull."

"You mean he ate its brains," summarized Calish.

Stenrak, seeing that his companions were curious but not covetous toward his fist-shield, took it up and squeezed three of his claws from the base of the skull and through the eye sockets. He then swung the object around and struck a nearby wall, very hard. The skull's horns bounced off the stone solidly, without breaking. Stenrak turned back toward them with a proud expression, and a large grin on his face.

"A shield or battering club then?" quizzed Mishtas.

The boys shrugged, as if unsure.

Stenrak, seeing that he had an audience, proceeded to pretend he was fending off an invisible attacker by jostling the skull to and fro and waving the horns back and forth. Then, in a sudden burst of speed, he hit another nearby wall, punching it very hard again. *Crack!* The sound echoed along the tunnel corridors, albeit a bit too loudly.

"Both, u-uncle," Mosher stammered after flinching from Stenrak's violent demonstration.

"Sshshh," whispered Calish while cocking his ear in a certain direction. "Listen."

They did so.

Mosher could barely make out soft, moaning noises. The sounds filtered their way up through the dark tunnels, echoing back and forth, much like Stenrak's skull strike. The creatures, the Cult, were close. The groans they made were an unmistakable sound, and most likely were tied into the cracking sound they had just heard.

Mosher whispered anxiously, "They m-might have been alerted." He swallowed hard, thinking of how those brutes would tear him apart like they did to others at the altar.

Calish saw the worried expression on Mosher's face, but he held firm. "Do not fear, Moshe, I am with you. Be ready."

"I am," Mosher replied. But in his gut, Mosher was far from it.

The rescue party studied one another carefully. When everyone nodded in the affirmative, albeit Mosher somewhat hesitantly, they entered the chosen tunnel slowly, as quietly as their feet would allow. After turning around a corner, they could see a distant opening ahead of their position. At the farthest end of the tunnel there was a small light source.

Calish pointed. "Down there."

Stenrak glanced at him, nodding in agreement.

"There must be Crystallight stones in there, where Bishtar is, or at least a few of them, anyway."

"Good," said Mishtas, "Then we will be on an equal footing if we engage the beasts."

They gingerly moved forward. After traveling a short distance, Mosher's foot bumped into something. "What is that?"

Stenrak brought his gem closer, lighting up a lumpy form on the cavern floor. They all surrounded the shape, curiosity on everyone's brow. Most of the figure was covered with fine fibers, but there were parts underneath it that could be seen. There were whitish bones protruding out of the filaments. They bent down to examine it. Beneath the threads was some kind of body.

Mishtas used his bow to push aside more of the fibers. "It is sticky," he commented, while forcing the stringy stuff from the body's head.

"Look at the skull." replied Calish. "It is... or was, a Pon, long dead."

"See the rib cage," furthered Mishtas, "the bones are crushed inwards. It has been punctured with a great force. What on earth could have done such a thing?"

Stenrak suddenly sniffed into the air, wrinkling his nose. His thoughtful expression quickly shifted into one of fright as he turned to face Calish and Mosher. *Mestalor!* Stenrak screamed in mind-speak, but the humans did not understand. "Mestolar!" hissed Stenrak, out loud this time. With the horned skull he pushed the others to take steps back.

"What's he saying? What's he saying?" they asked hurriedly to one another.

"I don't know." "Don't k-know!" Mosher replied.

But before long they could see what Stenrak feared. From an adjacent ceiling corner, something moved. It was dark, almost as dark as the corner itself, but it was clearly alive. Stenrak, thinking quickly, flung his gem at the object. The illuminated jewel landed near enough to the thing that its silhouette was better seen. After a moment, parts of the object became clearer: it was large and there were many legs... long, nimble and bent at strange angles. The thing then sprang to life, came out from its niche and skittered along the cavern ceiling as if weightless.

"Oh sh-shi-shtu!" said Mosher.

There was no time to retreat; the large crawling thing was soon to be upon them. With his free claw, Stenrak readied his hammer. Calish held up Asher's spear. Mosher, with shaking hands, took out his sling and readied a stone within it.

Mishtas yelled, "Duck!" They did. Mishtas quickly pulled back the arrow with all his might and let it fly right at the beast's head. It missed the head, but struck the beast squarely in the bulky upper abdomen. The creature screeched so loudly that they had to cover their ears. The thing dropped to a place right in front of them, clicking its pincers madly and jostling its sightless, bulbous eyes to and fro.

191

Stenrak leapt into action, wildly swinging his stony hammer, striking the creature's front limbs and dancing out of the way as the monster lunged at him. Forward went the creature's legs, grabbing and reaching; in and out of its maw flew its spiky, hard-shelled fang, but Stenrak used his fist-skull to block the monster's lurching appendages. But the creature was large, much larger than Stenrak, so the monster sprang forward again, too close, and had Stenrak backed into a tunnel wall.

The monster poked out its singular fang again and again. *Clack! Clack! Clack!* it sounded after hitting the skull's horns. And Senrak's quick reactions deftly shielded his body against the poking projectile each time.

"Sheol," he voiced anxiously. The monster's thorn came forth but this time it struck the skull too hard, knocking the shield free from Stenrak's grip.

"Striggitzz!" Stenrak shouted, as he watched his shield fly into the tunnel's furthest, darkest crevices. The creature then extended its front legs toward Stenrak.

Mishtas let loose another arrow just as one of the creature's long legs grabbed onto Stenrak's foot, knocking him flat to the ground. But then the arrow sank into the beast, hitting it squarely on its front section. The beast recoiled enough to let Stenrak yank his leg free. The Pon warrior scrambled to his feet and quickly joined the others.

Mosher, while whipping his sling in a mad frenzy, looked at Calish. When Calish gestured, Mosher let loose his stone. It struck the beast very hard in one of its protruding bulbous eyes, splitting the fleshy thing into bits and pieces. The creature shrieked again and quickly lurched toward Mosher. But Calish was ready. He set his feet firmly on the cave floor and held tightly to the spear's shaft. As soon as the beast was close enough, Calish let the beast's momentum meet the spear's sharp, pointy end. The blade penetrated into the beast's open maw, pushing past its fangs, and squishing its way down the creature's throat. The monster jerked in response and jostled to break free. But Calish held on to his spear regardless of being pushed and pulled by the bucking creature.

Meanwhile, Stenrak jumped up and on top of the monster, straddling his legs and feet over the beast's front section, while facing the back end of it. Instantly, his hammer delivered crushing wounds to the creature's upper abdomen, most especially where Mishtas' arrows had already penetrated the creature's tough hide.

Mishtas quickly grabbed Asher's spear, buttressing Calish's efforts. The monster's pincers stabbed out at Calish and Mishtas, but they managed to stay just out of the creature's reach. The beast tried to poke its long pointy fang at Mishtas.

Just before it could hit him, Stenrak jumped up and spun around, while gracefully balancing himself on top of the creature's head. Immediately he sent his hammer crashing down at the creature's fang, smashing the thing's outer shell and causing it to bleed out all kinds of strange, smoldering liquids.

Stenrak didn't stop. Like a whirlwind, the Pon warrior took his mighty hammer and pounded it up and down on the creature's head, mercilessly beating the creature's eyes and skull to a bloody pulp. Eventually the beast started to sink lower and lower. After one giant blow, the creature collapsed, motionless, except for the gooey juices that continued to flow from all its open wounds.

Stenrak jumped off the Mestalor's back. He landed in front of the humans. His eyes were on fire. Exhilarated from his efforts, Stenrak's chest heaved in and out while sucking air. He studied the dead Mestalor, and looked wildly about for something else to destroy. He then feasted his bulging black eyes on Mosher.

"S-Shi-shtu," gasped Mosher as he took a step back. Thinking he was next, Mosher scooted behind Mishtas. Stenrak angrily eyed him too, but Mishtas did not flinch. He did, however, raise his bow in a defensive gesture.

Just before Stenrak raised his bloody hammer, Calish put his hand on Stenrak's shoulder. Stenrak turned on him, ready to fight, but Calish stood his ground, staring back and refusing to be intimidated. "No, Stenrak," Calish said aloud. In a calm yet forceful way, he said, "Friend. We are friends."

Suddenly, in his mind, Calish felt that his words were somehow being understood by Stenrak's mind too. Stenrak confirmed the notion by tilting his head in a way that said he had experienced a communication that went beyond hearing. Stenrak relaxed his striking arm slightly.

Good enough, thought Calish. In any event, for the time being Stenrak had been distracted from killing Mosher. *Whew, that was a close one.*

Then Calish noticed thin hairy spikes sticking out of Stenrak's skin. It was quite obvious and impossible to miss. The strange hairs were all over him. He tried to touch one and Stenrak flinched, as if it hurt very badly. Calish went to pull one free, but was stopped.

"No!" cried Mishtas as he stepped closer. "Do not touch them. The hairs must be from the dead creature, and will not come out easily. See, look closely." And the boys did. Luckily, Stenrak, who appeared to be growing angrier by the moment, let them come very close. "The hairs are barbed, and will not come out easily."

"What do w-we do then?" asked Moshe, clearly concerned, and still frightened that Stenrak would take his anger out on him.

The trio peered into Stenrak's eyes with compassion. He returned their gaze. But there was also a vengeful, unquenchable purpose inside the Pon warrior. Stenrak huffed, puffing up his chest to full capacity. He appeared to be even more exhilarated by the pain, as if it was fuel to a raging, burning anger that could not be stopped.

Calish took in Stenrak's demeanor and declared, "We direct his anger at our enemy." He pointed to the place where Bishtar was, and by force of will got Stenrak to turn there as well. "Stenrak, we go there," expressed Calish meaningfully.

"Hissss, Hisssss." Stenrak spit in ire at the place in question. He then moved into the tunnel and picked up his Crystallight stone. With venom in his eyes, the highly agitated, spike-punctured Pon warrior set out toward the cavern entrance, screaming in his mind, *The Cult lair. Destroy... Kill!*

Calish suddenly cocked his head as if he could hear something.

"W-What is it?" asked Mosher.

"I think I hear Stenrak in my mind. It sounded like he said, 'Cult lair, destroy, or kill.'"

Mishtas neatly answered, "Then let's follow."

Mishtas and Calish pulled Asher's spear out of the dead creature's maw, grabbed up the still shaken Mosher, and followed their very angry Pon friend down the tunnel. Stenrak's bloody hammer swung back and forth, sometimes striking the tunnel walls, causing sparks to fly. He was ready to crush anything in his path.

"S-Shi-shtu. Here we g-go."

But before Stenrak could completely enter the lair's spaces, Calish caught up and stopped him. Calish raised his finger to his mouth, and voiced, "Shhhh".

Luckily, the heated Stenrak obeyed, barely.

Calish turned to his companions, whispering, "Something is happening!" Just as he spoke, from the lair's area they could hear shouts, and the sound of clashing bodies. Through the clamor they could then hear a forceful, deep-throated command ordering, "Kill them all!"

"That's Gasheer," hushed-out Mishtas. "He's here!"

Soon thereafter, they heard the unmistakable sound of Gasheer's whip. *Snap! Snap! Snap!*

After each snap there was a corresponding yelp from the creature that had just been viciously attacked.

The trio of humans looked at one another, knowing full well what the sound meant.

Mosher most especially reacted to the sounds, fearfully jerking from each whip-cracking echo. Calish noticed it and braced Mosher's shoulder to comfort him. Mosher searched out his friend's eyes and found both sympathy and great strength.

Calish's confidence worked; Mosher's face changed from fear to resolve.

"Are we ready?"asked Calish. The group viewed one another, excitedly and resolutely.

Then Mishtas added, "At least we are not alone. Gasheer and his men are with us." Following Stenrak's lead, who could wait no longer, the rescue party rushed into the fight.

More shouts came from Gasheer's soldiers as they took on the Cult. Bodies collided, claws reached out, scratching and ripping at Gasheer's soldiers as they in turn swung their swords feverishly at the slower moving Pon monsters.

Calish and company stood off in a corner, assessing the situation. For the moment they were ignored by the combatants. Calish's intention was finding Bishtar; he looked wildly about, searching for her, but she could not be seen. He also tried to hold back Stenrak, but the young warrior could not be contained.

Stenrak broke from Calish's grip. Even though he was smaller than any of the Cult, he flew into the battle, swinging his hammer at any Cultist that was within reach. In a blaze of motion, he swung the club, striking blows all over their naked bodies, causing the Cultists to shriek in pain. They lurched at him, but Stenrak was far too swift for them, as he danced away, back and forth, in between, and under their flailing claws.

"Where is she?" asked Mishtas hurriedly, obviously shaken by the carnage.

Calish studied the area again. Then his eyes focused on one particular spot. "She's in there." Calish pointed with his spear at an alcove, not far from where they stood.

"Where?" asked Mishtas, "All I see are solid walls."

"There, see in that dark alcove."

Just then a Cultist appeared at the alcove's entrance. This one was clearly the biggest Pon specimen, and different from the others. He held a long-handled sharp club and he wore a distinct necklace made of bones. There was a strange scar across his face and one of his eyes was badly damaged. With the remaining eye he scanned the raging battle before him, but did not enter it.

Mosher stuttered, "That one-eyed m-monster is guarding Bishtar. He does not m-move from his spot."

Mishtas prompted, "He is the one who fought Gasheer at the altar. See that necklace of fangs around his neck, the huge scar that crosses his face, and his broken eye. Gasheer could not best him."

Yes, One Eye is the Cult's leader," stated Calish. "We must get past him."

"B-But how?" asked Mosher nervously.

"Together, we will."

They all knew what to do. Mishtas readied his bow; Mosher his sling, and Calish his spear. Then they carefully skirted around the battle, along the cave wall, trying to avoid interfering with Gasheer's men as they took on the Cultists.

Stenrak, seeing what they were doing, quickly moved to create interference for any loose Cultist that made a move to attack the trio, swinging his hammer at them, and jumping out of the way before the lunging beasts could scratch their hungry claws at him.

But Stenrak didn't see all of the Cultists; one of them snuck up behind him. Just as the creature sank a claw into his back, an arrow caught Stenrak's attacker squarely in the throat. The arrow sank clear to the backside of the Cultist's neck. The creature gurgled out a muffled moan and released itself from Stenrak, who quickly turned to see who had sent the arrow. It was Mishtas, who was already adding another arrow to his bow. Stenrak nodded to Mishtas, who nodded back.

"Let's keep going," prompted Mishtas. But it was not easy. Too many Cultists and humans were battling it out in front of them, slowing their progress.

Meanwhile, Gasheer was busy finishing off another Cultist. *Snap! Snap!* With even more force... *Snap!* The whip tore the Cultist to pieces; open cuts crisscrossed the Pon's bloodied body. The Cultist danced and jerked from each blow. Gasheer threw out his whip again, but this time using it to deftly wrap its tether around the cultist's throat. Gasheer neatly pulled him in like he was a rag doll. The huge man grabbed the Cultist's elbows and twisted them so hard that the monster's arms snapped out of their sockets. Not bothering to kill his foe completely, Gasheer tossed the damaged Cultist aside, because there was something more important that had suddenly piqued his interest.

"Ahah!" Gasheer exclaimed excitedly, as he noticed One Eye standing there all alone, watching the battle. Gasheer moved in on One Eye's spot. He quickly tied up his whip and unsheathed his sword. He banged the blade hard against his chest's brass armor, grunting like a bull. He then held the blade out and readied his posture to engage in battle. With spittle streaming out, Gasheer croaked, "Now we will finish what we started, snake beast!"

One Eye hissed in response, sticking out his long, forked tongue in the process. Then he too banged his club against his bare chest. One Eye focused a mind-speak message to Voice.

Master, we need you. After that, the Cult leader stepped out of the alcove to meet the large surface dweller.

Voice, through its mental link with the Telek, was drawn out of its sleepless void. The spirit instantly found its way up through the numerous layers of Father's sphere to the Cult lair. Voice hovered above the scene, assessing what needed to be done. The big human was on to Telek, so Voice decided to help its Cult leader.

Stop that big one! shouted Voice to some nearby Cultists.

Two of them stopped their efforts at fighting soldiers and moved in on Gasheer, forcing the giant to stop advancing on One Eye to deal with them instead. The Cultists ripped their claws against Gasheer's armor, but their efforts were wasted; the claws merely made clinking noises as they scratched at the shiny brass surfaces. Gasheer popped his eyes in anger, and proceeded to chop them open with fierce thrusts from his double-edged sword. He sliced apart their pale-skinned bodies down to the bone. But the Cultists kept coming: hissing, screeching, moaning, bleeding, and flailing away at their giant oppressor.

"Come closer, you dogs! Feel my wrath!" Gasheer reveled in the killing, grunting out sounds that were mixed with fevered exultations. As his mighty sword hacked his foes into disjointed body parts, Gasheer bellowed, "Sons of Cain! Snakes of Sheol! I cast you to Amheh's lake of fire!"

One Eye could not help but stand back and watch Gasheer fight off his attackers so fiercely and adeptly. His one eye was fixated on the surface-dwelling behemoth. The human was most impressive. It was mesmerizing, it was . . .

"Blood Vein," One Eye mumbled. Unexpectedly, the scar that ran across his face started to throb, sending its hot blood throughout his body and brain. One Eye's thoughts wandered, and meandered some more. Then suddenly he saw images flash in his mind. There were strange creatures, enormous beasts, and powerful warriors. He saw himself battling them, destroying their bodies, dispatching his foes into bloody pieces.

"Mestalor!" he screamed involuntarily. A giant one. The beast had grabbed him up, pulling him closer to its fang-filled maw. It was chomping its cruel mouth, salivating profusely, wanting hungrily to consume him. He fought the drag with every ounce of his strength, holding firm to the monster's limbs, pushing them away. The creature's pincers started feeling at him up and down, so he changed tactics and grabbed the monster's forceps, forcing them closed, covering the creature's mouth. The thing pulled him right over its head, but could not chew at him because of it. So the monster pulled on him more; his back ached from resisting its multiple legs. The nimble and strong appendages had surrounded him, they were everywhere, and they were tugging and twisting him this way and that way. Nonetheless, he kept fighting.

Suddenly the heavy beast lifted him up, and slammed him flat to the hard, cavern floor.

"Uomphhh!!" He sighed as the wind was knocked from his lungs. *It is over,* he thought. He could finally find peace in Sheol. *Let the beast feed on me.* But for some reason, he resisted. With his last bit of strength, he tore one of the pincers free from its mooring; he quickly turned it around and plunged the sharp, spiky thing into the monster's tiny ear canal, pushing past hard matter and then soft, mushy stuff. In a flash, the creature's eyes twitched nervously and flopped solidly down upon its small head. The creature's many legs lost their grip on him and the beast gradually sank on top of him... dead, but still crushingly heavy.

He gasped for air. He was still face-to-face with his opponent; its acrid smelling saliva was hard to avoid, but he was so desperate that he didn't care... he sucked for air anyway.

He went to push himself free from his captor, and suddenly the dead creature, out of instinct, threw out its last weapon. The monster's pointy fang flew out of its mouth, piercing his left eye. "Aahh!" he bellowed and pulled his head back. But the damage had been done. The fang's acidic juices burned up what remained of his eye's flesh; he tried to scratch the hot liquid away, but his eye continued to smolder and burn. There was mind-numbing pain, he roared again and lost consciousness.

His one eye opened. He heard crowds cheering very loudly. He looked around; he was standing and the crowd was all around him. They were cheering him! There was a mighty King who stepped in front of him. The King's son, whom he had saved from the giant Mestalor, stood close by. The King, *his* King, was there watching proudly as a Maana master placed a purple, pulsing vein across his face, and around his broken eye. He felt the bloody artery sink into his flesh, becoming one with him, making him stronger and more alive. He gazed into his King's noble eyes and was suddenly reminded of who he once was: *I was a great warrior... My name was Telek, First to King Sto . . .*

But before Telek could complete the memories, Voice sent a piercingly searing pain into his brain. Telek recoiled from it. Then Voice, while Telek's agony was still very present, interjected loudly: *Telek, never mind what you are thinking, do as I say. Attack!*

Telek blinked his one good eye. In an effort to eliminate the anguish, he tried to shake his head clear of any glimmer of independent thought. Nonetheless, regardless of the pain, some memories lingered, but they were just out of reach. But strong emotions remained, stifling his mind, restricting his range of motion. Like a statue, he moved forward, stiffly. Telek's pain receded, but something still held him back because he did not take on the giant human. Only confusion ran across his scarred, heavily wrinkled, throbbing face. He droned incoherently, "Who am I?"

"Now's our chance," said Calish, noticing One Eye's strange behavior. Calish took off and rushed to the alcove. Stenrak and Mosher followed, while Mishtas took up the rear, watching for any threat from behind them. But One Eye was suddenly in front of them, blocking them all, readying his club to crush them. They backed up a little, looking for a way past the huge monster.

Voice, seeing the group trying to rescue Bishtar, said, *Telek, do as I say. Grab the girl; threaten to kill her.*

While Telek started to turn back and re-enter the alcove, Voice spoke directly to a few nearby Cultists. *Stop the humans, now! Kill them all. Start with that son of Storn. He is there, helping the humans. Pon traitor. Kill that Pon child!*

Telek cocked his head, listening to Voice's instructions. While scrutinizing the enemies all around, he became more puzzled. *Who am I? Who do I fight?* Then he slowly turned toward Bishtar. Telek gazed into Bishtar's eyes and stopped.

Bishtar stared at him as well, but her glare was on a different level. It was filled with hate, determination… yet also with understanding, because she too could hear Voice talking. Regardless, she had had enough.

Telek, Voice commanded, *what are you waiting for? Grab the girl now!*

Telek reached for her.

"Do not touch me, Telek!" she shouted out loud. For the first time, Bishtar mind-spoke just as intensely. She then twisted her small, clawed hand into a ball and brought out her powers, directing them at the one-eyed monster hovering over her. She could see, feel, and move the elements within Telek's body, and by tightening her grip, she could likewise strangle his insides. The floating lamb was nothing compared with what she could do with Telek's innards.

Telek started shaking. He bent over, his bowels twisting in knots, causing such pain that bits of feces dropped free from his already stained and tattered loin cloth. He slowly brought up his sad, agonized eye to meet Bishtar's. Then, in a subtle way, Telek lowered his head in a sign of submission to her authority. Bishtar smiled cruelly upon seeing Telek frozen there, unable to peal his one-eyed gaze away from her.

Telek, you fool! screeched Voice. *Do As I command you!*

But Telek was not Voice's any longer. He now had a new master.

Voice, seeing that it was losing control of the situation, decided to take over a nearby Cultist's body. By sending its spirit-essence inside the Cultist's pliable mind, Voice could inhabit and control any of its Cultists. Once inside the Cultist's body, Voice went at Bishtar. *If I cannot have you, my dear, then no one will!*

But Telek, who was aware of Voice's methods, was ready to stop the advancing Cultist. He looked at Bishtar and she knew what he wanted. She quickly released him from her powers. Telek turned around and blocked the Cultist before he could reach her. He stood toe-to-toe with Voice's Cultist and readied his club.

The two Pon grabbed at one another. They tore into each other, claws and teeth ripping at anything they could find. When an opening occurred, Telek used his club to beat the Cultist bloody,

201

bashing his shoulders, arms, or hip. Telek was too strong, swift and fierce for his opponent. The Cultist was very soon becoming too damaged to continue fighting.

Telek, stop hitting us! The only thing keeping the bloodied Cultist upright was Voice's control over the flailing body. But eventually the Cultist was drifting back, further with each bashing blow, falling lower and lower. *Telek, you traitorous slime-bug!*

Meanwhile, Gasheer finished off his opponents, swatting the last of them with his beefy fist, roaring loudly in the process. He turned back toward the alcove and was taken by surprise. Strangely, his main adversary was fighting another Cultist, thus leaving the girl unguarded. As he set his sights on Bishtar, an evil expression crossed his face. "Diseased daughter of a traitor, it is your time." Gasheer moved in on Bishtar, his sword at the ready.

Calish, Mishtas, Mosher and Stenrak were busy fighting their way past more of the fray, when Calish saw what was happening. Calish yelled in disbelief, "Gasheer, what is he doing?!" But as he started to go to his sister, another Cultist stood in his path.

Stenrak saw it and he quickly engaged the Pon monster who was blocking Calish. Calish, in a burst of speed, then dodged his way past them, running like mad at the man mountain.

"No!" shouted Calish at Gasheer. He rushed at Gasheer with Asher's spear, directing it at the giant's body. But Gasheer pushed his sword at the spear's point, sending the weapon out of Calish's grip and to the cave floor. Gasheer side-armed Calish, pushing him hard at a cavern wall. Calish took the blow, and then sank to his knees in pain.

While Mishtas was busy fighting off one of the Cult, battering the thing with his bow, Mosher ran to Calish's side.

"Moshe," cried Calish, "I cannot stop him."

Both boys looked up at Gasheer, who was grinning at their feeble rescue attempts.

Gasheer turned again at Bishtar. Eager to finish his task, he took some heavy steps toward her. Bishtar stared up at Gasheer, terrified of his motives. She tried to direct her powers at the giant, but taming Telek had left her weak. She raised her claws at Gasheer, but could not see or feel his insides. Powerless, she could do nothing but back up into the cavern niche and cover her face. Gasheer grinned broadly and raised his sword, ready to chop the girl in two.

Then, out of nowhere, Telek jumped onto Gasheer's back, savagely clawing at his arms, neck and anywhere else Gasheer's armor didn't protect. Gasheer yelped and grunted, taking in the wounds, but he was forced to drop his sword. Now, with his hand free, he grabbed Telek's wrists, stopping the Pon from doing further damage. Gasheer turned around, and in a display of awesome strength, lifted Telek off the ground, shouting, "Wretched creature, I will rip you into a thousand pieces!"

But Telek wasn't done. In an equal display of sheer power, Telek broke one arm free from Gasheer's grip and sent his club across Gasheer's upper chest, hitting some of Gasheer's brass armor... hard. The armor held, but Telek's blow was strong enough to force Gasheer to release his hold and back up a few paces.

Gasheer was then compelled to assess his opponent once again. Telek hissed loudly at the huge human and raised his club, ready to do more damage.

Gasheer growled in kind, and quickly took up his sword again. The two warriors squared off, jostling for position, circling each other, like they had in the Crystallight cavern.

Was I seeing correctly? Voice wondered. *Is the huge human here to kill Bishtar?* The spirit was again hovering above the battle, having been forced to leave the Cultist's body it had inhabited because Telek's fierce blows had done too much damage.

Calish, now seeing a clear path, ran to Bishtar's side. She put her arms around his neck in a way that said she was glad to see him. He too held onto her to reciprocate the gesture. Their reunion, however, was short-lived.

They both watched as Gasheer shouted and feigned a sword attack at Telek. The Pon recoiled a bit, and Gasheer used his free hand to punch Telek in his one good eye. Telek shrieked in pain. Now temporarily blinded, Telek quickly moved off, slashing his club madly in an attempt to keep the human from further attacks.

But Gasheer had other intentions. He turned from the one-eyed beast and set his sights on the twins. "Ha, ha, ha," he laughed cruelly as he stepped toward them, salivating at the prospect of destroying his enemies. "Two for the price of one."

Calish quickly opened his pouch and retrieved the Minthuru stone. In a last-second act of desperation, he thrust the stone into Bishtar's hand. Suddenly a flash of blinding light escaped from the stone. The radiance cascaded throughout the lair's spaces, stunning all who looked upon it. Within an eye's blink, all motion began to slow to a crawl. Then it completely stopped.

But Calish and Bishtar were unaffected. They looked around, visibly surprised by what they were seeing. Everyone was frozen in place, mid-motion; arms, swords, claws, everything had stopped. Around each combatant there was a glowing band of transparent colors, vibrating and swirling its way over everything. It was dazzling, brilliant, and miraculous.

Even Gasheer, whose brutal face hovered over them, was frozen. The twins gazed at him, fearfully wondering if the giant was indeed still animated. But no, he did not move. Even his drool had stopped flowing in midair.

"El, be praised," whispered Calish.

"What is happening, Calish?"

"I do not know, Sister, but whatever it is, we must leave." They got up, and while still holding onto the Minthuru stone, gingerly made their way past the mountain known as Gasheer. Bishtar inadvertently started to remove her hand from the stone. "No, Sister, keep your hand on mine. We must not let go of the stone yet."

"Okay."

Seeing Mishtas and Mosher nearby, Bishtar asked, "What of them?" So the twins went closer.

Calish, unsure as to what to do, used his free hand and touched Mosher's shoulder. Like magic, the swirling colors evaporated around Mosher's body.

As if waking from a deep sleep, Mosher gradually opened his eyes. "What h-happened?" he asked Calish. But Mosher thereafter ignored his friend as soon as he took in Bishtar. Then his curious appearance turned into a glad one. He swiftly took up his small flask of water and offered it her. She drank from it and handed it back to him, smiling in thanks. Mosher latched it back on his belt, while never taking his eyes off of hers.

"Oh, no I wasn't thirsty, Moshe, don't worry about me," Calish snarked, "but thanks for thinking of me anyway."

Bishtar accepted Mosher's love-struck attention and returned his gaze with a kind and caring one of her own. The pair stood there watching each other, spellbound.

Calish rolled his eyes. "Okay, you two, back to business."

The trio went to Mishtas. This time Bishtar did the honors and tapped him on the shoulder. The man woke up and said, "Bishtar, Calish, Mosher! What has happened?" The children merely glanced at each other and shrugged.

Mosher finally said, "Don't worry. Uncle, w-we must leave."

Calish brought the group to Stenrak, but when Bishtar could see that her brother was about to nudge him, she cried, "Brother, what are you doing?"

"Don't worry, Bishtar, he is one of us."

Bishtar scanned the battle scene. She soon found Telek, mid-motion, still ready to attack Gasheer. She thought to herself, *So is he, so is he.*

Calish touched Stenrak and the Pon warrior woke up. Dazzled, he took them all in curiously. Stenrak then cast his gaze upon Bishtar. Noticing her very Pon-like features, a funny expression crossed his brow. Unintentionally, he mind-spoke. *Female, what are you?*

Then in his mind came a surprising answer: *I am this.* Bishtar, feeling energized once more, took her free hand and twisted her claws into a fist.

Stenrak felt it in his gut; a singe of pain that coiled-up his insides. He glowered at Bishtar, knowing it was her doing, but he refused to show it on his face. Pain and discomfort was Pon reality. Showing its effects to one's enemies was a sign of weakness, and something he would not let happen. So he returned her gaze stoically. By her actions, the human girl, the *Harsha,* had made it clear that she *was* an enemy.

"Hey, you too," interrupted Calish, "we need to go."

Stenrak and Bishtar broke their mental connection. Stenrak quickly looked away, relieved and now free from pain, while Bishtar continued to watch him out of the corner of her eye.

"W-Wait," said Mosher impulsively.

"What?"asked Calish.

Mosher cautiously circumnavigated the various combatants, most especially around Gasheer. He stopped very close to the mountainous man. He waved his hands at Gasheer's massively grotesque face, making sure the brute was still frozen. When the brute's eyes did not blink, Moshe took a swift kick to the man's shin. "Ouch," Mosher cried. Kicking solid stone might be softer than striking the giant. Mosher hobbled away to complete his task. Eventually he picked up two items and made his way back to his companions. But before returning, Mosher stopped again as he was about to pass by Gasheer, since he realized that the giant was bent over in a rather gluteus-vulnerable position. *Interesting.* He stared at one of the items he had picked up. *This too is interesting.* He took the object, which just so happened to be long and sharp, and summarily poked Gasheer very hard in the butt with it.

Boink. Everyone laughed. Even Stenrak hissed in enjoyment.

Mosher acknowledged his audience by holding up the device very high. To go along with their laughter, he boldly proclaimed, "Electrum, the finest m-metal in all the kingdom." Of course his companions laughed some more. When he got back to his group, Mosher gave the ceremonial butt-poker to Calish.

"Thanks, Moshe," Calish said happily as he took up Asher's spear.

"You're w-welcome."

Then to Stenrak, Mosher gave the second item. Stenrak bowed his head while admiring the gift. It was a beautifully made flint dagger.

"Where'd you get it?" asked Bishtar.

"A d-dead soldier, I'm afraid."

The group started travelling toward the same tunnel they had taken to enter the Cult's home. Once near the exit, seeing that their escape was assured, Bishtar and Calish stopped.

"Should we let go of the stone?" asked Bishtar.

Calish thought for a moment. "Once we do this, everything should return to normal, I'm guessing."

Bishtar released her grip on the stone. They looked around and the freezing effect was still in place, but after a few seconds the shimmering lights started to fade.

"It appears that the freezing takes time to dissipate," observed Mishtas.

"It should give us more time to make our escape," added Calish.

Mishtas asked, "Should we not stay, to help Gasheer fight those things?" He pointed at One Eye. "We should at least help him fight One Eye."

Bishtar corrected him coldly, "His name is Telek." There was something in the way she said the name that discouraged the group from questioning her any further.

"No, Uncle," replied Calish. He took in his sister, and she too nodded her head in the negative. "Gasheer is not to be trusted."

"I understand," said Mishtas. He turned toward the Pon. "And what of Stenrak? We might be able to remove the barbs."

They all scrutinized the Pon warrior and his new hairy spikes. Redness and swelling were now at the base of each one.

"It must hurt like Sheol itself," uttered Calish.

Stenrak took note of what they were discussing and made a dismissive gesture, as if to say *Such is life for a Pon.*

Mishtas offered, "It seems like Stenrak already knows what he must do to remove the spikes. His people must have ways of dealing with such things."

Even though Stenrak could not understand the words, he somehow gathered their meaning. He nodded to Mishtas as a sign of gratitude for his concern.

Calish interjected, "Okay, Uncle, then let us be on our way."

"Yes, my kin, let us return to our tribe, where we belong."

CHAPTER 22
The Return

"Gasheer, report." Dathan was seated in his grandly designed chair. He watched keenly as the titan approached. The man mountain stood before his master like a soldier should, straight and still. The giant had some bandages along his neck, but Dathan didn't really care, it was Gasheer's job to fight. A few scrapes here and there were to be expected.

"Our trackers, following the trail of the creatures, led us to their lair. We killed many of those things. One of my men was killed, one injured." Gasheer hesitated before saying, "But I was unable to kill the girl."

Dathan was visibly distressed to hear the bad news. "How were you able to track them?"

"Their droppings, mostly. Occasionally they left behind bits and pieces of our people they took from the altar, partially eaten along the way." Gasheer poked at his butt, rubbing it for some reason. Dathan noticed the gesture but decided to ignore it; Gasheer's personal hygiene, questionable though it might be, was his business.

"Cannibals then?" Dathan queried.

"Yes, my Lord."

"Barbaric."

"There is more."

"Tell me."

"Calish, that boy Mosher, and Mishtas were there. They were in league with one of those creatures. I clearly saw them defending each other, working together and..." Gasheer paused and buffed his behind once again. Dathan raised his eyebrow at the brute's odd movements.

"Go on," barked Dathan.

"Also, before the battle ended..."

"Yes, what is it?"

"I am unclear in this, but... they suddenly disappeared."

"Disappeared? Are you mad?"

"No, my Lord, I speak the truth. You can ask any of my soldiers who saw the same thing."

"Saw what exactly?"

"One second they were there, and another second they had vanished. Bishtar and Calish were right before my eyes... gone in a flash."

Dathan looked very unconvinced. "Magic?"

"I know not, but before it happened I saw Calish remove something, a glowing object, from his pouch."

"A glowing object that looked like what?"

"A stone."

"Stone?"

"Yes, my Lord, a glowing stone that I have never seen before. Calish brought it up to meet Bishtar's hand."

"Interesting in so many fascinating ways, my rather large friend."

"What does it mean, my Lord?" Once more Gasheer started stroking his derriere and wincing at the same time.

"It means, my dear fellow, that we have within our midst a gift of unparalleled proportions. A gift that will yield fortuitous and prophetic results. A gift that someone close to us has kept hidden since our fall from the world we once knew."

Gasheer's expression looked confused, but Dathan, seeing he was talking with a limited intelligence, stated, "Never mind. We will find a way to turn this to our favor. And we must try to find out what this object, this stone, is."

Gasheer, while seeming to listen, was still poking at his rear end. Dathan stood up, for he had had enough of Gasheer's butt-rubbing. He demanded loudly, "Why do you keep stroking your ass, Gasheer?"

Gasheer's face became sorrowful. "I know not, my Lord."

"Well, stop it this instant. It is most disturbing."

"Yes, my Lord." Gasheer promptly pulled his hand from his butt and brought it to his side nervously, like he really wanted to keep scratching.

"Most likely," summarized Dathan sarcastically, "your butt scrape, or whatever it is – and please do not tell me the details – is a phantom pain, much like the phantoms that mysteriously disappeared in the creature's lair... or so you claim."

"It is true, my Lord, they disappeared," Gasheer objected vehemently, "I swear it."

"Hrumpph," Dathan responded derisively.

He turned away because he could hear the clamoring sounds of many people approaching. Dathan, of course, expected the visit, so he put on his well-practiced smirk as he watched the large ensemble of folks approach his tent. Korah, Abiram, and their closest relatives were in front, leading the group.

Dathan walked forward to meet them, opened his arms, and took the first swing at commandeering the whole event. "Well, well, it appears that the gods are with us. We have done battle with our enemies and have prevailed, of course. And I see, Korah, that your lovely granddaughter is safely in our arms once again."

With gladness Korah gazed at Bishtar, who was at his side. Her expression was not pleasant as she glowered with hatred at Dathan.

"It is a sign, it is a great sign," blabbered Abiram. As he glowingly peered at Bishtar, Abiram spewed, "The gods are truly with us."

For her part, Bishtar stared back like only she could. Abiram quickly turned from her, visibly distressed at seeing her venomous, dark eyes.

Dathan advanced toward the group. "Gasheer, our brave defender, has returned your granddaughter, as I promised he would, Korah."

"Is that all that happened, Dathan?"

"What could you possibly mean?"

"My grandson tells me your man Gasheer tried to *kill* Bishtar."

Dathan turned to the hulking man and said with mock surprise, "Gasheer, my good fellow. Is this true?"

"It is not, my Lord. The boy is mistaken. He is unaccustomed to battle, and was blinded by the shock of it."

"You lie!" shouted Calish impulsively.

"Hurmpph," grunted Gasheer.

Dathan took that moment to interject. "It seems clear, Korah, that unbeknownst to me, your grandson and his friends apparently took it upon themselves to take an unsanctioned journey into finding Bishtar. Tell me, Korah, are there other secrets your people have kept from us?"

"Meaning?"

"Well, from what I understand, your little band of would-be warriors were accompanied by the very enemy my soldiers were fighting." Dathan directed his gaze upon Calish. "Tell me... tell *us*... are you in league with those creatures that sought to kill us at our altar worship?"

At that comment, many in the crowd gasped.

Calish was about to defend himself when Korah pushed him back. "Dathan, Calish has explained this to me. The person Gasheer saw is called Stenrak. His people are called the Pon. They look alike to us, but just as we have differences, so do they. Stenrak, and apparently his people, his tribe, are not the same as the creatures that attacked us at the altar. The altar attackers are of a different tribe altogether."

Taking on an air of haughty nobility, Dathan responded, "Interesting, but tell us why we should believe such a thing?"

Calish, unable to control himself, blurted out, "Because, if it were not for Stenrak, we would surely all be dead by now."

Visibly shaken by this, Dathan squared off and prepared his rebuttal. "Are you telling us that one of those creatures *saved* us? This is nonsense. Our gods Osiris and Isis have saved us."

Korah responded, "I will not speak to that... not now, at any event. But it was Stenrak that showed Calish how to find this Crystallight cavern; the place we are living in right now."

"How exactly did he do such a thing?"

"In a vision. Calish had a vision from Stenrak."

"In a vision?" voiced Dathan incredulously. "Stenrak. Stenrak?! No, my dear fellow, if there was any so-called vision, then it was not made manifest by one of those creatures. It was made real by Osiris and Isis. Claiming one of those Pon monsters did it is pure folly. And possibly even blasphemy."

Many in the audience spoke aloud in agreement.

Feeding upon the crowds' approval, Dathan said, "My friends, clearly our gods are the only ones that could have saved us.

Creatures... monsters, Pon, whoever they are, cannot have any power over the chosen. *We* are the chosen."

Once again there were more nods and sounds of union from the assembly.

"Tell me, Korah, are there any more secrets you have kept from your fellow tribesmen?"

"No."

Dathan smirked knowingly and turned again to Calish. "Then tell me, Calish, how could you have met with, and or communicated enough to conspire with, this Pon creature?"

Korah cut in, "Apparently Calish, to some degree that I do not fully understand, can communicate with Stenrak."

"Communicate how?"

"Through some kind of mental talking."

Dathan turned on Calish. "Is this true?"

Calish stood up and boldly answered, "I am able to understand him. Yes."

"And what does he want? Why help us, as you naively propose?"

Calish was careful to parse his words. "I am not sure, but for now Stenrak's people know about us. They are undecided as to what to make of us."

Korah added, "Like us, they are divided. There might be some who are in favor of us being here, and others opposed. Like the ones who attacked us."

"The attackers are not like Stenrak, or his people!" Calish said.

"*We*, young man," argued Dathan, "cannot take your word on that. If Stenrak belongs to a larger tribe, then it stands to reason that there might be some, or many, of his people that have ill will toward us."

That comment brought signs of agreement throughout the crowd.

"These Pon creatures are an unknown, and as such must be seen as a potential threat, to all of us." Dathan then faced Gasheer. "Post your soldiers at every cavern entrance."

"Yes, my Lord."

"We must ask for our god's help in this." Dathan turned to the crowd and raised his hands in authority. "For now, let us disperse while we take some time and come up with our future plans."

The assembly nodded in acquiescence and turned to go. As the crowd dissipated, Gasheer went to Calish. The two squared off, elephant to mouse. But the wiry little mouse showed no fear of the behemoth in front of him.

Gasheer went first. "My spear, whelp, return it now."

"What makes you think I have it?"

Gasheer angrily made a fist, then glanced at Mishtas, who was very near and ready to come to Calish's aid.

"Don't you remember?" said Calish cleverly, "It was you that knocked it from my grasp. If it is lost, then it is your fault, not mine."

"Grrr," groaned Gasheer. He was visibly perplexed because he was unable to counter Calish's logic. "Your time will come, pup."

"As will yours," stated Calish coldly.

Then Mishtas forcefully took Calish by the shoulder and led him from the scene.

After that, Dathan approached Gasheer. Seeing the hatred in the brute's eyes, he said, "Don't worry, my big friend, don't worry. The time will soon come when the tribe of Korah will vanish from our memories."

Gasheer grinned broadly while thinking of how he would carry out his brand of justice upon all of Korah's tribe. To Dathan's extreme consternation, Gasheer then began rubbing his butt one more time.

* * * *

"I was thinking..." Dathan said while sitting at his tent's entrance, drinking Maana tea, watching his people go about their normal routines. Gasheer stood by Dathan's side, making sure his Lord was well protected, as usual.

"Yes, my Lord?"

"If this Stenrak character is a member of a Pon tribe, then it stands to reason that, just like us, there must be many other Pon who may or may not agree with what Stenrak has done; allying with Calish and that wretched creature Bishtar. If that is so, and I am sure that I am correct, then there will be Pon that might want to side themselves with something that benefits our way of thinking, if given the right incentive. And we might, in fact, find common cause."

"Yes, my Lord, but how will we make contact? We do not speak their language. And much time has passed since the altar attack. In the interim these creatures have made no attempt at further engaging us."

Dathan studied his charge with a curious expression, as it was uncommon for the brute of a man to be so... articulate. Dathan pondered, *Maybe there is more to Gasheer than I perceive.* But then he studied Gasheer a bit closer. The giant stood there staring blandly forward; his hair disheveled, mouth open, broken teeth exposed, his fat tongue and drool barely contained within his mouth... and of course, emitting the foulest of odors. *On second thought, maybe not.* "Do you not see, Gasheer? Is Bishtar the only child that has shown signs of changing, looking more and more like those Pon creatures as time goes by? And is it not true that nearly all newborns look more Pon than human?"

"Yes, my Lord, I have seen this, and do not know what to make of it."

"Of course not, but it is clear to me now. There will come a time when our tribe will be split into two parts; one still human like us, and the newer generation becoming like them... Pon. There will therefore be one of our tribe who looks like a Pon that can be recruited to stand for us, blend in with the Pon, and make contact to further our cause."

"Who?"

"I have grandchildren who are already changing into these Pon creatures. Have my sons come to me. I will instruct them to draft the best candidates among my grandchildren. He, or she, will make contact with these Pon and find those among them that are willing to work with us, and against those on Stenrak's side. My little grandchild Faester, for example; there is something about him, something in his eyes.

"Yes, my Lord, he is different, he is..."

"Like Bishtar? Is that what you are trying to say? Yes he is," Dathan said too eagerly, "I will tell my sons to train him well."

"How will our recruits talk to the Pon?"

"Calish has already alluded to the fact that he communicated with Stenrak. And as you have seen, Calish is now more Pon looking than human. It stands to reason that his physical changes correspond with other abilities, like being able to speak Pon. My recruits should have the same abilities. We can then strike a deal with these Pon creatures that benefits us."

"But what can we offer them in return for their favor?"

"Ah, my giant friend, that is really very simple. The Pon have shown no signs of being on par with our machinery, our weapons, our metallurgy, our crafting. They are primitive, to say the least, by comparison."

"But what if they have powers, like Bishtar?"

"If she is like all of them, then we would have been easily defeated at the altar battle. And Stenrak's tribe would have surely overcome us by now. No, if Bishtar has 'powers' as you say, then it might be rare, an aberration, even among the Pon. And if Bishtar has powers, then as I have already alluded to, we could find one of our recruits with equal gifts."

"Who, my Lord?"

Dathan became pensive. "Let's hedge our bets, my good fellow. As we have already discussed, my grandson Faester is, how shall we say, unique, is he not? Let us then treat him as such, and guide him accordingly. Have Hathar come to me."

"The witch, my Lord? Are we not warned to shun such creatures?"

"Warned by whom?"

"Moses, my Lord."

Dathan's smug expression swiftly changed; he angrily looked up into the face of Gasheer. "Do not speak to me of Moses! Are you defying my orders?"

Gasheer straightened his stance and stared forward. "No, my Lord."

After a moment Dathan relaxed. "Very well." Having settled his dominance over Gasheer, he went about straightening his superbly tailored robes. "And one more thing, Gasheer. Have our best seamstress prepare the finest robes for Faester. He should look the part, after all. And tell her to only use the blackest of fibers. Somehow black suits the child. Yes, I can say black is his color."

"It shall be done, my Lord."

Dathan nodded imperiously. "In the meantime, ask your best scouts to gather intelligence on these Pon. It would appear that they have spied on us; let us not be remiss in returning the favor. Eventually, I am sure we will find Pon that will see things our way. This process, however, will take time and will require patience and cunning on our part."

"But my Lord, my men wait, but we have seen no more Pon. Why do they not attack us now?"

"Yes, something keeps them at bay. It could be the fear of our weaponry. It could be they are waiting to properly gather their forces. But whatever the reason, we have been safe for quite some time. This is most curious and could be a means of furthering our agenda. A way of convincing our people of the power of our gods..."

"But what of our gods?"

"What of them?"

"Will they not help us? Will they not show us another sign?"

Dathan glanced up at Gasheer and grimaced, for he was truly saddened by the giant's ignorance. He reached out to his table, picked up a shiny mirror, brought it to his immaculately manicured face, and retorted, "My good fellow, they just did."

CHAPTER 23
Our First Home

Calish and Mosher stood alone in the Hidden place, waiting. Calish's dream had prompted their journey. That was fine by the boys, because they were very curious to learn of events from the Pons' perspective since their last meeting.

Soon enough, they could hear the sound of soft footsteps approaching them. They need not be alarmed, nor be frightened of the new arrival. They could sense his presence in their minds, and knew he was their friend.

"He is coming; I hear his mind working." said Calish while concentrating. "Can you understand him?"

"I am starting to, yes," answered Mosher. "And w-when I am close enough, I am also able to h-hear others in our tribe, our age or younger, as they voice their thoughts."

"I do as well. The language sounds more like what Stenrak speaks than ours."

"Or kind of like b-both mixed together. Strange." Mosher became thoughtful. "The adults, they cannot m-mind-speak like us."

"No, it appears that only the younger ones, the ones who are changing, can do so."

Calish turned toward their guest and mind-spoke as Stenrak walked up to them. *We are starting to understand you now.*

And I you, Stenrak replied. *You are much more like me now. We can talk in our minds. Because we are close to one another, we can hear each other's thoughts. As you might have observed, greater distance limits the ability to mind-speak. And if necessary, you can also keep your private thoughts, private.*

The boys nodded, showing that they had noticed the truth of Stenrak's description.

It is the Pon way. You are communicating the way we normally do. And of course you look like us now as well. If I didn't know better, I would say that you look like distant cousins of mine; the ones my family doesn't like, of course. Stenrak started hissing at what he thought was very funny.

Calish and Mosher smiled politely but still raised their eyebrows skeptically.

Both Calish and Mosher had changed a lot. If they were still in Egypt, they would not recognize themselves; furthermore, they would most likely be horrified by their present appearance. But time and the inevitability of eating the Maana had left them in a reluctant acceptance of something they could not control.

Calish reasoned, *Since we have been eating the Maana, we have changed a lot. Especially the young ones.*

Stenrak was intrigued by Calish's choice of words, but for the moment, kept his thoughts to himself.

Then, to follow Stenrak's cousin joke, Calish mocked, "And luckily you look just like me now, Moshe," and he patted Mosher on the back.

Mosher's curly black hair was all but gone; he had grown slightly leaner and more muscular. His skin was a pale white, his eyes as black as Calish's, and nearly as big as Stenrak's. At first glance one would say that all three boys were twins, but there were actually stark contrasts in their particular features, if one looked close enough. Only time and living in their new bodies had given them a type of recognition of the differences. "Thanks a lot," replied Mosher. "That makes me feel really g-great."

Calish faced Stenrak, business on his mind. *You asked for this meeting. What do you wish to discuss?*

We were successful in rescuing your sister, but I must warn you, the battle is far from over.

Battle? quizzed Calish.

There are many things I must tell you; there is much to learn. Now that we can more easily communicate, I will try to explain the most important things that you should know.

The place you now inhabit was once ours. It was our first home; our Holy Place, the sacred place of our First Ones.

Calish and Mosher exchanged curious glances. Then Calish mind-spoke. *Then why don't you live there any longer? It seems to be a better place in comparison with where we first arrived in the underworld.*

A good question my friend, a good question.

Go on then. We are anxious to hear what you have to say.

218

I do not know all the history, but I can tell you this... My people would have attacked you by now had you settled in any other place. But when you ended up where you did, it gave my people a reason to pause, and delay what should have been a certain death for you. Your new home is sacred to us. And yet it carries with it much divisiveness, anguish, and history. But more importantly, we have reverence for it.

Reverence?

When you first arrived, our Maana masters had visions of your presence. We felt the Earth move too. Many were frightened. The masters told us you had arrived very close to the sacred place, our Holy Place, and that you carried a sacred object. This caused derision between our clan. Some wanted to attack right away. Others said it was a great omen; a prophecy fulfilled. Some said that we should avoid you. And others wanted to wait and see. You are surface dwellers, or were. This is key.

We were... Calish said sadly looking at his clawed fingertips.

For us, you still are. Surface dwellers are legendary to us. We believe our First Ones, like you, were born as surface dwellers to the glorious surface world. I am not sure why, but for some reason the First Ones were punished. Their fate was to start anew in the underworld. They spawned the Pon; me and my people, as I have already told Calish when we met in the Valley.

Over time, our first tribe splintered into many competing groups. They fought over scarce resources, theology, and gods of all types. Many Pon worship Hull, our god of the underworld. Hull is the world. He is its many layers and he controls all the beasts contained therein. But there are many that disagree, fervently, violently. They say Hull is not the true God; that there is another greater God, lost to us when we were cast down. But many reject this notion because it is a difficult burden to bear. The idea that we are mere outcasts of an unknowable god is a hard meat to digest. It is easier to worship things we can see, touch, or change.

Of these things I am not sure, but long ago the disagreements turned very heated. This culminated in a great war that happened in the Holy Place. Legends say Hull was angered by our fighting... angry enough to punish us. The death toll was so great that the survivors had to flee, vowing to never return, leaving the sacred place isolated, as if it was taboo to live there. And there is powerful magic in the Holy Place, as you have already seen.

Mosher interrupted with, *But you have already attacked us in your Holy Place, or those creatures that look like you a-attacked. They took Bishtar. And by the way, Calish and I want to thank you for helping us rescue her.* Calish nodded to Stenrak in agreement with Mosher's words. Mosher then said, *To many of our people they are 'Pon' like you. Our people have not met others of your tribe. Many of us still lump you all together.*

Stenrak turned his attention on Mosher. *They are not like us, as I've explained before to Calish. Your people and mine will eventually meet, one way or another. When it happens, you will know I speak the truth. But when we rescued Calish's sister, you saw for yourselves that the Cult are slow-witted and aimless, their clothes in tatters, or nonexistent. They listlessly move about, moaning incoherently, because their minds have been washed from remembering who they once were.*

Mosher wished that he could forget. *Yes I r-remember. They are not like you.*

They are what we call the Cult of the Insane. And I must warn you again, those monsters, the ones who took Calish's sister, are controlled by a very powerful spirit we call Voice. This spirit is evil; it calls to Pon minds, forcing those who are weak-minded, or evil, to follow the spirit and carry out its wishes.

Calish refuted, *But there was one Pon who led them. You helped us avoid him during the fight. He was not listless; he was very powerful, and fought with purpose against Gasheer.*

Yes, agreed Mosher. *He had one eye; the other was badly d-damaged.*

And he had a necklace made of bones, furthered Calish, recalling that Mishtas had pointed it out.

And he had a strange purple s-scar crossing his face. It was g-gruesome.

Stenrak nodded. *I know him. He is called Telek. He was once my father's First.*

First?

My father's greatest warrior. His necklace was earned by killing my father's enemies. The scar on his face is actually a reward for achieving the highest military rank, but that is another story. My father should have killed him, after it became clear that Telek was under Voice's influence, but in a moment of weakness my father let him go. You see, Telek had saved my brother Stilik from a giant Mestalor. My brother was my age at the time and under Telek's tutelage. My brother took on the Mestalor alone, and was close to death when Telek arrived. Telek defeated the beast... but not before losing one eye in the process. He was, or is, a great warrior.

Mosher nodded. *He took on Gasheer, matching him in every way. G-Gasheer could not best him.*

Stenrak nodded with pride. *Their fight was indeed a sight to behold. Voice will chose the best soldier to lead the others. The spirit gives some autonomy to this chosen one, Voice's First. But Telek is not the real enemy; our real enemy is his master, Voice. You must remember this always.*

What should w-we do? queried Mosher.

This spirit must be repelled. You must watch out for signs of Voice trying to take control of your people.

How will we know? asked Calish.

If you see your people acting strangely, as in not talking, shedding their clothes, eating things that cannot or should not be eaten, acting violently for no reason, and finally going off on their own, know that you have most likely lost them to Voice. At that point, either let them disappear, or do what we do... kill them before they can join the dark spirit.

Kill them?

If they join forces with Voice, as you have seen, they will only cause further destruction. Kill them and avoid the deaths they will create.

Calish stated, *We have not seen any of us act as you described.*

Stenrak paused, thinking. *It could be that Voice has difficulty taking over your minds because you are surface dwellers. But you are changing, so how long could it be before Voice finds a way?*

Mosher asked worriedly, *Will this Voice and the Cult a-attack us again?*

No. As I said, they normally never enter the Holy Place. Voice knows better. We, the Helons, would certainly destroy them. The Maana masters believe the Cult was there to further Voice's influence over your people and to take the sacred item your people possess. Your sister was....

Yes? prompted Calish protectively.

Stenrak stared into Calish's eyes with resolve. *Beware of her. She is a Harsha.*

What? asked Calish incredulously. *Why? What is a Harsha?*

She has mind-motion powers... Harsha.

Mind-motion? Calish looked at Moshe, and they shared a thread of consternation. Ever since the altar incident, many believed Bishtar was different. Some believed her to be a witch, with great powers, but the boys refused to accept it. A twin brother would know if such a thing were true, so Calish didn't accept it. For Mosher, Bishtar could do no wrong. So Stenrak's theory was just that, a theory.

Calish finally stated, *We don't believe it.*

Stenrak decided to not push his companions on that particular issue. So he attacked the larger point from another angle. *The Pon also have a spoken language. It is simple, instructive, but it is not our preferred method of communicating. Pon talk to one another with our minds, as we are doing now, and mind-speaking is how we normally share information. But it has been known that some Pon can also harbor mind-motion powers as well: the power to move the elements to one's will. It is very rare, and in our history those with mind-motion powers have used it for evil purposes, often allying themselves with Voice. Beware if your people display such powers, for Voice will truly desire their power. So we are naturally vigilant in recognizing the Harsha. In contrast to the Harsha, our prophecy says that a Pon will be born with those powers, and that he will establish a new age for Pon... our Savior.*

A savior?

Yes, our savior. In our language he will be called O'oviss.

Your future mind-motion leader?

Yes. But sadly, here is where it gets conflicting for us. When Pon display mind-motion powers, they will claim ownership over that prophecy, saying they are the O'oviss, only to find out later that they are false profits. They are Harsha and using their power to dominate and kill us. So as I've said, we are very wary of mind-motion Pon.

Calish, still defensive, decided to speak his mind, literally. *That might be how it is for you Pon, but my sister is not like that. She is no 'Harsha' as you say.*

Agreed, buffeted Mosher very strongly.

Stenrak paused. He was about to mind-speak something, but stopped himself. He knew that the humans could not understand that Voice had chosen to take Bishtar for a reason. And it wasn't a good one. Even though Bishtar had used her powers to turn his guts upside-down during her rescue, Stenrak's new friends were not ready to hear of it. Mosher and Calish cared for Bishtar too much. They could not, or would not, accept that she had changed, and was, in fact, a Harsha. He hoped that the humans, and Pon, would not come to regret saving her.

So Stenrak decided to once again change the subject. *The reason we have not attacked, although many, like my older brother, called for my father to do so, is because you are surface dwellers. As such, you hold a kind of mystery to us. There is a longing for what you have, as if we should have it too. As I said, I do not fully understand it. I do know this; if you had been any other Pon tribe, living anywhere near the Holy Place, you would already be dead, or worse. Even the Cult dare not transgress near the sacred place. My father would have crushed any who dare trespass it. The Helon tribe is one of the largest and most powerful. We inhabit caverns relatively near the Holy Place, watching over it.*

Calish was still unsatisfied *It still doesn't add up yet. A lot of time has passed. Why have your people not tried to make contact?*

Our greatest Maana master says that because you inhabit the Holy Place, it proves to be an omen. He says we should leave you alone; be wary of you even. He won the debate, and convinced my father to stay his hand, for now. But know this; if you stay in the Holy Place too long, you will be destroyed. Your scared object will be taken. It is only a matter of time.

But it was you Stenrak that brought us there, Calish argued. *Without you I never would have found the Crystallight cavern, your Holy Place, on my own. We would still be in the first place we landed. Does your father know these things?*

My father did not know of my plans, nor did I until I watched you for a time. My father did not know I traveled to find you. Of course he had others who spied you out as well, but my travel was not sanctioned.

Why did you do it then?

My vision showed me your dreaming spirit; it led me to direct you through one of the entrances to our sacred place, our First Home. Do you remember when we first met in the chambers?

Yes.

I was consuming a special Maana called Sklon. That substance helped guide my visions and helped me contact you. In a way, I did not really show you anything; the Sklon, the Maana-induced vision, did. In fact, the name 'Maana' is our word. It must have been transferred to you through our shared vision. When you said the word Maana earlier, I was surprised. I did not know you used the same word, like us, to describe the same thing.

Calish agreed. *By the time I saw you eating it, your Maana Sklon, I had already named it Maana. It happened when Moshe and I first found the Crystallight caverns. I didn't know where I got that word. Moshe asked me to name the plants we saw. Maana came to my mind. The name Maana might have been taken from the vision you showed me.*

Stenrak agreed. *It seems clear that the legends of our common heritage are true. For example, when we first met, I heard your friend Mosher use the term, 'Sheol'. We Pon also know this word. I don't know exactly what it means to you, but for us it denotes something like a bad thing, usually. My mentor has told me that there were many surface memories we carried with us when the First Ones were cast down. Possibly this is a surface word we remember somehow. But over time, we forgot what it meant.*

Mosher added, *"For us Sheol is a curse, usually. But the Elders have explained that it also means a place for the dead, in the underworld. As far as I know, we are not dead, but I guess this is that place, even for the living, unfortunately. I remember my grandfather also told me there are seven gates guarding Sheol. I was wondering; could the portal to the Valley be one of those gates?"*

The boys looked upon one another, thinking hard about what Mosher had told them.

Calish was first to express his thoughts. *The Valley is like the surface world, but different. The small sun does not move across the sky. Could the Valley be here with us, in the underworld?* He shrugged his shoulders to answer his own question.

Stenrak replied, *The stones joining together to create one of your seven gateways within Sheol is very possible. I do know our underworld is vast. I am taught that there are other strange realms that are housed within Hull's walls. Your Valley could be one of them.*

Mosher, always thinking, added, *If the Valley is but one gateway, then what awaits us in the ones we have yet to traverse?*

Stenrak nodded thoughtfully. *There are, it appears, many mysteries we have yet to uncover. And I too have noticed that occasionally I somehow also learned words from your language. Valley, for one; sun for another; spear, and so on. Visions are remarkable things. Even the gem I gave you was also transferred to you because of a vision by my Maana master.*

Calish retrieved the stone in question from his second pouch, letting Stenrak clearly see it. Stenrak bowed his head, acknowledging that the boys had kept it safe. Stenrak had let them keep it after Bishtar's rescue, to help guide them back to the Crystallight caverns. *We call it the Crystallight stone.*

Stenrak repeated the word. *Crystallight... very well.*

Mosher asked, *Besides the vision, was there another reason you sought us out?*

Stenrak looked slightly surprised. *Calish, your friend is very insightful.*

Mosher was happy to hear the compliment; he smiled broadly. Calish, however, merely shrugged and put on his best 'yeah sure' frown.

Stenrak replied, *My brothers and I compete for father's inheritance, for his throne. As you might have guessed by now, my father is king of the Helons. My older brother Stilik is ruthless in his endeavor at first succession; my younger brother, for now, is willing to follow my lead. Of course if I could ally myself with you, it could only help my cause to be First.*

But I am also very different from my older brother. In fact, I am unlike many in my tribe. I am more curious than most. My teachers say it will be the death of me. They say I am impulsive, immature, lacking the wisdom of experience. But they have trained me in Sklon visions. Through those insights, I saw myself with you. I merely acted upon those insights. I did not know where it would lead.

Your father, is he angry with you for what you have done? Calish had to ask.

No. But my older brother is. My father sees it as our way to fight over his birthright; just as he once did to vanquish his brothers. It is our way.

How long do we have, to be safe where we are?

I know not. For now my older brother is kept busy by father, fighting in other places against our enemies. But Stilik knows victory over you is his ultimate chance to prove his birthright as first in line to be king. Moreover, his objective is to take your resources as well. So if anyone attacks you, it will be my brother Stilik. The good part is that as long as he lives, no one dare attack you first.

This brother... your older brother Stilik... how old is he?

Two.

He is two? Mosher and Calish were surprised.

Two? asked Mosher. *To us you look n-near our age. Calish and I are twelve; and you don't appear m-much older than us, so how can your older brother be two?*

I do not know how surface dwellers count the passing of time. One way we Pon do is by counting these. Stenrak pointed at an area just below one of his eyes.

Okay, quizzed Mosher skeptically, *we see your eye, but w-what does it mean?*

Look closer.

So the boys did.

Calish remarked, *I see a wrinkle, I guess.*

Yes, if you look even closer, you will see the beginning of yet another wrinkle.

226

So you're... ah, one wrinkle?
One and a half, to be precise.
And your father? How old is he?
Seven wrinkles strong.
Wow!

Seeing that the boys were interested, Stenrak decided to offer one of his best and most well renowned humorous anecdotes. *My teacher, Ashkolon, has many wrinkles . . .*

How many? the boys asked as if on cue.

They say that Pon do not have a name for a number that high. But that comment is only voiced when Ashkolon is asleep from Maana berry wine, or when he is not wielding his dagger. After that, Stenrak started hissing and shaking up and down. "Hiss-ss, hiss-ss, hiss-ss."

The strange sounds put a curious face on Mosher. "Is he l-laughing again, Calish?"

"Oh yeah, Stenrak is a real riot when you get to know him."

"I can s-see that."

Calish poked Mosher in his flabby belly and smiled, getting Mosher to smile with him. They soon joined in with Stenrak to share in his humor, each boy laughing in their own way.

As I said, father will listen to Ashkolon, for now. King Storn accepts prophecy. He knows what you carry is sacred. Stenrak said this while indicating Calish's other pouch, where the Minthuru stone was.

Mosher and Calish went to him, and Stenrak instinctively tensed but did not go for his weapon. Calish slowly handed Stenrak the Crystallight stone.

This gem, Calish offered, *is it special too?*

Yes, it was given to me by Ashkolon. He is my primary teacher and my Maana master. He is the one who had the vision directing me to give you the Crystallight stone. As I have described, he is very old, the last of his generation. Some say he was a disciple of a Maana master who fought in the great war, where the gem's fate was in question. Some say Ashkolon was that Maana master. Some say he is the first son of the First One. And a few even dare say he 'is' the First One. He is a mystery. But in any event, Ashkolon told me that this stone belonged to the First Ones.

227

Calish mulled over all he had heard. *The things you have told us... is there no good news for our people?*

For now, your people are safe. I believe the Cult retreated to their sad, dark holes, and will leave you be. But be wary of Voice, as I have told you. And know this, my friends; this truce will not stand forever. War and death are this world's constant companions. Be on your guard always.

At that statement, Mosher and Calish shared a look, thinking the same thing. *We will.*

Calish asked, *Will we see you again soon?*

Now and then? Stenrak focused his gaze on Mosher and mind-spoke to him: *I have a gift for you, in return for the dagger you have given me. The human weapon has made my older brother lose sleep, and for that I am truly grateful.* He held out the Crystallight stone to Mosher. Calish and Mosher exchanged curious expressions as if the gesture didn't make sense.

Take it, Stenrak said, *and you will understand.*

So Mosher picked it up into his hand. Sure enough, as Mosher held the stone, it started humming softly. Then Mosher received a vision. He saw a place that he had only heard about but had not seen. There was a small sun, lush green hills, water, and strange looking beasts. His tribe was nearby, working, eating, the children playing. Naturally, he scanned the crowd, but could not find Calish or Bishtar. *Strange,* he thought, *Where are they . . .?*

"What happened?" asked Calish as he nudged Mosher, "You had this weird, far-away stare on your face."

Mosher suddenly found himself back in the Hidden place, standing beside Calish and Stenrak. Mosher shook his head clear and muttered, "I saw the Valley. It was so real, so b-beautiful, just as you described to me."

All three boys smiled at his insights. Even though Stenrak could not understand Mosher's words, by inference and observation, he knew Mosher had received a powerful vision.

Mosher added worriedly, "But you were n-not there, Calish."

Calish shrugged and slapped Mosher on the shoulder. "Ah, don't worry about it. It's not important." Mosher took in Calish's casual dismissal, sort of anyway. At face value it sounded okay, but deep inside Mosher was bothered by it.

Satisfied, Stenrak began his final instructions. *There is something very important I must tell you before we part. The Crystallight gem, as you call it, is one of twelve gems. They say it is one of the children of the great gem, given to the First Ones. It has great power. The masters say Hull sees through the gems; Hull's eyes to our world, they say. Watching us, and intervening only when necessary. But Ashkolon has told me Hull answers to another god, the God of all. But that knowledge was lost to us. In any event, Ashkolon has revealed to me that the stone you carry is also one of the twelve. Before we rescued your sister, you showed me your power stone. When I saw it, I recognized that your gem is part of the prophecy; Ashkolon confirmed this. Ashkolon then explained that your jewel is, in fact, the great gem, and because it derives from the surface world, it is the key to unlocking the true power of the other eleven gems. Ashkolon also told me that the gems are attracted to certain people; not anyone can wield their power.* He stopped talking. He looked at Mosher with a serious expression. *This must be why you received a vision. And legends say that if all twelve gems are ever reunited, then Pon destiny will change forever.*

Mosher stared in awe at the energized, brilliant jewel that was presently making a soft melodious noise to enhance the humming. He twirled it in his fingers, matching motion with the melody.

Stenrak grinned. *Ashkolon was right to give it to you, my friend.*

B-But why me?

As with many things, Ashkolon would not say. All he said was to give it to you. He also told me that if upon receipt of the gem, it changes shape and color, then the holder is indeed the stone's true master.

It is humming, but it has not changed s-shape or color. It is still greenish. Then I am n-not its master?

No.

Then why give it to m-me?

You would have to ask Ashkolon. But I warn you, he does not like too many questions. And if he goes for his dagger, it is best to remain real quiet. "Hiss-ss, hiss-ss, hiss-ss."

Okay, I g-guess. Thank you, answered Mosher gratefully.

After Stenrak stopped shaking from laughter, Mosher took note of Stenrak's smooth skin, as it was so different from when they had last met. *The barbs stuck in your skin, Stenrak. We were worried about you. How did you remove them?*

Stenrak reviewed his arms up and down, flexing his wiry muscles in the process. *Ah yes, those. Mestalor hairs, somewhat difficult to remove. My father was very proud when I did not lose consciousness during the forceful plucking of each and every one of them. Luckily, they were actually very useful, because they helped me fight the Cult. It was... painfully stimulating. Perhaps if we ever fight another Mestalor, you two could experience the pleasure of their rage-inducing pain? I am sure you will enjoy it as much as I did. We could join together on the hunt if you wish . . .*

Calish and Mosher exchanged a not-in-this-lifetime expression.

Calish said, *Ah gee, I guess me and Moshe will pass on the Mestalor hunting, prickly spiky thing. But thanks anyway.*

Very well, my friends, very well. Stenrak bowed slightly. After that, Stenrak eyed them cautiously and walked backwards while facing them, holding onto his dagger's handle. When he was a few paces away, he abruptly turned and walked back the way he had entered.

"Not much for loving g-goodbyes, is he?" asked Mosher.

"It's just his way." Calish became puzzled for a moment. "Stenrak told us lots of stuff, Moshe."

"Yup, and were you p-paying attention, Calish?"

"Yeah sure, of course I was. Gee, what do you think of me? There's lots of stuff he said like, gobs of stuff, like you know, like well like..."

". . . like Hull, Holy Place, Ashkolon, First Ones, twelve Stones, Harsha, Telek, Stilik, mind-motion, Voice, Helons, King Storn, O'oviss?"

"Yes! Exactly right, Moshe. You see, I knew it all along."

"Oh brother, Calish. What would y-you do without me?"

Calish performed his standard pat-Moshe-on-the-back while saying, "Now you know why I brought you along, Drinkle ol' buddy."

Mosher rolled his eyes and Calish laughed, as usual.

Then Moshe started scrutinizing the brilliant stone in his hand. He started turning it over and over, like it was a delicate flower and the most beautiful thing in the world. Calish couldn't help but notice that Moshe was up to something, well beyond appreciating something fine-looking. *No,* the gem twirling, lamb-defending, stuff-remembering Moshe had some personal intentions for using the sparkling jewel.

Calish voiced dubiously, "You're not thinking what I think you're thinking."

"Wha–Wha–Wha... What?"

Hearing Mosher stutter that badly meant only one thing – or only one *person*, to be precise. "Oh shishtu, you *are* thinking what I think you're thinking."

"No, I ah, ah, I am not! Well... maybe... ah, so wh-what if I am?"

"Moshe, you're such a sap."

"Calish, don't say anything. Promise me!"

Calish could see that Mosher's little scheme was very important to him, so he spit in his hand and held it out. Mosher smiled, doing the same. Clasping hands firmly, they said aloud, while mind-speaking, "Cal-Moshe."

CHAPTER 24
A Small Item

Beefy hands pulled back the tent folds. The lumbering giant slipped under the barrier and into the dark spaces. He began his task by opening various belongings – trunks, packages, nick-knacks – and he also managed to crawl, rather clumsily, under tables. A small lantern barely illuminated the area, but the intruder could see well enough to recognize the item he was charged with finding. He also spied-out the old man who lay sleeping on a nearby cot.

"Old fool," he whispered.

The old man suddenly breathed louder, then began snoring. The intruder thought about taking steps not yet sanctioned. It would be so easy. *Not yet,* he thought glumly, *not yet.*

The hulking thief moved further into the tent, each step bringing him closer to the sleeping figure. Then he spotted the old man's pouch at the base of the cot, and knew the item was most likely in there. He crawled to it and suddenly froze.

"Who is there?" asked the old man in a creaky voice. He looked around with half-open eyes.

The burglar remained a statue, hoping that the old man would see nothing and return to his sleep. But the intruder's shear bulk, which dominated just about everything, made him impossible to miss.

"What are you doi..."

Instantly an enormously meaty hand covered the speaker's mouth, cutting him off. The old man struggled to break free, but the prowler was too strong, easily keeping the old man pinned to the cot, pushing harder and harder with each passing moment. The old man desperately clawed at the intruder's hands, but there was no contest. The old man's eyes were open wide with great fear. He tried to call out a muffled sound, "H... help."

"Shshhhhhh, shhhhhh," whispered the villain mockingly. While one of the thief's giant mitts covered the old man's mouth, the other slid around his victim's jaw, then over the old one's skinny throat. The aggressor could not control his emotions; a burning hatred seethed within him. He would tolerate the old one's disrespect no longer. The monster squeezed tighter, and twisted just as much, until... *Snap!* The old man's eyes blankly stared forward, lifelessly dead, his fragile neck broken.

"It is done, you old fool," said the intruder meanly, "it is finally done." The giant returned to the task of item-finding. He grabbed up the old man's pouch and excitedly rummaged through it, but the sack was empty. "Damn it!" The thief looked around some more, getting increasingly frustrated. He became enraged when the magical object was nowhere to be seen. He glared into the old man's dead eyes, and suddenly had an idea; unusual, but true. The brute could do nothing at the moment, but he took solace in knowing how he would eventually complete his task. "Yes, yes, I can see it clearly," he mused. In anticipation of acting out his rather violent daydream, the murderous thug spat out, "I will now have to take your little secret from your loving grandson. Ha ha."

CHAPTER 25
The Vision

Calish was troubled. His body tossed and turned, but he remained stuck within a very deep sleep. Inside of that, he battled against a relentlessly engulfing dream. His mind was spinning with shapes, colors, and the hearing of strange noises. A loud *whooshing* noise caught his attention. Everything suddenly became calm, clear, and he saw the glowing wall appear directly in front of him.

The Doorway. Within its shimmering edges, beyond its surface plane, lay something he had not seen in a long time. "The Valley!"

Calish started to walk closer, but was stopped in his tracks by another person that abruptly walked in front of him. It was a Pon man. Calish scrutinized the figure. There was something familiar about the man; his stocky build, the way he walked, and the way he looked at things.

"Moshe?" Calish called out curiously. But the man did not respond. The man continued to move closer to the doorway, ignoring the dreamer's call. "Moshe, do you not hear me? Moshe?" The man peered into the doorway with a serious, yet sad expression. He then turned back to look at Calish. And Calish was now sure that the Pon man was indeed his friend Mosher. Calish was also glad to see that Mosher had finally heard him.

"Moshe, what are you doing?" But Mosher did not answer. "Moshe!" Still, Mosher did not answer.

Calish suddenly realized that Mosher wasn't looking *at* him, but *through* him, like he wasn't there, as if he were studying something behind him. So Calish turned around. "My people. The tribe of Judah."

Lined up, coming to their spot, was everyone Calish knew. They were carrying their belongings, and they were closing in on the doorway. When they got very near the portal, Mosher was directing them to enter it. One-by-one, his tribe ventured through the doorway. Beyond it they emerged into the Valley.

"Moshe, why are they going there?" Calish went to go closer, for he too wanted to follow, but something kept him frozen where he stood. He couldn't budge his feet; they were stuck to the cavern floor. Try as he might, nothing moved. Calish started to panic. "Moshe, wait. I am here. Moshe, do not leave without me. Moshe!"

But Moshe could not hear Calish's cries; it was as if he wasn't even there. All Calish could do was stand there and witness everyone pass by, ignoring him in the process.

Soon enough, the last of his people walked through the doorway. Mosher prepared to take himself through as well.

Calish called out in desperation, "Moshe, please stop! Do not leave me here." Suddenly Mosher stopped, just as one of his feet breached the doorway's threshold. Mosher turned, and Calish felt a sudden excitement. His friend had heard his pleas and would wait for him too. "El be praised," he whispered.

Mosher stepped away from the portal, as if he had suddenly remembered something. He walked past Calish's spot without stopping. Calish's feet were suddenly free to move so he followed his friend. They walked forward, Mosher in the lead, Calish close on his friend's heels. Together they both moved deeper into the Crystallight cavern.

"Where are you going, Moshe?" Calish asked along the way.

But Mosher ignored his follower, as if he had heard nothing at all.

Soon enough the pair approached a very familiar and extraordinary location. "Why are we here, Moshe?"

Mosher bound up the flat side of the monument, in a similar way he had done years before. When he got to the exact place, in the center of the huge boulder, Mosher reached into his pouch. To Calish's surprise, Mosher took out the Minthuru stone. But the gem was different somehow. Calish wasn't sure how it was different; he just knew that is was. Mosher then said aloud, "Thus Saith El our Lord, let the Water of Life come forth."

Suddenly the ground, the whole cavern rumbled, and from the fissure at Mosher's feet a geyser sprang up. Its glistening waters flew high into the air. The water had the most intense blue and turquoise color; it was magnificent. Mosher smiled broadly and basked in the showers that soon thereafter drenched him. He then put the Minthuru stone back into his pouch and took out a small flask. He started filling it with the water. When he was done, he capped the flask and proceeded to jump off the colossus.

Mosher faced the monument and said, "Thank you, El. Thank you, Sky Rock. The Water of Life will be ready for O'oviss."

Mosher made his way back to the portal, with Calish close behind him. The duo soon approached the portal. Mosher kept walking toward the glowing doorway, but at a certain distance Calish discovered that once again his feet were frozen in place. He struggled mightily against the invisible force that kept him pinned to the cavern floor, but no matter how he tried, his feet would not budge.

"Moshe, stop. Wait for me." But Mosher kept moving closer and closer to the doorway. "Moshe, stop! Please wait for me!"

Just like before, as Mosher's foot breached the portal's entrance, he suddenly stopped. Like he had heard something, Mosher turned around to see what it was. Calish's heart jumped out of chest. *Yes, my friend, yes*, he thought gladly. "I am here, Moshe, see me." But once again Mosher looked at Calish with the same glare as he had done before, as if Calish wasn't even there. So Calish was forced to turn around one more time.

"Grandfather." Not far away Korah stood there, all alone, peering at his grandson. It was clear that the old man was waiting for him. That same loving and gentle smile was on Korah's face, the one that said he was happy to see his beloved grandson.

Calish called out, "Grandfather, what are you doing here?" But Korah did not answer. Suddenly Calish found that he could move his feet, so he went to Korah. "Should we not be going too? We must follow Moshe to the Valley."

But Korah merely stood there, staring at his grandson without speaking. Calish got closer, within touching distance. The two shared smiles and then Korah reached down into his pouch and pulled out the Minthuru stone. The jewel shone brightly with the same dazzling blue-turquoise colors that had showered over Mosher. Korah met Calish's eyes intently, and said, "No, my son. Ours is a different path. Always remember our one true God, El."

Calish was drawn to touch the magical stone. Everything vanished.

* * * *

Calish suddenly woke. He sat up, while feverishly looking about their hidden place. It was brutally dark all around him, but that was okay; he was already adept at seeing in its mysterious spaces.

He had to spit, badly, so he did many times. He reached for his jug of water, took in some gulps, swished it around his mouth and spit some more. His stomach ached and churned, so he drank again, swallowing some of the cool liquid. But the water didn't help much. His whole body reeked from the stench of what he had eaten.

"Sheol, this stuff is awful." He frowned as he looked into the package that contained the gift Stenrak had given him, wondering if indeed it was a 'gift' after all. "Sklon. Blech. Shishtu," he cursed. "Why did I take it?" Stenrak had warned him about Sklon. He had said its effects, its visions, could be... disturbing. Calish was now certain his Pon friend had been correct.

Moshe too had advised caution. In fact, he had said to not take it. "Do you not know w-what we were taught by Moses about communing with v-visions, divination? The Sklon stuff Stenrak has offered y-you isn't natural, isn't of El. Calish, do n-not take it."

But curiosity had been a greater force than following his best friend's advice. Calish very much regretted not listening now. He wished he had never eaten the horrid stuff.

He crumpled up what was left of the dark and course plant and let it drop from between his claws. Then he buried his head in hand with worry. Calish dared not think about what the Sklon-induced vision had revealed.

"It can't be true. Not all of it, anyway. No, it was just a dream. Just a crazy dream." Desperately trying to encourage himself to forget the whole business, Calish resolved, "No, I don't believe it..."

Suddenly his pouch started vibrating, and a humming came from within it. He reached for the pouch's flap, opening it quickly, withdrawing the glowing, sacred object. He had never seen the Minthuru stone act that way. "Something is wrong." So he turned and shook Mosher awake.

"What is it, Calish? I w-was sleeping."

"We must go to the Crystallight caves."

"Why?"

Calish held up the glowing stone. Mosher blinked at it. "What does it m-mean?"

Calish said one word and Mosher understood everything. "Grandfather." Soon enough, Calish would come to know that his harrowing vision was all too real.

CHAPTER 26
Where Is It?

3 Years Later

"I don't know what you're talking about," Calish voiced hurriedly.

Gasheer's sly expression got even sharper. The brute eyed Calish confidently. "Last chance, whelp." He casually reached for his Paingiver. The giant unwound the whip and let its furthest tether fall to the rocky ground. "How say ye?"

Calish looked all around, wide-eyed and very anxious. He was alone; Gasheer had cornered him in a neat alcove niche. He could run, but when he spied an opening to Gasheer's left side, the giant merely grinned. The mountainous man shifted his weight away from that direction, as if to say *Go ahead, try to get past me.* But rather than taking Gasheer up on his less-than-kind offer, Calish backed up, getting even closer to the cavern wall, unfortunately. Calish glanced past Gasheer's other side but that way presented even less hope. The titan stood firm, in all his spectacular armor, nearly as big as the cave itself.

"The exit is this way," Gasheer suggested disingenuously while waving to his side.

Shishtu! Calish chided himself for being so foolish. To go off alone was bad enough, but to let the hulking giant follow him was really stupid. *Where's Moshe?* he thought desperately. Calish called out in his mind, projecting his thoughts as far as he could. *Moshe, I need your help, come quickly!* But he received no response. Even though Calish was relatively near the settlement, Mosher must have still been too far away to hear his cries.

Gasheer went back to business. "I won't bother asking about Asher's spear. Oh yes, I have heard you call it such. And I'm sure you hid my javelin in the same place you are hiding your grandfather's precious item." Gasheer asked derisively, "Is Korah's little secret a glowing stone, perhaps? Is it the one you carried to the den of those Pon creatures we fought years ago?" Gasheer knew the answers, of course. He was merely enjoying the moment. "My Lord wants it, and you will tell me where it is, or else."

Gasheer started to take up his whip, while flashing that broken-toothed grin of his. "Your answer will determine how much love you receive from my Paingiver here. One or two gentle taps for a quick answer. And well, slightly more if you make me wait." He quickly lashed out the whip, snapping it very close to Calish's head. The cracking sound echoed in Calish's ear like a thunder shot and he instantly ducked, while bringing up his arms in defense.

Gasheer merely laughed. "Scared? You should be, little one." The brute brought around his whip again, whirling it back and forth; snapping it very close to the Calish's shrinking form. With each go, the whip's momentum was building, fracturing the air, while Gasheer relished every savory snap!

The bully was about to unleash its fury when out of nowhere a stony hammer struck Gasheer's helmet. *Ping!* It sounded as the weapon bounced off Gasheer's protective crown. Gasheer jostled his head slightly in response and quickly turned to see who had dared throw the object. From a nearby dark alcove Stenrak suddenly appeared. In a flash, the nimble Pon warrior ran like mad at the monster. Stenrak screeched in rage as he jumped up to slash at Gasheer's face.

But Gasheer was ready; he easily caught the flying figure in mid-air. Stenrak struggled to break free, but was not nearly strong enough. Stenrak lashed out his claws and his feet, but struck nothing but Gasheer's heavy armor. With one hand, Gasheer grabbed Stenrak by the throat and started to squeeze his meaty grip tighter. Stenrak's eyes popped and he was forced to try and pry loose Gasheer's fat fingers. But Gasheer merely smiled. He dropped the whip from his other hand and unsheathed his sword. He reared the blade back, ready to chop off Stenrak's head, when Calish jumped on his back. He grabbed Gasheer's sword arm, holding it up with all his strength, keeping Gasheer from bringing it down upon Stenrak's neck.

"Get off me, dog!"

Meanwhile, Stenrak, struggling to breath, frantic for air, focused his bulging eyes at the monster. With his last bit of strength, Stenrak focused his mind. He sent vivid mind-speak images into Gasheer's brain: *Sleep, sleep, eyes closed, sleeping . .*

Gasheer's eyes stared to collapse, but then he shook his head. Again he did this, jiggling his massive noggin back and forth. He growled in protest, fighting the urge to sleep, but Stenrak kept up the mental suggestions, sending more images of how Gasheer looked and felt to be blissfully sleeping. *Sleep Sleepy-Sleep.* Gasheer continued to struggle to keep his eyes open.

Suddenly Gasheer opened his eyes wide with fury. Realizing that the Pon creature had played a mental trick on him, Gasheer snarled at the figure in his grip. He squeezed Stenrak's throat tighter and spewed, "I will enjoy this, vile snake. Your little mind games will not work on me!" He reared back the arm that held his sword.

Calish quickly reached over and latched his whole weight onto Gasheer's sword arm. But Gasheer held him aloft, while Calish's feet dangled well above the cavern floor. Calish scratched his claws at Gasheer's arm, but mostly struck the armor. The giant barely noticed anyway.

Calish looked to Stenrak. His friend was starting to fade for lack of air. Calish found a bit of forearm flesh that was not covered by the armor. In desperation, he bit hard onto Gasheer's skin, sinking his sharp teeth as deep as possible.

"Grrroahhh!" Gasheer yelled, but the behemoth did not let go of Stenrak.

As Calish was biting, Gasheer's blood caressed his taste buds. It tasted good. He wanted more of it. Suddenly he felt insanely hungry; it was a desire unlike he had ever known. It gave him strength to bite even harder, and so he did. The hunger burned in him, and he growled in defiance as Gasheer tried to shake him off. But Calish, like a ravenous wolf, would not let go.

Gasheer was forced to release his grip on Stenrak's throat. Stenrak fell, gasping for air. Using his free hand, Gasheer punched Calish as hard as he could. Calish took in the head blow and was propelled to the ground. But he quickly righted himself, snarling. With blood dripping from his mouth and head, Calish glowered up at Gasheer as if the meaty giant was a feast that was already bought and paid for.

But Gasheer was not impressed. He glanced at his open forearm wound like it was nothing. He bent his arm to his lips and lathered his own tongue with all of it. The beast-man held out his torn flesh toward Calish and tempted, "Come and get your meal, diseased dog."

"I hate you!" Calish roared.

"So what?" spit Gasheer. "Now tell me your secrets, Calish, before I crush your little freak friend."

"Never!"

Stenrak, while still holding his throat and sucking in air, scrambled to gain some distance. He also reached for his pouch. As the giant and Calish conversed, Stenrak quickly stuffed a bit of Sklon into his mouth. He swallowed, struggling mightily to force it down his swollen throat. Soon enough it was in his belly and its effects took over him. He saw the translucently bizarre images, and his whole body shook from convulsions.

"Ha ha," laughed Gasher as he studied Stenrak's shaky form. He turned to Calish and prompted, "Hurry up, pup, see how the freak trembles. I will break him in two before your eyes. Hurry, before I do." The giant took some heavy steps to grab up Stenrak. "Now tell me what I want to know!"

Stenrak suddenly held out his hand at the giant and projected these words into his face, "Sassitass Sassitass."

Gasheer suddenly stopped.

Without wasting time, Stenrak mind-spoke in a language familiar to both the human and the Pon, *Go back home. Your master calls, can you hear it?*

Gasheer's face went blank. Moments later, Gasheer whispered, trance-like, "Yes, I hear it."

Then go, hurry!

Gasheer hesitated. Unexpectedly, he shouted to the open air, "I am coming, my Lord!" The giant looked all about, slightly confused, but still determined to follow his Lord's instructions. He picked up his sword and whip and went lumbering off toward the Crystallight caverns.

"Grizzlist, *Sheol*," squeezed out Stenrak. The Pon warrior started to collapse, gasping for air.

Calish ran to him and caught him up, bolstering him in the process. The Sklon, still in Stenrak, reeled in his gut, and twisted throughout his mind. He trembled much more, but Calish held him steady.

Eventually, the Sklon's effects began to slowly disappear from his body. His breathing gradually steadied.

When Stenrak appeared to have recovered enough to speak, Calish mind-spoke, *Are you okay?*

Between breaths, Stenrak finally answered, *Yes, but I am tired from mind-speaking to the man-beast, and from the Sklon.*

Calish understood his friend's plight, for he too had dealt with the Sklon's side effects; not the least of which was coming to terms with a vision that had predicted a dire future. That bit was still haunting Calish's dreams, and often his every waking moments of would-be normalcy.

As he watched Stenrak struggle and quake, Calish reflected, *Sklon, what a horribly powerful...* well he still didn't know what to make of it. But seeing that Stenrak had just used it to overcome Gasheer, Calish mind-spoke an obvious question, *How did you know to find me? Did you receive a Sklon vision saying I needed help?*

"I did n-not. I came to find you for another reason... to warn you that Stilik plans on attacking your people. As I told y-you long ago, Stilik will attack."

Calish answered aloud in Stenrak's tongue, "When?"

"I am not sure, but I will try to find out more. And I will come to help when it happens."

Thinking of why Gasheer had just attacked him, Calish said, "He wanted the stone, and my spear!"

"Do not worry. They are where you left them."

Calish was a little surprised to hear this. It must have shown on his face, so Stenrak explained. "I know you hide them both in our hidden place. Do not worry, my friend. Both items are yours, I understand this. We are allies."

Stenrak waved off Calish's support and stood up straight, more or less fully recovered from the Sklon's influences.

"Thank you, Stenrak." Calish inadvertently licked at his lips, bringing in more of Gasheer's blood, tasting it again, and wanting more of it.

Stenrak duly noted Calish's small gesture. "You are becoming more like us, Calish. Even much more than when we last discussed this topic in the hidden place, and even more than you might want to know. Not only can you now speak Pon tongue as well as me, but you have also tasted living flesh. And because of it you know its power over us. Pon call it the blood-longing."

It scared Calish to think of such a horrid thing. *How can I like living flesh? Nonsense.* Even though the craving was still within him, Calish still found it unbelievable.

Then all at once, without wanting it, Calish thought of everyone he knew. Their faces, their bodies, images of their glistening skin streaked across his mind's eye. When he did this, how they might taste also crossed his mind. It intrigued him. *No!* he argued with himself. He must squelch this awful yearning, forceably if necessary. But it wasn't easy. In fact, what should have disgusted him, fascinated him. *Why am I thinking this? Stop it. Stop it!*

Knowing what Calish struggled with, Stenrak offered his best advice. "Yes, it is the same for us, Calish. We find ways to inhibit our desires for raw, living flesh, even if the meat we crave is from our own kin. Some do this better than others. The Cult not at all. You will eventually find your own way of dealing with it. You are strong-willed, as I have always known, my friend. If you truly want to put the blood-longing away, you will do it. But know this, it will never be totally defeated; it is the Pon way... *our* way."

"Shishtu," Calsh muttered harshly. More for Calish to learn, and a sour lesson it was. Calish could do nothing but nod his head solemnly in response.

Stenrak likewise bowed his head in empathy.

To help reverse Calish's sad mood, he asked, "The Graxen?"

Calish knew Stenrak was referring to Gasheer; Pon called all behemoths Graxen. Gasheer certainly fit into those larger-than-large sandals. "I will be more careful around him from now on."

"He is truly a danger. But I believe he will leave you alone for now. I sensed from him that he had his fill of dealing with you. You are... a *clawful,* as your people say."

"It's a *handful,*" Calish corrected. "And I hope you are right. I am not yet strong enough to take him on, but I soon will be. And thanks for the save."

"My pleasure, Calish." More cheerfully, Stenrak observed, "It was a glorious fight, was it not?"

"Yeah sure, Stenrak, *real glorious.*" Calish rolled his eyes.

Stenrak hissed out his usual forked-tongue laugh, and Calish eventually smiled too.

"The spear..." continued Stenrak. "When we were younger you said that you had an important use for it. I now see it is the Graxen you plan on using it against. I envy you, Calish. And I pray that Hull lets me be there to witness such a fight. Calish vs. the Graxen beast. A battle of the legends."

"I'll reserve you a spot, front row."

Not really understanding Calish's humor, Stenrak merely nodded.

Calish put forth, "If possible, Stenrak, find a way to let us know when your brother plans to attack us. In the meantime, I will try to warn my people."

"Know this too, Calish... there are those in your tribe that conspire with Stilik. Among you is a Harsha priest. He is still young, but nonetheless capable of speaking on behalf of your people; or some of them anyway. The one you call Dathan, the master of the Graxen we just fought, is working to make deals with Stilik. The Harsha speaks for this Dathan."

Stenrak could have only been referring to Faester. To the Pon he was a Harsha; to the tribe Faester was a witch, and an evil one at that. Just about everyone was scared of the little serpent. It was rumored that Faester was exhibiting magical powers, so most folks avoided him. Apparently the Pon were also clued-into Faester's bag of tricks.

As far as Calish's promise to warn his people, the only adults Calish could turn to was Mishtas, and a few others that were still loyal to Korah's tribe. Unfortunately, Mishtas had little to no sway over Dathan, or even Abiram, for that matter.

245

Regardless of his near powerless tribal position, Calish answered, "I will do my best."

"I can see that our peoples are very much alike when it comes to politics, ambition and the love of power." Stenrak rubbed his sore neck. "One bit of advice, my friend. When you do battle the Graxen, whatever you do, don't let him grab you by the throat."

"I'll keep that in mind, Stenrak."

Stenrak nodded and made his usual side-ways shift, indicating that the discussion was over and that he was ready to depart.

Even though he expected no reciprocation on Stenrak's part, Calish added, *Goodbye, Stenrak. Thank you again.*

Stenrak bowed once more, and backed up a step. While keeping his eye on Calish, Stenrak moved further away before suddenly turning to exit the place. Like always, Calish watched him go. But this time, rather than silently leaving as usual, Stenrak sent a farewell message, *I will see you soon, my friend.*

Surprised, Calish thought to himself, *I guess you are becoming like us too.*

Calish wiped the blood from his own head wounds. Without thinking, he licked it from his claws and it tasted good, maybe too good. *Oh no.*

CHAPTER 27
Anubis

They stood together, young healthy humans clad in their own familiar clothing. The open air was fresh and inviting. "We can stay... can't we?" she asked softly. To secure the notion, Bishtar wrapped her delicate fingers around his forearm in a soothing and caressing way.

Mosher hesitated, not because he was worried about her touch making him uncontrollably stutter, but because her closeness made him rethink his initial response. He desperately wanted to say *Yes! Absolutely, we can stay.* Instead, he uttered sadly, "No."

"But this is our home," she argued. "I know it. I recognize the peak up there where Moses stood." She pointed to the ledge that both of them well knew.

He followed her direction, seeing the place where Moses watched over the Hebrew nation; where he gave El's instructions, and where he had come to after speaking with El at the mountain's summit.

"We c-cannot leave our people at this time, Bishtar. They need us. They need *you* even m-more."

It was true; Stenrak had recently warned them of Stilik's impending attack. Mosher had his doubts as to his own usefulness in the coming fight, but Bishtar's powers could easily tip the balance in the tribe's favor. He had a strong suspicion that it was her powers that had helped them escape from the monster. It was also her powers that had uncovered the golden stone, and it was her authority over the Crystallight gem that had opened the portal. That information made it clear that they could not forget what they left behind. More importantly, without her, there might be nothing left to return to.

"Stenrak's brother will attack our p-people at any moment. Would you leave Calish, Mishtas, and even your mother at their mercy? They will kill m-many of us, or even worse. You know this. Will you leave our clan to s-such a fate?"

Bishtar wanted to selfishly blurt out, *Yes.* But she did not. Mosher would not hear it. He could understand her impulsiveness, but Mosher would never accept such disloyalty. Her betrothed was a good-hearted young man, and no magically wonderful circumstance could change that fact. But that didn't mean she wouldn't try.

"Mosher, look at me."

He did. Her deep blue eyes glistened, sparkled. Her hair, long and brown, cupped her gentle face so perfectly. Bishtar was even more beautiful then he remembered, older too. She ran her fingers through his curly black hair, then over his handsome face, and through the peach fuzz that would soon become a man's beard. She moved very close, too close. It was a perfect moment.

Mind-speaking was not needed, and they didn't even try.

All at once, they kissed. He held her to himself, tightly, incapable of doing anything but that.

Suddenly a burst of energy surged between them; it was a greater magic than anything they had ever known; greater than the deepest mysteries any world could conjure up. Soon enough, they gave in to their desires.

When they woke, their arms were still holding on to each other. She kissed him gently and smiled. "We could stay, my love."

There it was! She had said the word he had longed to hear from her forever. His needy heart soared to peaks that even the mating could not achieve.

But staying? he mused, for too long apparently.

When he did not answer, she asked heatedly, "Do you not love me, Mosher?"

"Oh no, oh no, Bishtar. I m-mean y-yes, I d-do l-love y-you. I love you."

She was now stern and spat, "Then why do you stutter so badly when saying it?"

The naïve young man soon thereafter got his first lesson in dealing with the opposite gender. "I did n-not s-stutter... I mean, n-not more than usual."

She quickly got up, covering herself, and started to storm away. He grimaced, knowing he had put his clunky foot in his mouth, big time. He chased after her. "I am s-sorry, Bishtar. Please stop to listen."

"No! Now leave me be, Mosher, son of Judah!"

Oh Shi-shi-shtu, she gave me the son of Judah brand; she must be really mad.

Bishtar suddenly turned and snapped, "Did you use me, Mosher?!"

Yup, she's m-mad. "No, n-never."

"Then why do you follow me? Leave me be, I tell you." She took off again.

He ran in front of the very angry young woman, forcing her to stop. He stood his ground. "No I will not. I love you. And you know it."

Bishtar's cross expression soon softened. Nonetheless, she studied him, arms crossed, waiting to see what would happen. He approached gingerly and took up her delicate hands in his rather round, course and husky ones. At first she balked at his touch, but because he would not let go, she relented. "Then what are we to do?"

"We do what we m-must."

"What of this place, Mosher? Our bodies? Ever since we ventured through that glowing doorway, we have become what we once knew in Egypt. We are human once again. Mosher, I do not want to change."

"Bishtar, this place will be ours, but not now. Look around you. Where is everyone? Where is Moses? There is no sign that anyone has ever been here. Where are they?"

"I know not." Bishtar thought of the vision she had seen through Joseph's Cup. Mosher was right; her father was nowhere to be seen.

Mosher, doing his best to sound rational, explained, "I tell you they are long g-gone, or maybe they were never here, n-not yet anyway."

"What does that mean?"

"Think about it. The portal opens to this place yes, b-but when? If it was the time we knew, then our people would be here. We could be all alone at Moses' mountain, forever. What will we eat? How will we shelter ourselves? We are human, yes. But w-what have we lost? For instance, can we mind-speak?"

They tried, both incapable of sending their thoughts.

"What we once were n-no longer applies here. We know nothing of this place anymore. But what we left behind we d-do know."

"We are whole again, Mosher. I do not want to look like that again."

"Neither do I, but what choice do we have? Our people need us. They n-need you even more."

"I was wicked looking!"

He took her in his arms and whispered in her ear, "No, never." As she started to cry, he added, "No matter what y-you look like, you will always be the most beautiful w-woman who ever lived."

"Do you really mean it?"

"Yes."

Mosher re-absorbed her lovely blue eyes, thinking how wonderful it was to see her real beauty, a loveliness made possible by being on the surface world, and by being human too. Then he started to think about how the whole impossibly strange story started.

"I'm so glad I found you w-when I did."

They both cried together.

* * * *

Mosher watched as Bishtar disappeared down the dark corridor. *Where is she going, and why?* As was so often the case, Mosher couldn't help but follow her. Well, in his mind he was just keeping an eye on her… for safety purposes, of course.

Furthermore, where she had gone was definitely not safe; in fact, it frightened him. He quickly retraced his steps. *I must find Calish.*

When he found Calish, Stenrak was still with him, discussing something very important. They all greeted one another and Mosher got to business. "Calish, Bishtar has g-gone toward the forbidden place Stenrak w-warned us about."

"What? You must be mistaken."

"No. I just s-saw it."

Calish faced Stenrak and asked in Pon tongue, "Have you ever been there?"

"No, never. As I have told you, Ashkolon has said there are demons of unspeakable horrors down there. The Helons will not venture there. Your sister, Calish..."

"We know Stenrak; you do not have to remind us."

"We m-must call to her," voiced Mosher anxiously.

All three of them used their mind-speaking abilities to search for her. But she did not answer.

Calish declared, "She's either too far or cannot answer for some reason."

Stenrak nodded in agreement.

Mosher stuttered fearfully, "C-Calish, do w-we have time to find o-others to help us?"

"Moshe, there's no time. My sister is in danger; I can sense it."

"Then let's h-hurry."

Soon enough, they approached the place where Mosher had last seen Bishtar. He pointed to the passageway in question. "Down there."

Stenrak gave a regrettable expression, indicating that if she had gone into that particular tunnel, then Mosher was right; Bishtar had traveled to a location no sane Pon would tread. "Striggitzz Sheol." He grunted distastefully.

But never one to shirk from a battle, happy that he had his friends with him, Stenrak breached the tunnel's dark threshold without looking back.

Encouraged by Stenrak's bravery, Calish affirmed his grip on Asher's spear and Mosher retrieved his sling. The young men quickly followed their Pon ally into the dark void.

Not long after, they were close enough to hear a distant echo. It sounded like "Aaagh!"

"Did you hear that?"

"It's Bishtar! She n-needs us."

The trio ran like the wind, ready to beat back anything that dared to hurt her.

* * * *

Bishtar closed-in on where the vision had shown her. It was a cavern of sorts, not overly large; a few Crystallight stones adorned the walls, enough at least for her to easily see her surroundings. It was a cold and damp space. Lingering in the air was the fetid odor of decay.

What are those?

Bishtar moved closer. Bones of many creatures littered the ground in front of her. She carefully stepped over them. Some she recognized as Pon, but other bones were oddly shaped, quite large and broken as well. She followed the white trail and the bones gradually became more densely packed. Ultimately they formed a ringlet of sorts, like a circular arrangement that had been purposely made. At the ringlet's center was something very dark. She could barely make it out: it was a large, lumpy form. She watched it long enough to notice its mass lifting up ever so slightly, then lowering too, repeating that gentle rhythm over and over.

The thing breaths, it is alive.

Bishtar used her mind-motion powers to lift a small stone. It hovered aloft for a moment. She tossed it at the sleeping form with the flick of her foreclaw quite effortlessly.

Then she ran for her life.

* * * *

"Mosher, what about that thing that followed us here? Where is it?"

They scanned over the base of the mountain, just like they had when they had first arrived, but there was no sign of the brutal beast.

"It's gone. It didn't seem to like it h-here. Remember? The monster looked up at the sun, screeched and vanished. Bishtar, I'm not sure but I thought it looked a bit like y-your father Zebulun, in a very, very scary kind of way."

"I thought so too. I guess. I have been thinking about him recently." That was true enough, but what she didn't say was how the golden jewel had shown her a vision of her father *after* she had used Joseph's Cup to divine his whereabouts. But she didn't want Mosher asking about Joseph's Cup, so she kept quiet.

252

Luckily for her, Mosher circumvented the issue in his own way. "Why did you t-travel to that place where you found the g-golden jewel?"

Bishtar hesitated before answering. She could tell him some things, but not everything.

* * * *

She didn't think it would work. The chalice had done miraculous things, but what she sought was surely beyond the magical device's abilities. Bishtar tried anyway; or rather she was *willing* to try. She was a little older than the last time she had braved its insights. The Cup still frightened her, but the reason for using it far outweighed those childish concerns. She peered deeply into the cup while wishing for her heart's desire.

Father.

Zebulun could be with them. After all, there were many missing people after the Chasm event; maybe her father was among them. Perhaps he had survived. Maybe, if she could find him, she would have someone who would die protecting her from a tribe that was growing increasingly wary of her; that evil Dathan especially. If her father were around, Dathan dare not threaten her.

Father will crush Dathan; Gasheer too.

When the swirling blood stopped, in the Cup's center she saw a brilliant golden jewel. Even though it was partially covered with a black hulking blob, the shiny object was still spectacular. "What is that?"

She brought Joseph's Cup closer; wanting to better see the jewel's details. Then the display magically zoomed in a bit. The jewel was very near, and within one of its facets was a place she had not thought about in years. It was the meadow where she had last seen her father, tending to his herd right before that great and terrible day. He looked over to her, as he had done on that last morning, smiling and waving to her with his kind and loving eyes. Even though Bishtar was only watching the scene from a faraway place, and through the golden jewel's lens, she waved back, smiling too.

"Father," she sighed in longing.

Like a bird in flight, her view shifted slightly higher. There was a dark form that hovered over the gem. It moved. It was alive, but the details were hard to see; it was too indistinct for her big black eyes to gather. The view flew upward some more and she saw a path that led to the golden jewel. It was far, but she was confident she would find it, and that nothing could stop her.

After cleaning it, she placed Joseph's Cup back in the niche where she kept it hidden. From the same hole Bishtar retrieved her Crystallight gem. She placed the dazzling ruby-red jewel around her neck, like she had when Mosher had first given it to her. Joseph's Cup was no longer needed, but Mosher's gift could make all the difference in the world.

"Father, I will see you soon. I swear it."

* * * *

When Bishtar would not answer the 'travel' question, Mosher tried from a different angle. "Bishtar, what h-happened before Calish, Stenrak and I found you?"

That was a subject Bishtar was willing to discuss. "When I first saw the creature in the center of the nest of bones, I thought it was sleeping. I must have awakened it. When that creature stood up, it looked hideous; bear-like, but more as a man would with a hunched back. It had a dog head. I ran. It attacked me."

"Then how did you... what did y-you do?"

Bishtar wavered before replying. "I guess, I..."

"Yes?"

"...can do things, Mosher."

* * * *

The dark form caught up with her, soundly grabbing her by the shoulder. Its cold grip sent shivers down Bishtar's spine. "Aaagh!" she screamed before turning around.

The creature was massive, towering over her. The beast opened its long, pointy snout; sharp fangs stretched across its jaws. It was about to snap onto Bishtar's neck when she summoned her powers.

"No!" she shouted at her attacker. She raised her claws and lifted up the nest's sharpest, jagged bones. Instantly, she sent them hurling at the creature's backside. The cutting projectiles ripped through the monster's tough hide, many of them going clear through its torso. The dog-man screeched in agony and sank to the cavern ground. Before collapsing and closing its eyes in death, the beast stared at her, and moaned as if it was sad. Dog-man snarled one last time, showing its teeth, before it sank into oblivion.

After she recovered from fright, Bishtar stepped over the creature and moved to its nest. The golden jewel lay in the middle of the bones where she had seen it in Joseph's Cup. She reached down, grabbing it, wondering if the gem would somehow let her experience her old home, and most importantly show her where her father was.

Suddenly a shiver of energy flowed through her. She knew that something was behind her. She made a claw-like fist, readying her powers again. When that was done, she turned to face whatever it was.

"Father!" she cried in surprise. He stood very close, peering into her eyes. "What... how did you get here?" Then she realized that it *was* possible; her father had actually survived the Chasm event. Maybe he had gotten lost all this time, and she, or rather Joseph's Cup, had finally found him.

"Father!? Are you really here?" But the man said nothing; he merely kept staring at her. *Maybe he doesn't recognize me.* So she called out, sobbing, "It is me, Bishtar, your daughter."

The man's eyes sparkled with golden highlights, and he smiled brightly. He opened his arms generously, as if he wanted her to embrace him. Bishtar was all too ready to comply.

While they hugged, Bishtar wished that she could stay that way forever; in her father's loving arms, protecting her from everything bad that had happened.

But out of sight, the man's face suddenly changed expression, and his gentle smile vanished.

* * * *

While basking in the hot sun, Mosher looked down at his human feet, not really wanting to push, or not really wanting to actually know the truth of her powers. Bishtar being able to *'do things'* was an understatement, and something he and Calish dared not speak of. It scared them; him especially. Even the question of why she had travelled to that forbidden place scared him. But his love for her transcended those concerns and he would not let it interfere with what he felt for her. Finally, he whispered, "I know."

Bishtar, glad that Mosher would not press for more 'things' details, continued her harrowing story. "Anyway, I thought I had killed the dog-man. I was wrong. I had my back to it. Then I felt a strange presence. And when I turned around, my father was standing there right in front of me."

"Your father? The thing, the dog-man beast, changed? It became something you were familiar with. Did it, or rather *he,* talk to you?"

"No. But it was so kind looking. I mean, when it looked like my father. He opened his arms to me, and I wanted to hug my father... or *it* so badly. The need for his love took over me."

Mosher thought for a moment. "Anubis then? It sounds like Anubis, the Guardian of the Underworld, protecting a g-gem that allows for travel to the surface world. Anubis has a dog-like head. But I know of no legend that describes Anubis changing shape into people we know."

"But Anubis or n-not, maybe the creature uses a person's m-memories to lure its victims in close, to trust it, and then it attacks."

"Mosher, what was *Anubis* doing? When you showed up, I mean?"

"We heard y-you scream. When we came upon you two, we saw the creature, the Anubis thing that looked like your father, ready to b-bite its fangs in your neck. Calish readied Asher's spear, but I w-was first." He proudly gestured to his sling, still attached to his belt.

"I felt the thing jerk. Was that you, Mosher?"

"Yes. I s-struck it between the eyes." Mosher pointed to the bridge of his nose and poked himself accordingly. He scrunched up his face as if he had just been hit by something really hard and put on a silly, stunned expression.

Bishtar giggled and poked him between the eyes. "Boink."

"Ouch!" He decried in a wild, exaggerated manner.

They both laughed some more.

"It backed away from y-you after it got summarily 'boinked'."

"And you stood between me at that Anubis creature, Mosher. I have never seen such bravery."

"Or s-stupidity, maybe."

They both enjoyed the joke.

Then Mosher became curious again. "What happened after that? Did you use the stones?" He pointed to her ruby-red Crystallight gem that decorated her neck. "Did you let the golden one touch the one you wear?"

"I guess I did, yes. It all happened so fast. I saw the thing that looked like my father start to go at you, and I remembered that when you and Calish had rescued me from those Pon creatures, Calish and I touched our two stones together. I guess I thought the same thing would happen. But it didn't quite turn out that way, did it?"

"I'm n-not sure. I didn't see you touch the stones. I was too b-busy getting ready for that Anubis monster to devour me. But all of a s-sudden a glowing doorway opened, and as the monster jumped at me, I felt the two of us being tossed into the portal's threshold. And then we found ourselves here at the base of Moses' mountain. We stumbled to the g-ground and looked back from where we had arrived."

Bishtar retrieved the golden jewel from where she had set it down. She held it between them, and they both watched its many mysterious and sparkling facets of golden colors.

"Mosher? The two stones made that doorway then?"

"Yes, it must be. And the dog-man must of followed us here, b-but as soon as it passed through the doorway, it started to writhe in agony, s-screeching louder than anything I had ever heard. And then it vanished."

"Do you think Anubis is dead? Finally?"

"I don't know, Bishtar."

"What happened to it? Where did Anubis go?"

"Maybe back to where we found it." Moshe was pensive. He studied his hands, noticing how human they were, so different from being claws. "El has made our worlds separate, just as His realm is different from ours. So, too, the underworld is different from the surface world."

"Meaning . . .?"

"We cannot be here if not as humans, and we cannot exist in the underworld unless we are Pon. That is why we changed from being human. He made the underworld for the Pon… and even the Anubis creature. The surface world is for us, or rather what we once were. It is as Moses taught us; El made this world for man. Other beings are not welcome."

"But we were Pon moments ago. Why would El bring us here, make us people again?"

"Only El can answer such a question."

Mosher peered at the mountain's peak. It was so dark; much darker than he remembered it being. The mountain top looked as if its upper layers had been scorched by an unquenchable fire. But the black stones also appeared to be so old, like whatever had caused the blackening was long ago. Somehow that thought frightened him. It made him more certain that he and Bishtar did not really belong on the surface world anymore.

"But whatever the case, we m-must use the stones to reopen the doorway and return. Calish and Stenrak must be back there waiting for us. They will be very worried b-by now."

Bishtar's face became stern again. "Calish is one thing, but Stenrak? I don't care for him, Mosher."

"I understand, but know this: He came to warn us a-about his brother's impending attack. That was what we were discussing b-before we found you. Stenrak didn't have to do this. And Bishtar, if not for his help, I don't know that any of us would have s-survived our fall to the underworld."

"Maybe, but I still don't trust him. And I know he dislikes me. Would you take his side over me?"

Mosher could see was starting to get angry. *Lesson two:* She expected a certain answer and he knew all too well that he'd

258

better be quick about it. "Bishtar, I could n-never choose him or anyone else above you. I love you."

"And I you."

They embraced tightly then.

After a few moments, Bishtar raised a topic that definitely needed flushing out. "But what of this, Mosher? What of our people? They will not hear of what has happened here between us. We are not yet married. I will be scorned, reviled, an outcast even more than I already am."

He took her in his arms to comfort her. "Then what has occured here will stay with us. It will be as if nothing has happened."

She nodded, glad to hear him say it.

"Are you ready?"

"Yes." But instead of completing the stone-touching ceremony, she suddenly had a question to ask, so she did. "Maybe before we go, we could find our way back to Egypt, just to see it one more time. What do you think? Remember the sweet flowers, the fruit, the laughter?"

Mosher sighed. "Bishtar, I do not know the way, and even if I did, we do not have food, water, or shelter. It is very far from here. And how would we span the sea we once crossed? Do you not remember it?"

"I kinda' kept my eyes closed when I saw the giant walls of water," she said shyly.

"Well, a mighty sea separates us from Egypt."

"Maybe there will be a boat waiting for us!"

Lesson three: logic and a woman's emotions don't always go hand-in-hand. "Bishtar," began Mosher, being as patient as one could possibly be, "There will be n-no boat waiting for us. Please trust me. We must return."

"Very well, I will trust you... *this time.*" For emphasis, she gently poked him in his less-than-muscular belly.

Her touch inspired them to draw closer. They held each other for another long moment, and of course enhanced the embrace with an intimate kiss. Mosher was glad she could not read his thoughts; his desperate love for her would have surely passed between them. Having her know that secret scared him as much as the thought of losing her.

Before the longing could overtake them once again, Mosher reluctantly separated himself, ever so slightly. He then pointed at the stones.

Bishtar nodded. Then suddenly she had another important question. "Hey, wait a minute, I just thought of something. How did you know I needed help?" She wagged a cross finger at him. "Were you following me Mosher, son of Judah?"

Oh no, not the son of Judah brand again. "I ah, ah, ah, no of course n-not." He started looking around, as if searching for something, anything actually. As if to distract her, he rambled, "Gee, I think I s-see an almond tree up there. See it... see it, Bishtar?"

Before she could answer he said, "Did you know that the almond tree's wood is very s-strong? How strong, ask ye? Well, it was the only choice to b-be used for Asher's spear; practically unbreakable, I tell you. And Aaron's staff, they say, is also made from the almo . ."

"Mosher!"

"Y-Yes."

She smiled in a knowing way, and that was enough to settle the issue.

Lesson Four: Somehow women are always the boss.

"Bishtar?"

"Yes?"

"There is one more thing."

"Go ahead."

"There might come a m-moment when, well, you might be *needed.* Calish and I already discussed this." Before she could respond, he said, "We did not speak of this with anyone else, but he was g-going to ask anyway."

"Ask for?"

"We know you can do... *things.* If you see that Stilik's forces are going to overwhelm us, then we will n-need you to help."

"You're asking me to fight... to kill, Mosher?"

"If necessary, yes. Especially if they start attacking the children."

That comment hit Bishtar hard. "They would do this?"

"Stenrak has warned us, so y-yes. To make them slaves, or worse."

"They shall fail if they try to take the tents where the little ones are." She took her hand, forming a small fist to emphasize her point. On the surface world she sensed no power when making her grip. But once they returned to the underworld, Bishtar had no doubt that her mind-motion power would return to her. She would turn the attacking Pons' insides into mashed goo. Her wrath would strike enough fear in their hearts that they will be forced to retreat.

Knowing what the treacherous Pon intended to do was unnacteptable. It ultimately persuaded her to give up her human appearance for a far less than ideal one. Yes, she would go back, but that didn't mean she had to like it.

Mosher nodded his understanding. "Thank you."

"It is the least I can do."

One last time they gazed longingly at their surroundings. After a few long moments, Mosher grabbed part of the golden jewel and they touched the two stones together. The doorway came to life and the two young, vibrant lovers passed through the glistening wall of colors.

* * * *

"Bishtar! Moshe!" shouted Calish as he and Stenrak ran to meet them. They stopped just short of the barrier at the nest of bones, where they had just seen Mosher and Bishtar magically appear.

Bishtar pulled the golden gem away from the Crystallight jewel and the doorway closed to nothing. She took a step and lost her grip on the golden jewel. It dropped. All by itself the stone rolled back to a shallow niche in the nest's center.

She went to retrieve her prize when suddenly they heard a wild screech. All four of them had to cover their ears, it was so shrill and loud.

The young adventurers looked to the sound's source and saw a dark, menacing phantom grow out of a nearby pile of bones. The specter became solid and morphed into the beastly dog-man Bishtar had first seen.

"Leave it!" cried Mosher as he could see Bishtar reach for the golden gem. "Don't touch it." He grabbed her by the arm and pulled her out of the nest, toward the place where Calish and Stenrak stood.

Together, while holding up their respective weapons, the quartet moved off. As soon as the group backed away, the dog-man approached. But rather than attacking, the creature shuffled over to the place where the stone lay. It snarled at them ferociously, then proceeded to cover its body protectively over the golden gem. Its dog-like snout took one more ripping sneer at them and its eyes glistened with a dazzling display of golden colors. After that, the beastly thing tucked its head into its torso, forming a huge hulking ball shape that sank to a spot right over its golden possession. The dog-man then proceeded to sleep, as when Bishtar had first sighted it.

"Anubis sleeps," Mosher whispered.

"Anubis?" quizzed Calish, "Are you serious? That thing?"

Stenrak interjected by mind-speaking, *We call such things Sheol Demons.*

Calish raised his eyebrow. "That sounds kinda' boring. *Anubis* sounds better."

Stenrak made an expression of consternation as if his name should have been good enough.

"Yeah, Anubis," agreed Mosher, and Bishtar nodded too.

"Striggitzz," Stenrak cursed. *Crazy humans.*

"Anyway," cited Calish, "let's get outa' here."

Mosher followed with, "Let sleeping d-dogs lie."

The twins rolled their eyes at that one.

While the band of explorers returned to the better spaces outlying the Crystallight caverns, Stenrak mind-spoke to Bishtar, *Once more I have saved you, human.*

Bishtar glowered at him and spewed, *I didn't ask for your help.*

Stenrak, not liking her tone, unwisely went for his hammer's shaft.

Bishtar grinned at his impudence and started to make her standard clawed fist of power.

Calish immediately stepped between them, forcing both to take a step back. He turned to Bishtar, imploring, "He has come to warn us, Sister. We should thank him."

But Bishtar kept her steady gaze on Stenrak. She mind-spoke, *Tell your people that they will regret attacking the tents of our children.*

Stenrak *harrumphed* at the rebuke. But at the same time his eye's revealed that he had heard her threat and took it very seriously.

Calish forcibly led Stenrak forward and away from his sister.

As the two of them went up the tunnel, Mosher called out to them, "We will follow. Go ahead." Calish shrugged and grabbed Stenrak by the shoulders. The pair continued on their way.

When they were finally alone, Mosher faced his portal companion. Bishtar was passing her claws over her swollen head as if searching for her long brown hair. She was saddened that her fingers caught up nothing for the effort. She stared at him while touching her big black eyes in the process. Without mind-speaking, Mosher could tell that, in Bishtar's mind, she was 'wicked' looking again. But he did not let her think it; he returned her gaze with kindness and his heart went out to her. *Bishtar, I am here with you.* He went to hold her, and she let him. He wrapped his arms around her, but strangely she did not reciprocate the gesture. She stood there like a statue, stiff and unmoving. Mosher's gut screamed to him that something was severely wrong.

He released his hold on her, and took in her face. But it was blank, stoic even. He held onto her claw the way he had her human hand at the base of Moses' mountain. But she did hold onto his hand. Her little claws lay limp, refusing to clasp onto his.

"What is wrong, Bishtar?"

"Nothing," she said coldly.

"Then why..."

"Why what?"

"Why?... What of us?... What h-happened between us?"

"Nothing happened. Remember?"

She pulled her hand free and stepped back. Then she casually walked around him, as if he were just another obstacle in her way.

As he watched her disappear into the dark tunnel, his heart sank to depths that even the underworld could not fathom.

Lesson Five: You will never really know Bishtar, daughter of Zebulun.

CHAPTER 28
A Spear Inside

5 Years Later

Prince Stilik turned proudly to his First and commanded, "Send your best warriors to scout ahead. See if Stenrak stands with the surface dwellers."

"Yes, my Prime," answered First respectfully. First mind-spoke to a small group of soldiers, then two of them backed away and entered a divergent tunnel. First returned to face Stilik, and stood motionless, awaiting more orders. Two short red stripes rose over First's right eye, signaling his rank. To be First was a great honor, granted to him only after he had demonstrated great loyalty, bravery, and obedience.

Stilik nodded to his First and faced three other soldiers. "Take your men, go around the humans from behind, and when the main battle begins, kill the ones with the best weapons. Take the items and bring them to me. If possible, try to avoid killing Dathan's men. Try to remember they will be wearing red arm bands."

"Yes, Prime."

"And most of all," added Stilik, "avoid killing Calish. Their leader is mine; his death is my path to ascension. His spear is also mine."

"Prime!" they answered smartly. These foot soldiers, unlike First, merely had one short red stripe over their left eye. They promptly left.

Stilik turned his back on First and stepped forward to stand on a darkened ledge high above the Holy Place. It was a place very few knew of, most especially the surface dwellers. The battle was about to start. The humans were alert; their soldiers were strategically placed throughout the cavernous spaces. Many were tasked with guarding tents, which were another area ripe for the taking. Calish's soldiers were easy to spot, but in some areas they were very close to Dathan's troops. The fighting, therefore, would eventually get very messy.

No matter, pondered Stilik. *Once the battle begins, Dathan cannot fault me for collateral damage.*

The air was thick with anticipation. Stilik breathed in the odor deeply, flexing his broad muscles, expanding his wide shoulders even wider. He reached for and stroked his regal chest armor, taking in the strange blend of its smells, foul though they might be. The scents awakened fond memories. He felt over the shield's patchwork of various textures; all samples of the hides taken from his many kills.

"There you are, my old friends," he said while caressing the fleshy surfaces.

In one of his shield's corners was human flesh; soft, pliable and unfortunately too easy to get. He merely needed one thrust of the hammer on his victim's pleadingly wretched face. The skin had garnered an armor spot, not because the triumph was particularly difficult, but due to the distinctive fact that it was taken from a surface dweller. On that sad bit, cupped over his left shoulder sat Mestalor; a white skeletal shell that was painfully taken after the beast had scarred his back with its sharp pincers. Luckily for Stilik, the pincer bites exposed the monster's open maw to his stony sword. Underneath that bit was Kordeshu hide; hairy, fang-filled, and earned only after the small nimble creature had nearly severed his leg. The biting thing, while clenching its locked jaw on his thigh, had left its furry head vulnerable to a bashing blow. Near the other corner, covering his right shoulder, sat Pon hide; tough, gray, rough and carved from a rival clan's best fighter after he had mistakenly believed in Stilik's ruse of being hurt beyond recovery. Stilik was happy to see the surprised look on his opponent's face when at the last moment he sprang up and slit his attacker's over-confidently exposed neck. The armor's centerpiece, covering Stilik's heart was his prized pelt: Graxon. It was brown, supremely thick and practically impenetrable. Stilik's portion was bravely taken after he had plunged his best spear-stone through the titan's eye, making mush of its brain.

"Thank you," he whispered to his long-lost adversaries. "May you rest peacefully in Sheol."

He had won every one of the fragments in mortal combat. He didn't have to go on all of the dangerous missions, but if he did not, then others would, and to Stilik that was unacceptable. Stilik's father had collected the hides himself. When enough of them had been accumulated, he'd ordered their clan's best seamstress to tailor the breastplate. Stilik's reward was to wear the armor with honor. More importantly, it was proof to his father that he was worthy of acquiring the Pon's highest military rank.

Stilik ran a rugged finger along his face, tracing his bulging reward for achieving that rank. His pointy claw punctured up some of it. A drop of purple blood oozed out and he brought the metallic-tasting liquid into his mouth. *My Blood Vein. Delicious, yet bitter.*

This feature made Stilik very unique from any other Pon warrior. The Vein was taken from the heart of a live Sterga beast. Stergas were not particularly violent, so killing one never warranted an honorary place on one's breastplate, but the hard-shelled creature did have one very special trait – the Blood Vein. The thick, purple artery had the exceptional ability to graft itself onto other flesh, sinking deep into its new owner's skin and veins, taking in his or her blood, mingling with the Sterga's blood, and living again through its new host.

We have a treat for you, friend Sterga.

Stergas were fond of eating Pon. While devouring their favorite food, if the victim was animated enough, Stergas had a habit of grabbing up prey in their meaty little claws, chewing blissfully away, and rolling over on their thick backs, thus exposing their soft underbelly. Then it was a simple matter to cut into the beast, nearly killing it, but not causing death until the pumping heart with its central Vein could be removed. Of course, the Vein's recipient had to be there and would normally be the Sterga's main aggressor. He or she, if they chose, could also have their most trusted comrades by their side as proud witnesses. Once the heart was removed, a Maana master would quickly separate the Vein from the heart and attach the throbbing artery to the new owner's face. Within moments, the Sterga's Vein would sink its tiny tentacles into the recipient's skin and proceed to pump away.

Invigorating. Stilik's Vein ran diagonally from the corner of his white protruding cranium, past the bridge of his nose, down to his square lower jaw, ending in the side of his neck. Blood Veins were said to give their new masters enhanced skills: speed, endurance, and strength. In its wake one could see the purplish Vein darken and bulge out from Stilik's face, often throbbing or pulsing, especially when he was in the heat of battle.

The shield and Vein were proud accomplishments, but they paled in comparison with Stilik's truest inherent worth. Near the Blood Vein's apex, at his forehead's center, was Stilik's most distinguishing feature. It was very rare to see. It was a symbol of nobility and his family's crest; a jagged red circle with a black cross through it. At the cross's center was an imbedded golden-red crystal gem.

Hastisk spiders, little black crawlers that had a short and very strong central fang, were used to puncture a small hole into a noble's forehead. Hopefully the hole was deep enough to house a golden gem; if not, the recipient would have to endure the spider being reapplied for another go. If, however, the puncture hole was deep enough, a Maana master would insert the glowing gem into the noble's bloodied skull and skin. This ceremonial procedure was done with much pomp and circumstance, and was usually performed only under special conditions. Stilik had, by all his victories, more than met those conditions.

A prince and heir to the Helon throne.

If any other Pon were to see Stilik, they were to immediately bow, lest they be severely pummeled, or worse. For if their bend was considered insufficient, then the offender might be called upon as an unwilling volunteer to get more Blood Veins; especially if that individual was particularly animated, the way Sterga's liked.

All in all, the adornments reminded Stilik that he was more than ready to kill. "Must that include you, my brother?" asked Stilik to himself. "Will you too decorate my armor?" Reluctantly, Stilik factored his younger brother into the upcoming battle equation. If he got in the way, Stilik would not regret getting his claws around Stenrak's throat, but only if necessary. He looked over the Holy Place for the sly one, but Stenrak could not be seen. "I will find you, Brother," he hissed, while gripping his hammer's shaft.

Their father could no longer keep his people – keep him – from attacking the surface dwellers, prophecy be damned. They inhabited the Holy Place and it could no longer stand. Stenrak would have to pay the price for his so-called prophetic allegiance with the strangers. Even if Stenrak was right about the surface dweller's importance to Pon survival, the 'humans' as Ashkolon called them, at the very least had to be enslaved, and some of the more useless ones made food of. Furthermore, if the humans had a power stone, as the Maana masters had warned, then his Father should wield it. Or better yet, *he* should.

Stilik turned back around. As expected, First was still there: silent, rigid, like a motionless statue waiting for instructions. If possible, First barely blinked an eye, or dared to twitch his two red stripes. "Is their leader where he should be?"

First suddenly sprang to life. "My scouts told me the human Dathan is where we agreed upon."

"Yes, he should be. He wants our protection, and if we give it, he promises a sharing of all their science and weaponry. It will help make my rise to power assured. Make sure you keep him safe once the battle begins. But whatever happens, lead his followers to our chosen caverns. No matter the outcome, the surface dwellers can no longer stay in the Holy Place."

"It shall be as you say, Prime." First set out to do as he was told, leaving the Prince alone.

Stilik had hoped he could savor the last quiet moment before the battle in private, but that desire was soon squashed. From behind, another being approached silently. Stilik felt the intruder's presence before the individual could be seen. The prowler was like a dark shadow that crept into his heart.

Stilik turned to face the disturbance as the character emerged from the darkness, drifting toward him more like a ghost than an earthly man. The ghost stopped just short of getting too close. Then the two leaders stood on the ledge, face-to-face.

It angered the prince when the ghost did not bow his head immediately. Stilik waited, but still no deference. Violence should have been wrought upon the intruder for the insult, but Stilik had to stay his hand. For the sake of keeping the inter-species alliance, Stilik had to peacefully deal with the humans... for now. He usually didn't have to parley with their king Dathan, but he did have to put up with Dathan's chief negotiator, the ghost.

Faester, mind-spoke Stilk to the disrespectful little human-turned-Pon.

Faester was well adept at mind-speaking, but chose to say aloud, in Stilik's tongue, "My grandfather is ready, near the altar. Are we still in agreement as to our terms?"

Stilik glared upon the much smaller Ponman distastefully. Stilik had never trusted the human-Pon hybrid. Faester was diminutive in size, but that meant nothing really, for the little ghost was beyond dangerous. Faester, as usual, was immaculately attired in his black flowing robes. Faester's eyes were also black, but unlike other Pon, they were much thinner. More importantly, there was a tiny red dot in their center. The red dot was strange by any standard, and indicative of Faester's awesome powers.

Harsha slime worm, thought Stilik very quietly to himself, making sure the words did not broadcast themselves to Faester. Dathan's negotiator was duplicitous, cunning, and therefore a constant threat. He carried a small dagger attached around his waist. To Stilik, the tiny poking stick was superfluous and most likely a deceptive trick. Feaster didn't need to wield the tool because what Faester lacked in physical strength or fighting skills, he more than made up for with his mind-motion powers. These were powers that enabled Faester to do remarkable things. For example, Stilik knew that Faester used his mind-motion powers to help him travel so silently and smoothly, as if he walked on air, like a ghost. It also explained how the tiny creature could levitate enough to face him eye-to-eye. Faester's long black robe that skirted the ground only helped to foster that illusion, if it *was* an illusion. No matter, the human-Pon snake had powers that made him unlike any other Pon. In fact, Feaster was, as some misguided Pon believed, the O'oviss. But Stilik was not so easily fooled. Feaster was a Harsha, nothing else.

"We are in agreement," Stilik stated. "Dathan will be protected. Your new homes in our choicest caverns are ready. There will be plenty of food for your people. And they will be safe there. Are they ready?"

"They are," replied Faester. "Once you have finished off Calish's soldiers, my tribe will depart from your Holy Place as agreed. And speaking of Calish, what of the survivors from his people?"

"We will take their resources, and their lives."

"What will you do to them?"

"What do you think, Faester?"

"You cannot have all of them." Faester said this more as threat than a casual comment. A serious expression crossed his brow. "There will be many left over. They belong to me... or rather, to my Grandfather."

The survivors' fate had already been agreed upon, so Faester's new demands did not sit well with Stilik. The change in terms, combined with Faester's refusal to show proper bowing protocol made Stilik furious. He had had enough of Faester's disrespect. When challenged so egregiously, the warrior did what was in his nature and what he was trained to do. He slowly brought a claw to his hammer's shaft. His Blood Vein started throbbing too, black now.

Feaster, upon noticing the gesture and the pumping vein, glared intensely into Stilik's eyes. He was unimpressed by the threatening stance and was eager to remind the prince of his powers. Faester focused his mind. He envisioned how he could willfully move the surrounding elemental particles anywhere he wanted to: up, down... or better yet, twisting all around.

Striggitzz, cursed Stilik with trepidation.

Faester's beady black eyes blinked, and his eyes' red dots began glowing. Stilik instantly felt a trembling in his bowels. His guts started coiling over each other more and more with each passing moment. Stilik nearly doubled over, but did not; he would not give in to intimidation. The pain was Faester's doing; his powers. In defiance, Stilik tightened his grip upon the hammer. Stilik was sure he could mightily strike the small Pon creature, but could he do so swift enough, strong enough, before his own death came?

He finally relented and chose to be diplomatic... for the moment. With great effort, overcoming the pain, he defiantly squeezed out, "We can divide resources after the battle. I am sure we can come to some agreement then."

Faester released his grip on Stilk's insides, relaxed his expression, and the glowing red dots dissipated. "Why, thank you, Stilik. That is most agreeable."

"And the stone?" Stilik would not let that subject go, pain or no pain.

"I must remind you, as we have already agreed, the stone, once taken from Calish, belongs to Grandfather."

Stilik did not respond to Faester's stone comment and was careful not to mind-speak what he really thought. "Then we will meet after the battle."

"Agreed. And please remember my grandfather's forces will have a red arm band. I take it your troops have been advised and will act accordingly?"

Although Stilik hated Faester's patronizing tone, he nonetheless answered for the sake of ending the conversation before violent thoughts overcame him again. "Do not worry, Faester. My men know what to do."

"Very well indeed," Faester responded condescendingly. With that, he disappeared into a very dark tunnel, gliding effortlessly over the rocky surfaces, like the shadow he was.

Stilik grunted out his distaste for the slime-worm and returned to the ledge of the Holy Place. "We shall see, my friend, we shall see."

* * * *

"They are about to attack."

"From where?"

Calish pointed to the most obvious tunnels. "Over there, mainly, but the Crystallight caverns have many other hidden entrances, as you know."

"I understand," answered Mishtas. "And our soldiers are protecting what we can. Dathan has the bulk of his best soldiers around his camp, near the altar."

"Our men are few, Uncle."

"But they are loyal to you, unlike Dathan's. The older ones are still loyal to him; those that still look human. They know their time is coming to an end, but they stand by him. The younger ones, however, who look like Pon, are not as loyal, and have expressed sympathy for you, Calish. In any event, I have heard that Dathan's followers have readied their belongings, as if to leave this place. But our people are ready to move as well."

"Good. Do you think the sympathetic younger ones will fight with us?"

"I speak with them and some are willing to follow you if you decide to challenge Dathan. Two of Abiram's sons will also join us and they have sway over many. So it is possible. What you say about El has touched their hearts."

"I speak of what Korah taught me, Uncle."

Mishtas nodded sadly. "I miss him."

"I, too, miss him greatly."

"He stood for El, and against Dathan's gods."

"False gods, Uncle."

"And false promises, Nephew."

"Dathan has lost many believers over the years. Of this we should be thankful to El, and Korah's legacy."

"Dathan fears you, Calish. You have grown to be a fine young man, and he sees that you will challenge his authority over our tribe. His men rarely intrude upon our tents anymore. Thus, we are now a tribe more separated than we are united."

"On this wake cycle, our fate will be decided one way or another." Calish held up Asher's spear proudly. Since he had become an adult – tall, strong, and nimble – he no longer feared Gasheer, or that the bully would take it from him. In fact, he was quite fond of displaying the glistening lance in front of the brute's menacing face.

"Once the battle is over, you shall take your place as our leader." Mishtas waited a few moments, and when Calish did not answer, Mishtas started to wonder why.

Calish appeared pensive. Then he changed the subject. "Is Stenrak gone? I haven't seen him lately."

"I have not seen him either."

"I sense he is near, so not to worry. He and I have agreed to meet once more to discuss and implement our disposition."

"How so?"

Calish reached into his pouch and pulled out the Minthuru stone. "We will try and use this to doorway our tribe to another place."

"Doorway?"

The upcoming battle and its ramifications prompted Calish to tell his uncle about things he needed to know. "Many years ago, Stenrak and I combined our two stones; this Minthuru stone and his Crystallight stone. It created a doorway to another place."

"Back home to Egypt?" Mishtas asked excitedly, as his eyes lit up.

"Unfortunately, no. But it was beautiful, Uncle. Stenrak and I called it the Valley."

"And this doorway, how does it work?"

"It is like a shimmering wall or portal. Inside of it one can see the Valley. Stenrak and I passed through the doorway's threshold the way we walk through a tent's entrance. And then you will find yourself there, in the Valley, and no longer here."

"El, it is magic."

"I suppose so. A magical gift from the God of Moses to us."

"We really must leave then?"

"Our situation here is perilous at best. We are surrounded by the threat of death, as you are well aware. If we can open a doorway, then we must take the opportunity to explore the possibilities of finding a new home, even if it is temporary. Stilik's people will never leave us alone, here in what they consider their Holy Place. And you have seen how much Stilik's people desire our weapons, our machinery."

"Yes, during their first attack, by our reckoning five years ago, we saw many of them digging through our dead bodies for arrows, swords and knives. They even looked through unguarded tents for lamps, mirrors, and other miscellaneous items. Since then, other Pon must have seen those things, and decided to return for everything we have."

"Strategically, that was just a preliminary battle; to test our defenses. Stilik mostly attacked our outermost camps." That statement was very true, but Calish kept to himself another very thorny fact: Bishar's involvement.

What many in the tribe did not know was how she had used her powers. Bishtar decimated any of Stilik's forces that dared to attack the tents where the little ones were being kept safe. The Pon warrior's bodies were tortured, ripped open and strewn into mangled and twisted piles of so much waste. Witnesses on both sides ran in terror. It was even said that this event helped induce Stilik to withdrawal his forces. Unfortunately, Bishtar's help would not be available for the upcoming fight. She had become too indifferent as of late, far too mysterious, and often absent from the tribe's territory. This worried all of them greatly and was yet another example of the pressing concerns for the tribe.

Angry, Mishtas added, "They also destroyed tents belonging to our tribe... Abiram's too, before they killed him! Those devils."

"Of course."

"And yet somehow Dathan's tents were untouched and the Elder lives on."

"How coincidental," Calish said ironically. "Stenrak knew of the attack, but arrived after the battle had begun.

"So much death all around."

"For Stenrak too. His younger brother died defending us."

"More death. When will it end?"

"Soon, Uncle. The fight coming up will be the final battle. I know it."

"Do you think El stands with us? Will we survive?"

The Minthuru, which was still in his hand, started humming softly and Calish answered, "He is, Uncle, He is."

"I did not want to speak of this, but..."

"Out with it, my friend."

"I know you are fond of Stenrak, and his Pon folk, but during our first battle, some of Stilik's troops were seen eating our fallen. Some say they are no better than those beasts that attacked us at the altar so many years ago. Luckily, Stenrak fought them off before they could butcher the corpses, but the damage was done. It forced us to burn the corpses."

"I remember," Calish said sadly.

"My point is, they are not like us. Even though many of our people look like them, and all the youngsters look like them..."

Mishtas turned away from Calish while saying this, as to not offend him. "We could never do such things."

Calish became very worried. "I pray you are right, Mishtas." Calish kept to himself things he had heard some of the children mind-speak. The little ones, especially those born Pon, would often broadcast blood-curdling jokes about having a longing for flesh, human or Pon. *'Grandfather's toes look delicious,'* some would say. *'Yes, and Grandmother's are even more appetizing.'*

For now, tradition, cultural ties, and the human adults kept the young from carrying out their desires and turning those jokes into realty. *But for how long? Until the first generation is gone, perhaps?* What was even more troubling was how he himself was stifling urges for raw meat, what Stenrak had called the blood-longing. How long could he keep from acting out his growing desires for flesh? *But soon,* Calish accepted desolately, *those concerns will no longer matter to me.*

"We will find a way," interrupted Mishtas, after seeing Calish struggle with something that was obviously bothering him.

Calish made himself snap out of his dour mood. "Yes, my uncle, with Elders like you guiding our way, we will."

Mishtas was surprised to hear of himself described as an Elder. He never would have conceived of it on his own. Calish could see his puzzled expression, so he explained. "Are not Korah, Abiram, and even Dathan gone from us? Who then is better equipped, has more wisdom of years, to take their place than you? And who did Moshe and I turn to all these years for counsel but not to you? No, Uncle, our tribe needs, and must have, an Elder. You are that person."

"I am honored, but..."

"You must help our people... help Moshe."

"Why? What do you mean, help Mosher?"

As if on cue, Mosher joined them. Stenrak approached too. Both Mishtas and Calish looked anxious. Mosher asked, "What's g-going on?"

"Never mind for now," Calish answered. To quickly change the subject, he mind-spoke to Mosher and Stenrak. *The Cult? My sister? Are they here?*

276

The mentioning of Bishtar put a sorry expression on Mosher's face.

Yes, on both counts, my friend, answered Stenrak. *I hear them in my mind.*

Mosher added out loud for Mishtas' sake, "I have not seen Bishtar for many cycles. I asked her to s-stay, but I fear she is lost to us. She spends too m-much time off on her own. It is said she has explored very distant and d-dangerous places." He turned to Calish and said, "Your m-mother is worried she has been taken over by an evil spirit. Bishtar has changed so much, it s-scares her."

"My sister knows what is at stake... the doorway, the Crystallight stone she wears, and her role in our destiny. She understands, I know it, no matter how much she has changed." Calish grabbed Mosher's shoulders. "And you will see her again, my friend."

Mosher at first shied away from Calish's kindness, but it was also clear that the words brought hope to his eyes. Calish smiled broadly at seeing his friend's reaction.

Then he asked Stenrak, *And what of Voice?*

Unknown, my friend, but the spirit should not be underestimated.

How so?

Your sister is powerful; maybe too powerful for Voice to ever truly control. Ashkolon says that the evil spirit is wary of her and of what she might do, or rather will do, with or without Voice. But be assured, Voice will not let the battle pass absent its dark presence.

Calish nodded. For Mishtas' understanding, he both mind-spoke while speaking out loud. "And your brother, Stilik?"

He is near; I can sense him. Stenrak's expression looked almost eager. *He looks for me.*

"We stand with you."

At that comment, Mosher and Mishtas nodded.

"The battle will begin soon," continued Calish. To Stenrak he mind-spoke. *I see you wear a tattoo on your forehead.*

Stenrak brought his claw up to the red circle with its centralized black cross. He traced its outline. *I am old enough to carry the crest of my family in battle. My father, upon Ashkolon's council, agreed to let me wear it. And this brings up a subject we should discuss. I will tell you what to look for when the Pon warriors attack. It might help your warriors know friend from foe.*

Thank you, Stenrak. I was going to ask.

Stenrak nodded. *You might have noticed that most Pon soldiers carry red stripes on their foreheads. This denotes their rank and order. Usually there is only one short stripe over the left eye. This is the common class of warrior. They are dangerous, but not overly so.*

We have s-seen this, replied Mosher.

And so you can discern one Pon warrior from another, my men will have a black stroke over their eye. Stilik's will have a red one. If, however, you see a soldier with two red dashes, beware. He will be a seasoned warrior for Stilik and therefore very dangerous.

And your brother, how will we know him?

Stilik, my friends, will stand out. You will know him at once. To be more precise, since the last attack on your people, Stilik has earned two added adornments that will be most obvious and rare to see. You might recall Telek, the Cultist you call One Eye?

Mosher and Calish nodded.

He has a purple streak across his face. It is what we call the Blood Vein, denoting the highest in military ranking. My brother has since earned a Blood Vein. And his crest, unlike mine, will have a golden-red gem in its center.

The gem, what does it mean?

Stilik is a prince, next in line to be king of the Helons. Stenrak said this in a somber way, almost as if he regretted saying it. But rather than elaborating, he quickly changed the subject. *Are all your people ready to depart?*

"They are," answered Calish in mind-speak and out loud. "When the time comes, we will open a doorway to the Valley. Remember, Moshe gave the Crystallight gem to Bishtar. She wears it around her neck. She will give it to you so that you can open the doorway. And Moshe will lead our people from there."

Mishtas and Mosher both looked very surprised.

Mosher blurted out loud, "What do y-you mean by that?"

Calish, once again put a gentle hand on Mosher's shoulder. "Not now, Moshe. I will explain later."

Stenrak interjected before Mosher could further object. *Yes, and I will make sure to keep Stilik's forces at bay when the time comes.*

Good luck with him. From your description, he must be very powerful.

Luck is unfamiliar to us, Calish, my friend, but by now I understand your meaning behind it, so I will answer in a way familiar to your people... Thank you.

Calish and Mosher translated Stenrak's mind-speak to Mishtas and asked him to warn the tribe's forces. Mishtas acknowledged the message soberly. Then the group walked around the camp, checking the defenses, making sure the soldiers were ready to fight. Dathan's soldiers were easy to spot, whether they were human or Pon.

Mishtas observed, "Dathan's soldier's wear a red-colored arm band."

Mosher responded, "Yes, they think to f-fool us. No doubt Feaster has arranged for this."

Stenrak, understanding the topic of Faester, mind-spoke, *He is a cunning one, Calish. Ashkolon says he is in league with Voice. He has mind-motion powers. Beware of that Harsha priest.*

"I know my friend, I know."

Know this too. When the battle begins, arm bands will most likely mean nothing. My brother cannot, will not, fully guarantee any deal with your people. In the heat of battle, Pon warriors are known to fight anything set before their eyes.

"Does that include you, Stenrak?" Calish had seen first hand Stenrak's rage after it had been ignited by the heat of battle.

Stenrak paused to look at his friends. *Yes, my brothers, yes,* he said seriously.

* * * *

Gasheer, wearing his chainmail and brass helmet, took up the shofar and blew into it as hard as he could. The mighty sounds echoed throughout the Crystallight caverns. *Brr... Brr... Brr... Brr... Brr... Brr... Brr... Brr!*

His soldiers, positioned near and far, starting shouting out their call to arms. They were ready, weapons drawn, muscles tensed, invigorated by the sounds of Gasheer's shofar blasts. "Fight! Fight! Fight!" the tribe's soldier's yelled in unison.

Stilik's Pon soldiers were pouring in from every Crystallight cavern entrance. Screams and bodily clashes could soon be heard. Gasheer ordered some of his men to surround Dathan, as their Lord pulled back from the altar area and closer to his tents. Silently, Faester glided from a dark tent corner to stand behind Dathan. The red dot in Faester's eyes danced here and there madly, eager for any threat.

Faester whispered greedily, "I am here, Grandfather."

Dathan backed up a step, to be closer to Faester. "I trust that you are, my son."

* * * *

Deborah ran to where Gabeel stood on guard over some of Abiram's tents. Her small sword was at the ready, even though it might have been too heavy for her. She was dressed in warrior garb.

"Deborah," said Gabeel hurriedly, "Stay near the tents. Protect the little ones."

"No. There are others who will do it. I stand with you."

Gabeel was about to argue when they could hear the shouts of nearby soldiers as waves of Pon attacked. Swords were slashing, arrows flying, clubs swinging, and the enemy's claws were tearing at any flesh that stood in their way.

Gabeel turned to face Deborah. "Go back to the tents before..."

Suddenly one of Stilik's soldiers broke through the mass of flailing bodies. The Pon warrior threw his sharp hammer at Gabeel, striking him hard in the lower ribcage. Gabeel reeled back, clutching at his side, and dropped to his knees in pain. The Pon soldier, seeing he had the advantage, moved in to finish Gabeel off.

Deborah stepped forward, blocking the attacker's path. She brought up her sword uneasily, especially after noticing that the Pon soldier had two red dashes over his eyes. Everyone had been warned about the two-striped warriors. Deborah was not sure she could stop the much bigger, and obviously stronger, soldier from killing Gabeel, but two-dashes or no, she would die trying.

The soldier stopped for a moment and hissed out loud in anticipation of destroying both of his opponents. Two-stripes was even more eager to kill after seeing the shiny metal weapon in the female's shaky hands. He shuffled closer, grinning meanly, while taking out another club hammer from his belt.

When the approaching soldier was near enough to bash Deborah, an arrow struck the Pon squarely in one eye. The arrow's tip went deep into the soldier's skull. The soldier looked up, mouth open, and then dropped backwards, dead.

Gabeel and Deborah turned back to see the shooter. "Mishtas!" Deborah cried thankfully.

Mishtas ran to Gabeel and knelt beside him. He took out a spare cloth and used it to bind Gabeel's wounds. "Can you still fight?"

Gabeel grimaced, but got slowly to his feet. "I am ready." He grabbed up his sword and stared into Deborah's eyes defiantly. Seeing Gabeel's bravery, Deborah brought up her sword as well.

Shouts and clashing sounds were all around them now. "They are coming closer," Mishtas said as he readied another arrow in his bow. He looked at his companions. "For our tribe we fight together!"

Hearing the brave call, Gabeel responded, "Yes, Uncle, for the tribe of Judah!" The three of them shared nods. Like fierce lions with a common cause, they flew into the fray.

* * * *

Hurry, my sweets. Do not miss one moment of this pleasure.
From one secret, dark cavern entrance Voice ordered its Cult into the battle. They stumbled into the mêlée, moaning, claws outstretched. As was their custom, they began mindlessly

281

salivating at the prospects of eating anything that got within reach of their pointy claws.

Voice mind-spoke to its sweet little secret weapon. *My dearest, come now, we have work to do.*

Bishtar, walking slowly behind Voice's collection of killers, meandered into the battle zone. She could hear the dark spirit's commands, but showed no signs of truly listening. *Bishtar? Are you with us? Bishtar?* But the tiny young woman would not answer. Her mind, her thoughts, were her own.

Soon enough, the Cult moved in close to where Dathan's tents stood. The Cultists went to grab the closest victims. But Gasheer's archers were ready, letting loose their arrows tipped with fire. The first of the Cultists were struck hard. Some were instantly brought down by strikes to the head, but many of them were hit in the torso, arms or legs. The arrows were planted deep into the Cultist's tough hides. But the wounded Cultists barely registered any emotion or pain as they listlessly continued onward.

"Dispatch them now!" ordered Gasheer.

Gasheer's swordsmen swiftly ran forward to cut them down. The soldier's blades moved like lightning, hacking off the Cultist's limbs. Many of the appendages were still lit by the flaming arrows as they twitched nervously on the cavern floor.

Two of the crazed Cultists managed to slip by Gasheer's soldiers. Their eager, hungry eyes, and those slithering, forked tongues were set upon attacking an old man that stood very close to them. They went to grab him up in their lurching claws. Just before the Cultists tore into him, Dathan covered his face with his arms and backed up, bumping into his grandson. But Dathan need not worry, because the two monsters were suddenly stopped dead in their tracks.

"Aaahghh," Dathan cried in fear. When nothing happened, Dathan looked up from behind his arms with shock. The mindless beasts, mere inches from his face, were frozen in place. Only their open, gaping mouths continued to quiver as drool proceeded to fall freely down below. Dathan glanced behind him to see Faester peering over his shoulder.

Faester's beady black eyes were fixed forward and their red dots were glowing. His face was smirking, as if he was having the best time in his life. "Watch this, Grandfather."

Dathan turned to see his attackers and was taken aback again. The two Cultists were made to stand up straight and rigid, like the best soldiers in all of Egypt. They started to stretch more; their bodies elongating, their heads extending to the hilt of their necks. Crunching, snapping, tearing noises commenced, and their heads were suddenly ripped out of their sockets. Purplish blood splattered all over. Their bulging black eyes nearly popped out of their sockets as well. The two heads floated around a bit and were made to switch places. The heads were then drawn to squish their way into the wrong body, forcefully... very forcefully.

"Dance, my lovelies, dance," voiced Faester eagerly.

The Cultists were made to bob up and down and twirl all around, like they were made of straw... straw Pon dolls dancing a wild, crazy jig to the music of loud shouts and clashes from the nearby battle.

While Faester continued to grin at his dancing duo, Dathan could not help but be disgusted by the graphic display. He felt sick to his stomach; retched bile came up and he vomited. The old man felt faint and he reached back to grab hold of Faester's small shoulders. "Faester," he sighed in dismay.

Faester took note his grandfather's reaction and finally relented. "Very well, Grandfather, we are done with them." Faester released the mind-motion power he had over his victims. Immediately, the straw Ponmen flopped to the cavern floor. As soon as their bodies hit, the two separated heads fell away from their respectively wrong bodies and rolled to a stop right at Dathan's feet.

"Osiris help us," exclaimed Dathan. The head's four bulging black eyes were staring straight up at him. Dathan lurched forward a bit, unsteady and repulsed. "Thank you, G-grandson." But he quickly recovered his control.

"You are very welcome, Grandfather."

You are a devious little one. Yes you are. Of course Voice noticed Faester's handiwork, but decided not to intervene, even though the little human had just dispatched two of its Cultists.

Faester was, well, a work in progress as far as Voice was concerned.

Not really caring about Cult losses, the spirit scanned the battle arena for the real target of its desire. Soon enough, Voice spotted the human-Pon that carried Father's stone. Voice forced its First, Telek, to see where the spirit looked and commanded, *Telek, go kill that human-Pon. Take his pouch.*

But Telek ignored Voice's order because he was already employed by another force, a greater force. Telek's face went blank as he turned to gaze upon his real master.

Bishtar stared into Telek's one good eye and mind-spoke *Telek.* She then twisted her claws into a fist. Telek winced in pain, and his Blood Vein throbbed wildly. The Cult warrior looked to her sadly, blinking his one good eye, as if asking for mercy. *Telek, my One Eye. You are mine.*

Then Telek droned out loud, "Yes, Mistress."

Come to me. He did. Happy with Telek's compliance, Bishtar ordered, "Do not let anyone near me."

"Yes, Mistress."

Telek! screamed Voice. *What are you doing? Obey me!*

"Do not listen, One Eye," Bishtar commanded.

Telek bowed his head to her in total obedience.

Fool. Voice then turned on Bishtar, screaming in her mind. *I am tired of your disobedience, human! Let go of Telek before I hurt you!*

Instantly some of the Cultists under Voice's control went to slash Bishtar. But Telek stood in their way. He crushed them with his powerful swiping arms, claws, feet and teeth. Three more Cultists followed, moving in on Telek and Bishtar. To help Telek, Bishtar spoke to them the way she had with Telek.

You are mine now. She twisted her claws and the Cultists doubled over in agony. When they lifted up their heads to meet her stare, it was clear that they too would comply with anything she desired. In a voice as cold as ice, she told the three Cultists, *Take your place behind Telek.* They complied fully.

Telek mind-spoke to them. *You are one of us now.* Telek turned to Bishtar and waited for her instructions.

Bishtar nodded knowingly.

Telek faced his new recruits. *Enter the battle. Rage against other Cultists. Feed upon Stilik's troops as well.*

The three Cultists drooled in anticipation, moaned out sounds of compliance, then shuffled off to do as they were told.

Incredulous, Voice decried, *Traitorous, decayed slime. I will crush your mind.*

Telek immediately recoiled from the searing pain cascading throughout his body.

Having Voice hurt Telek was unacceptable; it made Bishtar furious. She stretched out her hand, as well as her mind. She closed her eyes and imagined how everything around her could move to her will. Soon enough, the ground shook, causing debris from the cavern's ceiling to fall all over Voice's Cult. Some were too slow to protect themselves and were crushed by falling rocks that pummeled their bare skulls and shoulders.

Voice screamed to the Cultists it still controlled, *Retreat, you fools. Retreat!!!*

They tried, only to be swallowed up by Gasheer's soldiers. Some of Calish's men took them on as well to good effect.

Fight! Voice shouted in their simple brains, but they were too slow, too overwhelmed by swinging clubs, metal swords, fiercely stabbing spears, and falling debris.

* * * *

Calish fought off any of Stilik's warriors put in front of him, stabbing them with his spear, kicking them down, or punching them senseless. As Stenrak had advised, they were for the most part foot soldiers carrying one red stripe and were therefore not particularly good fighters. Strangely, however, he had to take the fight to them, often chasing them down. It was as if Stilik's soldiers were cowards, or they were avoiding him. He had yet to take a wound.

They couldn't be that bad at fighting, could they? Nonetheless, soldiers of all stripes and colors ran back and forth, chasing each other. There were fights going on everywhere he looked. His best soldiers were still near him. Moshe was there too, doing well to take on all comers. But Stilik's forces had already stopped singling out Calish's men; they now attacked Dathan's red-banded soldiers as well.

"Shishtu!" Calish cried in dismay. It was turning into a free-for-all. Chaos, death, broken bodies were everywhere. He started to worry that there would be nothing left to save.

Stand aside!

In his mind, Calish could hear the authoritative sound of what could only be Stilik, Stenak's brother. Soon enough, Calish saw the Pon prince bash his way past everything in front of him, even his own foot soldiers. He was followed by two of his strongest looking soldiers, both bearing two red dashes above their eyes.

Stilik suddenly stopped at a respectable distance. He had his piercing black eyes set on one thing: Calish. But Stilik stood there, as if waiting for something. His two-striped soldiers got into tight formation, then got down on one knee and bowed their heads in deference. Stilik took note of their obedience. He lifted his chin at Calish magestically, as if expecting him to do the same thing.

When Calish did not bend, Stilik proclaimed, *Submit and spare your people further death.*

Stenrak was right, thought Calish while scrutinizing his opponent. *Stilik is easy to recognize.* The prince's golden gem of nobility, his chest armor, his Blood Vein, his powerful stature, and his expectation of servitude all pointed to one thing: a future warrior King. But Calish had no intentions of being subjugated. He would bow to no one, nor retreat from protecting his people. Instead, Calish readied his stance. He gripped Asher's spear tightly, proudly, yet nimble enough for any action, defense or offence. He lifted his chin too, but in a very different way.

Stilik grinned broadly at Calish's rebellious defiance. *Calish, you are brave, a worthy adversary. And your scalp shall adorn my armor.*

Fight me first, brother, hissed Stenrak as he bolted into view, blocking Stilik's path toward Calish.

Stilik, seeing his two soldiers stand up and get ready to take on Stenrak, waved them back. They promptly took up their places behind their prince, wary and ready.

Stenrak smiled after seeing his brother confront him alone, without his Firsts. Wasting no time, Stenrak flung himself forward, bodily tackling Stilik. But Stilik did not go down... almost, but not totally. Stilik was able to right himself and muscle his brother away, flinging him back, high in air.

Stenrak hit the ground rolling, while bringing forward his stony hammer. He grunted hard as he found his feet.

Stilik thundered, "Stenrak, I warn you!" He flexed his huge arms and chest and raised his club at his little brother.

"I will not let you pass," stated Stenrak, enraged.

"Leave now before father loses another son."

"Never!"

"You still have much to learn, little brother. Do not let this be your final lesson."

"Why do you talk so much? Fight me!"

Stilik grunted in distaste. Having enough of his little brother's disrespect, he croaked, "So be it." Stilik stomped his heavy foot on the ground and moved in to swat his brother to bits.

Just then, the caverns shook, and everyone hunkered down, covering their heads as rocks and debris rained down upon them. Calish bravely waded through the downpour and jumped up on the altar's raised base to get a better view. From his vantage point it looked like the brunt of the deluge was being poured out on the Cultists who were near Dathan's tents. "Good enough," he reasoned.

Gasheer, likewise ignoring the falling fragments, made a push into the heart of the battle; his men swinging their swords madly at anything Pon looking, even Stilik's men, who had already shown equal hostility. The human soldiers were making progress, especially as their giant leader was making short work of any Pon within his reach. Gasheer pummeled them mercilessly with powerful chops from his cudgel, bashing in their heads. The broken Pon were falling at Gasheer's feet, and those that still moved were beaten further by his soldiers. Gasheer soon thereafter stepped into an open space, where there were no Pon or humans close to him.

But Calish spotted him; the towering giant was hard to miss. When the shaking ground suddenly stopped, Calish knew it was his chance... at last. Calish stepped forward and threw Asher's spear as hard as he could. In a perfect arc, above the fray, the sleek and glistening lance soared at Calish's target, whistling loudly as it streaked through the air.

Mosher, hearing the unique sound, quickly pushed his dead enemy aside and watched as Asher's spear flew past him.

The spear slammed into Gasheer's side, piercing the titan's chain of mail. Gasheer immediately recoiled from the blow. Then he bellowed a thunderous-sounding growl. "Ggrrroahh!!!" Gasheer turned and focused his evil glare on Calish. He dropped the cudgel and grabbed the spear's shaft. With a mighty grunt-filled effort, he pulled and pulled until the spear-head came forcefully out of his side. Blood, chinks of his armor's metal, and bits of flesh were taken out as well. He looked at the spear like it was some kind of hateful poison and threw it down. "You dog!" he yelled at Calish.

One of his soldier's came to help, but Gasheer removed his helmet and used it to swat the soldier aside. While spittle shot forth from his twisted mouth, Gasheer eyed his own soldier away. Gasheer didn't want help; he wanted to get his beefy hands around Calish's neck. "Calish, you will feel my wrath!" Gasheer would make Calish pay by giving the gift of his Paingiver. The hulk dropped his helmet, reached to his belt and pulled out his bullwhip. He then began walking toward Calish while whirling it into action. *Snap! Snap!* The whip's crack echoed loudly throughout the cavern garnishing everyone's rapt attention. *Snap!*

Mosher looked into his pouch, selected the perfect stone, primed his sling and whipped the weapon into a frenzy of blinding motion. "El, give me strength." As Gasheer got closer to Calish, Mosher let loose one tether, and the stone took off. Then there was a loud *Crack!*

The projectile struck Gasheer in the center of his protruding forehead. Stunned and disoriented, he stumbled back a bit, shaky and unstable. He dropped the bullwhip and brought his hands to cover over his brow. Then blood suddenly flowed freely in between his swollen fingers and down his face. He took one more wobbly step back.

Just as it appeared that Gasheer would fall, he somehow righted himself. He stood up straight, wiped the excess blood from his face, and cast a wicked glare at Mosher. "When I am done with the whelp," Gasheer sneered, "I will take care of you… and I will feed both of you to the vermin that dwell here!"

Mosher made a move toward the colossus, but Gasheer's men blocked his path. Mosher readied his stance to take them on.

When Calish saw his friend about to fight Gasheer's soldiers, he shouted, "No! All of you stop!" Luckily, they did. In words and mind-speak, Calish commanded, "This is between me and Gasheer! You all know this. Do not interfere, any of you."

Everyone on both sides of the fight heard the words and relaxed their postures, somewhat. The soldiers then summarily made room for the two combatants to square off.

Bishtar too, seeing the spectacle, called off her three new Cultists from the fight with a wave of her hand and a powerful mind-speak. They soon thereafter shuffled to take places all around her and Telek.

By lifting his bloody club, Stenrak also held back his black-striped warriors. He then looked over at his older brother, waiting for him to do the same. Stilik, recognizing the significance of the moment, gestured to his troops, and they too stood down, for the moment obedient. But some few continued to feed, deep in the bloodlust.

Before the event could start, Stenrak quickly scooted to retrieve Asher's spear, fiercely growling at anyone who dared object to the taking of it, especially his older brother, who likewise saw the prize.

"Stenrak," barked Stilik. "Give that to me now!"

"No."

Stilik started to go to the weapon.

Just as the two brothers were about to clash, they heard another powerful message.

"I said stop, all of you!"

The two Pon brothers glared up at Calish as if they should really listen. There was no other choice. The power of Calish's words, and his charismatic presence, standing authoritatively upon the raised altar, at the center of the Pon Holy place, caused all to stop fighting.

"Calish, I..." called out Mosher. He made moves to push past the soldiers and go to his friend.

"No, Moshe, no," answered Calish. "It must be this way."

"Yes, little one," mocked Gasheer to Mosher. "Do as your master commands. And do not worry. The scars on your back will soon be joined by numerous friends. Ha, ha." Gasheer then stalked at Calish, his heavy feet pounding on the cave floor, his hands like claws, his muscular torso and arms tensed like an iron bull. The monster's face was bloodied fire.

In one very nimble leap, Calish jumped down from the altar. He circled around the brute, crouching low, looking for an advantage in Gasheer's stance. There was not much to find. Even with his side and head wound, the titan was like a steady, slow-moving mountain.

"Freak!" Gasheer spat at Calish, "I never did like you. And I will twist your neck till it snaps, just like I did to your beloved grandfather, ha ha. He died like a fool."

Calish opened his eyes wider at the remark. His suspicions were now confirmed; it was Gasheer that had killed Korah. Calish desperately wanted to get angry, and for a moment he nearly exploded and lunged at Gasheer. But at the last second, he stopped himself. Gasheer was playing with him, hoping to get him to commit a foolish attack. Getting close enough for Gasheer to grab him was a mistake. Once Gasheer had him in his grips, it would be over.

So Calish backed off and gingerly danced to the side of his opponent. The ponderous giant tried to follow, but could not compete with Calish's speed, so he threw out more venom. "What are you afraid of, little one? Come closer, or are you a whimpering coward, just like everyone else in your clan?" Gasheer took the time to spy-out Mosher as he was voicing the insult.

Mosher stared back sadly.

Calish looked hard at Gasheer, thinking. *Two can play this word game.* It was time for Calish to show the brute his persuasive skills. "Your time is done, Gasheer. Look around you, old fool. Your master has you at the mercy of the Pon... his sacrificial bullock so that he can make secret deals with them. Faester has taken your place, you useless piece of dung. Many of your men are dead; you are supposed to join them during this fight. Are you stupid enough to believe that Dathan has you in his future plans?"

Gasheer's face crumpled up more tightly upon hearing the sharp words. His expression was one of confusion.

Seeing the reaction, Calish continued. "Son of a Canaan dog, what are you really? Philistine, think for once. In Egypt you were nothing but a traitorous mongrel pet, and here you are but a stinking boil upon our unwashed asses. Give up now, you nit, and I might show you mercy."

"You insolent pig!" screeched Gasheer, his face distorting, twisting; his jaws distending out further than humanly possible. His teeth, broken and sharp, sprang up while frothy thick drool escaped through their gaps. Gasheer lowered his stance, leaned forward, practically on all fours, more ox-like than man, grunting out unintelligible sounds.

Unable to contain his rage, the bull lunged at Calish. But Calish was too swift, easily dodging out of the way... but not before using one agile leg to trip the huge man. Gasheer went down hard, and Calish immediately jumped on his back. Then he slammed a powerfully clenched fist into Gasheer's groin. The man bellowed. When he started to rise, Calish took his claws and slashed them across Gasheer's neck.

But Gasheer wasn't done. Like a raging volcano he reared up, while elbowing Calish in the ribs; a cracking noise emerged thereafter. Gasheer twisted his arms around while tossing Calish back several paces. As if he was weightless, Calish soared through the air, turning somersaults as he landed.

He got up slowly, holding his side, badly hurt from Gasheer's elbow punch. Gasheer followed and reached out his arms to grab Calish's throat, but Calish ducked beneath him and once again used his claws to slash at the wound from Asher's spear. His claws scratched across the metal shards of Gasheer's armor, digging in deep enough to cause further damage, as could be seen when more blood oozed from Gasheer's side.

Then Calish smartly backed away. The two fighters circled each other once again, both wary, both hurt, both looking for the advantage.

I haven't had this much fun in eons, said Voice, watching the fight unfold. It was shaping up to be most entertaining. But the spirit wanted what was in Calish's pouch, and that was what really mattered. *I will have all your stones, Father. The Pon are mine. Having the human's stone will guarantee my dominion forever.*

Voice took note of the spear that Stenrak held. Most interestingly, the Pon fool was so busy watching the humans fight that his grip on the spear was somewhat relaxed. *Bishtar, I beseech you, my dear. Redeem yourself to me. Use your powers, throw the spear now. Kill the giant beast of a man while his back is turned to us, then we will take Father's stone from your wounded brother.*

Bishtar thought about Voice's instructions, but did not act. She too wanted Gasheer dead, but she was worried that the spear might strike her brother instead.

Gasheer started making gurgling noises. Then blood started pouring out from his neck. At first he reached for his side, but then as he was having difficulty breathing, he grabbed his throat in an attempt to stop the bleeding. It seeped through his fingers and began to spray out in short bursts. Gasheer fell to his knees.

The giant was finally down... somewhat.

Calish unsheathed his knife. In a flash, he jumped forward and propelled its point into Gasheer's forehead. He pushed hard into the wound from Mosher's stone, but the blade got stuck. And Gasheer was still struggling. He reached over to grab Calish's throat, and with the last ounce of strength, he began to squeeze.

Calish ignored his lack of breath and continued to force his knife deeper into Gasheer's forehead. He made one final, strong push and an awful crunching sound came from Gasheer's head. The man mountain's eyes suddenly widened and went blank. His hands lost their strength and he started to fall, held back only by Calish's knife grip. Momentum and holding Gasheer's massive weight caused Calish to twist around, as he still held onto the knife's handle.

Now, Bishtar now, throw it, commanded Voice. But Calish had turned his back to her, so Bishtar hesitated after seeing her brother in direct line of sight.

But Voice did not care. In a fit of rage, the spirit overwhelmed Bishtar's senses with intense pain. It caused her to lose grip of her self-awareness. Without her consent, Bishtar raised her arm at Asher's spear. Voice used her powers to take the spear out of Stenrak's grip. The spear levitated, turned sideways in midair, and was sent hurling through the air.

The lance crossed the expanse, making an eerie wailing noise. The spear's tip sliced its way into Calish's exposed back, ripping through his chest, lodging its point into Gasheer's open mouth.

"No!" Bishtar cried. As the spear entered her brother, she too felt the pain. She recoiled from it... and in that moment regained her own self-awareness. Bishtar screeched at Voice, "What have you done!?"

She could see and feel that her brother was mortally wounded, and it made her crazy with anger. Then she remembered what Korah, Calish, and her mother had taught her about the tribe's true God. She screamed, "In the name of El, get out!!" All around, the ground, the walls and ceiling and everything else started shaking. Once more, debris fell from the cavern's roof as the combatants covered their heads.

In a fury that was unprecedented, she expelled Voice from her awareness. "Get out!" Then like an echo that thundered through the air, her voice rang louder and louder, pushing up against Voice's spirit, her cries pounding away at its nonphysical edges. 'Get out... Get out... Get out!'

Voice called out in desperation, *What are you doing, my dear? NO...* Then quieter, *No...* And barely audible... *no.* Voice was gone from her midst, banished to a deep and dark place that Bishtar could only imagine, but not readily see. The beautiful tiny female was awesome to behold. Her red gemstone was blindingly bright.

After that, her anger diminished, and Bishtar calmed her nerves, drawing a close to the shaking ground. Everyone stared at her, wondering what she would do next. She slowly walked forward, meandering haltingly past everyone around her. In awe of her powers, the crowd moved aside to let her pass. She then drew herself toward her dying brother.

When Mosher had regained his footing from the shaking ground, he ran to Calish and grabbed him. While still attached to Gasheer, Calish started sinking to the ground. Mosher, with help from a few soldiers, yanked Gasheer's dead body off the spear's tip and away from Calish. Mosher then gently laid Calish down, because Asher's spear was still inside his body.

Bishtar knelt at her brother's side with a somber, yet far-away expression on her face.

"Moshe," Calish said painfully as blood came up from his mouth.

"Yes, my friend. I am here. Be still." Mosher reached for Calish's shoulder, gently placing his hand there. "Hold on, my friend. I will go to Sky Rock and retrieve his w-waters. You will drink. Perhaps its p-power will heal you."

Bishtar's far away expression suddenly changed. She cocked her head quizzically while listening closer to what Mosher had said. But had she heard correctly? Was this the secret the boys had kept from her all these years? *What is Sky Rock?* she thought. *And where is this water with the power to heal? Is that how Mosher's scars had miraculously healed themselves?* For now she would say nothing, but her questions would have to be looked into eventually. She had the perfect tool to see the answers with... Joseph's Cup. *The cup is mine and I will use it.* The scared little girl was long gone. The mysteries of the unknown awaited and her great destiny would not be denied. She had real power.

"No, my brother," Calish responded, "Use it not for healing me, but for something else... something far greater."

"What? N-No." Mosher suddenly had a new thought. He reached for Calish's pouch and took out the Minthuru stone. "The stone then, maybe the s-stone can do something..."

Calish managed to hold back Mosher's hand. "Moshe, stop. The stone will not help me, but it will help *you.*"

"N-No. I can..."

"My friend, listen carefully, there's not much time. You must not let it be taken. After I am gone, take my pouch, protect the stone, and you will learn what you must really do with it. You are the leader now. Make the Minthuru stone your own. I believe in you, Moshe. I believe in you."

Meanwhile, Stilik, growing restless over the inaction, hissed at Stenrak and regrouped near his soldiers. The remaining humans and Stenrak's troops also quartered themselves and made ready to resume the fight.

Seeing this, Calish turned to Bishtar, "Sister, please. They will take our people and kill them... or worse. Please help me stop this carnage."

Bishtar reached down and replaced Mosher's hand with hers, thereby touching the top of the Minthuru stone. Then the stone glowed to life, even brighter than before. Its energy burst outward and spread quickly all over the cavern, enveloping the combatants and cascading its dazzling colors over all the people, freezing them in place. The strange light did not cast any shadows.

Calish studied his sister knowingly, and gestured at Mosher. Bishtar stretched out her free hand to touch Mosher's arm, waking him from the freezing effects. Mosher looked around and quickly realized what had happened.

Calish whispered, "Hurry, Moshe, the freezing will not last long. Gather our tribe, ready them for departure. Touch Stenrak first, bring him here. He will know what to do."

Mosher did as instructed, unfreezing Stenrak. He then ran around the combatants to find Mishtas. Once touched, Mishtas could see that the battle had been frozen, just as it had been when they had rescued Bishtar years before.

Mosher asked, "M-Mishtas, help me touch our people, recruit others to help. We must get our tribe ready for departure.

"Yes, I will," replied Mishtas. After seeing Calish's bad state, he decided to first run toward Hannah's tent.

In the interim, Stenrak came to Calish and knelt beside him. Bishtar and he exchanged heated glances, but did not act on their hatred for one another.

Calish mind-spoke: *My friend, help me open a doorway to the Valley we once visited. My people must leave now.*

Stenrak nodded understanding. By using his bloody claw, he reached out to Bishtar's necklace. She retracted, ready to strike back, but then stopped her mind-motion powers from activating because Stenrak had stopped moving as well. Stenrak was staring at the gem, his expression an extremely curious one. The jewel she wore was very different in shape and color from when he had given it to Mosher.

Stenrak mind-spoke to them both. *She must wield it, not I.* He turned to Calish. *Do you remember what I told you long ago?*

Calish, although weak, answered, *Yes, I remember.* He turned to his sister saying, "Bishtar, take your gem and touch the Minthuru stone with it."

Bishtar took the jewel from around her neck. She moved her other hand aside, giving space on top of the Minthuru stone for her ruby-red jewel. She touched the two stones together. Near to them a shimmering wall appeared. Within its facets one could see the beautiful landscape of the Valley.

Calish smiled upon seeing the beautiful Valley one last time. "Sister, you can remove your jewel now. When our tribe is through the portal, use your gem to touch the Minthuru stone once more and the portal will close."

"I will, my brother." She withdrew her ruby-red gem, while still keeping her other hand on the Minthuru stone.

Mosher returned by skipping around the shimmering portal. He gazed at it briefly, before running to Calish.

"Are we ready to go?" asked Calish.

"Mishtas gathers us. As you ordered, our people are r-ready. Many are already approaching." They looked up and saw Mishtas directing Korah's tribe through the doorway, one-by-one: women, men, old ones and children. They were carrying as much as they could hold. As they passed by, all of them gaped at the scene of Calish, lying prone, dying. They were sad to see it; many were crying.

Hannah broke through the crowd. Mishtas ran after her and tried to stop her, but could not. She ran to Calish, tears already falling.

"Mother," Calish choked out as blood came from his mouth.

"Calish, hold on, my son," she sobbed. She looked up at Mosher, waiting for him to do something, but all he could do was put his head down, afraid to meet her gaze. Hannah then cast her sights on Bishtar. "Daughter, do something!"

"Mother, I..."

Hannah's expression changed to anger and she screeched, "Bishtar, did you play a role in this? Why?"

Calish interjected quietly, "Mother, please, it was not her. Forgive her."

Hannah continued to stare angrily at her daughter. After a few moments, Calish's words sank in and her expression changed dramatically. "I forgive you daughter. May El have mercy on you, on all of us." Hannah turned to see her son for the last time.

Mishtas came to Hannah, gently pulling her away. "Hannah, it is time to go. Please." Hannah started to cry again and Mishtas more forcefully pulled her away. Then two nearby soldiers came and brought her nearer the doorway.

Stenrak stepped back a bit, allowing space for Mosher. Mosher knelt by his best friend. His face was full of sorrow. He did want Calish to give up, even though the end was near.

Calish's eyes were barely open. "Moshe?"

"Yes. I am h-here."

Calish coughed again, bringing up more blood up. "Promise me, once I am gone, Asher's spear... give it to Stenrak... it is his."

"I will."

Calish summoned enough strength to put on his favorite smirk. "My spear throw, was it... good?"

"It was a sight to behold, m-my friend. Asher would have been proud."

Calish smiled. "You are the stone's leader now. Take my pouch."

Mosher carefully pulled free the pouch from around Calish's torso and put it around himself. Calish nodded in approval. "Touch the stone, with Bishtar. And keep the doorway open long enough for our people to depart."

"I will, but..."

"No, my brother. You know what must be done." As Calish breathed in shallow, labored breaths, he took his bloodied hand and squeezed it into Mosher's hand, thus forcing his friend's hand onto the Minthuru gem. The stone started buzzing. It glowed with a new color: turquoise and blue, the color of a beautiful ocean. It made a uniquely different humming noise as well, signaling that the transfer of ownership had worked.

"One last oath, my friend?" Mosher reluctantly nodded in agreement. Together they softly voiced, "Cal-Moshe."

Calish's hand weakly dropped to his side. He took one more shallow breath and murmured, "Bishtar, Moshe, I lov..." And Calish died while staring into his sister's dark and mysterious eyes.

"No, no... no." cried Mosher, while burying his head into Calish's chest.

After a long moment, Mosher lifted his head to see Bishtar as she watched her brother... distantly. Then she forced herself to gaze at Mosher. Her face was unreadable, and still alien in so many ways. Although his eyes were also big, black orbs, there was a sadness within them that transcended his strange form, making him temporarily human once again.

Then, from the edge of Mosher's eye, a solid tear-drop formed. It got so big that it flowed like a mighty river down his face. He had broken his promise to never cry in her presence, but he didn't care. Things would never be the same again.

Bishtar also understood that their lives had irrevocably changed. She gazed down hard at the ruby-red jewel, her promissory gem, and for a moment its brilliant red colors twinkled like bright little dots in her deeply black eyes. But was it a reflection or were the colored dots coming from within Bishtar? The glowing spots of red reminded Mosher of Faester - *his* eyes lit up in a similar way. The thought of Bishtar having anything in common with that snake made Mosher feel beyond sad. He now had another reason for tears. *No,* Mosher wished to himself. *Not you too, my love.*

Bishtar made a move, as if she would toss her jewel aside, like it meant nothing at all. And Mosher felt as if his heart had been totally broken, shattered beyond belief. But at the last second, Bishtar stayed her hand and did not throw the gem. *What does this mean?* Mosher pondered. *Could she still care?*

"I... I... am sorry," she said finally.

Bishtar broke her connection with Mosher and the red glow in her eyes disappeared. She looked at the people around her, the ones waiting in line to enter the doorway; her mother too. They were once her clan, her tribe. Now they watched her cautiously, for many feared her.

She didn't disappoint them. "You and I are different now," she declared openly. "We can never be the same. I will leave now. Do not follow me, and do not try to interfere with my plans." She said this in words for her tribe, but also in mind-speak. The mind-speak was directed in particular to warn off Stenrak, because he was most eager to attack her still.

Mosher took in Stenrak, noticing his readiness to seek revenge for Calish's death. In both words and by mind-speak, he said, "Let her g-go. For now our fight is over."

Stenrak glared at Mosher, at first with anger, then with understanding. Even for him, the deaths had been enough. Then Stenrak angrily faced Bishtar, and said to her in mind-speak, *This is far from over, evil one.*

Bishtar answered him in kind. *I know.*

Bishtar and Mosher stood up together, while keeping their hands upon the Minthuru stone. They took a few steps away from Calish's dead body and toward the glowing portal. Stenrak, meanwhile, went to a few of his soldiers, touching them, and brought them back to stand near the doorway, as guards.

"We must make an end to this somehow," said Bishtar, indicating the stone, and the fact that they would soon release their hold on it, thus unfreezing everyone.

"I know." Mosher reviewed the situation. He called over two soldiers who were managing the exodus through the doorway. "Come," Mosher commanded, "take Asher's spear out from Calish, carefully." The soldiers did so and handed the bloody thing to Mosher. "Now take Calish's body through the portal. We will bury him in the Valley, properly." They picked up the body and proceeded to go through the portal.

Mosher then turned toward the Pon soldiers. "Stenrak!"

Stenrak came forward and Mosher handed the blood-soaked weapon to him. Stenrak bowed his head and took it up. He stepped forward to stand before his warriors. "Grizzlist, Shalatzz !" he screeched. As Stenrak raised Asher's spear in victory, his followers rejoiced enthusiastically.

299

Mosher stood up straight, tall and with authority to face the survivors of the battle. He gazed at Mishtas with a serious expression. It was clear Mosher wanted to say something, so Mishtas gestured to the crowd in a way that said they should stop entering the doorway and gather to form a circle in front of Mosher. They did so.

Upon seeing this, Stenrak's soldiers also quickly muted their hissing shouts. Some of the wounded, including Gabeel, who was supported by Deborah, were picked up so that they might hear what Mosher had to say. All eyes were upon him, as they waited to hear from their new leader.

Mosher scanned his audience slowly. Then, with great confidence, he started to speak. "Calish is dead. But we will not let his sacrifice be in vain. I ask you to come together as one people, united in our common struggle to survive in our strange new world. Let us never forget, we are the blessed children of El: His tribe of Judah, Benjamin, Zebulun, and all the others. Let me be clear, we will survive, but only as *one* people, one clan, one remnant."

Gradually the soldiers, both human and Pon, sheathed their respective weapons. Even Stenrak's soldiers, who could not understand Mosher's words, followed suit, and reluctantly nodded in agreement, lowering their arms.

"Our struggle is not over. But for now let us move forward and rebuild our lives in peace. There is hope for us. Our perseverance has proven that we were meant to go on living. Join me in that endeavor, and I can promise you that, together, we will endure and prosper."

Upon hearing the inspirational speech, everyone cheered and started clapping, shaking hands or embracing each other. Stenrak's soldiers hissed out their approval, though most of them were still confused. They even accepted a few hugs from the surface dwellers, while cautiously keeping a close eye on their weapons if a human got 'too friendly'.

Through the clamor, Bishtar whispered in Mosher's ear, "Nice speech, Mosher... no stuttering."

"Thank y-you."

At that, Bishtar rolled her big black eyes. She then pointed at One Eye, who stood nearby, frozen with his claws extended, waiting to slice open one of Dathan's men.

Mosher knew what she wanted, "No."

"Do not worry. Telek will do as I tell him. We will leave peacefully."

Mosher relented and they walked to One Eye, where Bishtar unfroze him. The monster looked about, confused, drooling a little, but soon enough brought his arms down peacefully. Telek took his place at Bishtar's side.

Stenrak approached Mosher and Bishtar, mind-speaking. *We will go now. When my brother and his soldiers awake, they will only see our bloody footprints.*

From where they all stood, they could still see Stilik with his raised club, ready to bash Stenrak's head, frozen mid-swing. Anticipating what Mosher would ask, Stenrak said, *No I will not kill Stilik, not like this. Our father will not yield his throne to a coward. I will have to postpone my fight to be First.*

Mosher turned to Bishtar. "Will you two be okay? Do not attack each other once I am g-gone." Bishtar and Stenrak glared at one another, suspiciously. *Truce?* asked Mosher via mind-speak.

Agreed, they both said.

Stenrak held up his new spear with pride, and in Mosher's tongue stuttered out, "Succ-cess... Moss-ess."

Bishtar raised an eyebrow at Stenrak's pronunciation of Mosher's name. A proud smile crossed her lips. She looked up into Mosher's eyes and announced, "Moses... yes... Moses, an apropos name for the man to lead our tribe." Her choice, her betrothed, as she had always known, was a very special man. The tribe would endure.

Once again, as when Mosher had offered her the promissory gem, Bishtar's approval increased Mosher's stature and somehow he was able to stand even taller than before. He smiled at her compliment. "I am ready."

Stenrak and his soldiers departed without saying anything else.

Bishtar and Mosher walked to be near the portal's threshold. They watched as the last of their tribe entered the doorway, until all were gone except Mosher, Bishtar, and of course One Eye; who was not really altogether there to begin with.

While still holding the Minthuru stone, Mosher and Bishtar faced one another; one tall reluctant leader, and one petite, chillingly beautiful young Ponwoman. They stared at each other, both thinking things that they kept to themselves.

Bishtar spoke first. "I will touch my jewel to yours as you go through the doorway, thus closing it behind you."

"I understand."

Bishtar let her hand that was upon the Minthuru stone drift over his, and she started saying something: *Mosher, my lo . . .*

Mosher saw Bishtar move her hand, he felt her touch, he heard her words. His heart jumped, but he could only say with great sadness. "Good... b-bye."

With her other hand, Bishtar brought the ruby-red gem to touch the Minthuru stone, thus closing the doorway. A humming noise commenced, signaling that the portal was slowly closing. "Goodbye," she repeated. Then, with the smallest of gestures, she twirled the promissory gem in her free claw, while releasing her hold on top of the Minthuru stone, but not before letting her hand slide along his one last time. Mosher's heart jumped again at her touch.

As the glistening doorway got smaller and smaller, Mosher entered it. He took one giant step closer to the Valley. He could see its wonderful landscapes, feel the warm breeze upon his skin, see the sun's beautiful light but nonetheless... the love-struck young man couldn't help but look back one more time.

But she was already gone.

* * * *

Bishtar and One Eye touched their three Cultists, thereby waking them from their motionless state. The small group then walked toward their place of exit. For the moment the people around them were all still frozen. She was not worried about more confrontations; her group would be deep into the tunnels before the freezing effect would dissipate.

"Come, Telek."

"Yes, Mistress." Telek smacked one of the slower Cultists in the head, just to make sure he didn't lag behind.

Bishtar suddenly stopped. The brood, too close behind her, bumped into one another clumsily, thus incurring a few more ardent slaps from Telek. But Bishtar ignored the comical display. She was too busy reviewing the battle scene, a small degree of concern on her face. There was still a smattering of Cultists intermingled with the tribe's various combatants. Some Cultists were feeding, others fighting, and a few doing their best to follow Voice's order to retreat. *Hmmm,* she pondered. *What to do?* This was a problem, but not overly so.

With resolve, the lithe beauty commanded, "Telek, take our three followers and awaken most of the other Cultists. When they are alert, order them to retreat immediately. But leave a few frozen." With a slight grin, she added, "Let Dathan's men deal with them."

"Yes, Mistress." Telek and his team set out to do as their new leader wanted.

Soon thereafter, Bishtar and her three followers continued on their way. They passed the altar, and after that, Dathan's tent. Dathan was standing there, frozen like everyone else. Bishtar thought about killing the Elder; it would be so easy, and the old bastard surely deserved it. But then she looked closer. Behind the Elder was Faester, lurking there like the black shadow he was.

"Viper," she spat at him.

As she spoke, Faester's frozen eyes twitched, and his tiny red dots glowed brightly. Suddenly they turned to look upon her. Instantly, Bishtar could feel his cold presence in her heart. Moments later, in her mind she could hear the combined sound of Voice and Faester saying. *Viper-ess, my dear.Viper-ess.*

After that, out of prudence more than fear, Bishtar hastened her pace, taking her shuffling brood of Cultists into their escape route. "Follow me, Telek."

"Yes, Mistress."

CHAPTER 29
The Promised Land

Gabeel was exhausted, breathing harshly, feint from his wounds. He fell to his knees, gasping for air. Purplish blood oozed from the gaping hole in his ribs.

"We are nearly there, my friend," encouraged Mishtas. He did his best to carry Gabeel's weight, but the wounded soldier could no longer take his own steps, and Mishtas was getting too tired to lift him anymore.

Deborah also held onto Gabeel, but the look on her face was grim.

Seeing that he was too weak to go further, they gently laid Gabeel down to the ground.

"He is bleeding out," she whispered anxiously to Mishtas. He nodded understanding.

Mishtas looked forward and back. There were many others around them, in varying states of disarray. Some were wounded, some were weary, but nonetheless whole, and there were others that were busy tending to the children or the elderly. The tribe shuffled forward through the undergrowth, carrying their belongings heavily, tiredly, moving slowly toward an unknown destination. Mishtas glanced ahead again trying to see exactly where his people were going. "I must find Mosher."

"Where has he gone?"

"Undoubtedly he has gone to the front of the tribe, to scout ahead."

Since opening the doorway to their present location, in all the confusion, Mishtas had lost sight of their new leader. They were in a large valley. Up ahead, far from their spot, were many mountains. There were forests of varying degrees of density sporadically situated all around them.

"The sun shines. It hurts my eyes. I am not used to seeing it," Mishtas said, while squinting. The sun was high above them, and *strangely*, he thought to himself, *it has not moved since we started walking.* By his reckoning, the tribe had been on foot for a half a day.

Deborah saw what Mishtas had noticed. "Mishtas, why is the sun not moving?" she asked rather naively. "Isn't the sun supposed to move across the sky?"

"You are right, Deborah, the sun remains still. Why does it seem smaller, and somewhat darker, than I remember it?"

"These trees and shrubs we pass..." Deborah reached out to pluck a nearby growth. Its yellow-blue leaves were multi-layered and shaped like giant tear-drops. "They are oddly formed and colored. Is this how it was in Egypt, Mishtas? I do not remember our old home so well."

"No, the plants are not like this in Egypt, or any land we found after that."

"And the mountains, they sparkle with reddish purples and other colors that I do not remember seeing."

"Yes, and look there..." He pointed toward the distant peaks. "I see shiny golds and silvers too."

She nodded and turned her eyes straight up. "The sky is filled with a mist. Are those what clouds look like, Mishtas?"

"No, Deborah, they are not like that."

"Where are we?" she finally asked. "Could this be the Promised Land my grandmother told me about when I was a child? The land Moses had promised us? Is that why things look so... different?"

Mishtas contemplated the beauty of their location, and compared it with all the dark and dangerous places they had seen since the day the Earth had opened and swallowed the Tribe. Deborah's question, although innocently stated, had a lot of merit. The doorway was an unknown. Although Calish had told him that it did not lead to Egypt, the shear majesty of the surroundings made Mishtas wonder if the doorway had indeed transported them to a Promised Land, if not *The* Promised Land.

In any event, Deborah's observation was well worth considering. He turned to her and stated, "Deborah, I believe you could be right. This could be the land Moses spoke of."

Mishtas bent down to examine Gabeel's wounds. He carefully removed a bandage Deborah had placed there. The gaping hole went deep into Gabeel's side; it soon started leaking out more blood. So Mishtas quickly pushed the bandage back into its place.

Gabeel needed attention or the brave young warrior would die soon.

"Deborah, let me find another to take my position, while I go and find Mosher."

She agreed, and Mishtas asked a fellow traveler, who looked able-bodied, to take his spot helping Gabeel. "I will be back soon," he said to both of them. Mishtas then left in a hurry. He wasn't sure, but maybe, he hoped, Mosher could help Gabeel somehow.

Mishtas ran to the front of the congregation, where he found some soldiers leading the way. "Have you seen Mosher?"

"Yes," one soldier answered, "he has traveled through that stand of trees. We follow him."

"Good, I must find him." Mishtas scurried past the trees and up a hill. Upon achieving the hill, he saw their leader. Mosher had found what looked like a raised meadow, where he had stopped. He stood there gazing around, while holding the Minthuru stone. Mishtas took off and soon caught up to him.

"I think I have found a g-good spot for our people," Mosher said upon seeing his uncle. "It has n-nearby water from streams, with fish in it. And there are plenty of s-small trees for wood. I even found fruit b-bearing bushes."

"Good, very good, but..."

"Yes, Uncle?"

"We have wounded," Mishtas stated, "some are close to death."

"As soon as we settle, we will ask our healers to see to them."

"Some cannot wait. Gabeel is soon to die if something isn't done now. He fought bravely, and saved many others while doing so."

Mosher looked puzzled, as if he wasn't sure what Mishtas was trying to say. Mishtas glared at the Minthuru stone, gesturing to it as if he wanted Mosher to use it.

"I do not know how, Mishtas. I am n-not a healer and do not know if this will help, or even how to make it help."

"There is no other choice, Mosher. It couldn't hurt."

Mosher thought for a moment, placed the stone back in his pouch and replied, "Very well, lead me to him."

306

Mosher bent down to examine Gabeel's wound as soon as the pair found the wounded soldier. He carefully pulled back Deborah's bandage and tossed the bloody mess aside. He then tore off a piece of his tattered shawl, wrapped the end of it tightly, and stuffed that bit deep into Gabeel's side. Gabeel groaned and cried out in pain. But the wound would not stop bleeding, as more of the purple liquid gushed past the cloth.

Gabeel barely cracked open his eyes. He glanced up at Mosher. He held his claw onto Mosher's arm and weakly whispered, "Say a prayer for me, brother, say a prayer." Then he coughed up some blood.

Mosher, shaking his head negatively, finally took out the stone, and with hesitation, held it near Gabeel's wound. But nothing happened. "I do n-not know what to do," he said in frustration.

Mishtas chimed in, "Try to say something, like a prayer, before using the stone."

Mosher thought about all he had learned from Korah, from Sky Rock, and tried, "El, please heal our friend Gabeel." Still nothing happened. Mosher tried again more earnestly, "El, we ask for Your help to heal Gabeel." But again nothing happened. The stone even refused to hum.

"Perhaps," offered Mishtas, "a blood sacrifice would work."

"How, and w-who's blood?" queried Mosher honestly perplexed.

Mishtas, Deborah, and Mosher studied one another, not knowing the answer. When no one responded, Mosher, in desperation, took out his wolf knife. He sliced open his palm and let a few drops of his purple blood drip onto the stone. He waved the bloodied gem over the wound, but again nothing happened.

"Gabeel is like a son to me," pressed Mishtas with a sense of certainty. "That might help." Mishtas took Mosher's knife and did the same, mixing his red blood with Mosher's purple bits.

They waited anxiously, but still nothing.

"Let me try." Deborah, getting impatient, abruptly took the knife. She barely flinched as the sharp blade cut open her palm. As soon as the first drop of her purple blood touched the stone, it started to hum. With the second and third drop, the buzzing got louder. Mosher and Mishtas looked hopeful, and Deborah pointed to the wound as if to say *Hurry.* Mosher promptly held the humming stone over Gabeel's wound.

The humming was a good sign, but still no healing took place. Mishtas gestured to Mosher, as if to begin saying something. Mosher thought for a moment, and proclaimed, "El, please, in Your mercy, heal our brother Gabeel."

The Stone suddenly glowed to life. Then the gem sent an intense stream of luminosity toward Gabeel's wound. The sparkling jewel soon thereafter hummed louder as more light shot forth from the stone, cascading its brilliance over Gabeel's ravaged side. Gabeel squirmed a bit in reaction, but it was clear that the light was mending rather than hurting. His blood was drying up, and Gabeel's torn flesh was gradually becoming whole again. Mosher also did his part to move the sacred object back and forth while the light did its magic to rebuild Gabeel's internal and external damages.

"It's working," cited Mishtas. "It's a miracle." He turned to Deborah. "Young alma, you are truly a blessing. Your sacrifice was acceptable."

Mosher and Mishtas shared a joyous expression. Deborah, for her part, shed a tiny tear. And Gabeel, after a few small coughs, took a deep life-affirming breath. Then he opened his eyes and looked up at them. He smiled, especially after seeing Deborah's lovely face.

Gabeel then focused on Mosher, who was still holding the stone. "I know you, do I not? I have seen you with Calish. Your name is ..."

Mishtas, grinning broadly, put his hand on their new leader's shoulder and proudly claimed, "They have called him Moshe. Praise El for choosing him to lead us."

"Moshe?" repeated Gabeel. "Is that your name, my friend? Praise El." Upon noticing the magical gem in Mosher's hand, Gabeel declared, "I am in your debt, Sir."

Mishtas agreed. "We all are. And yes, Gabeel, his name is Moshe."

Mosher, their supposed leader, smiled after hearing the kind words. His face had changed, why not his name as well? He further reasoned that if the name Moshe was good enough for Calish, than who was he to argue. He turned away from his companions and scanned over the Valley... *Calish's Valley.* As he took in the expansive, beautiful and verdant landscape, the man they wanted to call Moshe humbly replied, "For a little while, I am Moshe. M-Maybe just for a little while. Praise You, El, for a new home and a healing this day."

He smiled broadly and felt truly grateful. *Home. We have finally arrived.*

CHAPTER 30
Buttons

The tribe soon thereafter settled into Moshe's meadow. It was lush with vegetation, had water from many streams, and there were even small animals that scurried about. Mishtas asked those that were still able to set up their tents, build fire-pits, gather supplies, and establish areas for the wounded to heal. Gabeel, feeling strong once more, was given oversight of the remaining soldiers, and the task of having them create a defensive perimeter.

Once that undertaking was underway, many took a few moments to take stock of their new home. They were overwhelmed with happiness to see the sky and sun again. They cried out with joy and bent to their knees to give thanks. "El, we thank you."

After that, they waited patiently for night before sleeping. Even though they had come from dark underground places, they nonetheless looked forward to seeing the night sky again, with the moon and stars.

But night did not come, or at least what they remembered night as it had once been. The sun, as it was, never moved across the sky. They watched and waited, but still there was no solar movement and no night or stars.

After some time, the mist that permeated the upper atmosphere gradually drifted under the sun, causing the sky to darken enough so that there was the appearance of night. The subtle darkness was more than acceptable for the congregation to call it 'night'. For the first time, the exhausted tribe fell asleep in their new home.

By the following morning, the mist covering the sun had moved off to the horizon. But most of the tribe slept in. There were, however, some folks that were early birds.

"What the hell is that?" said one wide-awake clansman.

"I know not," said his companion.

A very large, fat, strange creature bumped into their tent. It proceeded to knock over the poles that held the tent upright, clumsily smashing everything in its path. The early birds quickly backed away from their tent, wary of the odd intruder. The creature stopped, jostling in the middle of the debris that had once been their tent, and looked at them with its sad, droopy eyes. The beast then summarily lay down. It burped and pawed at its furry head as if grooming itself.

"Should we sound the alarm?"

"Don't know, but I see the beast broke your table."

"And yet your table is untouched, so I'll answer my own question. Definitely sound the alarm."

After hearing of the uninvited visitor in the compound, Moshe, Mishtas, Gabeel and a few soldiers went to the tent in question. All the commotion had awakened other tribesman as well, and by word of mouth the crowd was growing. Some even brought out chairs to sit and watch what was happening.

And so the show began.

Moshe and company approached the beast, slowly. It was bigger than two camels put together, very furry, multi-colored, with a small short-snouted head that hung low to the ground. The beast had two round forward-facing eyes that were watery and glum. After noticing all the people around it, the beast got up and swiveled around its spot. It shuffled more than walked, its bulky body hanging over its short, stumpy legs. When it did move, tent debris of all sorts traveled in its wake. But for the most part the beast stayed where it was, relatively unmoving, watching Moshe's people with its sleepy friendly eyes.

"Has it hurt anyone?" asked Moshe.

"Not that we are aware of," answered a bystander.

"Has it destroyed anything?"

They scrutinized the tent debris. There were bits of food and ripped tent parts scattered about. There were also broken pieces of pots and smoldering food taken from the fire-pits, and that stuff was stuck to the creature's matted and crust-filled fur.

"Is there anything it *hasn't* destroyed might be a better question," responded Mishtas.

The beast yawned. After that, for some reason it focused its sluggish eyes on Moshe. The creature slowly and unabashedly approached him. It sniffed at Moshe's clothes. Moshe recoiled a bit but could not sense hostility, so he relaxed his posture. Then a long purple tongue with tiny yellow spikes slithered out of the creature's mouth. It wound its way up Moshe's tunic until it found one of the clasps that held his shirt together. With a gentle pull, the creature's tongue tore the clasp from his tunic. The animal took the clasp into its mouth and chewed the item for a few crunches, swallowed, and burped.

"Nice."

The intruder yawned again wider than before, this time exposing its tiny, square-shaped teeth and purple-yellow, gyrating tongue. It stared at Moshe, as if waiting for him to do something. When Mosher did not move, the creature snuggled up closer to him. Moshe, with really no choice, tentatively reached out and started stroking its fuzzy head and ears. As soon as he did this, the beast started making a soft chittering noise.

"I think it likes you," quipped Mishtas.

"Just what I always w-wanted, a giant fuzz-ball."

"Don't say I never got you anything, Moshe."

"Gee, thanks, Uncle."

The creature flopped most of its bulk on top of Moshe's feet. Moshe grunted from having the heavy mass practically crush his toes. He gradually wriggled his feet out from under the mound of fat, fur, and creature stuff. The beast subsequently fell asleep; but not before loudly producing one more foul-smelling belch and purring as it lay there.

While waving away the odor, Moshe retorted, "And if this is 'liking me', then I don't want to s-see hating me."

"It seems like your friend wants to stay," observed Mishtas, "What shall we call it?"

Moshe glanced down at his open shirt. "B-Buttons. Of course."

"Male or female?" Mishtas asked, not at all knowing the answer. They both bent over and looked, but only saw rows of flesh and clumps of fur.

"Go ahead and g-get closer."

"I'll pass."

"Figures."

Some of the people standing around suddenly jumped and moved away from the nearby tree line. "There's something behind us!" someone shouted.

"Watch out!" another person said excitedly.

Everyone watched nervously as the nearby weeds and shrubs shook and rustled. Soon enough, a small furry head poked out from behind a bush. It was followed by another similar head. The small black eyes of the beasts looked around at the folks who were likewise staring at them.

Just then, the first of the creatures saw Buttons. The little scrambler sprang through the brush, followed by its companion. They started squeaking out a high-pitched chattering noise, as their squat and furry little bodies stumbled into the encampment. Along the way, they bumped into anything put before them, including each other, while they approached Button's position.

Buttons, wakened by their insistently loud clamor, lifted its head and calmly raised one of its lumpy hind legs. The small creatures made their way beneath the mass of Button-stuff. Muffled sucking noises soon thereafter began. Buttons then calmly went back to sleep.

"I'm guessing female."

"Do tell."

"There's another one!" someone shouted.

"Where? I see nothing," said another.

"There, it is hiding below those tall weeds."

"Stand back, everyone," warned Moshe as he approached the sight and scanned the tall weeds. He could barely make out the two little eyes that were staring back at him. "This one is shy. Make r-room for it."

Everyone moved back a little. Soon enough, a small figure started making the same chattering noises, while popping its head further out of the weeds.

"Come, little one," prompted Moshe as he gestured to the creature.

The small animal stared at Moshe, squawked once and stuck out its slithering purple-yellow tongue.

"Okay little one, okay," relented Moshe as he backed away.

The creature spied Moshe one more time. When it was happy with Moshe's compliance, it scrambled its way over the weeds and shrubs, squeaking madly at some of the thicker plants that hindered its path. Once clear, it stopped for a moment to look at

313

the people. They stared back. Then, after hearing the sucking sounds from Buttons, it started stumbling its way over to her.

"Everyone, let the b-beast be," Moshe declared.

But no one really needed to be told that. One person however, as he was getting out of the creature's path, left behind the chair that he had been sitting on.

The animal didn't notice the obstruction until it bumped its head into a chair leg. The little critter stopped, jerked its body around a bit, lifted one hind leg, and suddenly a spray of liquid came shooting out from somewhere beneath its tail. The spray hit the chair and instantly it started smoldering. Soon thereafter, the chair started to melt and fall apart. When that was done, the curious creature sniffed at its handiwork, and then turned to join its siblings under Buttons.

"Okay, I'm guessing don't piss these creature's off," said the bystander.

"*Literally* don't piss them off," agreed the other.

"Everyone, listen," commanded Moshe, "It appears that we have m-made some new... friends. For now, these creatures do not appear dangerous, but I would advise caution. If anyone sees them do anything aggressive or d-dangerous, notify me or Mishtas immediately."

Everyone gave signs that they understood.

"Amazing," they said to one another.

"Nothing like this in Egypt, I dare say."

"We're not in Egypt anymore..."

"The Promised Land then?"

"If the Promised Land be filled with strange, acid-spraying beasts, then you might be right about that, my friend."

The gathering couldn't stop pointing, smiling, and watching for anything new that the curious animals might do, even though Buttons seemed quite content to do nothing but sleepily lay there while feeding her litter.

After noticing that the children in the crowd were obviously most intrigued by the creature's cute demeanor, Moshe called out to them, "Names for the offspring of Buttons?" As soon as he spoke, they started shouting and mind-speaking their numerous and boisterous suggestions.

314

Moshe mind-spoke and shouted loudly, "Alright, alright, let's s-settle this." The children soon quieted. Moshe thought about what he had heard for a second and concluded, "For the biggest of the three, we have a s-strong contingent of v-voices saying Stripes." It made sense because the creature did have a pattern of stripes that ran across its body. The boys gave out shouts of approval. "Okay, Stripes it is."

Moshe thought some more, remembering what he had heard. "For the second creature, we have Turtle Dove." The girls shrieked with joy. "And for the littlest, we have..." and he hesitated, not sure if he could recall the most popular choice.

"Scout!" shouted out a very small child. Then the other children gave their yeas of approval.

Moshe nodded, turned towards the suckling beasts and shouted, "Scout!" The furry little creature popped its head out, looked around, found the caller, squawked, burped, stuck out its tongue, and after a moment returned to its feeding.

"S-Scout approves."

"Better than the alternative," mocked Mishtas while pointing at the smoldering chair.

In words and in mind-speak, the children then chanted, "Scout, Scout, Scout." Sure enough, Scout reappeared. It seemed to know what they meant.

"Do you think he knows his name?" quizzed Mishtas.

As they watched, Scout slowly shuffled around in circles, moving in unison with the screeching children. Moshe gazed intently at the strange beasts. "I can sense something in the creatures, as if they can g-gather, deep in their minds, what we are thinking. Or maybe a better way to say it is: what we are *feeling*."

"Are you saying they understand us, the way we think?"

"Buttons found us, Mishtas, not the other way around. So maybe, yes, on s-some level, they understand us."

"This place is strange indeed."

"Do tell, Mishtas, do tell."

CHAPTER 31
Crickets

Moshe scanned their encampment with pride. Mishtas, Gabeel, and some of the other family leaders had done well to organize the tribe. *Valley Days*, a name coined by tribal members, consisted of the mist cycle that routinely covered over or retreated from their little sun. Amazingly, only three *days* had passed since entering the Valley. Yet within that short period, the gathering was making great progress.

We have even honored our dead, Moshe thought. They had quite appropriately taken time to find a good site to bury their dead. The tribe's official graveyard, sadly, included a prominent spot for Calish. Moshe had given the eulogy; it was well received, albeit through all the tears, most especially from Hannah.

Mishtas comforted her as best he could, but it was not easy; Hannah was inconsolable. And her loss was shared by so many others that had lost loved ones, making it a tough day for the remnant.

After the ceremony, Moshe asked the tribe's best builders to erect a stone monument for Calish with an etched message:

Here Lies Calish
son of Hannah
Beloved Leader
of the Judah Tribe

Later that day, by taking from nearby resources, the resilient and industrious people started construction of new tents and huts. They even found time to repair the damage done by Buttons; after, of course, they had used some delicious shrub-berries to lure the beast away.

As another Valley night approached, Moshe stood in the shadows of his tent, looking out at his sturdy tribe.

Soon thereafter his uncle approached. "The people like it here," stated Mishtas.

"Yes, and I hope we can s-stay."

"Why do you say that, Moshe?"

"You are the older generation, Mis-shtas. And as such, your c-changes are very few. Most of the young, and all the newborns, are P-Pon. Like m-me, they shun the light from our new home. It b-burns our eyes; our s-skin too. It hurts us-s to be in the open."

Moshe was stuttering much more than usual. Mishtas had seen the same affliction among many of the younger people as well. But out of respect for Moshe's already burdensome responsibilities, Mishtas decided to ignore it.

Therefore, Mishtas spoke to other matters. "Yes, I have noticed that many of them prefer dark places, often finding the shade of trees where they can spend their day, returning to the open only when it is necessary. And there is more to know of this. Scout found some nearby caves. The children followed. There was a small entrance to the caves that only a small burrowing creature could have discovered."

"Really?" queried Moshe, very interested to hear more about the strange creatures.

"The children like going into the tunnels and staying there, but Scout retreats back to the open soon after entering the dark places."

"Fascinating. The creatures prefer the open to the closed s-spaces."

"Then why do you think Scout would go there to begin with?"

"It is more proof of what I said before. They can hear us; know us-s, what we long for. It r-resonates with them."

"They are a blessing." Moshe nodded in agreement. "And there is even more that I must tell you."

"How so?"

"Our scouts tell me of what they have found in the distant valleys. The good news is that there is wonderful bounty; giant fruits, small game, and plenty of fish-filled waters."

"And the bad news?"

"They say that there are other much larger creatures there as well. 'Behemoths', they called them. The scouts said they thought of themselves as mere crickets in their sight."

Moshe became pensive. "That would confirm what I have come to b-believe about this place."

"Yes?"

Moshe thought for a moment about how he would explain his prior knowledge of the place they were in. Years before, when he had first touched the Crystallight gem, he had had a clear vision of the Valley, but Calish and Bishtar were strikingly absent from view. After the recent battle in the Pon Holy Place, Mosher understood why the twins were not part of his vision. Bishtar had simply gone away. She did not venture through the portal with the rest of the tribe. Calish, of course, was a different sad story. It was now clear to Moshe that Calish knew all along why he wasn't in the vision. His last stoic words to Moshe meant that Calish had already accepted his fate. In one of his own visions, Calish had seen that he was not destined to join them in the Valley.

But it is you who should be here leading us, my friend, reflected Moshe. Somehow Calish had enough strength of character to keep the secret to himself until the very end. Moshe could only wish that he had even one half of Calish's strength; or his natural leadership qualities. Calish's death was a deeply personal and sad fact that Moshe had not yet come to terms with, and it was something he was not ready to openly discuss. He looked hard at his uncle, thinking, *but at the very least, Mishtas needs to know some basic Valley history.*

So Mosher began his tale. "Many years-s ago, Calish, Stenrak and I, when we first met, combined the Crystallight and M-Minthuru stones. The two of them opened a d-doorway, that they traveled through, whereas I was left behind. Calish, upon his return, told me what he s-saw. The things he described are identical to what we are s-seeing here. The sun, the valleys, and the giant beasts.

"For now, advise your men to spread the word: do not approach the large Behemoths. We do not know if they are d-dangerous. So far the animals we've s-seen appear to be herbivores. That means..."

"That there are also meat-eaters as well."

"Yes-s, so let's be cautious. Tell G-Gabeel to remain vigilant and continue to post his soldiers at strategic p-points around our encampment as lookouts."

Mishtas nodded his understanding. "Moshe, I must also report what Gabeel has told me. And this might be even stranger than the sight of the Behemoths."

"Go ahead."

"He has explored the caverns that Scout uncovered. He tells me they are much more extensive than what the children found. He called them a 'labyrinth'. Furthermore, there are signs of an ancient Pon presence: old bones, leathery rags, broken pieces of their type of weapons, and cooking items. Some of the items look identical to things we've seen Stenrak's people use. He therefore believes the tunnels might eventually lead to where we once lived, in the Maana caverns."

"Interesting, but I am in no h-hurry to return there."

"Nor am I, Moshe, nor am I. But with everything we are learning, how long will it be before..."

"... Our new and wonderful h-home will be taken away from us, just as the s-surface world was."

"What shall we do?"

Moshe sadly responded, "I know n-not, Uncle, I know not."

CHAPTER 32
Golden Man

"Hello."

Moshe turned around, somewhat surprised, thinking he was alone on the edge of the precipice. He was even more shocked when he saw who was standing there.

"Peace be with you," the speaker said casually. The *man* gently raised his right hand, open palmed, fingers up. When Moshe didn't respond, the man said, "Do not fear, my friend, I am here to help you." The man bowed his head and gestured graciously.

After recovering from being surprised, Moshe studied his new companion. He could not help but notice how striking the man's features were. The man's skin was a sparkling golden color. His hair was more than just blond; it was also golden-colored too, and long. It flowed over his shoulders and down his spectacular robes. The man wore open-toed sandals that were very well-tailored. The Golden Man's face was very handsome, with piercing blue eyes and finely chiseled features. His smile was warm, and his voice was charmingly smooth.

"Who are you?"

"I am... and please don't be surprised... sent here by our Father."

"Our F-Father?"

"Yes, He has sent me with an important message, and with an even more important task."

"Go on."

"He tells me that the stone you carry can, if wielded by His representative, redeem your people."

"Red-deem?"

"Restore, deliver, rescue, save..."

"I unders-stand the w-word."

"Yes, very good," accepted Golden Man kindly. "You see, your changes, your presently grotesque features, are not permanent. The stone you brought here from the surface world, Father's stone, is very unique. It has the power to transform you back into what you once were. Better even, for if you follow my advice, your bodies will be as beautiful as mine. And of course, if you agree to the process, you will also eventually return to the surface world."

Moshe was not sure if what Golden Man had said was truthful or not. He reached down to pat his pouch. He was glad to feel the stone's outline. Calish had told him to protect the item, and that it would one day show its true purpose. Could this man represent that purpose?

"The offer, however," continued Golden Man, "must be accepted now, my friend, for if you hesitate, your people, your descendants, will not know redemption for a millennia or more, or quite possibly never."

"How d-do I know you speak truthfully, *my friend?*"

Then Golden Man levitated a short distance from the ground, right on top of the spot where the tribe had doorwayed into the Valley. If he were to take one step back, he would fall off the cliff's edge. His expression was one of confidence, as if the floating deed was a magical and yet easy thing to do.

Moshe was unimpressed. "We have seen m-much magic and s-strangeness since being here."

"I can demonstrate further." Golden Man drifted back down to the ground. "Father has given me dominion over this land and the creatures therein." He raised his arm and a shot of lightening sprang up from his fingertips. This was immediately followed by a loud, thunderous wailing growl. After that, an earth-shaking pounding emerged.

Moshe had to turn around to see where the pounding sound came from. Past a stand of trees, a giant beast suddenly presented itself. Moshe couldn't help but think of the behemoths he had recently discussed with Mishtas. The titan walked on its two hind legs, mostly upright, but still leaning forward. It had two shorter claw-filled hands that extended out of the front of its torso. Its large head and snout was covered with scaly spikes that cascaded along its spine and onto its tail. The monster opened its mouth, roaring, and displaying two rows of sharp teeth.

"El, protect us," whispered Moshe, watching the beast with caution.

Golden Man, in a sing-song way, proclaimed:

"Do not fear
do not fret
upon the ground
its feet are set."

Golden Man raised his hand at the monster. The beast came up to him and stopped dead in its tracks. But its enormous head however remained very animated: its nostrils flared, and its jaws snapped open and closed as it eyed Moshe suspiciously... and hungrily. Golden Man made a strange facial expression and spied Moshe to see if he had noticed the strange song-like word-play. Luckily, Moshe was so absorbed by the monstrous beast that he had barely noticed the odd rhyming words.

"There, you see," furthered Golden Man, "the beast is as tame as a common earth worm. And by the way, her name is Sweety."

The monster snapped again at Moshe, snarling its upper jaws, revealing a very nasty set of fangs.

"Isn't she just a dear?"

Sweety turned her cruel, hungry stare upon Golden Man. But oddly, the monster did not act out on what should have been its natural instinct to devour.

Moshe responded with, "Yes, I can see the w-wormy resemblance. And the name S-Sweety... well... s-suits her." He turned to Golden Man and asked, "What do you w-want?"

"Why, it is very simple. Return to me Father's stone."

"Return to y-you?"

"Yes, Father has given it to me."

"Why then do you still n-not have it?"

"A long story, my friend. Suffice it to say, there are entities that defy Father's will. And as soon as you found this wonderful valley – that I helped you discover, by the way – Father asked me to retrieve His stone. You see, I had promised Him to help you find this land; a promised land for a lost people."

"How did you 'help' us here, Mr. No-name?"

"The doorway you walked through can take you many places. But only I can open the doorway to *this* place. And to this spot,

322

along this particular cliff's edge, where such travel is made possible. And only I can wield the stone to deliver the offer I have already given."

Moshe wondered if what the man had said was true. How did it just so happen that the doorway led to their present location? Was this Golden character responsible?

"Tell me, friend," prompted Golden Man while gesturing to Moshe's body. "Do you really want to look this way? Does not the sun here burn you in ways that your eyes, nor body, will never adjust to?"

Moshe struggled mightily with Golden Man's arguments. Deep inside, he longed for things to be set right. His people, the children especially, did not deserve what had happened to them. He studied his clawed hands, thinking how bizarre they were. How many times had he gazed at his reflection in pools of water, wondering how or why he was so awful looking. Yes, even 'grotesque' as Golden Man had said. Moreover, the Valley's sun did indeed burn him.

"It d-oes burn, yes-s," he finally admitted.

"Yes, I'm s-sure it d-does," mimicked Golden Man, reviewing Moshe's stutter in a less than sympathetic manner. "Your speech, as it were, will only grow more twisted; as you have surely noticed. Your body will never adjust, nor will your Pon-looking tribe, I'm afraid. Is it not time to end the suffering of your egregiously punished people? Think of them as much as for yourself, my friend."

Moshe had to pause and mull over Golden Man's suggestion. Korah had told him of Moses, and his God, and how El was mad at their tribe for being disobedient. But how much rebelliousness could equate to such a cruel judgement?

Yet, had his people not survived all the terrible and awesome wonders put before them? In fact, during their recent exodus from the Crystallight cavern, he had told the clan how proud he was of their resilience against such impossible odds. Did he believe those brave words or not?

"I am uns-sure..."

"Do not be," stated Golden Man confidently. "Trust me. And I will ease your pain, my friend... Mosher. Or as your people call you now, Moshe. Your new name: *Moshe*. How apropos."

Startled, Moshe asked, "How do you know my n-name?"

"I know many names. For example, Bishtar."

"What of h-her?" Moshe asked a little too anxiously.

"Unrequited love, is it not? And why? Because, my dear friend, you have been unfairly judged for grievances you did not commit. Bishtar too. Think of it, Moshe. You could have a perfect body, better than before." Golden Man said this while gesturing to his own spectacular face and physique. "And Bishtar as well will return to you, much more beautiful than you remember, or could possibly imagine. And when she sees you in your glory, she will love you. The stone, if wielded by me, can doorway you back to the surface world, where you two will live out long and fruitful lives. Is this not what you long for... Moshe?"

Golden Man had touched upon something Moshe had tried to suppress; his desperate longing for Bishtar. It tore his guts to pieces to be reminded of her. But mentioning the doorway to the surface world also made Mosher wonder: could Golden Man have power over the golden gem he and Bishtar had discovered so many years before? Could he defeat Anubis? Strangely, Mosher's unusual new companion did not mention the phantom dog-man who guarded the golden jewel.

This was cause for concern. Regardless of his inner turmoil, there was yet another important question that made Moshe hesitate. "The s-stone was given to m-me by Calish. He did not mention you as part of its workings."

"The stone did not belong to Calish, so he would not know of all its properties. For example, its power to heal, as I've seen you have already stumbled upon. If you comply, Moshe, perhaps I could teach you of all its ways."

"But Korah had t-told Calish, told us..."

"Korah was an old fool. Was it not his own iniquity that brought your people here? It was his rebelliousness that caused you and Bishtar to be separated."

"He was my g-grandfather. He loved us, he..."

"...is not here to protect you, to care for you as he should have done. Puzzle this fine question, Moshe: Was it not Korah who stood by and watched as Gasheer whipped you? Is that love, Moshe? I dare to say no. But I am here to help you. And this is my valley. Everything in it belongs to me."

The despairing of Korah, the mentioning of Bishtar, combined with the whole confusing business, made Moshe suddenly angry. "Then w-why do you ask for the stone? Why not use your powers to merely take it s-somehow?

Truth be told, there was a huge part of him that wanted Golden Man to take it, use it, to be done with the whole insane situation. Calish was dead. Their real leader, his best friend, was gone. *Who am I to think I can take Calish's place? Damn this place and everything else!* All he really cared about was being reunited with his love. He was tired of the longing, and the endless aching pain of missing Bishtar.

"The answer to your rather heated question is really very simple," responded Golden Man. "If you give Father's stone willingly, you will receive the blessing I can bestow it with, to deliver on my promise. Salvation comes from a willing heart." After saying those inspiring words, Golden Man drifted on the air much closer to Moshe. He sent his piercing gaze into Moshe's eyes. He then reached out his golden arm and opened his hand. "Will your heart to me, Moshe, and I will ease all your suffering."

Moshe looked deeply into Golden Man's intensely brilliant and mesmerizing eyes. His glare was magnetic, and Moshe was drawn into it, like a moth to flames. He gradually reached for his pouch. To end the burden he carried... the weight of all his tribe depending on him was too enticing a prospect. Let Golden Man fix it once and for all. Golden Man was beautiful, dazzling; Moshe wanted everything about Golden Man. *Let it be done,* Moshe thought wishfully. *Let me be reunited with Bishtar, in our proper home, together forever.*

As if in a trance, Moshe retrieved the Minthuru stone and slowly brought it up to Golden Man's waiting fingers.

Seeing the brilliant stone so close caused Golden Man to take on a quirky, lustful expression, and he sing-songed:

"Give to me
your willing heart
endure the pain
before we part!"

With that, Golden Man's appearance of lust suddenly changed into one of shock, as if he did not mean to say such a thing. Then Moshe snapped out of his trance, and he eyed Golden Man suspiciously.

* * * *

Gabeel and Deborah ran to find Mishtas, frantic in their search. They ran past many huts and tents until they finally caught up with him. "Where is Moshe?" they asked excitedly.

"He went off... said he wanted to be alone."

"We must find him."

"Why?"

"Come and s-see."

At the outskirts of the encampment they found Buttons and her siblings. Buttons was very agitated, jostling to and fro, and when she saw Mishtas, she shuffled up to him while chattering much louder than usual.

"What is it, Buttons?" asked Mishtas.

She jerked about and started to move off into the undergrowth, only to stop, jolt around and look back at them with her sad and needy eyes.

"She wants us to follow," Mishtas said quizzically.

Deborah suddenly blurted out, "It's Moshe! I can sense it. There's something w-wrong."

"We must find him then." Mishtas turned and said to Gabeel, "Gather your soldiers. We leave immediately."

Gabeel whistled loudly, and sent out a mind-speak alarm. Soon thereafter, a small squad of armed soldiers showed up. "Where should we look?"

But they need not worry about that, because Buttons was already ahead of them, blazing a trail through the brush, clearly leading the way.

326

* * * *

Moshe was suddenly startled. He shook his head to clear his thoughts, and instinctively brought the hand that held the Minthuru stone closer to himself, out of the reach of Golden Man. Behind him came a thunderous pounding sound that shook the ground beneath his feet. It was followed by a loud chattering noise.

Golden Man peeked over Moshe's shoulder with trepidation to see what was approaching. He then nastily rhymed:

> *"Hand it over,*
> *you retched nit*
> *or from Sweety's bowels*
> *you'll be as shit!"*

Moshe turned back. Up from the valley a dust cloud was forming. Emerging from within the plume was a large, lumpy shape that was moving madly toward their spot. In a flash, the form broke through dust.

"Buttons!" Moshe said in disbelief. He had never seen the beast move so swiftly. He didn't even think she was even capable of such a feat. But she was. Behind her were Mishtas, Gabeel, Deborah, and others sprinting to keep up.

Within a short distance from Moshe, Buttons suddenly stopped and whirled around so that her tail section was facing him. She lifted her hind leg and immediately sent out her melting hot liquid. Moshe hunkered down and covered his head with his arm, thinking he was sure to be hit. But all he felt was the spray slightly singe his skin as it streamed past him. He braved a glance from under his arm to see where the spray was going.

It went right at Golden Man, then through him. Like a river, the poison cascaded all over and past the Golden figure, eventually falling over the cliff's edge.

"Awe – e-e! You evil beast!" cried Golden Man, while writhing in pain as if the spray was burning him up. "Awwww!" he groaned, twisting in agony.

327

Buttons continued her barrage until her spray of steaming hot liquid gradually faded into nothing more than but a few spits and sputters.

Golden Man peered up from behind his hands. His expression of terror abruptly turned into a vicious smirk. He voiced an evil laugh while singing,

> *"Ha, ha eeeel*
> *ha ha eel*
> *your broken spirits*
> *I will steal!"*

Golden Man glared at Moshe, then at Buttons, then at Sweety, and he coldly rhymed,

> *"Sweety my dear*
> *kill them all*
> *and before you do*
> *be sure to maul."*

As soon as Golden Man said this, Moshe could see Sweety ready herself, and her jaws, for a fatal charge. Golden Man also made a sudden lunge to grab at the Minthuru stone in Moshe's hand. Moshe saw the motion and instinctively gripped the stone tighter a second before Golden Man could reach it. When Golden Man's fingers touched the stone, everything shifted and disappeared.

* * * *

Sky Rock loomed above him, above them, above everything. Then in a sudden rush, its waters gushed out from the crack within the enormous boulder's side. From there, the water ran into a shallow stream that extended right before them both.

Moshe and Golden Man found themselves in that place very near Sky Rock. They both stared in awe at the towering sight and sound of the mighty waters. In between them, in their respective grasps, was the Minthuru stone.

Golden Man looked closer at the water, and was soon frightened by it. He grabbed the stone tighter and forcefully pushed Moshe, along with himself, away from the water's edge.

"Let go, you fool!" shouted Golden Man, while glancing behind him to make sure he had achieved a better distance from the water.

"Never!" declared Moshe.

Golden Man's face became fierce and he howled,

> *"I will kill*
> *all of your tribe*
> *your fate unknown*
> *to any scribe."*

Golden Man suddenly transformed into a hideous, hairy monster. The revolting beast growled and bore its teeth at Moshe. But Moshe would not let go of the stone.

Then Moshe remembered what Bishtar had screamed when Calish was murdered, and out of desperation, he did the same. "In the name of El, I command you to be gone!"

The Minthuru stone started humming.

Golden Man instantly returned to his golden appearance. He backed up a little, releasing his hold on the stone, and stood there anxiously waiting, as if he was unsure if Moshe's words would have any effect upon him.

In a few moments, Golden Man took on an aggressive stance as he could see that Mosher's prayer had not hurt him. So he started to advance, as a violent, hateful expression crossed his brow. He lifted his golden hand; it turned a fiery red. Electricity sparkled from his fingertips. Flames erupted, and those elements coalesced into a bolt of pure lightning that extended high above both of them. He eyed Moshe viciously; his target, his victim, could do nothing to stop the oncoming bolt of destruction.

But before Golden Man hurled the arc, he readied a hateful message. His voice became deep, gravelly, and with venom he spewed out,

"Son of Adam
Father's ol' plan
will be for not
in Pon or man

Son of Adam
know thy place
share my void
in time and space

Son of Adam
redeem thee never
Eden is lost
for now and forever."

Golden Man raised his hand higher and was about to throw the flaming bolt of lightning when Moshe, in a daring attempt to avoid the strike, used the hand holding the Minthuru stone to push Golden Man further away. Golden Man was twisted unsteadily back by its force. He tried mightily to right himself, but he lost his balance and stumbled closer to the water's edge. His face showed great fear as one of his jostling feet accidentally breached the stream. Then his wetted foot immediately started smoldering... and melting.

"Aaah!!" he screeched in agony. As Golden Man screamed, his mighty bolt of lightning fizzled and blinked out to nothing.

Suddenly, throughout the cavern's spaces, Moshe could hear a mysterious melodious song that said:

"In the name of El
Balize Voice be gone
cast you into Sheol
once hearing this song!"

"Noooo-ooo!!!" screeched Golden Man in total shock. Upon hearing the rhyme, he looked wildly about the cavern, trying to find the song's source. "No-o-o-o-!" he shouted to the open air. His perfect body began to be ripped into thousands of shreds. The

330

golden pieces spun and twisted over and over, and one by one were sucked into a whirling blackness that encompassed his shrinking, disappearing silhouette. Golden Man then gawked straight up while pleading, "Father! No-o-o. Voice asks You for forgiveness. Do not be angry with Your angel of light, VOICE!!!"

Nonetheless, Golden Man's form continued to be drawn into the dark void. As the last vestiges of Golden Man's appearance and his screeching, eerie, agonizing wail dissipated into the emptiness, Moshe suddenly realized who, or what Golden Man was: Voice, the evil spirit Stenrak had warned them of so many years before.

Another sound then emerged. Replacing Golden Man's cries was: "Hoo, Hoo-oo." The sound had the same tenor and melodic ring as the singing Moshe had just heard. The *hoo* sound merged with the hum of the Minthuru stone. "Hoo, Hooo," it rang for a second time. Upon the third, "Hoo, hoo-o-o," a form started to take shape, and then become solid.

"Yike-shtu," Mosher stuttered in astonishment. Directly in front of Moshe was another mysterious man. He calmly stood at the water's edge, not at all bothered if the waters touched his feet. Moshe did not recognize the man. He was young, somewhat tall, well built, and slender. His smooth hair was long and black. His cheekbones were highly set. His eyes were dark, piercing, and oriental in nature. His skin was a reddish brown. He was very handsome in a rugged way. Moshe had never seen a man like him before. But what was the most strange were his clothes. They were tailored to fit neatly around the man's body and legs in a way that was totally unknown to him. The man's shoes bore no signs of obvious stitching, and its fine leather covered all of his feet. The pharaohs would have truly envied such garments.

Again the cry rang forth, "Hoo, hoo-oo-oo."

Mosher searched out the sound and suddenly saw its source. Perched above the young man, as if clinging to an invisible branch was an enormous owl. Its feathers were beautifully colored and patterned. Its head was pure white, plumed at the neck. It had tall, fluffy ear tufts, and its deeply intense eyes were as big as melons.

"The g-guardian of the underworld," Moshe whispered in awe, remembering well his Egyptian lessons. *How fitting*, he thought as he reflected on all that had happened since the day the earth opened.

Moshe called out to the magnificent creature, "Bubo, are you to take me to the l-land of the d-dead?"

The great owl gazed at Moshe keenly. The mighty bird then directed its huge eyes at the dark-haired man.

Moshe followed suit. He was startled to see what was in the man's hand. It was the Minthuru stone! Moshe looked to his own hand. Rather than seeing the stone, he saw a glowing light where the stone should have been. He lifted his head toward the man, watching to see what he would do. The man turned to face Moshe, holding the stone at him so that Moshe might see it better. Moshe noticed that the Minthuru stone was different from what he remembered; it was now slightly bigger and it appeared to have sections to it, as if it was comprised of numerously colored gems that fit together like a puzzle. Yet the stone somehow intrinsically remained the Minthuru stone he was familiar with. The man then twisted the whole stone to hold it with both hands, end-to-end.

Then the man boldly proclaimed, "Chedel Shaar Chedel Qodesh El." To the side of Moshe's position another doorway opened.

"El, be praised," Moshe said in wonder.

Moshe approached it. Through the glowing doorway he saw the world he had once known as a boy. Egypt, glorious Egypt. More importantly, he could see himself, or rather what he should have grown to be, as a *human* man.

The other Mosher stood there staring back into Moshe's Pon-like eyes. Mosher's human face was sad to see the Pon double, but not so much that his human self could not smile in a gentle and generous way. Moshe couldn't help notice how striking his double was. Moshe's human self had curly black hair, and there was a sign of a scruffy, yet well-suited beard. Mosher's body, as it had always been, unfortunately, was a bit stout, but in a good, sturdy way, he eventually concluded.

"That is m-me?" Moshe said in disbelief, and a touch of gladness. All in all, his human appearance was most gratifying to see.

Then from somewhere nearby, another young man emerged. He was wiry and muscular. His head was covered with long brown hair. He carried a very familiar spear as he went to stand beside Moshe's human double. The two men greeted one another with great affection.

Then the two friends beckoned for yet another to join them. From another place nearby came a third person. She was a young woman and she was beautiful. She walked to stand near Moshe's other self. When she got close, she held onto the human Mosher's arm warmly.

"El, let it be," he voiced fervently. Moshe knew who she was; he knew who the other young man was, for there was no mistaking the family resemblance between twin brother and sister.

The young lady turned toward Moshe, and a glittering light around her neck caught his attention. The gem attached to their necklace of promise sparkled with the brilliance that could only derive from El's true sun.

As Moshe watched the trio, sharing in their harmony and togetherness, his dry Pon eyes somehow formed yet another drop of moisture. Moshe shed one more tear…this time, one of joy.

The dark-haired man turned the Minthuru stone over and repeated the words, "Chedel Shaar Chedel Qodesh El."

A new doorway opened, replacing the first one. This time Moshe could see people very much like the dark-haired man, with the same features. But these people had very simple garments that looked like they were sewn together in a way that he was much more familiar with. Nearby there were tents made from animal skins. But the shape of them was very different from what his people built. The portal tents were tall cone shapes that were pointy at the top.

The great owl, somehow transcending the doorway, flew to a place nearby the pointy tents. Bubo landed on a tree branch and pivoted its massive head toward him. Something telling in the bird's expression made Moshe think to better examine the portal's details, so that is what he did. Beneath the owl was a young woman tending to a pot that hung over a fire pit. Bubo hooted and the young woman turned to see Moshe. She was strikingly beautiful, with long black hair, dark red skin, and tender features. If he didn't know better, he'd guess that the young man who held the Minthuru stone and the beautiful woman were brother and sister. They looked so much alike. The lovely woman continued to stare at him and her eyes penetrated into Moshe's heart. She then smiled warmly as if she knew him. More than anything in the world, he wanted to know her too.

"Chedel Shaar Chedel Qodesh El," spoke the man, and the Sky Rock world disappeared.

CHAPTER 33
Sweety's Flight

As soon as Moshe reappeared, Sweety took an enormous stab at chomping down on his head. At the last second, Buttons knocked him out of Sweety's way, replacing Moshe with her bulky torso. Moshe went flying in the air, his Minthuru stone flying even further into the brush. Sweety sank her teeth into Button's back and she let out a loud squeal. Sweety squeezed her teeth harder into Button's furry hide as Button tried mightily to break free.

"Buttons!" Moshe shouted in fright. He recovered his footing, took out his wolf knife, and with careless abandon, flew at Sweety. He scooted around her back side and used the spikes along her spine to climb up near her neck. With all of his force, he started slicing his knife into Sweety's thick hide, anywhere and everywhere he could reach.

Sweety soon started to jerk from the stabbing wounds and eventually had to release her grip on Buttons. She danced and reached out her snout to try to nip at Moshe. But he rode her like a bucking horse, nimbly staying out of the muzzle's way. Then, in one serious jolt, he could not avoid landing hard on some of Sweety's spikes. They pierced his chest skin but Moshe held on, continuing with his assault.

"No!" commanded Gabeel, as some of his soldiers readied their arrows and spears to shoot at the monster. "You might hit Moshe. Wait until I give the order."

The soldiers held back.

Gabeel ran to join Moshe. Thinking to copy Moshe's Sweety-climbing stunt, Gabeel jostled for position near Sweety's tail and reached out to grab her spikes. But Sweety saw him coming, and with a swift motion, flicked her tail at the new intruder. Gabeel was catapulted over the cliff's edge.

"Stay back!" shouted Moshe to the soldiers.

But Stripes, Turtle Dove and Scout did not listen. They shuffled over to Sweety, and from three sides started spraying their poison all over the beast's legs and feet. Sweety shrieked in pain as her skin started smoldering from the burning fluid. The giant danced back a few steps. Then she focused her fierce eyes on the three little attackers.

But the brood kept up the attack until they had used up all their spray. Mere dribs and drabs sputtered out as they aimed their last bits at Sweety's feet. Then they backed up from their position and started trembling from fear, because they had no more fight in them.

Sweety, seeing the creature's helplessness, initiated her efforts to chomp onto them.

Stripes and TurtleDove, being a little quicker, were able to scoot out of the way. Scout, however, was not as swift, so Sweety made a lunge to grab him. Just before Sweety was to latch onto the little beast, Moshe sent his claws deep into the fleshy part of Sweety's skull in a final assault.

In his mind, Moshe screamed *Stop!*

Suddenly Sweety stopped. The beast stood there, frozen in place, her toothy mouth prevented from closing right over Scout's prone and vulnerable body.

Scout chattered loudly, and shook violently upon seeing the rows of fangs all around him. Large drops of Sweety's drool streamed down on Scout's furry little body.

As Moshe touched Sweety's mind, he could sense many things from her: hunger, anger, cunning, and most immediately pain. The litter's burning fluid was still smoldering and scorching into her skin. Because their minds were linked, Moshe also felt the beast's agony. Therefore it was not difficult for him to command her to do what he himself wanted to do: *Run – find water – fast.*

Sweety turned, and with a purposeful gate stormed away from the battleground.

As soon as Sweety got far enough away from the area, Mosher jumped off her back, rolling into the weeds and dirt.

He ran back straight to the cliff's edge. Everyone was there. Some of the soldiers were reaching down, clasping arms, legs, and body together, forming a line that extended over the cliff's side.

Moshe stretched his neck to see what they were doing. "Gabeel!"

Gabeel was holding onto a bunch of shrubs that grew out of the cliff's side. At the same time, he was struggling mightily to grasp onto a spear that had been passed down to find him. The spear and Gabeel's claw were close, but not quite close enough.

*Grab it, my love, m*ind-spoke Deborah while she hung herself as far over the cliff's edge as possible.

In a sudden thrust, Gabeel sent out his clawed hand to grasp the spear's shaft. He did grab it, barely, then he let go of the shrubs his other hand had purchased. He sat there suspended in midair, dangling over an empty space, with nothing below him but very distant rocks and boulders.

Moshe mind-spoke and shouted, "Hang on! Hang on!"

"Pull him up!" shouted Deborah, with authority.

And of course the soldiers did so. Soon enough, Gabeel reached the cliff's peak. They pulled him to safety and everyone latched onto him in a warm welcome; most especially Deborah.

Moshe squeezed Gabeel hard on the shoulder. "You were foolish to follow me, Gabeel."

Gabeel put his head down, as if humbled by Moshe's words.

"But thank you, m-my friend, thank you."

Gabeel was happy to hear it, as Moshe went to embrace the young warrior.

Mishtas called out, "Moshe, come quick! It's Buttons."

Buttons lay on her side, bleeding badly from her wounds. She moaned a sad cry. After seeing Moshe, she did her best to stretch out her snout to meet him. He came to her and stroked her ears, while lifting her head as gently as he could.

Mishtas asked, "The stone? Do you think it might work again?"

Moshe looked at him worriedly. "I lost it, M-Mishtas."

"Do not fear, we will find it." Mishtas went to gather Button's litter.

Moshe opened his pouch so that Button's brood could get a scent. Then the little creatures started moving into the underbrush.

Soon enough, Scout started making loud chattering noises. Mishtas followed and bent down to pick up what he found: the stone. He brought it back to Moshe.

Moshe took up the gem. "Once again, my friend, I have n-no idea if this-s will work, nor how to make it work."

"We must find a way." Mishtas remembered when they had cured Gabeel. "Blood! A blood sacrifice. It worked before."

"Yes, but w-who's blood?"

Mishtas scrutinized the creatures. "Or better yet, *what's* blood."

Then Moshe put together what Mishtas referred to. "No, they cannot possibly understand this-s. Moreover, how can this w-work on an animal?"

"Did not father Korah teach us that we are all creations of El, even the beasts?" Mishtas pointed to his head. "Speak with Buttons; tell her your idea."

Moshe hesitated, but then calmly reached out his clawed hand to touch Button's head. He showed her the Minthuru stone and in his mind he said, *Blood.* He also did this while showing her the blood from his own chest wounds. But all he could get in return from Buttons was sensations of pain and sorrow.

"It's n-not working. She doesn't understand me." He retracted his hand from her head and stood straighter. His sadness at seeing Buttons suffer was palpable, and it was forcing him to contemplate the unthinkable. In Egypt, if a beast was that badly damaged, it would be immediately put down so as to release the animal from suffering. He reluctantly started to plan the quickest, most efficient way of ending Button's anguish. He retrieved his wolf knife, looked at Mishtas knowingly, and readied his posture to do the awful deed.

But just before he raised the knife, he felt a bump at his calf. He moved his head down to see Scout nudging up against his leg. Then the little creature willfully turned over to expose its soft underbelly.

Mishtas observed, "I think she does understand, Moshe."

Moshe nodded in agreement. He knelt down and held the Minthuru stone close to Scout's body. He took the wolf knife and very carefully snipped open a small cut on Scout's soft belly skin. Scout squirmed a bit, but otherwise let Moshe do his task. A greenish gray blood soon began to trickle out and onto scout's fur, and he was quick to collect it onto the stone.

The Minthuru stone started to hum. Moshe brought to stone over to Buttons, and as soon as it was close to Button's wound, the same healing light that had coursed over Gabeel's body started to emanate and work its magic. "El, we ask that You heal Your creation called B-Buttons."

Within a few moments, Buttons began to tremble. Then, as the wounds closed, she started to rise. Buttons lifted her snout at Moshe. After that, she brought out her yellow tongue, licking Moshe's face in the process. The people all around rang out with shouts of joy.

Mishtas announced gladly, "You have done it, Moshe!"

"No," Moshe argued as he bent over to retrieve Scout. With the little creature at his bosom, Moshe stood tall. He proudly gazed at everyone, and at every being around him. In mind-speak, and in a loud commanding voice, he proclaimed, "*We* have done it. El has done it."

CHAPTER 34
The Strangled Goodbyes

Mishtas said sadly, "I will miss you, my friend. Do you really have to go?"

"We mus-st," Moshe said. His difficulty speaking aloud was becoming more and more labored. His pointy tongue, thin lips and sharp teeth seemed unsuited for what was once his native language. The Valley somehow seemed to exacerbate the problem immeasurably. "The children... those m-my age, are uncomfortable h-here. I can no-no spea... say our words we-ll."

To help Moshe, as much as agree with him, Mishtas continued Moshe's thoughts out loud. "Yet another example of how our clan, or part of it, is separating itself from the Valley. The little ones spend their days and nights in the nearby caves. Very few play in the open field anymore with Scout and TurtleDove. And the animals, likewise, shun the caves. They will not follow the children into them; they get nervous and run back into the fields. But the children seem more at home than ever in the darkness. I've followed them once and I've seen them gladly enter tunnels that would cause terror in my heart if I were to dare enter them."

"The light h-here and openness bothers-s them. I als-so find myself longing for the dark spaces-s of our underground home before we discove— found the Maana caves-s. Hmpph," grunted Mosher in disbelief. "Fun-ny, I wish for the closed t-tunnels I once feared."

"Soon the older generation will be gone," cited Mistas. "Those that still remember Egypt will die of old age. And they will forget Moses, our tribe's original Moshe. The new generation will have to find greener pastures, I hope. Speaking of which, where will you bring our Pon-looking tribe, Moshe?"

"Back t-t-o the Maana caves, and from t-there we mak cont-tac with Stenrak's tribe."

"To what end?"

"Hope Sten-rak accepts us-s and we can integra— be one with them. The Maana caves-s, just temporary. Not ours b-but a Pon Holy Place. No, we need more options-s, alternate foods and other survival techniques-s. Stenrak's people help us-s." After that, Moshe had to pause to collect himself.

Mishtas warmly patted him on the shoulder. "It is okay, my friend, I still understand you. And you are not alone. I hardly ever hear the children speak our language anymore."

"Yes-s, I hear the-em, in my mi-n," he stammered while pointing to his head.

Mishtas studied him with kind eyes. He loved Moshe too much. To see him go meant that he would lose touch with everything he once knew about the tribe's life on the surface world.

"And Gabeel? Will he travel with you?" asked Mishtas.

They both watched as Gabeel and Deborah approached.

Gabeel stuttered, "I will s-stay, and..." He too loved Moshe, but felt a tremendous loyalty to Mishtas for saving his and Deborah's life during the battle in the Pon Holy place. Gabeel looked at Deborah to see what she would say.

"I wi-ill st-ay, t-t-oo," she stammered. She held Gabeel's hand as if she would never let go.

Moshe faced the loving couple and said in mind-speak, *I will miss you both greatly.*

They bowed their heads in deference, and clasped their arms around Moshe. Then Moshe thought to them, *We will be waiting for you if...* He wanted them to know that if, or rather, *when* they were to venture back into the tunnels, they would be welcomed. It was only a matter of time before they too would be forced to leave the Valley.

He then mind-spoke his final words to them. *If you try to find us, I cannot think of a way to directly help guide you. You will have to find your own way. The journey will undoubtable be fraught with danger. The only thing I can promise you is that I will ask Stenrak to ask his Maana masters to use their powers to help you.*

Gabeel and Deborah nodded that they understood.

Moshe turned back to Mishtas. "You are the Elder of the R-Remnant, Mish-sh-tas-s. Take c-care our people."

They embraced one last time before Moshe began to walk toward the cliff's edge. Before reaching into his pouch, Moshe looked past Mishtas, Gabeel, and Deborah. The tribe; *his* tribe of Pon, were waiting patiently for him to reopen the doorway. They were standing in line, holding their belongings, ready to go. Around them was the older generation; the human ones that would stay in the Valley. The goodbyes had already been given, but the sadness on everyone's face was clear.

"You know I will," answered Mishtas resolutely.

Moshe took in the Valley's beautiful landscape one last time, defiantly ignoring the burning light of the small sun. Buttons and Scout came to his side, chattering away. He reached down to stroke little Scout. The creature rolled over to allow him to rub its belly, and the small nick where it had given up its blood.

Moshe mind-spoke to him. *You're a kind little creature, aren't you?*

Scout chattered louder upon hearing the sounds.

"Where T-Turtle Dove and S-Stripes?"

Mishtas answered, "Yesterday they played with the children for a little while, and then they disappeared into the forest. No one has seen them since."

Moshe stood up to face Buttons. He stroked her matted fur and fuzzy ears. She watched him carefully with eyes much sadder than normal. "Goodbye, But-tons-s," He said with as much joy he could muster.

After that, Buttons cocked her head at a strange angle. Suddenly in Moshe's mind he could hear an echo sound repeating. *Goodbye, But-tons-s.* She snuggled up to him and reached out her tongue to stroke his claw-like hand. Her touch prompted an exchange of emotions, and inside he could feel what Button's felt. There was such a profound sadness in her spirit. Then from around her sunken eyes moisture formed. Soon enough, the drops started to fall.

"She will miss you." said Mishtas. "But not as much as I."

Moshe stroked Buttons on the ears one more time, and in his mind he told her, *I understand.* Then he retrieved the Minthuru stone from his pouch. It immediately started to hum, as if it somehow knew that its power was needed. Then the hum got louder as Moshe held it very near the cliff's edge. He turned it over and held it the way the black-haired man had shown him.

342

Moshe solemnly spoke, "Chedel Shaar Chedel Qodesh El."

Suddenly, at the cliff's precipice, a sparkling doorway appeared. Through some of the shimmering facets one could see the images reminiscent of the Maana caverns: the Crystallights that littered the rocky walls, murky Maana plants sprinkled here or there, the great altar, endless streams of dark alcoves and tunnels... and of course, Sky Rock. The threshold's view of the dark cavern corridors was in stark contrast to the brilliance of the light-filled Valley. It was heart-breaking to think that the tribe would give up the light for the dark. But what could one do?

Nothing.

Moshe, upon seeing their old home, nodded to Gabeel. Gabeel in turn gave the mind-speak message for the new clan of remnant Pon to begin entering the doorway, one-by-one.

They did.

CHAPTER 35
O'oviss

2 Years Later

The lone traveler, hooded and cloaked by a long flowing robe, walked through the underbrush to the raised meadow. He looked up at the little sun briefly, covering his squinting eyes with his arm. His reach extended beyond the cloak's sleeve and where the sun's light hit exposed skin, smoke arose. The light burned him so he quickly had to cover up again. The cloak protected his pale, leathery skin from the sun's heat, the hood from a brightness his eyes could barely tolerate.

Moshe stared into it anyway. *The sun; it is where I remember, but was it always so strong, so intense?*

He scanned over the valleys, forests and ever so distant mountains. He felt lost in its immensity. The open spaces scared him a little. A big part of him wanted to retreat back to the dark caverns and tight tunnels that he now called home. That desire, Moshe sadly concluded, scared him even more. But he put those thoughts from his mind; he had a job to do and there was no time for giving in to his fears. He'd be better off thinking about something positive. So he hiked further, happily anticipating a joyous reunion. While smiling broadly, he overtook the meadow's crest. But he did not see what should have been readily apparent, and his smile instantly disappeared.

Where is everyone?

Moshe entered the meadow, stumbling a bit to overcome the tall weeds and dense overgrowth that was everywhere. Toppled stones littered the area as well. The rocks could have been where the tent posts once stood, but it was hard to be certain. He found torn pieces of tents, broken tools, and dismantled carts half-buried in thick grasses. But the folks were all gone, without a trace.

Did they move to another place? Yes, that must be it. I will look a bit more to see if they left a message somewhere.

He walked to the nearby tree stand, where his people had liked to gather, but saw nothing. He went closer to where the children once played in the caves, but the underbrush had covered over the entrances. Because there were no more clues, he decided to try the tribe's burial site. There were placards there; maybe his clan had left a note saying where they had gone. He expected the site to be no more populated by graves then when he had last seen it.

He was wrong.

He passed through the graveyard's post and lintel entrance and was taken aback. Countless headstones filled the area. Many were disheveled, falling down and buried under thickly knotted shrub brush. It was a mess; something his people would never tolerate.

"Shi-shi-shtu," he gasped. Why were there so many plots? Did his tribe suddenly grow, and then just as swiftly die off? There were more than enough markers for everyone who had stayed behind. He started searching for headstones with names that were etched upon them. He soon found some. He pushed back the overgrowth to read the inscriptions.

Durious. *Yes... he was old, it makes sense.*

Claras. *She was not old. What happened to her?*

Obediah. *He was one of the few Pon who had stayed behind. He was my age!?*

On and on, Moshe went, finding more names. Most he knew, but some he did not. He looked for but did not see a memorial for Gabeel and Deborah. But he was sure their names would not be there. The young warriors were brave and adventurous; they would have stayed to help Mishtas for a respectfully appropriate time, and then they would have left to find the rest of their Pon tribe.

He called out to the open air, "We have not yet found you, my friends, but we will never stop looking."

At the bequest of Stenrak, who represented Moshe, the Maana masters had ventured into Sklon visions and searched for Gabeel and Deborah. But so far they saw no sign.

There was, however, one master who had voiced some enigmatic ramblings during his particularly harrowing vision. While in a Sklon trance, the master mumbled out something about a young Pon couple that had stumbled upon a very deep and unknown habitat. Apparently, within the haunt's strange walls were frightful creatures that did not take kindly to Pon mind-speakers, especially those who intruded into their space from visions. That unfortunate Maana master never properly woke from his traumatic vision. He became comatose, only able to eat, defecate and mutter over and over the words: "Death to all outsiders."

Eventually, after his family had tired from feeding and cleaning his excrement, they decided to offer his living body to the clan's Sterga beasts. It was a sad event for the family. But at least the Sterga's were happy, for they truly enjoyed their treat.

Moshe then spotted two memorial stones that were much taller, larger and more elaborately designed. They stood side-by-side and very close to one another. Even from a far distance he could tell that they had writing upon them that was much more descriptive than the others. He moved closer because whoever lay there was obviously important. When he got there, he anxiously read the inscriptions:

Here lies Mishtas, our beloved Elder
Loving Husband of Hannah
Father of Eleazar
Lived to the age of 93

Here lies Hannah
Loving wife of Mishtas
Mother of Calish, Bishtar, and Eleazar
Lived to the age of 92

"No... no," he cried in disbelief. Moshe knelt down in front of both tombstones. He reached up, tracing the various engravings with his fore-claws, rereading the words again and again. "How can it be? At the m-most, only two years have p-passed since we left the Valley. Hannah, I am s-sorry. You will be missed. Mishtas, my d-dear friend. Uncle, how can you be g-gone?"

By his estimation, Mishtas should have only been in his late forties. Moreover, how long after his death at ninety-three did the survivors last before everything had turned to disarray and to dust?

"How can over fifty y-years have p-passed?" If it were possible, Moshe's dry Pon eyes would have shed a tear.

Before he exited the graveyard, Moshe stopped by the yard's first and most central occupant. He couldn't leave without seeing it one more time. He found the place and went to his knee in front of the stone that held the name of his one true friend.

"I am here, C-Calish," Moshe said solemnly. "We are living with Stenrak's people now. As you m-most likely could have guessed, those of us who l-look Pon had to leave your Valley. The ones who were still human stayed h-here, and by the looks of it, are now your companions. I hope that w-wherever you are, you are h-happy."

"So far we are surviving: you would b-be proud. And I still have Korah's gift. I have kept it s-safe, as you asked me to." Moshe reached down to his pouch, bringing out the Minthuru stone. Its blue highlights sparkled brightly from the sun's rays, but did not hum the way it had when he had doorwayed into the Valley. He stared at it, wondering about its true powers, something he had barely come to know.

Then he thought about what he had read on Mishtas's tombstone. *Time has progressed differently here... or where I was. Or maybe El's stone transcends time as well as space.*

He suddenly started to worry. "Will s-she still be there?"

Ashkolon told him that he must travel through the doorway to meet his destiny; to meet his mate, and bring her to the underworld. He didn't say exactly who she would be; Ashkolon didn't know. All he knew was that it had to be done; Ashkolon's Sklon induced vision had said so. The Pons' future was at stake.

At first Moshe had hoped his mate would be Bishtar. But that was a young man's wishful thinking. She would not be in the Valley. She already lived in the underworld, so fitting her into Ashkolon's vision didn't make sense. Besides, there were Pon drifters that had told stories of a distant tribe, led by a powerful mind-motion queen; a terrible Harsha empress that was not to be stopped. Somehow he knew that terrible queen was his Bishtar. "My love."

So that only left one other candidate. Two years earlier, Bubo the great owl had shown him a beautiful, long-haired young woman. She had stared into his eyes as if she knew him, and as though they were meant to be together. Of course Moshe wanted the same thing.

But if time was ever-changing, then would she still be there? Would she still be young, or old, or what? Would she still remember him? If so, how would he convince her to follow him through the doorway? And for heaven's sake how could he coerce her into mating with him? He looked grotesque by human standards.

He had asked the Maana master, but once again Ashkolon did not know. *Leave me be, human! I have told you all there is.* This was Ashkolon's last comment before he brandished his dagger and threatened an extremely painful death if Moshe dared to ask another question. The very old prophet was not the most patient of creatures and did not take kindly to incessantly unanswerable questions.

Luckily, Stenrak's family was there to placate him with the finest Maana berry wine and some choice pieces of Mestalor, otherwise the fate of the Pon would have been in more serious doubt than it currently was. Apparently, Maana masters got very hungry, and thirsty, after having visions.

But who could Ashkolon's vision be pointing to?

Logically, bringing someone to Pon territory meant that the person was not already in the underworld, so the woman Bubo had shown him had to be the one. Somehow it made sense. The beautiful, dark-haired, red-skinned woman made sense.

"I m-must get r-ready for her."

He took one last look at Calish's marker. "Goodbye, m-my brother. Wish me luck on w-what I am about to do. And may El bless and protect you."

Moshe then set out toward the meadow. On the way, he passed by the densely overgrown and dark place where the children had liked to play hide and seek with Scout, TurtleDove, and Stripes. He scanned the area, wanting desperately to see the curious little beasts. Of course there was no sign of them, so he thought of their mother.

"Buttons!" he shouted impulsively. "B-Buttons!" But how could Buttons be there? If fifty-plus years had passed, she would be gone and her offspring would have perished as well. "S-

Scout?" he whispered, knowing the sad truth of the lovely little creature's absence.

He collected himself, retook the meadow's spaces, and set to the task of building a home. Just in case he was successful in finding someone to bring back into the underworld, she would need shelter, and a nice place to live. He started by gathering bits and pieces of left-over tent debris, and anything else that was needed. He cobbled together the structure nearest to the heavily forested area, close by the Valley's caverns. He could venture out during the Valley's misty night, but during the daylight hours he would have to be in the shade, or if necessary, retreat to the darkness of the caves.

It appears my body can no longer tolerate the sun's rays.

The structure was for her, whoever she was. Taking her directly into the underworld would be too stressful for a human, far too strange. On that count he well understood. It would be better to bring her to the Valley first, where they could get to know one another, and learn to communicate, until the mating time came.

"El, g-give me s-strength."

When the building task was done, he donned his cloak, took up his pouch and ventured back to the Valley's precipice. He took out the Minthuru stone and turned it over end-to-end, holding it the way the strange dark-haired man had shown him years before. Then he recited the words the red-skinned man had spoken. "Chedel Shaar Chedel Qodesh El."

The shimmering doorway emerged. Its edges glowed and hummed to life with many colors, as he well recognized. Moshe approached it; he glanced through its portal, smiling broadly from what the doorway revealed. Within its borders he could see the forest habitat where the simple people lived. Once again, he recognized their cone-shaped tents made of animal hides, their fire pits, and their basic tools. Some of the dark-haired, red-skinned folks were also walking about. It was as he had remembered it; he became excited, and very anxious to see her. But no matter where he looked, he did not see the beautiful young woman.

"I am too late. El, I am too l-late."

Then, from somewhere in the nearby forest, he heard, "Hoo. Hooo."

Moshe quickly turned his eyes up to see Bubo, who was as magnificently plumed as before, perched on a branch high in a tree. Bubo took note of him. Then the mighty bird swiveled its huge head down, directing him to look beneath its spot. Out from the trees emerged the woman. If possible she was even more beautiful than he remembered, and it melted his heart once again. She looked at him, and he, of course, at her.

Now what? How do I get her to follow me here?

But he need not worry, for the woman reached down and picked up a leather sack that was stuffed with what could only be her belongings. Then she walked to the doorway, in a straight line, and stopped just short of its threshold. She gazed at him and smiled, warmly, knowingly. He could do nothing else but return her generous smile.

He stepped forward, extending his clawed hand through the shimmering boundaries of the doorway. In his old Hebrew tongue, he said, "I am Moshe."

She took up his claws with her delicate little hand and did her best to speak in kind, "Ta'al Zera-eesh, ka Moshe."

Moshe nodded in understanding and for the first time, spoke her name, "Zera-eesh." And the beautiful young woman went to Moshe through El's doorway.

****

Nine Months Later

Moshe let the tent flap down as quietly as he could. He stood up straight and stared wistfully at the place he would need to go. Zera-eesh lay sleeping finally, after succumbing to exhaustion from labor pains. Her time was near, so he knew, or rather dearly hoped, that his old friend, his powerful ally, would give-up the precious gift once more.

Pon encampments surrounded him. Some were of his tribe, but most belonged to Stenrak's people. Luckily his and King Storn's camps had peacefully integrated themselves, for the most part. Stenrak had seen to the arrangement. After the battle in the Holy

Place, he and Ashkolon had petitioned the King to allow Moshe's people to settle in Helon-controlled territory – if and when the Judah tribe ever returned. Stilik, of course, had objected vehemently, but because of Ashkolon's council, the King ultimately decided to let Moshe's tribe take up a place relatively distant from the main settlement, and even further from Dathan's encampment.

Of course Dathan strongly objected. He wanted Moshe's people enslaved... or worse. Moshe hated him for that – for many things, actually. But as long as Dathan and Feaster kept their distance, he was willing to keep the peace. Besides, he had more important concerns on his mind, not the least of which was fulfilling prophecy.

Upon the tribe's return from the Valley, Stenrak had explained it to Moshe in this way: *Ashkolon and I told King Storn of the battle, of Voice's interference, and of the portal. Our message was that everything, including the stones, had a purpose in prophecy. Ashkolon also advised the King to let the prophecy play out, for there was still more to come. King Storn was eventually convinced; he ordered Stilik to stand-down for now. And Dathan was instructed to give way and not interfere with Pon business.*

It wasn't long after the King's royal decree that Ashkolon had his vision concerning Moshe's role in venturing to the Valley. Once Moshe and Zera-eesh had returned from the Valley, Stenrak helped the situation along even further. He made certain that his people gave them a respectable amount of privacy, and whatever else they needed.

Moshe carried a small clay flask his mate Zera-eesh had given him. It was crafted by her people. The sides had small carvings on it of animals he had never seen. She told him their names, and was intrigued by her animated stories about how the animals lived. Her home was, by his reckoning, very far from Egypt. Moshe didn't understand the connection between his people and hers, but then again, it was just one more example of the many mysteries posed by the underworld, and by extension, the surface world.

Moshe moved through and around the various huts, nodding peacefully to each Pon citizen that he passed. Most of them gestured back in kind. But there were those that couldn't help but display their forked tongue and hiss out their suspicion of him. Obviously there was still work to do on overcoming interspecies relations, even though everyone looked the same, more or less.

"Peace be with you, friend," Moshe voiced in Pon tongue to a person he passed by.

"Hisss –ssss!" came the hostile reply.

"Okay then, I'll just be on my w-way." Moshe quickly scooted past the rather angry citizen.

He made his way to the tunnel that led to the Pon Holy place; what he had once called the Crystallight cavern. When he finally arrived, he was stopped by a guard who wanted to know where he was going. But once Moshe identified himself, the guard let him pass. Stenrak had already seen to this and had ordered the guards to give Moshe clearance to the tunnels. Stenrak didn't know all the details of Moshe's trek, but he trusted that Moshe had a good reason to breach the Holy Place's domain. Stenrak was becoming a true brother... much like Calish had been.

"C-Calish," he said to himself reflectively. That life had seemed so long ago and so far away. And yet Calish's memory was never completely out of his mind, nor his heart, because thoughts of Calish always corresponded with overriding memories of Bishtar. "No, don't think of her, not now," he chided himself, "I have s-something important to do."

Besides the flask, Moshe carried the Minthuru stone. Once again, because of Stenrak's influence, it was still in Moshe's possession. He hoped that the stone's presence would help encourage his old ally to remember and honor his puzzling instructions: "The time will come; you will know what to do."

But was this that time? Without the Water of Life, the upcoming birth might very well be nothing but a normal event. That could put the unborn child's life at risk because some would say they had been tricked into believing a false prophecy. Ashkolon is the one who had told King Storn of the birth's significance. But could his influence be enough to protect the child? Maybe at first. But would Ashkolon's sway last indefinitely? Moshe could not afford to take chances; any edge he might have at protecting the child had to be employed because there were many who saw the birth as a threat.

Stilik, for starters, was one very big threat; he intended on capturing the throne, and once in that seat... well, who knew how he might see competing forces. Then there were other hostile Pon clans, some of whom did not like the idea of Storn's Helon tribe rallying around a supposed prophetic leader.

There was also Voice, who as Golden Man had warned that it would allow nothing to take the Pon from its dominion. Was Voice gone forever? Moshe could not be certain that the evil spirit had been totally vanquished. No, the spirit still lived unfortunately, and Stenrak had agreed with that assessment.

Beyond that there was Dathan, who was predictably arrogant and extremely ambitious; and by extension Faester, who was definitely in the Voice category of evil. Moreover, Faester, as some Pon believed, was the O'oviss.

The enemies were lining up.

"El give me strength."

After exiting the tunnel that led to the Holy Place, Moshe made his way to the cavern where he and Calish had discovered the monumental boulder. He soon found himself standing in front of his old ally, Sky Rock. As expected, it was as impressively overbearing and powerfully enduring as he remembered.

Now what? He took out the Minthuru stone. He tried holding it up to Sky Rock, as if its presence could magically force Sky Rock to open once again. But nothing happened.

While holding out the stone, Moshe tried reverently saying what he hoped would be the magic words, "Chedel Shaar Chedel Qodesh El." But again nothing happened.

He tried climbing up to the place on Sky Rock where the fissure had released its waters. He bent over and called into the small crack that had been there since the moment he had first smote the rock so many years before. "Sky Rock, it is m-me, Moshe. Hello?"

But still nothing. Why didn't Sky Rock offer the waters the way it had done when he had fought Golden Man? Surely this time was just as important as it had been then. Could it be that Ashkolon was wrong and everything he and Zera-eesh had done together was for nothing? Or maybe he had unknowingly done something wrong.

He reached his claws into the crack and offered, "I am s-sorry, Sky Rock." But still nothing.

He soon became frantic and started scratching his claws into the fissure, calling out again, "Sky Rock, w-where are you? You helped m-me defeat Voice. Why did you do so if n-not for this moment? I do not understand. I know y-you are in there. Do you not know the birth is n-near? Is this not the time you told m-me of?"

Everything was in the balance; the fate of his people, his mate, and most importantly, the unborn child. He sat down, feeling despondent, wanting to cry. Then he started to. And even his dry Pon eyes could not stop a few tear drops from forming.

While he was sobbing, he suddenly realized that he should try repeating the most crucial words Sky Rock had taught him. But what was it again? "Yes, yes I r-remember now: Thus Saith El, our Lord, let the Water of Life come forth."

Immediately Sky Rock trembled and the waters gushed forth. Moshe quickly stood up again, somehow keeping his balance despite the trembling. The waters showered over him. He gladly let some of it enter his mouth while smiling widely, enjoying the moment. He quickly opened the flask, letting the waters enter it. His tears of sadness were washed away by the gloriously refreshing liquid. The water again restored his body and mind. Moshe's thoughts were fully clear for the first time in his life, a new miracle.

"I am whole, I am whole," he cried, overwhelmed with joy. "I can now speak clearly." He touched his lips as he spoke, still trying to believe it was real.

The sounds of the spraying waters were loud. But then something much greater emerged. A mighty voice rang out, "Take the water, Moshe. Father has seen to this. His will be done."

"I will, Sky Rock. El be praised, I will." Moshe raised up the flask, thus allowing the sprinkling waters to fill it to the brim.

"Peace be with you, Moshe, and to the son, peace. Goodbye for now, my friend, goodbye."

"Goodbye, Sky Rock. Thank you."

* * * *

A slender delicate claw rotated around and around in the thick red liquid. Soon enough, the blood began swirling on its own. The watcher's claw retracted. As expected, it was no longer needed. The watcher waited, somewhat patiently, for something to appear within the confines of the silver vessel.

Joseph's Cup had done well to show the secret of Sky Rock's water. Now the watcher needed to know how that secret was to be used. It had to be done; her true dominion over the underworld could never be accomplished if something as powerful as a Pon prophetic destiny came to pass.

The blood swirling slowed. Then it stopped and the redness started to dissolve. The liquid soon become as clear as the air itself. The watcher stared with keen interest as the images took shape. Soon thereafter, the images magically transformed into a place that was very familiar. The vessel's power allowed the watcher to witness anything that was important, like a bird that slowly flew over everything. The view was at first well above the scene and the watcher was shocked by the sight. There were many Pon, great and small, surrounding the Holy Place's altar. The bird flew closer. Moshe was there; Ashkolon too. The view was drawn even closer again. Beside them, on her back was a woman, a human woman! At first the watcher was incredulous by the woman's presence.

The woman suddenly screamed in agony. The watcher soon recognized why. Immediately the watcher was filled with a great and terrible, burning jealousy.

* * * *

"Aaaahhh!!" screamed Zera-eesh loudly. Again her voice rang out across the cavern. The spectators took note of the noise, but they were not overly concerned with her pain. They were only there to see if the prophecy would be true.

"Her time is near," croaked Ashkolon coldly. A servant Pon approached him, and in deference bowed greatly while offering the high priest his headdress. Ashkolon took it up and placed it over his pale grey, bulbously large head. The circlet was forged from a roughly rune metal band that was dull and flawed. In contrast, there were shiny, bright crystal gems that adorned it. He then arranged his ceremonial robes and pulled back the sleeves, exposing his gnarled and vein-riddled forearms and claws. He made one small gesture and the Pon nurse-maids moved in close and readied the woman's legs.

Thousands of onlookers scanned the event. Their dull, whitish-gray faces looked up to the raised altar, to where the momentous birth was taking place. Their expressions revealed anticipation; their bulging black eyes were opened wider than usual, if that were possible.

Zera-eesh screamed again, her body convulsing in pain. The nursemaids reached in to grab the emerging form. As soon as the woman gave birth, the nursemaids cut the cord and took the child, delivering it to the high priest. Ashkolon accepted delivery; his clawed digits cupped the child in a less than gentle way. He looked upon his charge, scrutinizing and assessing, up and down. Then he probed the newborn's mind.

"Gryi-iiki!" Ashkolon was stunned by what he found. Power unlike he had ever known was within the baby.

Suddenly a shocking bolt of energy shot out from the child. The painful force entered into his hands, throbbing its way up through his old arms. Somehow he did not lose his grip, though a trembling fear engulfed him. For a moment he contemplated the unthinkable. *No,* he decided reluctantly, the infant must live, no matter what; it was prophecy revealed.

Ashkolon composed himself enough to complete his task. The ancient prophet turned to his audience and delivered the words they were waiting to hear. He also sent out his message via mind-speak. "The baby is Pon. It is a boy." Hisses of delight criss-crossed the Holy cavern. Ashkolon then lifted the infant up so all could see and declared, "Yaanai is born. Prophesied child of the Spirit; he will see Father's light. Your savior is here!"

The hisses of delight became gasps of awe.

Summoning more courage, the priest performed his final job. To bring the infant to life, he plunged the sharpest of his claws into the infant's ribs. The baby suddenly jerked and took its first gasp of air. The infant screeched out a deafening sound. The thunderous call echoed through the chambers and the caverns shook in response. Debris and stones fell from above as the followers covered their heads and cowered in fear. But many ignored the onslaught, choosing to grandly prostrate themselves before their new master. Some of those beings, unfortunately, were struck down hard by falling rocks.

"Gryi-iiki, alee, shagool," whispered Ashkolon uneasily, wondering if he too was to be killed by the power within his grasp.

When the shaking stopped, Ashkolon glared at Moshe strangely. The old priest's expression was a mixture of fear and amazement. The greatest symbol of all Pon history was in the cup of his claws. He nodded at Moshe in reverence. Strangely, for the first time Ashkolon mind-spoke to Moshe politely. *Human, it is done.*

Moshe gestured in kind. Then he turned to see his benefactors. Not far away, King Storn was seated upon his throne, watching carefully, a ponderous expression covering his face. His crown, which was much more elaborately sprinkled with jewels than Ashkolon's, also differed in another important way. The metal used to forge it was a shiny gold: perfect and unblemished. It was a gift from Dathan. His human craftsmen had forged it as the first of many concessions the surface-dwellers made for their safety and security. The Pon/human relationship was, for a time, an uneasy and delicate affair that had yet to be fully explored.

Moshe mind-spoke to King Storn respectfully. *My Sovereign.*

King Storn nodded slightly. The royal one turned to cast an intense gaze upon the child. The birth put into question his kingship, his legacy, and his sons' birthright. If he made the newborn his adopted son, would that fulfill or negate prophecy? For now, he heeded Ashkolon's council and would do nothing to harm the infant boy. But could he learn to accept the child? Could his sons do the same?

To Storn's right stood Stilik: tall, powerful, and as usual, menacing. He wore his body armor, but his favorite club-hammer was sheathed in its belt, and his Blood Vein was eerily calm and deflated. This was not a time for fighting; the warrior understood that. But Moshe knew the prince did not agree with the prophecy. Stilik wanted the Pon to live-out their destiny devoid of any human intercession. Of course, that is exactly what the prince intended on making happen, as soon as his time came.

To Storn's left was Stenrak, resolved to finally accept his place as second in line to be king. Stenrak, of course, held proudly onto Asher's spear. Unlike Stilik, Stenrak believed in the prophecy; after all he had been instrumental in living it. He trusted Ashkolon, his Maana master. Moreover, Stenrak highly valued the growing relationship he had with his newest family member, Moshe.

With that in mind, Stenrak projected, *I am happy for you, brother Moshe.*

Thank you, my friend.

Moshe peered deeper into the dark alcoves, well behind Storn's throne. He scanned every nook and cranny, intently searching for the dark creature he knew was lurking there, somewhere. Stenrak followed Moshe's lead and turned to see if their common enemy would dare to make his presence known. There was nothing there. But what they couldn't readily see, they could surely feel.

He is there, watching, warned Stenrak.

I know, replied Moshe uneasily, *I know.*

Do not worry, Moshe. Even with his ardent followers at his side, Faester will never interfere. At least for now.

As a symbol of his resolve and union with Moshe, Stenrak raised Asher's spear very high. Then he stepped forward so that all could see it well. *Let this show the dark shadow Harsha what he faces if he were to come ahead too much.*

The sight of Stenrak proudly raising Calish's spear to protect his new family made Moshe proud and hopeful. But more than that, it reminded Moshe of Calish. There was something in the way Stenrak wielded Asher's spear that was so gloriously reminiscent of his best friend. Moshe couldn't help but believe that somehow his friend's vibrant spirit lived on in Stenrak's powerful body.

Stenrak finally said, *One day we will battle him, but not now. Faester's time is not yet. But when it is, my friend, know this, I will stand with you.*

Funny, thought Moshe to himself, Stenrak's words *sound* like Calish too. *Thank you, brother.*

Ashkolon delivered the infant into Zera-eesh's bosom. She gladly took him in, encircling the little boy in her arms. Moshe approached Zera-eesh's side and took up her hand gently within his own. They looked at each other, smiling and happy. Together they gazed at their son.

Then Moshe took the flask from his pouch; he opened it and let a few drops of its precious water flow into the child's mouth. The infant sucked at it fully; it made his little face glow and shine.

"Gryi-iiki!" Ashkolon whispered to himself while recoiling from the sight. Moshe had the water! *The* Water! Now the child had it. *Why?* he wondered in astonishment. Ashkolon had only tasted it once. The Holy Monolith had given it to him. It had also mysteriously spoken to him. But since then there was nothing; no more words... and no more life-extending water. *What did it mean?*

Suddenly in his mind Ashkolon saw a disturbing vision of his own death. After untold eons... death! "Sheol shagool. No!" Ashkolon was forced to recognize that somehow the prophecy did not include him, not anymore.

As a tumultuous rage built up inside of him he fumed, *This is not acceptable, I am the First! No I will not allow it!* The old priest reached for his dagger, pulled it from his belt and moved toward the child.

Nearby, at the top of the altar's newly built crystal monument, the Minthuru stone suddenly started to glow. Its deep blue radiance grew stronger, cascading a brilliant light across the Holy Place, pushing out the darkness, forcing it to retreat into the furthest corners and tunnels. The light became so strong that almost everyone was blinded. The Pon onlookers covered their eyes and turned away.

The mighty Minthuru stone rose into the air and moved to be beside the infant. The baby's tiny hand reached out and his forefinger touched the stone. A special and separate white sliver of the stone's radiance washed over the infant's body. The light changed him. As he turned to face his mother, for a moment, in a beautiful flash, the Pon baby looked... human.

But no Pon could see it; they were still blinded by the pure and divine white light. Only Zera-eesh could see the perfect face of her little boy, with his piercing brown eyes, red skin, and silky-smooth black hair. The infant and his mother locked eyes. The child was so much like her. Peering at him was like seeing her reflection in crystal clear water. She saw innocence, kindness, uniqueness, and great strength of character. She smiled the way mothers do and whispered proudly, "Son of White Eagle."

Darkness once again crept in from the cavern's furthest edges, and as the blinding light faded, the Minthuru stone returned to its spot upon the altar. So too the little human baby became a Pon once more.

Moshe and Zera-eesh returned to sharing in the moment with their infant. But Moshe suddenly felt as if something else was happening. So he turned his head to see Ashkolon, who was strangely standing much too close. The Maana master's expression had dramatically changed. He was no longer amazed; he was angry, very angry... at the baby! He was glaring at the child, baring his sharp teeth, as if seething with hatred. More importantly, he held a dagger! Moshe thought the old priest would kill the child, so he instinctively used his body to shield the baby from Ashkolon's sight. He hurriedly mind-spoke, *Ashkolon, what is wrong?*

Ashkolon hesitated upon hearing the words. He clenched his mouth closed, and while still staring at the infant, mumbled out loud, "After all this time Father, after all this time. Why?"

Stenrak, seeing that something was wrong, leapt from his place by King Storn's side, and swiftly made his way to the altar. He approached Ashkolon cautiously. When the priest would not give way, he then bodily moved between Ashkolon and Moshe.

Stenrak stared into his mentor's eyes, anxiously asking, "Master, what is it?" He carefully gripped Ashkolon's wrist, staying the hand that held the dagger.

Ashkolon eventually broke from his trance to gaze at Stenrak. There was such disillusionment and pain in Ashkolon's tired old eyes; it made Stenrak scared to see it. The priest trembled and started to fall; Stenrak had to bolster him. He called to the priest's assistant to come forward and help Ashkolon away from the altar site. The helper grabbed Ashkolon. The pair then haltingly made their way down the altar's steps. Ashkolon's head was sunk low. He never looked back, and was still mumbling to himself as he made his way from the altar.

Stenrak turned to Moshe and gently put his claw on Moshe's shoulder. *It is alright. This is your time, my brother. Do not think of anything but your new family.*

Moshe gestured in thanks. Then he turned to his mate. "It is fine, do not worry."

Zera-eesh smiled at Moshe lovingly and used her free hand to grasp onto his. The new parents then went back to admiring their new creation.

After a few moments, Moshe suddenly had a new thought. It was very important after all. He gazed into the chosen woman's beautiful eyes and asked, "His name, how shall we call him?"

Like magic, Zera-eesh understood what he meant. Without hesitation, the proud new mother declared, "O'oviss. His name will be O'oviss."

Epilogue

Long after the others had departed, a discrete shadow drifted its way in and among the bloodied and broken corpses. The shadow, like a ghost, a black one robbed in the finest of fibers, floated slightly above the dead. But this specter was not dead. He was very much alive, and he alone breached a space no sane being dare trod. The smells, pungent and foul, put a cruel and yet hungry expression upon the ghost's wicked little face.

Fascinating, he pondered greedily, while scanning the abundant meat and booty around him.

He was surprised that so much was left behind. "Hiss-sss, hiss-ss," he sniggered gleefully at his good fortune. While hissing, a forked tongue popped in and out of his slit-like mouth. The black slithering thing also had the ability to take in the odor of decay, thus making him hungrier.

"And where is everyone?" he asked sarcastically.

They had all fled, out of fright, and out of obedience. After the battle, Stilik's army was stunned to find that Calish's people had simply disappeared. Stenrak appeared to vanish into thin air as well. 'Evil magic', some Pon soldiers fearfully decried. Others said it was done by the god of the underworld; a being the simple-minded Pon reverently referred to as Hull.

Hull? What poppycock.

Prince Stilik chalked up the disappearances to his own theory of Pon mysticism concerning the Holy Place. Ultimately, though, as his soldiers continued to tremble, Stilik ordered an immediate withdrawal. The Pon were so primitive and naïve, their uncomplicated brains could not fathom what he knew to be a rational explanation: Calish had utilized a crystal stone and or stones, to create some kind of temporary freezing effect. He had clearly felt himself being frozen in place when Bishtar and her brood had passed by him. If the stones could freeze people, then it wasn't far-fetched to consider they could also open portals to other places. While that freezing effect was in place, a portal was opened to transport Calish's clan somewhere else.

Simple, really.

Hathar had told him of such things. She used her powers of astral projection and had seen portals opened to other places; enticingly enigmatic and fascinating places. She said there were great stones in play. Very insightful, she was... Oh how he wished, sometimes, but not too often, that the smelly old hag was still with him, still tutoring him in the dark arts. It was too bad how she ended up, so sad, really... *Hathor, can you hear me? Hathor? Oh well, what is one to do?*

In any event, a portal was the only sensible explanation as to why Calish's clan vanished so quickly. The ghost also had a strong suspicion that there was more than one stone in play and that they somehow worked collaboratively. There was the one Bishtar carried around her delicate little neck, combined with the stone Dathan coveted. Regardless, it was the Pons' pagan fears that had left the Holy Place's bounty to the underworlds scavengers. Or better yet, to him.

"But that can wait." His furtive imagination conjured up some interesting prospects. "Maybe I will celebrate my treasure with a dance. Grandfather doesn't appreciate my keen sense of humor, so I guess I'll just have to enjoy it all by myself. Ah well, such is the burden I carry." The ghost raised his thin little claws and his eyes' red dots glowed. His claws quivered and all of a sudden a collection of nearby severed arms, heads and torsos started levitating, bobbing up and down, then of course twirling all around. It would not be a true dance after all without the twirling all around.

It was most entertaining.

There was nothing to stop him from doing whatever he wanted. The Pon Holy place was as still and quiet as a graveyard... well, except for the shuffling sounds of the dancing body parts. "It is too quiet." *Music,* he mused, "What is a dance without music?"

"Nothing, I tell you, nothing." To coincide with his twitching fingers, he spit out a hissing tune to match the gyrations of the various limbs; high notes for the arms and heads drifting their way up, and low notes for the heavier portions that floated beneath the smaller bits.

363

"Ah, so many possibilities. And no ninnies to stop me. In one way or another, they are all subdued."

Stilik and his simple-minded soldiers were long gone and they would not return to the Holy place, as per the final command of that dithering fool, King Storn. "Osiris, give me the strength to deal with fools."

Calish's clan, as already calculated, had most likely fled through a portal. "Calish?" *Hmm, what of Calish?* the ghost asked himself. *Well, maybe not Calish anymore.* Calish had suffered a mortal blow during the battle; it would be difficult to imagine he had survived Asher's spear after it nearly cut him in two. That meant their clan was now led by that stuttering oaf Mosher. "The proverbial blind leading the blind."

How long could it be until Mosher's group fell into disarray? *Not long,* he imagined. Furthermore, Mosher was bound to have one of the stones; most likely the one Dathan had always wanted. But one or two stones didn't matter because he was intent on commandeering all of it. Yes, every last stone was destined to be his.

"And Ashkolon, you ask?" Well, that wrinkled old busy-body stumblebum was hard at work having his so-called visions. When not doing that, he was drunk from Maana berry wine. "The useless delusions of an impotent Pon mythology. Poppycock, I tell you, poppycock."

His grandfather and the tribe's remnant, mostly older humans, had settled into their new caverns, very far from the Holy place. As promised by Storn, there was food and water, so for the most part they were content to stay where they were. "A successful negotiation, yes, indeed. And in no small measure due to my rather persuasive and charming personality."

"How true, my friend, how true."

Voice and the spirit's brain-dead Cult had slithered their way back to one of their dingy little hovels and were most likely busy licking their wounds, something they were sure to enjoy. "Oh Isis, they are truly deranged."

And finally, what of that female dog Bishtar? Well sadly, her slinky-sly self, along with her little crystal gem, were beyond his furtive reach; at least for now. "But I will get you, my pretty."

"All gone. No one to stop me I tell you." The ghost glared again at the bounty, the dancing limbs, and voiced selfishly, "I have every right to this."

He had warned Stilik that after the battle many of the leftovers belonged to him. The prince, therefore, had no say in what he was doing. Nonetheless, he stretched out his mind to make sure that he was indeed alone. With his powers he sensed that there was no other living presence. Giving in to the hunger, he quickly drew-in one claw, thus forcing a nearby dancing arm into his waiting grip. He took up the meat, brought it to his mouth, and started chewing into it savagely.

"FEAR ME." Abruptly, the loud bellicose words rang out across the caverns.

Startled, the ghost quickly threw down the torn-up food and started searching for the source of the sounds. On guard now, his beady black eyes glowed very bright from their red dots. He used his mind-motion power to clear a circle of empty space around him; the dancing body parts forcefully flew away at a great speed.

He snarled, stretched out his claws and hissed out a warning to whoever had the audacity to confront him. "I am Faester!" he shouted to the air. "Show yourself if you dare."

On impulse, Faester looked straight up. To his astonishment, there were twelve great eyes amongst the darkened recesses of the cavern's roof. The eyes, like giant crystals, made up of various sparkling colors, were staring down at him. Faester gawked at them too, not believing what was clearly above him.

It must be a trick, he imagined finally. *It can only be Voice or Bishtar playing a game with me. Well, if so, it is a dangerous game... for them.*

Faester called out again, "Show yourself! I am not afraid of you."

As if his words had been heeded, an enormous pillar suddenly, loudly, forced its way up through the cavern floor, stretching up high, then all the way to the ceiling. The pillar's walls glowed with hot molten lava. But strangely, the red, yellow and black steaming liquids flowed *up* the column's sides, defying gravity, and earthy rules.

"What is this?" Faester asked incredulously. For the first time in his dark little life the ghost really felt fear.

Once again, to his astonishment and regret, his question was answered. "HULL..."

The thunderous word vibrated throughout the Crystallight caverns, shaking Faester to the core. His body lost its ability to float above the ground. Faester sank, and his feet touched the rocky surface – a sensation he had not known in many years. Then a great unseen power surrounded him and Faester was forced to his knees shaking uncontrollably.

"YOU HAVE DARED TO DISTURBED HULL'S SLUMBER. HULL WATCHES ALL THINGS INSIDE OF ME. YOU ARE AN EVIL LITTLE CREATURE THAT DELIGHTS ONLY IN WICKEDNESS, THUS INCURRING HULL'S WRATH."

After that, two giant stone hands cracked their way out from nearby walls. The mighty hands stretched across the cavern's expanse and swiftly grabbed Faester up, lifting him aloft, squeezing him tightly. Faester felt his arms, legs, and bones compress to a near breaking point. He screeched in agony as Hull's voice thundered aloud once more. "WHY SHOULD HULL ALLOW YOU TO LIVE?"

"Please, please, my Lord, spare me!" Faester pleaded, "Augghh!!"

HULL IS NOT YOUR LORD, VILE INFECTION. HULL IS CHAMPION OF THIS REALM."

"Augghh!! Please master, please." The crushing continued, and he could no longer breathe.

Just as Faester was about to lose consciousness, a lilting tone - a ringing melodic series of notes swam across the air, echoing in and out of every space. The sounds were beautiful, as if made by heavenly harps, flutes, and instruments beyond description. Faester heard the sounds, the wonderful music, and was almost moved to tears by their purity, their majesty... but something inside of him kept him from truly accepting their message. Faester's would-be tears were soon thereafter retracted, and his heart only hardened and blackened more.

366

Hull, however, well heard and understood the divine sounds. Before too long, the stony hands relaxed enough to allow Faester to breathe at last.

"HULL REALEASES YOU. BUG. WORM. ENEMY OF LIGHT. FATHER HAS COMMANDED IT AND STAYS HULL'S HANDS. BUT KNOW THIS, WICKED ONE, HULL IS WATCHING YOU. THERE WILL COME A TIME OF YOUR RECKONING."

Hull's fingers relaxed some more and Faester dropped away from between the massive digits. He fell swiftly to the cavern floor, where he collapsed upon himself. Sharp pains streaked through his feet, ankles and knees.

Faester looked up, and hovering above him were the large cruel hands, now making a fist. The colossal mitts were shaking and trembling, as if they were all to ready to come crashing down upon his head. Faester raised his arms in a feeble attempt to protect himself.

After a few moments, he braved a glance between his wobbly claws to see the giant fists still in their place, stayed by a force Faester dare not think about.

"Shishtu," Faester whispered terribly to his would-be destruction. When death did not come, Faester carefully and cautiously, got up. Even though his body ached all the way down to his feet, he started slowly hobbling away from beneath the awesome, threatening fists.

"RUN!" boomed Hull's voice.

He turned his sights up again only to see the giant crystal eyes fiercely glowering at him. *Oh no!*

The ghost, although in great pain, somehow quickened his pace. He grabbed-up his long black robes and stumbled toward the nearest cavern exit. Unwittingly, he tripped over some of the corpses that lay in his path, falling face-first into their swollen, torn-open torsos. Maggot-riddled guts and gore got smeared across his twisted face, and some of the bile was forced into his open mouth. Having now lost his appetite, he clawed the putrid stuff away in revulsion, gagging and choking from it. He stood up awkwardly and listed forward again, sucking in heavily labored breaths because his body... his aching muscles and feeble joints, were unaccustomed to generating motion.

"RUN!" came the thunderous sound again, echoing across the chambers.

But Faester didn't need to be told twice. The little black shadow, the ghost, the vile infection, was already on his way to being gone.